Arranging Gershwin

October 2014

To Morgan,

Thanks for reading the book!

All the best,

ARRANGING GERSHWIN

Rhapsody in Blue and the Creation of an American Icon

Ryan Raul Bañagale

OXFORD
UNIVERSITY PRESS

Oxford University Press is a department of the University of
Oxford. It furthers the University's objective of excellence in research,
scholarship, and education by publishing worldwide.

Oxford   New York
Auckland   Cape Town   Dar es Salaam   Hong Kong   Karachi
Kuala Lumpur   Madrid   Melbourne   Mexico City   Nairobi
New Delhi   Shanghai   Taipei   Toronto

With offices in
Argentina   Austria   Brazil   Chile   Czech Republic   France   Greece
Guatemala   Hungary   Italy   Japan   Poland   Portugal   Singapore
South Korea   Switzerland   Thailand   Turkey   Ukraine   Vietnam

Oxford is a registered trademark of Oxford University Press
in the UK and certain other countries.

Published in the United States of America by
Oxford University Press
198 Madison Avenue, New York, NY 10016

Publication of this book was supported by a grant from the H. Earle Johnson Fund of the
Society for American Music and with the generous support of the AMS 75 PAYS Endowment
of the American Musicological Society, funded in part by the National Endowment for the
Humanities and the Andrew W. Mellon Foundation.

Library of Congress Cataloging-in-Publication Data
Bañagale, Ryan Raul.
Arranging Gershwin : Rhapsody in blue and the creation of an American icon / Ryan Raul
Bañagale.
    pages cm
Includes bibliographical references and index.
ISBN 978–0–19–997837–3 (alk. paper)—ISBN 978–0–19–997838–0 (alk. paper)
1. Gershwin, George, 1898–1937. Rhapsody in blue.   2. Grofé, Ferde,
1892–1972—Criticism and interpretation.   3. Bernstein, Leonard, 1918–1990—Criticism and
interpretation.   4. Ellington, Duke, 1899–1974—Criticism and interpretation.
5. Adler, Larry—Criticism and interpretation.   I. Title.
ML410.G288B36 2014
784.262—dc23
2014007171

9 8 7 6 5 4 3 2 1
Printed in the United States of America
on acid-free paper

To Shermy and The Bean

CONTENTS

Acknowledgments   *ix*
Credits   xiii
About the Companion Website   xv

Introduction: Arranging an Icon   *1*

1. Complex Compositional Origins: Ferde Grofé and
   Rhapsody in Blue   14

2. Living Legends: George Gershwin and *Rhapsody in Blue   47*

3. From Camp to Carnegie Hall: Leonard Bernstein and
   Rhapsody in Blue   73

4. Rearranging Concert Jazz: Duke Ellington and *Rhapsody in Blue   96*

5. "It Ain't Necessarily So": Larry Adler and *Rhapsody in Blue   119*

6. Selling Success: Visual Media and *Rhapsody in Blue   148*

Epilogue: Arranging on Multiple Levels   *174*

Endnotes   180
Bibliography   196
Index   201

ACKNOWLEDGMENTS

Like *Rhapsody in Blue*, the arrangement of this book resulted from the contributions of many. I would like to thank everyone at Oxford University Press who assisted in bringing it to fruition, especially Norm Hirschy, who provided friendly guidance and enthusiastic support from our initial correspondence and onward. I am deeply indebted to the anonymous reviewers who took time with both the proposal and the full manuscript, offering invaluable and insightful feedback that has allowed me to assemble as strong a book as possible.

This project emerged from a casual comment made by my graduate advisor, Carol J. Oja, and flourished under her guidance at Harvard University. Thank you, Carol, for your unwavering support, mentorship, and friendship. Members of her American music "diss'n group" kept the process of writing both invigorating and on track: Emily Abrams-Ansari, Davide Ceriani, Elizabeth Craft, Glenda Goodman, Jack Hamilton, Sheryl Kaskowitz, Drew Massey, and Matthew Mugmon. One of the great joys of graduate work at Harvard was the community of faculty, students, and staff. Special thanks are due to Professors Kay Kaufman Shelemay, Ingrid Monson, Thomas Kelly, Sindhumathi Revuluri, and Anne Shreffler; librarians Sarah Adams, Liza Vick, and Kerry Masteller; and my "G" cohort Corinna Campbell, Katherine Lee, and Anna Zayaruznaya. I am extremely grateful to the American Musicological Society, which provided two full years of graduate funding by way of the Howard Mayer Brown and Alvin H. Johnson AMS-50 fellowships.

I could not have completed this book during my first years as a professor at Colorado College without the wide-reaching support of my institution and colleagues. I am particularly grateful to Victor Nelson-Cisneros and the Riley Scholar Program. My faculty colleagues in the music department offered constant support and encouragement: Richard Agee, Ofer Ben-Amots, Dan Brink, Michael Grace, Susan Grace, Victoria Lindsay

Levine, and Stephen Scott. Other members of the Colorado College community whom I wish to recognize include Susan Ashley, Stormy Burns, Helen Daly, Aju Fenn, Scott Krzych, Corina McKendry, Corinne Scheiner, Patti Spoelman, Daryll Stevens, and the students of my Spring 2013 seminar on George Gershwin, one of whom made a particularly timely dubstep arrangement of the *Rhapsody*. The Humanities Divisional Committee provided support for my final research trip to the Library of Congress as well as my dedicated and resourceful student research assistants, Ella Vorenberg and Connor Rice. Under the direction of Professor Anne Hyde, the Crown Faculty Center made possible a book manuscript workshop with an illustrious panel of American music scholars: Larry Hamberlin, Beth Levy, Jeffrey Magee, and Drew Massey. Thank you all.

I have benefited from the generosity of those working in and around the field of American music. Thank you to the Gershwin scholars who have been welcoming, receptive, and supportive: Richard Crawford, Howard Pollack, David Schiff, Wayne Shirley, and James Wierzbicki. Among this group, I would like to single out Larry Starr, the advisor of my master's degree work at the University of Washington, who helped me find my way in the field of musicology and remains a valued mentor. Ongoing conversations with friends and colleagues from my time at the University of Washington contributed greatly to my work: Vilde Aaslid, Benjamin Albritton, Lincoln Ballard, Gwynne Kuhner Brown, Rachel Mundy, and Susan Neimoyer. I also wish to acknowledge the assistance of Ayden Adler, Anthony Brown, Humphrey Burton, Jean-François Charles, Judith Clurman, Todd Decker, George Ferencz, Gary Fry, Phil Gentry, Ferde Grofé Jr., Dave Paul, Joe Powers, Tamara Roberts, Cameron Rose, Douglas Shadle, Travis Stimeling, and Judy Tsou. For their archival assistance and insights, I thank Raymond White and Mark Horowitz at the Library of Congress; Michael Owen formerly of the Ira and Leonore Gershwin Trusts; Shannon Bowen at the American Heritage Center; D. J. Hoek at the Northwestern University Music Library; Barbara Haws at the New York Philharmonic; and Barbara Perkel at the Boston Symphony Orchestra. The Society for American Music and the American Musicological Society provided generous support for the final stages of this book through their H. Earle Johnson Publication Subvention and AMS 75 PAYS Subvention, respectively.

I am grateful to those scholar/editors who assisted in the past publication of portions of this book, including John Howland, Lita Miller, Jeffrey Taylor, and Walter Van de Leur. A portion of chapter 2 first appeared as "Isaac Goldberg: Assessing Agency in American Music Biography" in *American Music Review* 34/2 (Spring 2010), published by the H. Wiley Hitchcock Institute for Studies in American Music. Chapter 3 has drawn upon material from "'Each Man Kills the Thing He Loves': Bernstein's

Formative Relationship with *Rhapsody in Blue*" in *Journal of the Society for American Music* 3/1 (February 2009), © The Society for American Music, published by Cambridge University Press, and reproduced with permission. An earlier version of chapter 4 appeared as "Rewriting the Narrative One Arrangement at a Time: Duke Ellington and *Rhapsody in Blue*" in *Jazz Perspectives* 6/1–2 (Spring/Summer 2012), © Taylor & Francis, and reused with permission.

Much like Leonard Bernstein, I received my first copy of the sheet music for *Rhapsody in Blue* as a teenager. Similarly, I begged my mother to buy me the score. She agreed with the condition that I commit to learning the piece—I hope this book suffices. Along with her, my father, brother, sister, and brother-in-law have each provided encouragement and levity. Likewise, I am grateful for the personal assistance and professional advice offered by my mother- and father-in-law.

My wife and I have two amazing sons. The first was born as I completed my dissertation and the second arrived as I completed this book. Felix and Theo are constant reminders of what is really important in life, and with this project completed, I look forward to enjoying moments with them as effusively as possible. Seeing the world anew through their fresh eyes continues to be the most profound of experiences.

Finally, eternal gratitude, love, and appreciation go to my wife Katie, who has been supportive and patient over the course of this extended endeavor. From her willingness to make multiple cross-country moves down to the witty doodles that accompany her meticulous edits of my prose, she has kept everything in perspective and maintained a healthy dose of humor. I am fortunate to have her in my life and eagerly anticipate what the future holds for our fabulous family. May our rhapsody be never-ending.

CREDITS

ABOUT THE COMPANION WEBSITE

www.oup.com/us/arranginggershwin

Oxford has created an open-access website to accompany this book that provides access to additional audio and visual materials. Throughout the text, recordings and performances of various *Rhapsody in Blue* arrangements are signaled with the ◐ symbol. Additional figures, including color reproductions of selected charts and photographs, are signaled by the ▤ symbol. The reader is encouraged to access these online materials while perusing the book in order to provide as fulsome an experience of these multifaceted arrangements of *Rhapsody in Blue* as possible.

Arranging Gershwin

Introduction

Arranging an Icon

So suppose I did give George a hand with his opus. . .
              —Private Joe Fingers, *I Won't Play* (1944)

A short film about a marine with a penchant for narrative braggadocio might not seem like the most obvious place to start, yet it highlights the three central concerns of this book: arrangements, mythmaking, and the recursive power of George Gershwin and *Rhapsody in Blue* in narratives of America and its music. In November 1944, Warner Brothers released *I Won't Play*, which would go on to receive an Academy Award for best live action, two-reel film ⬧. Although not directly about Gershwin or the *Rhapsody*, it reveals a great deal about the standing of both as the United States found itself ever more ensconced in World War II.

In some respects, *I Won't Play* could have been easily mistaken for a true-life newsreel, rather than a work of fiction. Screened prior to the start of a feature film, it opens with a booming voiceover accompanying black-and-white stock footage of a marine base surrounded by palm trees. The narrator informs us that we are on a remote island in the South Pacific, "maybe Tarawa," referencing the then-recent battle known now as the first major victory by the United States over Japan in the Pacific Theater: "It was tough to take. But it *was* taken. And our guys are still there hanging on. It's hot and it is dangerous and it is lonesome as—it's very lonesome. Entertainment or diversion of any kind is manna from heaven. Even a good liar is not likely to be dismissed. . . ."[1]

That supposed liar is Joe Fingers, a Marine Corps private with seemingly endless show business connections. Private Fingers incessantly impresses and entertains with tales of his illustrious associations. He "gave George [Gershwin] a hand with his opus," helped Frank Sinatra get his start with Tommy Dorsey, played piano with Benny Goodman, and "invented" the Hollywood starlet Kim Karol—the very pinup girl who adorns the wall of his barracks. The extravagance of his accounts—including his claim to have written a portion of *Rhapsody in Blue*—raises suspicion among his fellow marines, who unceremoniously declare him an impostor. To make a short story shorter, a fortuitous series of events reveals his genuine relationship with Kim Karol, which is good-enough evidence for the boys that Joe Fingers is for real.

In the final scene of the film, a fellow marine asks Fingers if his story about Gershwin and *Rhapsody in Blue* is "on the level." Setting aside his cigarette for dramatic effect, he details the account: "Look, the guy comes to me and says 'Fingers, I got a problem. . . . I'm stuck on the first passage'—you guys know the phrase." He turns to the piano and regales the men with an instantly identifiable theme from the *Rhapsody*. Reemphasizing the impasse faced by Gershwin to the men gathered before him, Fingers continues his tale: "So I says, 'Look, if you treat the middle part something like this. . . .'" His words dissipate into the performance of a flashy, cadenza-like passage, after which he proudly declares, "And he was OK!" Private Fingers then hammers out the final six bars of the *Rhapsody* as he winks directly at the camera. As the shot dissolves into the Warner Brothers closing logo, a symphony orchestra swells. The film ends with the final triumphant chords of the *Rhapsody*.

The casual observer might not notice the sonic sleight of hand that has just occurred. As a set, these fourteen bars of music outline what has become known as the "ritornello" theme—one of five central melodies in *Rhapsody in Blue*. In reality, each of the three phrases introduced by Fingers in less than a minute comes from a different part of the *Rhapsody*. The first phrase is a piano reduction of the first full orchestral statement of the ritornello theme [R. 3 to R. 4].[2] For the second phrase—that section that he supposedly authored—Fingers jumps to the middle of the second piano cadenza, transposed up a half step from what appears in the score [R. 6-4 to R. 6]. This barely audible modulation sets up a satisfyingly appropriate dominant to tonic conclusion for the film. In the final phrase, Fingers offers the final six bars of the piece with the added accompaniment of the full orchestra [R. 40+1 to R. 40+6].

Joe Fingers is no more real than his connection to *Rhapsody in Blue*—both are the invention of Hollywood screenwriters Laurence Schwab and James

Bloodworth, the first of many individuals encountered in this book who have tapped into the iconic power of George Gershwin and *Rhapsody in Blue* to tell their stories. Their film *arranges* both Gershwin and the *Rhapsody* on multiple levels. The most apparent type of arrangement occurs through the sonic manipulation of disparate portions of the *Rhapsody* while maintaining its fluidity and familiarity. More subtly, *I Won't Play* arranges Gershwin and his music into the narrative action, relying heavily on the associative value of both. The presence of the *Rhapsody*—often thought of as *the* quintessential piece of American music—provides that sense of familiarity that both the characters on screen, as well as the movie-going audience, would have craved in a time of war. At the same time, the film arranges perceptions of Gershwin and the creation of *Rhapsody in Blue*, contributing to the mythology of both. The compositional abilities of Gershwin were called into question long before his sudden and untimely death in 1937. Here that impression is extended. Because of his apparent involvement in the development of the *Rhapsody*, the film situates Private Fingers *dextera domini*—as the right hand of the divine spirit known as Gershwin. Of course, a moment's reflection reveals the arrant absurdity of this facet of *I Won't Play*: The early twenty-something Fingers would have been a child when the *Rhapsody* premiered in 1924. This detail may explain the deliberate wink offered by Fingers in the closing credits. Unfortunately, in narratives about the history of American music, most stories about Gershwin have not received such tongue-in-cheek presentation. Indeed, anecdotes plague the history and reception of *Rhapsody in Blue*.

A central premise of this book is that arrangements participate in the assemblage of music history, tempering the mythmaking that typically accompanies constructions of the past. Musical arrangements reconfigure an existing piece of music through any number of techniques, including the reorganization or removal of thematic material, the alteration of instrumentation, and the modification of tempo, rhythm, and dynamics. As historical documents, arrangements record processes of creation, interpretation, and performance, serving as musical vehicles for the delivery and maintenance of individual and communal narratives. In this way, they function as historiographies in their own right. They also go hand in hand with biographical arrangement.

The iconic status of George Gershwin and *Rhapsody in Blue* emerges only from their respective arrangement by others in a multitude of forms. The various ways that musicians have shaped Gershwin and the *Rhapsody* reveal the centrality of both to musical creativity in America over the course of the past century, while providing insight into the priorities and practices of those musicians themselves. Each instance of arrangement retroactively shapes the meaning of the original work and its composer, as well as influences its reception in the future. In the case of *Rhapsody in Blue*, however, identifying the "original work" and the "composer" presents some challenges.

ARRANGING A MUSICAL ICON

One of the fundamental problems with studying *Rhapsody in Blue* is that it is not a composition—at least not in the way musicologists typically conceive of such. Unlike a Beethoven symphony or even subsequent works by Gershwin for the concert hall, the *Rhapsody* existed as an "arrangement" from the very start. When Gershwin first wrote the score to the *Rhapsody*, he did so in two-piano form. Because of time constraints, inexperience, convention, or some combination thereof, Gershwin relied on arranger Ferde Grofé to prepare the full score for performance by the unique instrumentation of the Paul Whiteman Orchestra, the ensemble that debuted the work on February 12, 1924. The American public first experienced the *Rhapsody* through Grofé's arrangement. Although Grofé's role in the initial creative process of the *Rhapsody* has never been denied, the extent of his contributions to the origin and ongoing life of the piece have been sidelined due to his status as an arranger.

Arrangers have long played second fiddle to composers, though in effect they do the same thing. In the study of Western classical music, composers are typically considered the originators of a musical work, while arrangers simply manipulate an existing creation. Liszt, with his celebrated keyboard arrangements of symphonies and arias might represent an exception to the rule, but even these works are referred to by academics as transcriptions or paraphrases—rather than compositions in their own right.[3] To this end, jazz and musical theatre scholar Jeffrey Magee observes that the "*functional* distinction between an arranger and a composer is embedded in a *hierarchical* distinction among kinds of musical creativity."[4] That distinction has deep roots in the tendency of musicological studies to privilege the so-called masterworks of the classical and romantic eras, pieces of music created by a single auteur. Although the purview of historical music scholarship has widened significantly since the introduction of critical and popular music studies of the 1980s, composers maintain their privileged status over arrangers. The piece will forever remain George Gershwin's *Rhapsody in Blue*, but the creation and maintenance of its iconicity results only from its arrangement by a host of other musicians over the course of time. In this sense it is a "work in movement," to borrow a phrase from semiotician and philosopher Umberto Eco.[5] The *Rhapsody* remains an open text for musical interpretation.

Countless arrangements of *Rhapsody in Blue* have appeared during the past eighty-five years, many even during Gershwin's lifetime. As early as 1931, Isaac Goldberg, Gershwin's first biographer, remarked that the *Rhapsody* "has been subjected, as is the usual fate with classics, to adaptations both wonderful and fearsome."[6] As evidence in support of his observation that the *Rhapsody* had achieved "classic" status less than a decade after its premiere, he identifies a modernist performance by the Ballets Russes at the Théâtre des Champs-Élysées in Paris, a Grecian ballet staged at the Hotel Metropole in London, a tap dance routine by Jack Donahue, and an arrangement for Borrah Minevitch's harmonica ensemble—arrangements representing both ends of the highbrow/lowbrow musical spectrum. A few years after Gershwin's passing, biographer Edward Jablonski sent Ira Gershwin a discography of *Rhapsody* recordings then available in the United Kingdom. Ira responded: "Thanks for the English listings. Yes, I have most of them. Not, however, that Banjo Octet of 'Rhapsody in Blue' which I probably would like to hear once and then promptly forget."[7] Forgettable or not, countless arrangements of the piece over time have been eclipsed by the ubiquity of a symphonic arrangement of the *Rhapsody*, also prepared by Ferde Grofé.

First published by Warner Brothers in 1942—five years after Gershwin's death—Grofé's symphonic arrangement has become the "standard" version of *Rhapsody in Blue* in many respects. This arrangement standardizes the instrumentation of the *Rhapsody*, making its performance possible by any number of orchestral ensembles around the world—as opposed to the unique instrumental combinations of the Paul Whiteman Orchestra. Accordingly, it dominates performances of the *Rhapsody*. Between 2000 and 2005, for example, 376 ensembles rented the orchestral performance materials from European American Music Distributors, the company that manages performance rights for the piece.[8] Leonard Bernstein used this symphonic arrangement of the *Rhapsody* when he recorded what Gershwin biographer Howard Pollack has identified as "perhaps the best-known performance of the piece in the later twentieth century"—a recording released on the Columbia label in 1959.[9] As considered in chapter 3, part of the popularity of this recording has to do with the veneration of Bernstein. At the same time, the symphonic arrangement of the *Rhapsody* is appealing because of its connection to traditional American narratives of ingenuity and promise. Through its classicization, the piece is picked up by its proverbial bootstraps, elevated from its roots in 1920s jazz, and placed front and center in the imaginary museum of American music.[10] An important parallel exists here between such representations of the *Rhapsody* and narratives of George Gershwin himself.

ARRANGING A BIOGRAPHICAL ICON

The appearance of this symphonic arrangement of *Rhapsody in Blue* during the opening ceremonies of the 1984 summer Olympics exemplifies the taut connection between Gershwin's music and his life. Under the sunny skies of southern California, the Los Angeles Memorial Coliseum hosted the opening ceremonies of the Games of the Twenty-Third Olympiad on July 28, 1984. More than 100,000 people—spectators, athletes, and performers—gathered in the majestic stadium to the newly composed strains of John Williams's now-ubiquitous *Olympic Fanfare*. The variety of American musical forms encountered as the pageant unfurled on the field below left little doubt about the commanding and captivating power of the United States, or the culturally imperialist ambitions of opening ceremonies producer David Wolper and the Los Angeles Olympic Organizing Committee headed by Peter Ueberroth. Iconic American imagery accompanied each musical offering. A colonial-era fife-and-drum corps accompanied the initial entrance of the stars and stripes. The University of Southern California marching band, expanded to 800 musicians, paraded around the field to a medley of Americana that included John Philip Sousa's "Washington Post March" and Woody Guthrie's "This Land Is Your Land." The final formation of the massive band outlined a map of the United States whose borders were then flooded by an equally large troupe of dancers. Escorted by a dozen oversized covered wagons, men, women, and children erected a small frontier town, cavorting about to Aaron Copland's *Rodeo*, as well as the nineteenth-century folk song and minstrel show mainstay "Turkey in the Straw." Etta James emerged and sang a gospel rendition of "When the Saints Go Marching In" surrounded by a chorus adorned in red, white, and blue robes.

Grofé's symphonic arrangement of *Rhapsody in Blue* formed the artistic climax of these opening ceremonies ◑. As an orchestra seated in bleachers at the east end of the field began to play the *Rhapsody*'s famous "love" theme, dozens of women draped in elegant pale-blue-and-white gowns cascaded from the coliseum's central archway high above. Suddenly, seemingly appearing from nowhere, eighty-four grand pianos materialized from the majestic peristyle, six in each of fourteen archways (see figure 0.1).[11] The audience gasped in astonishment before breaking into thunderous applause. Each piano had its own male pianist dressed in a blue tuxedo with

Figure 0.1
Performance of *Rhapsody in Blue* at the opening ceremonies of the 1984 Los Angeles Olympics, © Bill Ross/CORBIS.

tails. Their synchronized arm gestures and dramatic head nods emphasized the theatricality and refinement of the performance to the utmost. Like every other aspect of the opening ceremony, organizers designed the *Rhapsody in Blue* spectacle to instill a sense of wonder and pride. Distinct from all other musical performances, however, they did not stage the *Rhapsody* on the field of the stadium. Rather, its physical relocation to the upper archways of the coliseum placed both the piece and its composer on a pedestal. This celebration of America's musical past elevated the *Rhapsody* above all else.

The preeminent position of *Rhapsody in Blue* in the history of American music results not only from its hallowed presence in the orchestral repertory, but also from a cultural fascination with what the work represents. The booming preamble heard over the loudspeakers just before the performance of the *Rhapsody* at the 1984 Olympics sums up this sentiment: "Jazz made its way from the streets of New Orleans to the finest concert halls of New York, and inspired George Gershwin to write this American classic."[12] This vision of the composition's upwardly mobile fusion of distinct musical traditions—from the streets of New Orleans to the concert halls of New York—conveys an experience not unlike Gershwin's own rags-to-riches story. The *Rhapsody in Blue* stands as a musical manifestation of the American Dream.

Such biographically oriented observations about Gershwin and the *Rhapsody*, simultaneously poignant and problematic, are by no means new. In fact, they are well rehearsed. The narratives surrounding Gershwin's meteoric rise from the rough-and-tumble streets of the lower east side of Manhattan to become a composer of international renown first emerged during the composer's lifetime. Isaac Goldberg did much to set this legend in motion with the publication of his 1931 biography *George Gershwin: A Study in American Music*. He presented Gershwin as a man of humble beginnings who elevated the popular music of his youth to unprecedented heights. Following Gershwin's death just six years later, anecdotes about his life—sometimes emerging several times removed from the man himself—supplemented Goldberg's observations and crystallized into accepted truths. Aspects of Goldberg's biographical arrangement of Gershwin and *Rhapsody in Blue* resonate throughout scholarly and popular narratives about American music, including the only other book-length consideration of the piece, David Schiff's *Cambridge Music Handbook*.[13]

Schiff's 1997 text evidences the canonical status of the *Rhapsody* in the realm of Western art music by the close of the twentieth century. The fifty-six handbooks in the Cambridge series seek to "provide accessible introductions to major musical works."[14] A majority of the offerings focus on the usual suspects, with composers such as Bach, Mozart, and Beethoven receiving multiple volumes. Thirteen books—the same number given to Bach, Mozart, and Beethoven—are dedicated to the works of twentieth-century composers. Schiff's *Rhapsody in Blue* text is one of only two American music handbooks; the other is on Charles Ives's *Concord Sonata*. Although sensitive to the ongoing collaborative nature of the *Rhapsody*, Schiff identifies the piece as a composition and Gershwin as its composer throughout. The central role of Gershwin as composer comes to the fore in Schiff's third chapter, which describes and names each of the main musical themes comprising *Rhapsody in Blue*.[15]

The thematic vocabulary Schiff devised for *Rhapsody in Blue*, with the accompanying characterizations that they impart upon the music, forms a sort of biographical arrangement of the piece in and of itself. Rather than identify the five separate themes by number or function, he assigns each a memorable and programmatic title: ritornello, stride, train, shuffle, and love. The incipit for each theme, as well as a tag motif based on the "Good evening friends" melody, appears in figure 0.2. The ritornello theme is so named because it returns seven times over the course of the piece. The stride theme relates to the "oom-pah" Harlem stride piano style of its accompaniment. The train designation also results from the rhythm of its accompaniment, which suggests the sound of a locomotive moving

Figure 0.2
Five themes and tag motif for *Rhapsody in Blue* with names as assigned by David Schiff.

at full speed. Likewise, the shuffle label derives from its rhythmic contour—although the term itself was not regularly used for such a rhythm until the end of the 1920s. Finally, Schiff titled the love theme—the grand *andantino* melody that emerges midway through the piece—because of its similarities to the love theme in Tchaikovsky's *Romeo and Juliet*. Schiff is careful to emphasize that these names are of his own invention, and that they, with the possible exception of "train," have no historical origin or significance.[16] Regardless, the names have become common parlance in scholarly considerations of the *Rhapsody* and are used throughout this book to facilitate quick identification of the musical material under discussion.[17]

REMAPPING THE TERRAIN

Rather than introduce and examine every existing arrangement of *Rhapsody in Blue*, the goal here is to demonstrate a variety of approaches to a few specific interpretations of the piece so that all future encounters with the *Rhapsody* can be situated within its broader environment. Taking a cue from philosophers Gilles Deleuze and Félix Guattari, each arrangement of the *Rhapsody* stands as its own plateau. These geologic entities are "continuous regions of intensity constituted in such a way that they do not allow themselves to be interrupted by any external termination, any more than they allow themselves to build toward a climax."[18] In other words, though a plateau is neither a nadir nor a zenith, it offers an energized plane for investigation. Surveying the horizontal space that lies before each arrangement charts a new conception of the *Rhapsody*. No single plateau offers the ultimate or pinnacle interpretation of the larger landscape. Rather, it is only when they are taken together that a representative topography emerges. The arrangements addressed in this book remap the terrain of the *Rhapsody* in this way and ultimately reflect a broader vision of the work, George Gershwin, and music-making in America—its people, their pursuits, and their processes.

Emerging out of a fabled moment in American music history, the complex and communal creative origins of *Rhapsody in Blue* lie at the center of its flexibility and adaptability. Chapter 1 considers the initial creation of the *Rhapsody* in a way that challenges existing assumptions about its genesis and reveals considerable intervention on the part of Ferde Grofé. When calculating the contributions of Grofé to the initial arrangement of the *Rhapsody*, previous studies have superficially compared instrumentation indications in Gershwin's original two-piano manuscript in pencil to Grofé's full score for the Paul Whiteman Orchestra.[19] However, such considerations are incomplete because they do not account for the role of a third source in the initial preparation of the *Rhapsody*: an intermediary fair-copy manuscript in ink, introduced here for the first time. This document is one of several previously unconsidered manuscript arrangements of *Rhapsody in Blue* that appear throughout the course of the book. The analysis of such documents demonstrates ways that traditional musicological methodologies participate in arrangement studies. Here, a detailed comparison of all three original *Rhapsody in Blue* manuscript sources revises the *Rhapsody*'s timeline of creation, clarifies the roles of Gershwin and Grofé in that process, and ultimately places significantly greater emphasis on the role of the arranger in the life of the piece from its point of origin. In the process, such considerations call into question many of the assumptions and anecdotes that have long accompanied narratives about the origins of the *Rhapsody*.

Arrangements contributed greatly to the living-legend status of both Gershwin and *Rhapsody in Blue* in the years before his death. A multitude of commercial arrangements—recordings and published sheet music— emerged by the early 1930s, and chapter 2 considers how they shaped the iconicity of Gershwin and the *Rhapsody*. Royalty and copyright documents from the Library of Congress collections divulge new information about prominent and lesser-known iterations of the *Rhapsody* in circulation during the decade following its 1924 premiere. The study of arrangements in this book, however, is not confined to the musical sources alone, and each chapter examines biographical arrangements as well. Chapter 2 undertakes this task in two respects. First, it considers early film usage of *Rhapsody in Blue* and the narratives about Gershwin, the *Rhapsody*, and American music conveyed through their visual representations of the piece. Second, the chapter explores Isaac Goldberg's portrayal of Gershwin and the *Rhapsody* in his 1931 biography, exposing the personal agency of Goldberg vis-à-vis his unfulfilled musical ambitions and personal vision for American music.

As witnessed in *I Won't Play*, the arrangement of Gershwin's biography and music allows musicians to position themselves within the history of American music. The three subsequent chapters consider the way musical arrangements by a core set of interpreters—Leonard Bernstein, Duke Ellington, and Larry Adler—allowed them to establish their identities as musicians in America while operating under the tall shadow of George Gershwin. The *Rhapsody* played an ongoing role in the careers of these three men, who each created multiple arrangements of the piece over the course of time. Every individual arrangement provides a snapshot of what the *Rhapsody* meant to a particular musician at a particular moment in his career. They provide an opportunity to track the role of the piece in their personal and professional development, as well as witness how they wrote themselves into the historical narrative through the multivariate process of arrangement.

Through arrangements of *Rhapsody in Blue*, Bernstein, Ellington, and Adler each portrayed Gershwin and his music in a particular light. Chapter 3 locates the origins of Leonard Bernstein's polemical statements and presentations of the *Rhapsody* in his youthful encounters with the piece by exploring two recently discovered documents: a copy of the solo-piano sheet music for *Rhapsody in Blue* that he acquired in 1932 and a previously unknown arrangement of the work that he prepared for a group of summer camp musicians in 1937. Not only did Bernstein have a particular vision of how the *Rhapsody* should operate, he also identified deeply with Gershwin and the piece. His arrangement of the *Rhapsody* in print and in performance became an outlet for profound personal and professional anxieties as he rose to prominence during the 1950s.

The *Rhapsody* also came to bear on the professional development of Duke Ellington. A cluster of *Rhapsody* arrangements performed by Ellington over the course of his career form the focus of chapter 4. These include a recorded version released in 1963 and two previously unknown arrangements that date to the mid-1920s and early 1930s, respectively.

The presence of the *Rhapsody* at the outset of Ellington's compositional output in the realm of concert jazz raises some important questions about the role of the piece in Ellington's development of extended forms, as well as its role in the remapping of jazz history that occurred during the 1960s.

Remapping history of another sort emerges in chapter 5. Harmonica virtuoso Larry Adler was an exceedingly popular arbiter of classical composition for the general public, until he found himself blacklisted in 1949 as a result of his supposed communist affiliations. The fifth chapter considers the ways in which Adler used the *Rhapsody* to build a career performing on a nontraditional concert instrument during the 1930s and 1940s and then attempt to revive that career following a period of exile. Starting in the 1980s, Adler spoke often of his close personal and professional relationship with Gershwin. Accepting Adler's narratives at face value—like so many other anecdotal accounts of Gershwin and his music—masks a more extensive and dynamic history documented by his musical arrangement of the *Rhapsody*.

Arrangements of *Rhapsody in Blue* not only assist in the deconstruction of the mythologized musical past, but also hold the potential to establish new narratives—myths in their own right—about American culture more broadly. Visual representations of the *Rhapsody*, wherein arrangements of the piece serve a narrative function, figure prominently in this respect. As an extension of the early cinematic treatment of the *Rhapsody* in chapter 2, the final chapter focuses on film and television encounters with the piece from the last quarter of the twentieth century to the present. Over time, a consensus emerges from such visual representation that closely aligns with conceptions of the piece as a sonic symbol of American ingenuity and success. Such formulations of the *Rhapsody* are precisely what United Airlines had in mind when it selected the piece as its corporate jingle in the late 1980s. However, the inherent flexibility of the *Rhapsody* has resulted in its seemingly limitless adaptability for the company. From commercial advertisements to terminal soundscapes to pre-flight announcements, United has imbued the *Rhapsody* with a host of associations beyond those employed by Hollywood.

From the very beginning, *Rhapsody in Blue* has existed as a variable idea and not a fixed text; the same might be said of Gershwin as well. Shifting the emphasis away from a centralized composition and the sole agency of a single composer reveals new narratives. When cast together, these narratives reshape conceptions of the *Rhapsody*, George Gershwin, and music-making in America. Exploring the cultural work of the *Rhapsody* in this way suggests future directions for studies in American music as the field enters a new generation of scholarship—a field that in the second decade of the twenty-first century has a substantive body of musicological literature on which to stand. At the same time, it prompts a reassessment of that scholarship with respect not only to Gershwin's life and music, but also to the status of the arranger and arrangements. And the arranger that started it all was Ferde Grofé.

CHAPTER 1

Complex Compositional Origins

Ferde Grofé and Rhapsody in Blue

The precise chronology of the *Rhapsody*'s writing is somewhat misty, clouded as it is in anecdotal mythology. . . .

—Biographer Edward Jablonski (1987)

In the boardroom of the American Society of Authors, Composers, and Publishers (ASCAP) hang framed letters from its notable members. A letter from George Gershwin to ASCAP general manager J. C. Rosenthal, which at first glance appears to be little more than historical bric-a-brac, holds special significance:

> Mr. [Jerome] Kern at lunch the other day brought to my attention that Ferdie Grofe had listed among his compositions "The Rhapsody in Blue." Mr. Kern said he objected to this at the last meeting and he advised me to write to you about it. Mr. Grofe made a very fine orchestration from my completed sketch but certainly had no hand in the composing.

Just above the salutation, Gershwin added, "Hoping you will straighten this out."[1] This seemingly simple request has occupied critics and scholars for more than eighty years. On paper—in the composite record made up by the copyright registry, published copies of the sheet music, and even the program from the work's premiere—Gershwin remains the sole composer. But the fact remains that he had assistance in the creative process and that assistance came from Ferde Grofé, the primary arranger for the Paul Whiteman Orchestra.

General accounts of the *Rhapsody*'s initial creation are well known. As the story goes, during the fall of 1923, bandleader and self-appointed "King of Jazz" Paul Whiteman commissioned Gershwin to write a piece for his upcoming "Experiment in Modern Music." Occupied by preparations for his new musical *Sweet Little Devil*, Gershwin supposedly forgot about his commitment to Whiteman. Younger brother Ira pointed out a news item in the *New York Tribune* on January 4, 1924, that unassumingly announced: "George Gershwin is at work on a jazz concerto."[2] With less than five weeks until its February 12 debut and with the Broadway premiere of *Sweet Little Devil* taking place in the interim, Gershwin would have to make haste.

In order to deliver his concerto on time, Gershwin did not complete a fully fleshed out score for the Whiteman Orchestra. As remains true in the present day, Broadway songwriters rarely arranged their music for public performance, leaving the task instead to professional orchestrators. Keeping with convention, Gershwin prepared a two-piano "short score" for *Rhapsody in Blue*—the fifty-six-page "completed sketch" to which he refers in his letter to ASCAP. This manuscript in pencil places the solo piano part in one grand staff system and the accompanying jazz band in another. Gershwin would create similar short scores for each of his subsequent works for the concert hall prior to preparing the final orchestration himself.[3] With the *Rhapsody*, however, the task of arranging fell to Grofé. Although accepted practice for a man of the theatre such as Gershwin, such assistance departed significantly from traditional expectations for classical composition.

Without Ferde Grofé, the world would not know *Rhapsody in Blue* as it does today. In an account repeated often in historical writing on the piece, Grofé stated that he traveled "daily" from his apartment seventy blocks north of Gershwin's residence on West 110th Street, retrieving "more pages of George's masterpiece."[4] As Gershwin notated sections of his two-piano manuscript for the *Rhapsody*, he passed them along to Grofé, who prepared the work for performance by the instruments in the Whiteman Orchestra. Grofé was well aware of the unique timbres and talents of the twenty-three-member ensemble, which included several musicians who doubled on multiple instruments. The original jazz-band version of *Rhapsody in Blue* came together this way, page by page, leading up to its much-celebrated debut at Whiteman's Experiment in Modern Music on February 12, 1924, in Aeolian Hall.

Debates about the extent of Grofé's creative contributions to the *Rhapsody* are as longstanding as the piece itself. One frequent line of inquiry compares Gershwin's pencil manuscript—the "completed sketch"—to

Grofé's full-ensemble jazz-band score, drawing upon numerous instrumental assignments in various hands and types of pen and pencil. One point of view underplays Grofé's role, assigning greater credit to Gershwin. As early as 1931, Gershwin's first biographer, Isaac Goldberg, affirmed that "an appreciable part of the scoring had been indicated by Gershwin."[5] Toward the end of the twentieth century, Alicia Zizzo, a well-known interpreter of Gershwin's piano works and editor of *The Annotated Rhapsody in Blue*, asserted: "Two manuscripts exist. . . . Both scores are identical. Grofé did not alter a single note, chord or any other directive of Gershwin's."[6] More recently, musicologist Howard Pollack determined that "Grofé scrupulously honored Gershwin's intentions," adding that Grofé "stayed extremely close to the notes and rhythms, and heeded orchestral suggestions as well."[7] Working with the same pair of manuscripts, others have assigned greater agency to Grofé. Jerome Schwartz declared in his biography of Gershwin that "in the final analysis, it was Grofé, not Gershwin, who determined which instruments were used in the score."[8] Whiteman scholar Don Rayno asserted that "while remaining faithful to Gershwin's composition, Grofé contributed immensely to the rhapsody [sic]; in many cases he revised George's marginal recommendations for instrumentation—always, it seemed, for the better."[9]

Authorities on both sides of this debate missed a key piece of evidence: a fair-copy manuscript held in the Ferde Grofé Collection at the Library of Congress. It represents a crucial third source document heretofore unconsidered in analyses of the *Rhapsody* (see table 1.1).[10] While Gershwin completed portions of his two-piano pencil score, various copyists—including Gershwin himself—compiled an additional manuscript in ink. Grofé worked from this fair-copy text when he began his arrangement of *Rhapsody in Blue*—not from Gershwin's pencil score as previously believed. The manuscript documents the *Rhapsody* in the midst of its development. It captures a stage of the *Rhapsody* that subsequent revisions to the pencil score—the emendation of dynamics, accents, instrumental assignments, and even countermelodies—obfuscate. It

Table 1.1. THREE MANUSCRIPT SOURCES FOR *RHAPSODY IN BLUE*.

Author	Description	Nickname	Library of Congress Location
Gershwin	Two-piano manuscript	"Pencil"	George and Ira Gershwin Collection
Various	Fair-copy manuscript	"Ink"	Ferde Grofé Collection
Grofé	Jazz-band manuscript	"Grofé/Whiteman"	Ferde Grofé Collection

illuminates the pace with which the *Rhapsody* came together; the time-line of completion was even faster than previously believed. Perhaps most important, it confirms that Grofé played a larger role in the genesis of the *Rhapsody* than typically allowed. Introducing this fair-copy ink manuscript draws out Grofé's significant contributions to *Rhapsody in Blue*, further complicating the issue of composition that Gershwin himself raised in his letter to ASCAP.

COMPOSING *A RHAPSODY IN BLUE*

Patrons attending Paul Whiteman's Experiment in Modern Music on February 12, 1924, received two different programs as they entered Aeolian Hall, leaving the cold behind them on 43rd Street. The first was the venue's standard black-and-white program. It featured, among other items, advertisements for the Aeolian Company's Duo-Art reproducing piano, announcements of upcoming concerts, and classified listings for vocal and piano teachers. The second, more elaborate program had a gold-and-blue cover printed on thick, marbled stock that was hand-stitched with a blue cord. Whiteman reportedly spent nine hundred dollars to cover the expense—there were no advertisements inside.[11] Rather, the contents included an explanation by Whiteman about his concertized "experiment," composer biographies, a list of concert patrons, and set of program notes by jazz sympathizers Gilbert Seldes and Hugh C. Ernst.

Much has been said about the musical programming of this now famous event, including its steady march through the history of jazz, its re-presentation of popular tunes in an unfamiliar environment, and even its connection to the variety-show or revue format of the day.[12] Yet no one has ever commented on the peculiarity of the title given to the most famous work on the program: *A Rhapsody in Blue* by George Gershwin. Note the indefinite article used here. The piece does not appear as *The Rhapsody in Blue* or simply *Rhapsody in Blue*, but rather *A Rhapsody in Blue*. The semantic difference is significant. It also directly connects to the new source manuscript under consideration here. This very title appears in big block lettering at the top of the fair-copy ink score given to Ferde Grofé. Identifying it as *A Rhapsody in Blue* suggests that neither the ink manuscript nor the arrangement heard at Whiteman's concert represented the definitive iteration of this work. Rather, they offered distinct presentations of a musical idea to be encountered in multiple interpretations. Revelatory or not, *A Rhapsody in Blue* arranged by Ferde Grofé quickly became known as *The Rhapsody in Blue* by George Gershwin.

A close consideration of the three original manuscripts for *Rhapsody in Blue* reveals how the initial arrangement took shape in a more rapid and less collaborative process than previously assumed. Although Gershwin's pencil short score and Grofé's full score arrangement for the Paul Whiteman Orchestra remain among the most prized items in the archives of the Library of Congress, the fair-copy ink manuscript emerges as the invaluable missing link between them. This ink manuscript has been the most directly accessible of the three manuscripts located in the Library of Congress holdings, but for various reasons—including the historical fetishization of the other *Rhapsody* manuscripts—it eluded consideration until now.[13]

The Pencil Manuscript

The exalted status of Gershwin's two-piano manuscript for *Rhapsody in Blue* ("pencil") within the Library of Congress holdings likely obscured the significance of the ink score in the past. Gershwin's mother Rose maintained possession of the document until her death in 1958. Five years later, the Gershwin estate donated it to the Library of Congress. The document has been bound in a blue leather cover with a gold-leaf title that identifies it as Gershwin's "original manuscript." Because it is written in pencil on brittle manuscript paper, the surviving score is extremely fragile. In the interest of protecting and preserving documents such as this, the policy of the music division of the Library of Congress is to provide researchers with a microfilm of the manuscript first.[14] They show the original manuscript only when a patron has questions that this surrogate document cannot adequately address. Even though this microfilm represents a scratchy, poor-quality duplication of Gershwin's pencil score, a majority of past studies of the *Rhapsody* appear to have relied on it exclusively. Direct consultation of the pencil manuscript recasts nearly all past assessments of the *Rhapsody* and its compositional process.

Many annotations by several different hands using a variety of writing implements appear in this manuscript. Based more on the content of individual annotations and their layering above or below other markings in the score than on the handwriting itself, some general observations emerge. A plain pencil inscribes instructions like "cue in leader," which reminded Gershwin, who performed from this score, to alert Paul Whiteman that a piano solo was nearing its end. A black ink pen clarifies accidentals, dynamics, tempo indications, and notes, likely representing revisions entered by Gershwin. A red pencil, probably belonging to Grofé, adds rehearsal numbers and provides instructions, which were subsequently erased, for the copyist. At least two sets of blue pencil markings appear, with one providing additional copyist information through hash marks, circled numbers, and the occasional "x." A second set, likely added in preparation for the initial publication of the solo-piano sheet music, adds various accents and dynamics.

The layout of the piano and jazz-band parts in the pencil manuscript offers insight into Gershwin's notational and compositional process. Each of the fifty-six pages in this manuscript has twelve preprinted staves that the composer utilized in various ways; no two pages contain the same distribution of piano and jazz-band systems. Both of the four-line systems on the first page of the manuscript, for example, contain two grand-staff piano staves: The upper is assigned to the jazz band and the lower to the piano solo (see figure 1.1). With the exception of a key signature, the piano staves on the first page remain blank, suggesting that when Gershwin began composing the *Rhapsody*, he left open the possibility for the piano to be a part of the introduction. Obviously, he changed his mind. To conserve space, on page two of the manuscript, Gershwin began to omit the piano staves altogether until the instrument's first entrance at measure 19 [R. 2+3 (see figure 1.2)]. This consolidation of the score persists throughout the remainder of the manuscript. For passages where one part or the other is absent for an extended period—the piano cadenzas, for example—Gershwin left a blank line as a buffer between systems in the manuscript. Several points exist where Gershwin squeezed music into this buffer line, having decided to add the piano to a section that was initially intended just for jazz band or vice versa. Some of these additions were made prior to Grofé's scoring of the work. Others, including various piano fills and countermelodies, were introduced at a later point, either through consultation with Grofé or at his suggestion as Grofé prepared his full-score arrangement for the Paul Whiteman Orchestra.

The Grofé/Whiteman Manuscript

Much to the chagrin of Paul Whiteman, Ferde Grofé donated the manuscript for his full-score arrangement of *Rhapsody in Blue* for piano and jazz band ("Grofé/Whiteman") to the Library of Congress in 1946. While in the midst of preparing his own collection for deposit in the archives of Williams College that year, Whiteman realized that he was no longer in possession of the original full score of the *Rhapsody*. Although he conducted from this manuscript at the premiere of the work, as well as at subsequent performances around the country, the score passed back and forth between Whiteman

Figure 1.1
Page one of the *Rhapsody in Blue* pencil manuscript, Library of Congress, Music Division, George and Ira Gershwin Collection.

and Grofé as the latter prepared the *Rhapsody* for various arrangements and publications. Varying accounts indicate Whiteman's intent to sue either Grofé or the Library of Congress for its return. But as Grofé scholar James Farrington notes, "Whiteman's lawyers pointed out that Williams College would have to become party to the suit. Not wanting to impair relations with the Library of Congress, the trustees of Williams decided to decline involvement, thus forcing Whiteman, still furious, to drop the suit."[15]

Figure 1.2
Page two of the *Rhapsody in Blue* pencil manuscript, Library of Congress, Music Division, George and Ira Gershwin Collection.

The score as received by the Library of Congress from Grofé was in extremely poor shape. Years of use had taken its toll on the document. According to the detailed preservation report that accompanies the score, the manuscript remained with the conservation department between November 1976 and April 1987. During this time, cellophane tape that had been applied to reinforce the delicate paper of this well-used score was removed from the outside edges of several pages. The solvents used in the process caused the red and blue grease-type pencil markings to fade in locations near to where the tape had been. The preservation process culminated in the hermetic encapsulation of each individual page in laminated plastic, permanently protecting the brittle paper from further deterioration.

Like Gershwin's pencil score, thorough assessment of the Grofé/Whiteman score requires direct access to the original document itself, which was not possible for the duration of its conservation. The available microfilm has the same readability issues as the pencil score. A published facsimile of this fifty-three-page score, released in commemoration of the fiftieth anniversary of Gershwin's death, became available commercially in 1987.[16] However, since it was photographed and printed in black and white, distinguishing one type of ink or pencil from another remains nearly impossible. Many of the pencil indications added after Grofé completed his scoring in ink are either illegible or too faint to make the facsimile copy of much use in reconstructing the initial creative process of the *Rhapsody*.

Although the document remains significantly less marked up than Gershwin's pencil score, a variety of indications in different types of pencil and ink appear throughout. Grofé provided clarifying indications to his copyists: A red pencil supplies rehearsal numbers; A blue pencil inserts brackets to separate systems on a crowded page, appends performance directions not initially notated (such as bowing instructions for string instruments), and indicates deleted measures with heavy strike-throughs. Performance indications, likely inscribed by Whiteman, hastily appear in dull pencil. These include hairpin dynamics, large arrows pointing to various ensemble entrances, and a reminder to "wait for nod" from Gershwin at the end of the extended piano cadenza that precedes the start of the love theme. For commentators such as Edward Jablonski and Susan Neimoyer, this indication implies that Gershwin improvised this particular solo at the premiere performance.[17] However, a firmer understanding of Grofé's working process suggests otherwise.

The Grofé/Whiteman manuscript, produced at a relatively early stage in Grofé's career, reveals the markings of a meticulous and methodical orchestrator. Grofé laid out his staff systems prior to entering any music on a given page. Instruments and brackets were done first in ink. Then Grofé added evenly spaced measure lines in pencil. Only after taking these steps did he begin to enter the music. Whenever possible, Grofé employed a copyist to save time in the process of notation. A series of measures containing the same music as previously notated received sets of letters in red or blue pencil to indicate corresponding measures to be written out in full by his copyist when preparing individual parts for performance. For example, the first three bars of the full-ensemble presentation of the stride theme at measure 115 [R. 12] are marked C, D, and E respectively, and correspond to the C, D, and E in the otherwise-empty measures 119–121 [R. 12+4 to R. 12+6]. Through use of this shortcut, Grofé avoided writing out nearly forty individual bars of music—no small feat considering the time constraints under which he worked.

Similarly, Grofé did not take time to enter extended piano solos. Rather, he approximated the amount of space it would take for a copyist to transcribe such passages. In their place, he left instructions to enter a certain number of bars from the piano solo score into his orchestral manuscript. In some cases, Grofé left just the right amount of space, such as the end of page twenty-five and the entirety of page twenty-six where a copyist entered the twenty-eight bars of piano solo that begin at rehearsal eighteen. Elsewhere, however, Grofé overestimated; this was the case with the "wait for nod" indication on an otherwise-empty page thirty-two. The six bars of the supposedly improvised piano cadenza that precede the love theme are fully notated in Gershwin's pencil manuscript, but are absent from the Grofé/Whiteman score. They are also absent from the fair-copy manuscript ("ink"), providing the first of many suggestions that Grofé worked from this intermediary document when preparing the premiere arrangement of *Rhapsody in Blue*.

Introducing the Ink Manuscript

Unlike the pencil and the Grofé/Whiteman scores, the ink score has had neither special bindings nor attempts at preservation; it has not been published in facsimile or edited form; and it has not entered into any previous study of the compositional process of the *Rhapsody*. Yet of the three manuscripts located in the Library of Congress archives, over the course of the last quarter century, it has remained the most readily accessible for direct consultation. The manuscript, visible in a publicity photo of Grofé taken in 1967 (see figure 1.3), remained in his possession until his death five years later. It eventually arrived at the Library of Congress in two stages. The first—largely comprised of solo piano passages—arrived with the Grofé collection items in 1972, and the library acquired the remaining pages— the orchestral passages that introduce the major themes—two decades later.[18]

The ink manuscript holds the key to deciphering information coded in both Gershwin's pencil score and Grofé's full score for the Whiteman Orchestra. First, it illuminates many of the instrumental assignments found in the pencil manuscript that have governed a majority of past

Figure 1.3
Ferde Grofé in 1967 at age seventy-five with the ink manuscript of *Rhapsody in Blue*.
Associated Press, used by permission.

studies on the *Rhapsody*, clarifying which of these indications are original, secondary, or subsequent. In total, there are twenty-six specific instrumental indications, although more general indications such as "solo" and "orch." appear throughout. Those assignments appearing in both the pencil and ink manuscripts represent those originally indicated by Gershwin. The clarinet annotations found in measures 1 and 73 [R. 6+1] of both scores, for example, represent such indications. Assignments that fall into the secondary category include those that appear in the pencil and Grofé/Whiteman scores but not in the ink score. Such additions may have been entered onto the pencil score in the middle of rehearsals. They appear to have functioned as cues for Gershwin—who performed from his pencil score—rather than as specific orchestration directions. One example is located at the start of the stride theme (m. 91 [R. 9]) where the notation "trpts" (trumpets) appears above the melody line. Subsequent assignments, the final indication category, were added to the pencil manuscript at various unknown times after initial performances of the *Rhapsody* in

1924. The precise dating of each one is not possible, but those annotations in blue pencil were likely made by Grofé when the time came to arrange the work for ensembles with more standard instrumentation than that of Paul Whiteman's.[19]

Additional clues about the initial creation and compositional timeline of *Rhapsody in Blue* emerge from the individual pages of the ink score, which fall into distinct gatherings. A gathering (or fascicle) is a group of individual folded pages of music, often nested within each other, that demarcate a particular portion of the larger manuscript. Traditionally, the analysis of gatherings provides an understanding of the piecemeal construction of chant books related to the medieval Catholic liturgy, such as the missal and the breviary. Although nearly a millennium removed from such processes, the seven distinct gatherings of the ink manuscript (see table 1.2) similarly reveal just how much of the *Rhapsody* Grofé received from Gershwin each day while scoring the piece. From a compositional standpoint, passing along a copy of the score rather than the original pencil manuscript makes a good deal of sense. It seems questionable that Gershwin would want to continue composing the *Rhapsody* without referencing what he had already completed. Biographer William Hyland ventured as much: "It is possible that the separate sheets Gershwin supposedly was handing over to Grofé every day were discarded—if they ever existed."[20] Fortunately, these

Table 1.2. PAGE GATHERINGS FOR THE INK MANUSCRIPT OF *RHAPSODY IN BLUE.*

Gathering	Pages	Measures	Bifolia	Notes
1	1–4	1–29	i=1,2,3,4	Water stained
2	5–12	30–109	ii=5,6,11,12	Bifolio iii sits inside of bifolio ii
			iii=7,8,9,10	
3	13–18	110–187	iv=13,14,15,16	Gershwin's hand enters at
			v=17,18	bottom of page 13; bifolio v has
				same water stain as bifolio i
4	19–30	188–334	vi=19,20,29,30	All pages remain connected in
			vii=21,22,27,28	collection
			viii=23,24,25,26	
5	31–32	335–353	ix=31,32	
6	33–36	354–415	x=33,34,35,36	
7	37–50	416–558	xi=37,38,50,[51]	Page 51 blank; page 48 omitted
			xii=39,40,47,49	from numbering; bifolio xiii
			xiii=41,42	taped to bifolio xiv
			xiv=43,44,45,46	

separate sheets did survive, and their gatherings communicate a great deal about how the *Rhapsody* came into existence, including insights into the creative processes of both Gershwin and Grofé.

The initial gathering of the ink manuscript reveals that Gershwin took his first break from composing the *Rhapsody* after completing only twenty-nine measures. This opening portion includes the introduction of the *Rhapsody* through the tag motif prior to the start of the first piano cadenza [R. 4+5]. As with the pencil score from which it was copied, this passage of the *Rhapsody* is the most detailed of the entire score. It is also the only ink manuscript gathering that appears identical to the pencil score. Both manuscripts designate particular instrumental assignments for the melody, provide articulation and accent markings, and specify dynamics for individual parts. Such care suggests greater attention paid—and perhaps greater time allotted—to these opening measures. The first gathering comprises four pages, but the last of these is blank. Assuming that the copyist notated all available music at the time of its preparation, it is reasonable to conclude that Gershwin had only completed the first twenty-nine measures of the *Rhapsody* when the ink score was begun.

If Gershwin indeed began to notate the *Rhapsody* on January 7, preparations for his newest musical, *Sweet Little Devil*—originally titled *A Perfect Lady*—soon intervened. The creative team rewrote the opening sequences for the second and third acts between the end of its Boston out-of-town tryout on January 11 and its Broadway opening ten days later. Two new songs emerged—"Hey! Hey! Let 'Er Go!" and "Quite a Party"—as well as additional dance arrangements. These arrangements prepared by Robert Russell Bennett do not survive, but the songs by Gershwin remain. Hints of *Rhapsody in Blue* are found throughout the score of *Sweet Little Devil*, and the connections that emerge in "Hey! Hey! Let 'Er Go!" are of special interest. The verse resembles a less syncopated inversion of the *Rhapsody*'s stride theme. Likewise, the song's refrain employs a melodic contour strikingly similar to that of the train theme.

Regardless of how long Gershwin neglected work on the *Rhapsody* to attend to *Sweet Little Devil*, the pencil score documents the ensuing pressure to compose quickly. A distinct shift in Gershwin's notation appears between the careful outlay of the first twenty-nine measures and those that followed. When he returned to the *Rhapsody*, he wrote out what became the first piano cadenza. This passage began confidently enough, with six highly rhythmic and chromatic measures tonicizing the key of A major. At the moment in the published score that corresponds to measure 37 [R. 5-4], however, Gershwin struggled with exactly how to proceed. In the pencil score, he wrote out a rapid, two-measure chromatic ascent in

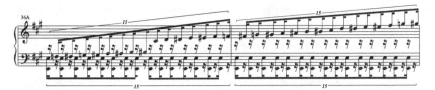

Figure 1.4
Two excised bars (following m. 36 [R. 5-4]) from Gershwin's pencil manuscript of *Rhapsody in Blue*.

the right hand of the piano over a repeated dominant pedal (see figure 1.4). This dramatic segue led to a four-bar, fortissimo jazz-band presentation of the ritornello theme with a "marked and jazzy" performance indication. However, in the service of compositional variety, Gershwin changed his mind. He crossed out these six exuberant measures, opting instead for a more subtle pianissimo echo of the descending figure in measure 36 followed by a simple seventeen-note scalar ascent to a sparse reintroduction of the ritornello theme by the solo piano at measure 38 [R. 5-3].

Given that Gershwin seems to have had no plan as to what would come next, it should come as no surprise to find Grofé in the same boat. The Grofé/Whiteman full manuscript reveals that he completed his scoring of the first gathering of the ink manuscript before Gershwin decided to start with a piano cadenza in gathering two. Consistent with his working methods, Grofé prepared page six of his full score with systems and bar lines for the continued presence of the full ensemble while waiting for additional pages from Gershwin. However, as documented by erasures, when Grofé received the solo-piano-dominated second gathering, he had to rebar page six of his full-score manuscript accordingly. Another example of a rebarring due to an unexpected change between gatherings appears on page twenty-five of the Grofé/Whiteman score, which correlates to the shift from the third to the fourth gathering. Here too, Gershwin suddenly introduces a piano cadenza.

Although four different copyists took part in the preparation of the ink score (see table 1.3), the appearance of Gershwin's hand remains the most

Table 1.3. COPYIST HANDS IN THE INK MANUSCRIPT OF *RHAPSODY IN BLUE*.

Hand	Measures	Key Indicators
Scribe 1	1–29	Narrow accidentals; horizontal quarter-note rests
Scribe 2	30–121	Flat note heads; broad beaming lines; tiny bass clef
Gershwin	122–174	Two-stroke white notes; disconnected beams
Combattente	174/175–559	Evenly spaced and unrushed; very straight beams

illuminating. The first change in copyist maps directly onto the division between the first and second gathering. The second copyist continues onto the first page of the third gathering, but ends abruptly in the midst of a new theme. At this point, music notated by Gershwin suddenly appears. He begins in the middle of the first appearance of the stride theme, where a descending line in the bass clef moves the theme into the subdominant (m. 122 [R. 12+7]). The fifty-two subsequent measures in Gershwin's hand carry several markers of his notational style: The black notes have small, round heads; the heads of the white notes, typically composed of two separate semicircles as opposed to a single circular motion, remain unclosed on one side; beams connecting eighth notes are straight and frequently do not connect to one or more stems in a series; downward beams often appear to the right of a note head; eighth-note rests are curved rather than angular; and ledger lines are narrow and not evenly spaced. Gershwin's notation appears rushed albeit precise.

Given the time constraints under which Gershwin prepared the *Rhapsody*, it is curious that he took the time to copy out this passage himself. In a 1930 article, Gershwin noted that he routinely composed in the evening and tended to "physical labor—orchestrations, piano copies, etc." in the afternoon.[21] He may simply have decided to pick up where the most recent copyist had left off. However, nearly half of the eighty measures of music in the second gathering are for piano solo, and Grofé likely scored them quickly. Gershwin probably assumed responsibility for copying out this passage in the third gathering because he was under pressure to deliver additional pages to Grofé—but first he needed to figure out how to compose his way out of a corner.

Gershwin crafted portions of his *Rhapsody* to avoid clichés of typical jazz-band arrangements, such as the standard unfolding of verse and refrain or the minimal development of those themes beyond a slight harmonic shift. As the date of the premiere drew near, however, such considerations may have fallen by the wayside. One example of Gershwin's attempt to avoid such a formulaic presentation of the *Rhapsody*'s themes appears at the end of the aforementioned piano cadenza in gathering two, where he opted for a pianissimo return to the ritornello theme in the piano as opposed to the fortissimo "marked and jazzy" full ensemble.

A similar attempt at compositional variation took place in the midst of writing the stride theme, the point in the third grouping where Gershwin's hand appears in the ink score. Up to this point—through the first eight measures—the theme resembles a standard AABA Tin Pan Alley tune, with each phrase lasting four measures. Gershwin began with a four-measure B section (seen in figure 1.5) when he eventually returned to complete the rest of this theme. Rather than repeating the A phrase as expected, however, the last four measures of this theme dissipate. The rhythmic pulse and the block melody heard in the initial A sections evaporate into a thrice-repeated linking theme punctuated by four chords and a cymbal crash (mm. 127–137 [R. 13-3 to R. 14]). These compositional choices result in an elision of standard AABA song form and move the piece forward with rhapsodic finesse.

In the midst of transferring this newly completed passage from the pencil to the ink score—as well as the forty-odd bars that follow—Gershwin introduced various revisions. Other copyists involved in the preparation of the ink score did not introduce such modifications. For example, in addition to adding slurs and accents, he also filled in the octave beneath the triads that accompany the B section of the stride theme discussed earlier (see figure 1.5). This method of maintaining the inner notes of a chord, but changing its harmonic configuration through the motion of the outside notes, is characteristic of Gershwin's idiomatic writing for the piano. Such piano-oriented revision in a passage for jazz band suggests that Gershwin was not thinking specifically in terms of ensemble writing, but rather in terms of performance on his own instrument.

Gershwin also introduced a seemingly trivial change that reveals additional evidence that Grofé depended on the ink score rather than the pencil score. This modification occurs at measure 145 [R. 15-1], which links the A and B sections of the shuffle theme. In the pencil manuscript, the transition consists only of an eighth-note D7 chord in the treble clef on the first beat, followed by an ascending eighth-note scale in the bass clef

Figure 1.5
Mm. 123–26 [R. 12+8 to R. 13-3] of the stride theme as notated in ink (top system) and pencil (bottom system) manuscripts of *Rhapsody in Blue*.

Figure 1.6
Mm. 144–146 [R. 15-2 to R. 15+1] of the shuffle theme as notated in ink (top system) and pencil (bottom system) manuscripts of *Rhapsody in Blue*.

(see figure 1.6). In the ink score, however, Gershwin added three ascending quarter-note dyads to the treble clef. These notes subsequently become a brief trumpet solo in the Grofé/Whiteman score. Had Grofé been working from the pencil score at this point, no such solo would have appeared.

Speed Dictates Form

A comparison among the pencil, ink, and Grofé/Whiteman scores makes clear that Gershwin—and as a result, Grofé—encountered several starts and stops in the process of setting the *Rhapsody* down on paper. Scholars tend to agree that Gershwin began notating the *Rhapsody* on Monday, January 7, the date that appears at the top of the first page of the pencil score. However, a closer inspection of the manuscript itself reveals that the "7" was squeezed into an original "Jan. 1924" indication at some unknown point after the month and year notation (see figure 1.7). This addition may indeed represent the actual date of Gershwin's commencement on the pencil score. It may also constitute a later addition to substantiate the now-celebrated anecdote about learning of Whiteman's commission from the January 4 *New York Tribune* article. Regardless, it appears that Gershwin only got as far as page three of his pencil score before setting it aside for a period of time, probably so that he could attend to *Sweet Little Devil*, which ended its Boston tryout run on Friday, January 11. Assuming a return to work after its Broadway premiere on the night of January 21, Gershwin would have had only seven days to write before traveling to

Figure 1.7
Date as it appears on the first page of *Rhapsody in Blue* pencil manuscript (above) and with the subsequently added "7" digitally removed (below).

Boston for a recital with Eva Gautier on the evening of Tuesday, January 29. Might Gershwin's impending departure for Boston have prompted the appearance of his hand in the ink score? Either way, the sudden departure of his hand after the third beat of the solo-piano line in measure 174 [R. 17+4] coincides with a request from Grofé to accelerate his efforts. In a little-known interview from the early 1960s, Grofé recalled:

> At first [Gershwin] would write out a pencil sketch and would then take the trouble of making me a nice neat piano copy in ink. But time was getting short, so I told him that it wouldn't be necessary for him to take all that time to copy it in ink, but to just give me the pencil sketch, and I would have the chief copyist for Harms, Inc., whose name was Combattente, finish copying it, which he did.[22]

Indeed, Fred Combattente's hand enters the ink manuscript at the very moment when Gershwin's departs. It also coincides with the point in the *Rhapsody* at which the careful balance between piano and ensemble begins to break down.

The third and final public rehearsal for Paul Whiteman's Experiment in Modern Music—where the *Rhapsody* received its first performance—took place on February 5, exactly one week after Gershwin's performance with Gautier in Boston. If the appearance and departure of Gershwin's hand in the ink score aligns with this trip to Boston, it would mean that Gershwin and Grofé completed the remaining 300 measures of the *Rhapsody* within the span of seven days. The notion is not as extreme as it may first appear. Following measure 176, nearly two-thirds of the remaining measures (238 out of 382 bars) are given over to piano solo.

The continual return to solo piano passages, one of the hallmarks of the *Rhapsody*, would appear to be a practical decision rather than an aesthetic one. Whenever Gershwin felt pressure to quickly compose additional sections of the *Rhapsody*, he defaulted to piano solo. This is the case at the outset of the second gathering—where Gershwin began writing after a break to work on *Sweet Little Devil*—which represents the start of the first piano cadenza. Likewise, at the end of the third gathering—where Gershwin turned completion of the ink score over to Combattente—a piano cadenza emerges, marking the onset of 142 consecutive measures of piano solo with little instrumental accompaniment for Grofé to score. Only 30 total measures in this passage required any active scoring, saving Grofé a significant amount of time in the preparation of his arrangement for the Whiteman Orchestra. As indicated by Gershwin in his pencil manuscript, a single horn line accompanies the piano for fifteen bars in the middle of a presentation of the stride theme (mm. 204–218 [R. 20 to R. 21]). The next instrumental entrance, the sixteen-bar ritornello theme at measure 242 [R. 22]—given as a single melody to be played by the clarinet with bass drum and cymbal accompaniment—provides a stable background for Gershwin's filigree piano extemporization. An additional sixty measures of piano solo begin at measure 257 [R. 24], representing another instance of Gershwin turning to piano solo to fill out the *Rhapsody*.[23]

Such economy also extends into the love theme. For all its fame and splendor, this passage of the *Rhapsody* required only 44 measures of scoring on Grofé's part. The eighteen-measure melody repeats twice, with a four-bar linking motif assigned by Grofé to a solo violin and celesta, respectively, following each statement of the love theme. At the start of the second iteration of the theme, the ink score contains no instrumental suggestions, and the pencil score simply indicates "full." Here Grofé expands the first and second violins from a single melody line played *sul G*—entirely on the lowest string—to a four-part *divisi*. The brass completes the midrange harmonic sonorities, while the alto, tenor, and baritone saxophone combination heard in the first iteration becomes a trio of soprano saxophones complementing the upper register of the strings.

In strong contrast to the first half of the piece, after the love theme passage, the compositional thoroughness of the pencil score (as preserved by the ink score) becomes reduced to little more than a basic outline of melody and harmony. Only six instrumentation assignments were provided by Gershwin, of which Grofé adhered to three: a solo horn line during the piano's presentation of the stride theme (mm. 204–218 [R. 20 to R. 21]), a cymbal encountered in the "Orientalist" presentation of the ritornello theme (mm. 242–256 [R. 22 to R. 24]), and a brief passage given to the celesta (mm. 357–360 [R. 31 to R. 32]). All remaining instrumental decisions, including the sixty-two-measure orchestral build to the climax of the *Rhapsody*, would seem to be the work of Grofé on his own.

The musicians in Paul Whiteman's ensemble were celebrated for their ability to play multiple instruments, an aspect of the ensemble Grofé relied on extensively in his initial arrangement of *Rhapsody in Blue*. Grofé capitalized on such doublings as the instrumentation timeline chart located on the companion website makes clear ●. In this timeline, occurrences of the various themes appear at the top and measure numbers appear below. The piano solo appears in red, woodwinds in blue, brass (including tuba) in green, strings (including bass) in yellow, and rhythm section (including banjo) in purple. Black horizontal lines within a particular color indicate the location of the melody at any given point in the piece. Black vertical lines indicate an instrumental assignment originally notated in Gershwin's pencil score and the subsequent ink score that Grofé carried forward into his Paul Whiteman arrangement. In the first eighty-five measures, Ross Gorman, whose five instruments appear in the top lines of the chart, cycles from Bb clarinet to bass clarinet to oboe and back to clarinet. Donald Clark and Hale Byers switch between various saxophones. Likewise, Albert Armer alternates between tuba and string bass. Such changes provided not only visual interest as the musicians switched from one instrument to the other but also a great degree of sonic contrast.

The woodwind combinations on their own demonstrate the variety of orchestral colors available to Grofé. For example, the alto and tenor saxophones join the bass clarinet—in its only appearance in the score—to interject statements of the tag motif during the first statement of the ritornello theme (m. 39 [R. 5-3]). The clarinet joins two soprano saxophones through the stride theme (m. 115 [R. 12]), before pairing with the baritone saxophone alone to present the main melody of the shuffle theme (m. 138 [R. 14]). These unique sonic combinations make the unified timbre of the alto, tenor, and baritone saxophones at the commencement of the love theme (m. 317 [R. 28]) a welcome release. During the four-bar violin solo that precedes the theme's second iteration (m. 339 [R. 30]), the reed players quickly substitute their instruments with saxophones in the soprano register. These two statements of the love theme represent the only point in the entire arrangement when three saxophones are heard together—something to keep in mind when considering later arrangements of the *Rhapsody* by Grofé for theatre and symphony orchestra.

ASSESSING GROFÉ'S CONTRIBUTIONS

Acknowledging that Grofé scored the *Rhapsody* with a significantly greater degree of independence than previously assumed allows for a more direct consideration of how his selection of instruments and implementation of other jazz-band arranging techniques transformed Gershwin's so-called pencil sketch into a full-fledged, musically engaging "composition." In his study of Don Redman's work for Fletcher Henderson's band (circa 1922–29), Jeffrey Magee observes that, "[l]ike a composer, an arranger gives an original shape to a piece of music, creating unity and contrast through a variety of musical elements. . . . Like an improvising soloist, an arranger takes existing material. . . and uses it as the framework for a fresh, new conception."[24] One reality of the *Rhapsody*—and one of its most recurrent criticisms—is that large passages offer little more than AABA Tin Pan Alley-style tunes, despite Gershwin's attempts to avoid such formulations. The decisions Grofé made in transitioning the *Rhapsody* from Gershwin's two-piano pencil score to the Whiteman arrangement lent the piece a necessary level of "unity and contrast" expected of a composition. But in addition to instrumentation choices, exactly what decisions did Grofé make?

Grofé's Pre-*Rhapsody* Arranging

Looking at Grofé's past clarifies his approach to the *Rhapsody* in 1924. He prepared his first arrangements in 1919 during a brief stint with Art Guerin's band—considered by James Farrington to be the first true jazz band on the West Coast.[25] Guerin and his musicians relied on the "huddle system," or what jazz musicians would later call a "head arrangement." Like a football team before a play, the musicians would gather together before each number to determine who would take the melody, the harmony, and the solos. Critics such as Carl Engel praised the results of such performance practice: "Jazz is abandon, is whimsicality in music. A good jazz band should never play, and actually never does play, the same piece twice in the same manner. Each player must be a clever musician, an originator as well as an interpreter, a wheel that turns hither and thither on its own axis without disturbing the clockwork."[26] The style made for an exciting and unpredictable musical experience. Grofé was taken by the ephemeral timbral combinations made possible by such performance practice, but perhaps due to the classical side of his musical upbringing, he favored somewhat more order and permanence.[27] While working for Guerin, he began to write down what he heard. He replaced the improvisatory performance style of the huddle system with notated arrangements that highlighted the unique instrumental combinations inspired by such performances.[28] This process made it possible to recreate the most thrilling moments with greater consistency. It also allowed further exploration of the individual abilities of each performer and the refinement of the various instrumental mixtures.

Grofé's foray into arrangements paralleled a contemporary move by music publishers to make their most popular songs available as "stock" arrangements, which offered straightforward settings of songs for performance by a standard combination of instruments. Throughout the 1920s, ensembles routinely turned to such charts to keep up with the demands for social dancing. Publishers were more than happy to oblige, providing generic settings of hits of the day. The use of a stock arrangement by an ensemble did not necessarily imply a canned, note-for-note performance, however. For certain ensembles, the stock arrangement served as a point of departure. Fletcher Henderson's 1924 recording of "Copenhagen," as Jeffrey Magee has demonstrated, reveals how the "doctoring" of the published stock arrangement by Don Redman resulted in a dynamic and complex transformation.[29]

Two years before Redman began to prepare arrangements for Henderson, Paul Whiteman hired Grofé for his ensemble in March 1920.[30] Whiteman had just received a contract for his nine-member band to play three sessions each day—more than five hours of music—at the Alexandria Hotel in San Francisco. Grofé's services were immediately put to use. The Whiteman ensemble's success from this point forward owed much to the arrangements Grofé provided. Rather than rely on stock arrangements, Grofé customized popular songs for performance by the specific musicians within the group. In May 1920, two months after Grofé began to work for Whiteman, the ensemble relocated to the East Coast to perform at the Ambassador Hotel in Atlantic City. Their immediate popularity resulted in a quick change of venue to the Palais Royal in Manhattan. Record companies took note of the reputation and musical proclivity of Whiteman's ensemble. Their first disc, released in September 1920 and featuring "Whispering" and "Japanese Sandman," sold in record numbers, prompting Victor Records to sign the group to an exclusive two-year contract.[31]

Grofé was well acquainted with Gershwin by the time the *Rhapsody* forever linked the two in the history of American music. Whenever Whiteman wanted to add a new song to the band's repertory, it became Grofé's job to track down the published piano-vocal sheet music and create an arrangement. This practice kept him in constant contact with various publishing houses and the musicians they employed. After the 1920 success of "Whispering" and "Japanese Sandman," Whiteman sent Grofé in search of their next hit. Along the way, Grofé encountered Gershwin at the T. B. Harms publishing company, where Gershwin worked as a staff composer.[32] Gershwin also had his first major success that year when Al Jolson recorded his song "Swanee."[33] As Farrington notes, "it became Grofé's habit to visit Gershwin (who was already somewhat successful) and go over George's most recent songs. If Grofé thought the song was effective, he would take the music and make an arrangement of it for Whiteman's band."[34] During the early 1920s, before the premiere of *Rhapsody in Blue*, the Whiteman Orchestra performed seven Gershwin songs. Grofé prepared arrangements for each of these. Although the notated scores and parts for the early songs have long since disappeared, the surviving original recordings offer a sonic glimpse at his approach during this period.[35] Two signature components of Grofé's style emerge that provide insight into his ultimate arrangement of the *Rhapsody*: the harmony chorus and the use of thematic echo.

The creative consistency of Grofé's arrangements soon lent Whiteman's ensemble a characteristic sound: "warm and luscious," in the words of pioneering jazz critic Henry Osgood.[36] In *So This Is Jazz* (1926), the first book-length treatment of the subject, Osgood noted that Grofé's arrangements contained "no noise, no unrest. It was delightful to listen to and yet it was perfectly danceable."[37] Grofé purposefully reigned in the rhythmic restlessness of typical jazz-band performance through what he termed the "harmony chorus." As Osgood observed:

> In the harmony chorus, when the melody did not need special emphasis, Grofé gave it to the solo saxophone, supporting it with sustained chords, *piano*, on the brass (used like horns); if the melody needed to stand out more, he reversed the process, giving the melody to the first trumpet and using the two saxophones and the trombone for the sustained harmonic support. The rhythm was lightly indicated by the piano, the banjo, a light pizzicato bass or perhaps merely a whispered drum tap. That was an absolute innovation in jazz.[38]

At first glance, such arranging may not seem as innovative as Osgood reports. However, Grofé's approach offered a pleasing middle ground between the dominant opposing performance practices of the time: stock arrangements, which were repetitive and predictable without doctoring, and the huddle system, which led to potentially un-danceable musical chaos. In his earliest arrangements for Paul Whiteman, Grofé prepared charts with a greater degree of variety than a stock arrangement, while maintaining a timbral uniformity that appealed to listeners. The departures that Grofé makes from Robert Russell Bennett's stock arrangement for the Whiteman ensemble's recording of Gershwin's "Do It Again" serve as a case in point.[39]

Recorded for Victor Records during the spring of 1922, "Do It Again" was the first Gershwin song put on disc by the Whiteman Orchestra that was not part of a medley (Victor 18882) ◐.[40] Grofé stayed close to Bennett's stock arrangement through the first verse, assigning the violin and trumpets to the melody over a sparse-yet-steady rhythm section. His first departure from the stock occurs at the onset of the chorus (also known as the refrain). As a means of adding motion to the whole-note-heavy melody played on the violin and trumpets, Grofé inserts an echo of the "Do It Again" theme following each instance of its appearance. The theme itself consists of a series of four eighth notes that descend stepwise from the third-scale degree to the sixth, passing right through the tonic (see figure 1.8). [41] Grofé transposes the subsequent return of the verse into the relative minor. He accomplishes this transition through a four-bar modulation featuring the celesta—an instrument Grofé favored and incorporated into his initial arrangement of Rhapsody in Blue. When the chorus enters again, the melody is now played on the tenor saxophone. Although the harmony returns to the original major key, the "Do It Again" thematic echoes remain in the relative minor. A four-bar bridge, with an ascending line reminiscent of the passage that precedes the grandioso finale of the Rhapsody, ushers in the third and final occurrence of the chorus. Here the trumpet and violin return to the melody while the trombone provides a countermelody. On the recording, each instrument introduces a small degree of improvisation to its respective line. Given the otherwise innovative approach offered by Grofé's arrangement, his four-bar codetta feels a touch mundane. However, since the piece was performed primarily for social dancing, a clear cue that the song had reached its conclusion was certainly in order.

Grofé also prepared an arrangement of Gershwin's song "(I'll Build a) Stairway to Paradise," which became the unexpected hit of George White's *Scandals of 1922*.[42] Whiteman's ensemble featured prominently in this

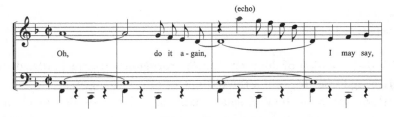

Figure 1.8
Gershwin's "Do It Again" melody with thematic echo added by Ferde Grofé.

annual iteration of the *Scandals*, and Gershwin later stated, "I'll never forget the first time I heard Whiteman do it. Paul made my song live with a vigor that almost floored me. . . . There was no stopping 'Stairway to Paradise' once Whiteman got his brasses into it."[43] The "vigor" that Gershwin experienced resulted directly from Grofé's arrangement. Since the song was composed specifically for *Scandals*, Grofé likely prepared the arrangement from Gershwin's manuscript or from a copy of it; neither the published sheet music nor the stock arrangement existed at the time.[44] The Paul Whiteman Orchestra recorded Grofé's arrangement for Victor Records on September 1, 1922 (Victor 18949) ◗.

Multiple techniques contributed to the success of this particular arrangement, including novelty effects in the brass and percussion, a near textbook application of the harmony chorus, and the dramatic use of group improvisation. The eight-bar introduction begins with a swooping trombone line (likely the moment that struck Gershwin so assuredly) and concludes with a cymbal-accented descending figure. This trombone line becomes the glue that holds together the continuous secondary-dominant chord progression (C-Eb-Ab-E7-A-F7-Bb) found in the verse, over which the violins and trumpets carry the melody. The first iteration of the chorus features the saxophone ensemble over a sustained descending trombone line. The sonorities are reversed for the second chorus, where Grofé draws special attention to the melody by locating it in the solo trumpet, using the saxophones to provide additional harmonic support through various fill figures. Following a trumpet solo taking the form of a twelve-bar blues, the final "out chorus," as the last refrain of an arrangement was commonly called, offers a nod to the huddle system of performance: All of the instruments enter, each adding its own independent line to the mix. Grofé's arrangement likely instructed the musicians to "fake jazz band," and the constant threat of collision between the parts certainly adds to the thrill of hearing the final chorus.[45] Just when the arrangement seems to have strayed too far from its otherwise ordered presentation, a tidy four-bar clarinet codetta concludes the piece.

Variety Is the Spice of Life

With the exception of duration, Grofé's scoring of *Rhapsody in Blue* does not go significantly beyond the techniques of his arrangements of other Gershwin songs for the Whiteman ensemble at the time—despite observations, even by Grofé himself, to the contrary. Grofé recalled that scoring the *Rhapsody* "took me out of the realm of dance music arranger and into the concert field."[46] Gershwin biographer Isaac Goldberg concurred: "[Grofé] may be said fairly to have originated, on the afternoon of February 12th, 1924, a school of jazz arrangement."[47] However, Grofé's original arrangement of the *Rhapsody* was consistent with his prior work on Gershwin's songs. Vernon Duke would observe some years later that "Grofé's orchestral translation was a good, honest job in the typical early-Whiteman-concert-jazz tradition."[48] Instead of "inventing a new school of orchestration," Grofé applied his versatile understanding of jazz-band arranging to a longer piece of music—a medley of tunes perhaps. Although some scholars no longer consider the themes of the *Rhapsody* to be mere tunes, Grofé made no such distinctions in scoring it.[49] Without Grofé's inventive treatment of Gershwin's recurring themes, several passages in the *Rhapsody* might have simply fallen flat.

Such variety sustains multiple repetitions of the ritornello theme. Three complete statements of this theme reveal techniques used by Grofé to sustain its appeal over the course of several recurrences, including his use of thematic echoes and the harmony chorus. Although segments of the ritornello theme arise throughout the introductory twenty-four bars of the *Rhapsody*, a complete presentation of this AABA theme does not occur until measure 38 [R. 5-3]. It follows the first piano cadenza. Gershwin initially specified a full-ensemble presentation of the theme at this point, which he crossed out in the pencil manuscript, opting for a subtler introduction. The piano plays the first three measures of the A portions of the theme. Two-measure statements of the tag motif by the jazz band round off the A section of this theme, while the piano arpeggiates chords in rhythmic consonance with the band. Despite his careful construction of this passage, Gershwin provides no indications for instrumentation.[50] Respectful of Gershwin's decision to take a more subtle approach to the theme, Grofé limited the jazz-band orchestration to the three reed players: Ross Gorman played the melody on a bass clarinet, and Donald Clark and Hale Byers provided harmony on the alto and tenor saxophones, respectively. The piano completes the theme unaccompanied. It plays the B and final A sections in an equally sparse texture before launching into a seventeen-bar cadenza at measure 55 [R. 5+14].

Having delayed a full-ensemble presentation of the ritornello theme by more than thirty measures, Gershwin assigned the theme to a *fortissimo* jazz band at measure 72 [R. 6]. A pair of blank staff lines appears beneath the jazz-band line in his pencil manuscript, which remained empty when copied to the ink score. Such a move implies that Gershwin intended to add a piano part at a later point. Indeed, a piano fill—block chords that accent the offbeat—eventually came to occupy the empty lines beneath the tag motif at measures 75–76 [R. 6+3 to R. 6+4] in the pencil score. When writing out the B and final A portions of this theme (page eleven of the pencil score), Gershwin left just one blank staff line (as a buffer between jazz-band systems) instead of two. As in other sections of the pencil manuscript, this line suggests that Gershwin's initial impulse was to have the jazz band play the second half of the theme on its own. However, a piano echo of the B section melody—added at some subsequent point in time—came to occupy this originally empty buffer staff line.

The solo-piano echo heard in the B section of this melody (mm. 81–84 [R. 7 to R. 7+3]) may have come at the suggestion of Grofé. In an interview, he claimed to have added "counter themes where necessary."[51] Here Grofé may have conceived such thematic echoes—located in the piano rather than the ensemble—to be counter themes. The addition of this piano echo provides both motion and variation within the second presentation of the ritornello theme. It remains unclear at what point this echo was squeezed into the pencil score and by whom. The same is true of its incorporation into the ink score, where it was entered into the treble-clef staff line of the jazz band with a different pen. Such an addition on the part of Grofé would be consistent with his demonstrated addition of thematic echoes in arrangements like "Do It Again."

Grofé also made use of the harmony chorus when scoring this second full iteration of the ritornello theme (mm. 72–90 [R. 6 to R. 9]). The A melody appears in the oboe, alto and tenor saxophones, trumpets, and violins, with the harmony provided by the horns and trombones through a pulsation of quarter-note chords (see figure 1.9; a color version of this timeline appears on the companion website 🔊). The rhythm section (tympani, banjo, bass, and accompaniment piano) further reinforces this steady beat. Placing the woodwinds over a brass foundation recalls the harmony chorus often used by Grofé in other early arrangements for the Whiteman ensemble. The remaining four bars of this presentation of the ritornello theme—the final A section—are marked "fill up" in pencil in the ink score. Here Grofé inverts the melody and harmony, staying true to Osgood's observation that in a harmony chorus, "if the melody needed to stand out more, [Grofé] reversed the process."[52] In the final A section, the horns and trombones take the melody while the remaining instruments play quarter-note chords on the offbeat.

The jazz sonority of the B section of this AABA theme (mm. 81–84 [R. 7 to R. 7+3]) stands in marked contrast to the harmony chorus sound that precedes it. Grofé situates the melody among the alto saxophone, tenor saxophone, and one of the horns, with the aforementioned piano echo. The removal of the oboe from the melody here allowed Ross Gorman to switch

		72	73	74	75	76	77	78	79	80	81	82	83	84	85	86	87	88	89	90
Gorman	Eb Soprano Sax																			
	Bb Clarinet																			
	Oboe																			
	Alto Sax																			
	Bass Clarinet																			
Clark	Bb Soprano Sax																			
	Alto Sax																			
	Baritone Sax																			
Byers	Bb Soprano Sax																			
	Tenor Sax																			
	Piano																			
	Horns in F																			
	Trumpets																			
	Trombones																			
	Violins																			
	Percussion																			
	Tympani																			
	Banjo																			
	Tuba																			
	String Bass																			
	Acc. Piano/Celeste																			

Figure 1.9
Instrumentation timeline for second full statement of ritornello theme in the Grofé/Whiteman manuscript of *Rhapsody in Blue* (mm. 72–90 [R. 6 to R. 9]).

instruments quickly for the clarinet entrance four bars later. The second horn, trombones, and accompaniment piano, which had been providing support for the melody, also fall silent. Meanwhile, the violins, banjo, and bass maintain the steady pulse through pizzicato quarter notes—another important scoring effect to keep in mind with respect to Grofé's subsequent arrangement of the *Rhapsody* for symphonic orchestra. Grofé's push to add as much variation as possible within the different choruses, then referred to as arranging "inside the strain," reflects a growing trend among contemporary arrangers like Don Redman.[53]

The third full statement of the ritornello theme represents the only instance of this particular melody—and one of only a few moments in the pencil or ink manuscripts as a whole—where Gershwin indicated a specific instrumental combination. Likely to appeal to the Orientalist vogue of the 1920s, Gershwin initially suggested clarinet, violin, and baritone saxophone for this passage—the same combination heard throughout Whiteman's "Japanese Sandman." Grofé opted for a slightly different combination that honored Gershwin's sonic intentions while avoiding a direct reference to the hugely popular recording. He assigns the jazz-band melody line to the upper registers of soprano and baritone saxophones, creating what sounds like a Mozartian Turkish band. Pizzicato violins, a cymbal, and bass drum complete this effect. Notably, in the B section of this iteration, Grofé omits a whole-note melody similar to that heard in the presentation of the stride theme in measures 204–217 [R. 20 to R. 21]. Rather, he assigns the harmony to the pizzicato violins as eighth notes on beats one and three. The shift removes a drone effect that becomes particularly dissonant in the third and fourth measures of the B section, a sonority encountered recurrently in Tin Pan Alley references to "The Orient" by Gershwin and other composers of the time.[54]

Though it would have made sense to contemporary audiences of the time, out of all the instrumental and scoring effects used in the piece, the Orientalist presentation of this third instance of the ritornello theme sounds the most out of place today. In fact, regardless of the particular arrangement being used, this passage is frequently omitted in performances and recordings of the *Rhapsody*. Part of this results from the fact that in the published two-piano score, this passage and a majority of the extended piano solo passages that precede and follow it [R. 19 to R. 25-4] are part of an optional cut. However, it is worth questioning whether this passage would be skipped as often today had Grofé departed from Gershwin's instrumentation suggestions and arranged it so that it aligned better with the sonorities of the rest of the arrangement.

The examination of each of these three instances of the ritornello theme reveals that scoring for an ensemble such as Whiteman's extended beyond the task of doling out the parts. The art of arranging for jazz band developed rapidly during the 1920s, promoting innovation and variety. Gershwin knew enough to write such variety into his two-piano version of the *Rhapsody*. Some of it worked, such as the first full instance of the ritornello section. Some of it did not work, such as the Orientalist third instance of that theme. Yet large passages appear that present nothing more than an AABA Tin Pan Alley-style tune, the second instance of the ritornello theme, for example. It became Grofé's responsibility to keep such passages moving through the same kinds of textural and timbral choices that he had used in previous arrangements of Gershwin's songs.

AFTER THE EXPERIMENT

Beyond his contributions to the original arrangement of *Rhapsody in Blue*, Ferde Grofé should also receive credit for the longevity of the piece. As David Schiff notes, "Grofé's intimate knowledge of the band's personnel contributed to the success of the piece, but the *Rhapsody* has outlived the Whiteman band."[55] Grofé's role in the continued popularity of the *Rhapsody* cannot be overstated. He created subsequent arrangements that served to maintain the *Rhapsody*'s popular place in American culture throughout the twentieth century and beyond. Grofé prepared at least five additional arrangements of *Rhapsody in Blue* after the first one for Paul Whiteman.

Two were for his own use: the first at a Gershwin memorial performance in 1937 and the second for Grofé's Novachord Orchestra at the 1939 World's Exposition. Three were prepared for widespread use: theatre orchestra (1926), concert band (1937), and symphony orchestra (published 1942). Although only the arrangements for theatre and symphony orchestra are considered here, the other arrangements underscore the continued presence of the *Rhapsody* in Grofé's career.

Whereas Grofé's original arrangement for the Whiteman ensemble was scored for a specific set of musicians performing on a specific combination of instruments, his subsequent theatre orchestra version allowed for performances of the *Rhapsody* by more generic ensembles (see instrumentation in table 1.4). Grofé completed this rendition, which resides in the George and Ira Gershwin Collection at the Library of Congress, on February 23, 1926, and T. B. Harms subsequently published it as a stock arrangement. This score removes the necessity for instrumental doubling at the same time as it alters the overall scoring of the *Rhapsody*. For example, three of the five instruments played by Ross Gorman (oboe, alto saxophone, and clarinet) are assigned to separate musicians. The remaining two instruments (Eb soprano saxophone and bass clarinet) are replaced by flute and bassoon. Two of the four violin parts are removed in favor of viola and cello. By making allowances for its performance by multiple combinations of standard instruments, the work became usable by a wide variety of ensembles. The flute and bassoon were found more commonly in theatre orchestras than either the Eb and Bb soprano saxophones or bass clarinet. Likewise, the baritone saxophone, tuba, and second piano parts were removed. Since most theatre orchestras included a full string section, Grofé added cello and viola parts. Most of the published parts contain cues to be played in the absence of a particular instrument. For example, in the opening measures, two of the saxophones carry the horn parts where they would not have otherwise been played. Likewise, a cue for the bassoon appears in the trombone line. Additionally, the arrangement contains the same set of optional cuts located in the published two-piano score, allowing an individual bandleader to decide how long or short the piece should be by omitting large portions of the piano solo or the aforementioned third statement of the ritornello theme.

These practical changes initiated the classicization of the *Rhapsody*. Although the theatre orchestra score calls for three saxophones, its overall design provided a template for Grofé's subsequent symphony orchestra arrangement.[56] In fact, when the time came for Grofé to expand the *Rhapsody* for this latter ensemble, which occurred at some point before Gershwin's death, only a few small instrumental changes needed to be

Table 1.4. INSTRUMENTATION FOR THREE ARRANGEMENTS OF *RHAPSODY IN BLUE* BY FERDE GROFÉ.

Grofé/Whiteman Scoring	Theatre Orchestra Scoring	Symphony Orchestra Scoring
Reed 1: Eb Soprano saxophone ----->	Flute	Flute 1 & 2
Reed 1: Oboe	Oboe	Oboe 1 & 2
Reed 1: Bb Clarinet	Clarinet 1	Clarinet 1
Reed 2: Bb Clarinet	Clarinet 2	Clarinet 2
		Bass clarinet
Reed 1: Bass clarinet ----->	Bassoon	Bassoon 1 & 2
Reed 1: Alto saxophone	Saxophone 1 – Alto	Saxophone 1 – Alto (optional)
Reed 3: Tenor saxophone	Saxophone 2 – Tenor	Saxophone 2 – Tenor (optional)
Reed 2: Alto saxophone	Saxophone 3 – Alto	Saxophone 3 – Alto (optional)
Reed 2: Baritone saxophone		
Reed 3: Bb Soprano saxophone		
Horn 1 & 2	Horn 1 & 2	Horn 1, 2, & 3
Trumpet 1 & 2	Trumpet 1 & 2	Trumpet 1 & 2
Trombone 1 & 2	Trombone 1 & 2	Trombone 1 & 2
		Tuba
Piano Solo	Piano/Conductor	Piano Solo
Piano Accompaniment/Celesta		
Percussion	Percussion	Drums
		Tympani
Banjo	Banjo	Banjo (optional)
Violin 1	Violin 1/Conductor	Violin 1 (two stands)
Violin 2	Violin 2	Violin 2
Violin 3 ----->	Viola	Viola
Violin 4 ----->	Cello	Cello
Tuba/String Bass ----->	Bass	Bass

made. The flutes, oboes, clarinets, bassoons, horns, trumpets, and trombones were each given an additional part, and the bass clarinet and tuba were reinstated (see table 1.4). Doublings resulting from these additions render the three saxophones unnecessary and, as Schiff opines, "obscure the idiomatic colors of the original."[57] Since most orchestras do not regularly employ saxophonists or banjo players, these last remaining vestiges of the original jazz scoring frequently go unrealized in symphonic performances of the *Rhapsody*. Another point of classicization occurs in the piano's first introductory passage (mm. 24–27 [R. 4 to R. 4+3]). In the jazz-band arrangement, bells, strings, and percussion accompany the piano. In the symphonic arrangement, these are omitted, giving the piano its own solo and yielding a more concerto-like introduction.

The decisions Grofé made in transitioning the *Rhapsody* from Gershwin's two-piano score to the Whiteman arrangement lent the piece a necessary level of consistency through instrumental variety. This variety is lost in his subsequent arrangement of the *Rhapsody* for symphonic orchestra, which some critics feel suffers as a result of the smoothed-over orchestration. A degree of sonic coherence is expected of a classical symphonic work. Yet it was the sonic novelty of Grofé's scoring upon which Gershwin relied when assembling the various themes of the *Rhapsody*. When this novelty is removed—indeed, the incorporation of saxophones (which remains optional) or trumpets with "wha wha" mutes represent the near extent of the novelty heard in the symphonic arrangement—the piece loses a great deal of momentum. This lack of sonic interest is precisely what encourages the introduction of cuts in modern performances of the *Rhapsody*.

ARRANGER, COMPOSER, OR BOTH?

To put it simply, without Grofé, there would be no *Rhapsody in Blue* as we know it. Although a significant claim, the details that lie in support of it are perhaps even more important. At particular moments throughout both his initial Whiteman arrangement and subsequent versions for theatre and symphony orchestras, Grofé made contributions that shaped the compositional makeup of the *Rhapsody*. Does this equate his role with that of Gershwin? Isaac Goldberg, Gershwin's first biographer, seemed conflicted on this issue. After claiming that Gershwin had indicated "an appreciable part of the scoring," Goldberg observed that "the contribution of Grofé was of prime importance. . . . It is strange indeed that he was not represented on [Whiteman's] program as a composer."[58]

Gershwin, of course, strongly disagreed with such a notion. Even before his letter to ASCAP, Gershwin affirmed this detail publicly. In a 1926 article in *Singing Magazine*, he reported that "Mr. Grofé worked from a very complete piano and orchestral sketch in which many of the orchestral colors were indicated." Such an assertion serves to bolster Gershwin's status as composer. Further separating his contributions from that of Grofé, he continued, "The ability to orchestrate is a talent apart from the ability to create. The world is full of most competent orchestrators who cannot for the life of them write four bars of original music."[59] For Gershwin, then, it was the themes rather than the overall sound of the *Rhapsody* that counted as the composition. His point of view conforms to his experience as a songwriter and as a man of the theatre. The composer provides music (sometimes nothing more than a lead sheet) to the orchestrator, who in turn arranges it for performance onstage. In Gershwin's estimation, it would seem that orchestrators offer little more than a paint-by-numbers approach—the casual addition of color to a fully outlined work.

From the start, the reception of *Rhapsody in Blue* has hinged on its arrangement. If Grofé had been a lesser arranger, would the *Rhapsody* have become the success that it did? Ultimately, such speculation is akin to asking what Gershwin's *next* opera might have sounded like. Grofé's original orchestration for Paul Whiteman's ensemble made history, and his subsequent arrangements of the *Rhapsody* secured its ongoing place in American culture. But as the next chapter considers, the reputation of the *Rhapsody* and Gershwin resulted not from Grofé's efforts alone; musical and biographical arrangements of both proliferated in the years before Gershwin's passing.

CHAPTER 2
Living Legends

don't fear the real world, but reimagine it.
—Dr. Clague

George Gershwin and Rhapsody in Blue

Music has a marvelous faculty of recording a picture in someone else's mind. In my own case, everybody who has ever listened to *Rhapsody in Blue*—and that embraces thousands of people—has a story for it but myself.

—George Gershwin (1930)

George Gershwin became an icon in his time, and arrangements of *Rhapsody in Blue* participated greatly in his rise to fame. These took many forms after the 1924 premiere of the *Rhapsody*, and each contributed to the mythic status of both Gershwin and the piece itself. Recordings by the Whiteman orchestra with Gershwin at the piano disseminated the work widely and supposedly made Gershwin a very wealthy man. The sale of sheet music and stock arrangements allowed for the performance of the *Rhapsody* by a range of ensembles and skill levels—professional and amateur musicians alike could make the piece their own. The public accessed the captivating power of the *Rhapsody* not only through live performances but also through its cinematic arrangement in films like *King of Jazz* (1930). The publication of *George Gershwin: A Study in American Music* by biographer Isaac Goldberg in 1931 provided an intimate look at the man and the ways his life influenced his music, establishing narratives about the *Rhapsody* in particular that resonate into the present. These various arrangements of *Rhapsody in Blue*—musical, biographical, and historiographical—became important parts of Gershwin's legacy during his lifetime and in the years and decades following his death. Considering each in turn reveals the multitude of individuals responsible for the early success of *Rhapsody in Blue* and draws out the role of arrangement in the creation of a living legend.

MAKING A MOLEHILL OUT OF A MOUNTAIN

The early public success of *Rhapsody in Blue* remains one of the most mythologized aspects of its legacy. When addressing the popularity of the *Rhapsody*, writings on Gershwin regularly highlight the remarkable sales figures associated with its earliest recording. David Ewen, author of several biographical studies of Gershwin, wrote in 1956 that the *Rhapsody* "first became known to the world through the blue label recording which Whiteman and his orchestra made for Victor. *A million copies were sold.*"[1] This statement is more false than true. Whiteman and his orchestra did record the piece for Victor's prestigious "blue label" on June 10, 1924, but this recording neither circulated around the world nor sold a million copies. Ewen further claimed that "the royalties from the sale of sheet music, records, and other subsidiary rights gathered more than *a quarter of a million dollars* in a decade. The *Rhapsody* made Gershwin a rich man."[2] Such appraisals remain present in writings on the *Rhapsody*, in part because they promote the success and prestige of the work.

It is unclear where, when, and how these figures initially emerged. Ewen was conscious of the tendency to exaggerate narratives surrounding the piece, noting that "the *Rhapsody* has inspired not only controversies but also tall tales."[3] Nonetheless, his own statements ultimately contributed to the lore of the *Rhapsody* and inspired subsequent biographers to follow suit. David Schiff (1997) and Howard Pollack (2007) are two prominent authors who highlight this million-copy sales figure.[4] This information not only demonstrates the assumed popularity and omnipresence of the piece, particularly in the first ten years of its existence, but also attaches the *Rhapsody* to Gershwin's financial well-being, thereby marking its success as central to the composer's rags-to-riches story. What emerges when we look beyond received wisdom and focus on more concrete evidence?

Questioning the status of the *Rhapsody* by investigating the details behind such sales figures reveals that its status and enduring success result not only from its initial presentation and promotion by the Whiteman Orchestra, but also from the various recorded and published arrangements that followed. Royalty statements housed at the Library of Congress—for both recordings and sheet music—reveal significantly lower sales figures for the *Rhapsody* than previously reported. The piece simply did not make

Gershwin as rich, and so quickly, as was assumed. More important, these records uncover the presence of heretofore-unconsidered interpretations of the piece—recorded and published arrangements that participated significantly in the popularization of the *Rhapsody*.

The sheet music firm T. B. Harms faced a conundrum similar to that of the *Rhapsody*'s early critics: How to treat a piece of music that treads the middle ground between popular and classical? As the exclusive distributer of Gershwin's music, Harms managed all the mechanical (recordings and film) and publication (sheet music) royalties accrued in the sale of his compositions. Until the publication of *Rhapsody in Blue*, the works that Harms dealt with were exclusively in the genre of popular song. Whereas companies such as Boosey & Hawkes had generations of experience publishing and distributing more traditional classical compositions, Harms had no such infrastructure in place. In fact, it was not until June 12, 1924— four months to the day after the *Rhapsody*'s premiere—that it submitted the work as an "unpublished musical composition" for copyright deposit.[5] Gershwin subsequently received 15 percent of all sheet music sales and 50 percent of all royalties received by Harms from record companies.[6]

Before the availability of sheet music, recordings of the *Rhapsody* played a significant role in the dissemination of the piece. Paul Whiteman's two recordings of the *Rhapsody*—the 1924 acoustic-horn version and the 1927 electric-microphone (or orthophonic) version—remain the most often discussed in writings on the piece. Their historical allure arises from their proximity to the work's premiere, George Gershwin's performance of the piano solo, and their presumed popularity. Although both recordings sold quite well upon their release by Victor, neither attained million-copy status. In the case of the 1924 recording (Victor 55225) ◗, royalty statements reveal the sale of 15,611 copies during the first three-month period of availability (June–September 1924; see table 2.1). After this initial burst, consumers purchased an average of 2,600 copies per quarter for the next three years. Nearly 44,300 copies of this premiere recording of *Rhapsody in Blue* sold by the second quarter of 1927. Gershwin earned almost $800 (approximately $10,700 today) as a result.[7] This is no small sum, but these figures must be put into perspective: single-quarter sales for recordings of Gershwin's song "Somebody Loves Me" from *George White's Scandals of 1924* amounted to 254,481 copies, netting Gershwin $1,145 (approximately $15,600 today).[8] Recordings of this single Gershwin song generated more revenue in three months than the original 1924 issue of Rhapsody in Blue did in three years.

The second Whiteman recording of *Rhapsody in Blue* (Victor 35822) ◗ would become substantially more popular, but hostilities in the studio

Table 2.1. DOMESTIC AND CANADIAN SALES FIGURES FOR PAUL WHITEMAN'S 1924 RECORDING OF *RHAPSODY IN BLUE* (VICTOR 55225).

Year	Quarter	Copies Sold	Amount to Gershwin	Gershwin Total 2013 Equivalent
1924	3	15,611	$ 281.00	$ 3,837.80
1924	4	4,031	$ 72.56	$ 991.00
1925	1	2,981	$ 53.66	$ 716.12
1925	2	1,242	$ 22.36	$ 298.41
1925	3	1,211	$ 21.80	$ 290.93
1925	4	1,782	$ 32.08	$ 428.12
1926	1	2,411	$ 43.40	$ 572.65
1926	2	1,599	$ 28.78	$ 379.74
1926	3	2,227	$ 40.09	$ 528.98
1926	4	4,074	$ 73.33	$ 967.57
1927	1	5,061	$ 91.10	$ 1,222.76
1927	2	2,063	$ 37.13	$ 498.37
	Total	44,293	$ 797.29	$10,732.45

almost precluded its existence. By 1927, advances in technology, including the introduction of higher fidelity electric recording methods, propelled sales across the nation. Riding a wave that would result in Victor's best year ever—more than 34 million albums sold—the company reassembled Gershwin, Whiteman, and his orchestra in a New York recording studio on April 21, 1927.[9] Tensions between Whiteman and Gershwin had been on the rise for more than a year, largely due to disagreements about various tempi taken in live performances of the *Rhapsody*. The argument came to a head in the studio, and Whiteman refused to lead the performance. At the last minute, Nathaniel Shilkret, a music director at Victor who would go on to direct the premiere recording of *An American in Paris*, stepped in and saved the session.

This electrically recorded version quickly overshadowed the 1924 acoustic recording. It sold nearly as many copies in the first six months of its release as the earlier recording had sold in three full years (see table 2.2). By the second quarter of 1930, the 1927 recording of the *Rhapsody* had sold more than 110,000 copies, earning Gershwin just over $2,000 (approximately $28,000 today). This is a considerable sum, particularly during the early years of the Great Depression. However, Gershwin spent approximately the same amount ($2,058.30) to have orchestrations prepared for his 1933 musical *Pardon My English*.[10]

Table 2.2. DOMESTIC AND CANADIAN SALES FIGURES FOR PAUL
WHITEMAN'S 1927 RECORDING OF *RHAPSODY IN BLUE*
(VICTOR 35822).

Year	Quarter	Copies Sold	Amount to Gershwin	Gershwin Total 2013 Equivalent
1927	2	19,987	$ 359.77	$ 4,828.90
1927	3	20,211	$ 363.80	$ 4,882.99
1927	4	11,057	$ 199.03	$ 2,671.42
1928	1	8,197	$ 147.55	$ 2,015.19
1928	2	4,506	$ 81.11	$ 1,107.77
1928	3	4,658	$ 83.84	$ 1,145.06
1928	4	4,407	$ 79.33	$ 1,083.46
1929	1	3,781	$ 68.06	$ 929.54
1929	2	5,182	$ 93.28	$ 1,273.99
1929	3	5,187	$ 93.37	$ 1,275.22
1929	4	Figures	not reported	this quarter
1930	1	11,322	$ 203.80	$ 2,850.10
1930	2	13,151	$ 236.72	$ 3,310.48
	Total	111,646	$ 2,009.66	$ 27,374.12

The inflation of sales for Whiteman's 1924 and 1927 recordings in the
biographical narrative of Gershwin is clear. Rather than one million copies,
the 1924 *Rhapsody* recording sold approximately 50,000 copies. Even when
combining these sales with the approximately 110,000 purchased copies of
the 1927 *Rhapsody* recording, the total remains well shy of the million-copy
mark. In total, the *Rhapsody* earned Gershwin $3,758 in domestic and
Canadian mechanical royalties between 1924 and 1932 (approximately
$51,300 today). The twenty-six-year-old composer's financial standing
increased significantly during the mid-1920s and early 1930s, but it was
not from record sales of *Rhapsody in Blue* alone. Ewen's lofty calculation
may have accounted for all sales up until the point of his writing; sales
trends throughout the 1930s, however, do not suggest that Whiteman's
recordings ever sold in such numbers—certainly not before they were reissued much later in the last quarter of the twentieth century.

The supposed popularity of the Whiteman recordings obscures the fact
that other musicians recorded separate arrangements of the *Rhapsody* during these initial years. Many labels began to record and distribute their
own renditions of the piece in 1927 (see table 2.3). Notably, recordings by
groups other than the Paul Whiteman Orchestra accounted for one-quarter
of all *Rhapsody in Blue* discs in circulation in the closing years of the 1920s.

Table 2.3. COMMERCIALLY AVAILABLE RECORDINGS OF
RHAPSODY IN BLUE, 1924–1927.

Label/Number	Recorded	Ensemble	Soloist	Retail Price
Victor 55225	6/10/1924	Paul Whiteman	George Gershwin	$1.50
Victor 35822	4/21/1927	Paul Whiteman	George Gershwin	$1.50
Banner 696/	3/9/1927	Adrian Schubert	--	$0.35
Domino 4555				
Harmony 422-H	5/18/1927	Victor Irwin	Victor Irwin	$0.50
Perfect 14825/	5/25/1927	Willard Robison	--	?
Pathé 36644				
Edison 52145	11/4/1927	The Edisonians	Frank Banta Jr.	?
Brunswick 20085	12/2/1927	Frank Black	Oscar Levant	?

This included versions issued by labels such as Compo (705 copies), Pathé (5,972 copies), Edison (2,426 copies), and Brunswick (5,590 copies). Based on sales, the most popular of these non-Whiteman recordings were those by Adrian Schubert and Victor Irwin, which sold 14,400 and 8,600 copies respectively between the second quarter of 1927 and the first quarter of 1928. A review appearing shortly after the release of Adrian Shubert and his Concert Orchestra's recording of the *Rhapsody* noted that "it may not be as satisfying as the [Whiteman] original. . . [but] it is an extraordinary bargain."[11] At a retail price of only $0.35—compared to Whiteman's $1.50—its popular appeal seems to have resulted from financial considerations ($4.70 versus $20.00 today).

The recording of the *Rhapsody* released by Columbia in 1927 participates in the racialized marketing techniques that emerged in the recording industry at the time. The disc was distributed on Columbia's mid-priced Harmony label and featured an ensemble under the lead of Victor Irwin, a white bandleader and violinist who performed more often as Irwin Abrams. Under this pseudonym, he recorded for Okeh Records, known as a "race label" that released some of the "hottest" dance bands in America. These recordings were marketed to African-American audiences. In 1926, however, Columbia purchased Okeh and subsequently released Irwin's two-sided dance arrangement of *Rhapsody in Blue*. Its decision to release this particular recording as one by "Victor Irwin" on Harmony, as opposed to "Irwin Abrams," caters to the notion that the *Rhapsody* and its symphonic-jazz mode appealed exclusively to white performers and audiences. However, Duke Ellington's contemporary performances of the work, as discussed in chapter 4, run contrary to such assumptions.

The Irwin recording captures a version of what his band likely per-formed live ◐. As if to summon dancers to the floor, it begins with a quick statement of the tag motif played by the winds and brass. Only after this homophonic call to the audience does the familiar clarinet trill usher in the opening ritornello theme. When the clarinet reaches the top of its glis-sando, the band enters at a steady 110 beats per minute—as opposed to Whiteman's greatly fluctuating tempi—which it maintains until just before the conclusion of side one. The tuba and banjo keep the beat moving, while Irwin's violin trades the melody with the clarinet and trumpets—three instruments with piercing timbres well suited for both acoustic recordings like this one and noisy dance halls. Although a piano is present, its role is strictly as accompaniment. Instead of adhering to the solo-piano passages that link various melodic sections of the *Rhapsody*, which would pull the performance out of tempo, Irwin introduces new transitions to maintain the rhythmic flow of the performance.

It is ironic that a piece designed, in Isaac Goldberg's estimation, to place jazz "beyond the dance" found itself immediately fulfilling the needs of the dance hall.[12] These historiographically obscured recordings document alternative versions of the *Rhapsody* that were in circulation at that time. Ultimately, the recordings discussed here suggest only a faint outline of the non-Whiteman/Grofé interpretations of the *Rhapsody* performed by dance bands—both black and white—around the country. Victor Irwin's band was certainly not the only ensemble to perform the work as an accom-paniment for social dance. Reports of the *Rhapsody*'s appearance in clubs remain scant, and the exact number of ensembles that created their own arrangements of the work as its popularity increased remains unknown.

Nevertheless, royalty statements reveal that a significant number of bands purchased stock arrangements of the *Rhapsody* once they became commercially available. Harms issued a stock arrangement of the piece by the second quarter of 1926. The company had not immediately made a stock arrangement available, but eventually did so in response to the fact that many bands (including Duke Ellington's) were already playing the piece anyway; Harms simply wanted to be in on the profits. It was a wise decision. As discussed in the preceding chapter, the arrangement for the-atre orchestra prepared by Ferde Grofé allowed for a great deal of flexibility in performance. Nearly 1,500 full sets had been purchased by ensembles by the end of the decade (see table 2.4).

Prior to releasing its full-band stock arrangement of *Rhapsody in Blue*, Harms prepared and published a two-piano edition of the sheet music (Harms 7266-41). According to the Library of Congress copyright regis-try, this version for "pf., with 2nd pf. in sc." (piano with second piano in

Table 2.4. SALES OF *RHAPSODY IN BLUE* STOCK ARRANGEMENT SETS FOR THEATRE ORCHESTRA, 1926–1930.

Year	Quarter	Copies Sold	Av. Price Per Set	Total Sales	Amount to Gershwin	Gershwin Total 2013 Equivalent
1926	2	111	$ 4.24	$ 470.50	$ 70.58	$ 931.28
1926	3	56	$ 4.13	$ 231.28	$ 34.69	$ 457.72
1926	4	97	$ 3.90	$ 378.50	$ 56.78	$ 749.19
1927	1	135	$ 4.00	$ 540.50	$ 81.08	$ 1,088.27
1927	2	110	$ 3.80	$ 418.25	$ 62.74	$ 842.11
1927	3	164	$ 3.73	$ 612.50	$ 91.88	$ 1,233.23
1927	4	162	$ 3.82	$ 619.00	$ 92.85	$ 1,246.25
1928	1	182	$ 3.82	$ 696.80	$ 104.52	$ 1,427.50
1928	2	88	$ 3.83	$ 337.50	$ 50.63	$ 691.49
1928	3	71	$ 3.89	$ 276.50	$ 41.48	$ 566.52
1928	4	104	$ 3.90	$ 405.50	$ 60.83	$ 830.80
1929	1	62	$ 3.87	$ 240.00	$ 36.00	$ 459.07
1929	2	46	$ 4.08	$ 187.50	$ 25.13	$ 343.22
1929	3	33	$ 4.13	$ 136.50	$ 20.48	$ 279.71
1929	4	35	$ 3.90	$ 136.50	$ 20.48	$ 279.71
	Total	1,456		$ 5,687.33	$ 850.15	$ 11,426.07

score) received its copyright on December 31, 1924, despite the fact that original copies of this score bear a copyright date of 1925.[13] In subsequent printings, Harms would refer to this two-piano/four-hand score as the "original" to distinguish it from simpler solo-piano versions on the market. Sales of the resulting two-piano/four-hand arrangement were steady from the start (see table 2.5). However, due in part to a retail price of $3.00 (approximately $40.00 today) and the challenging nature of the piano part, they remained less substantial than the sales of many of Gershwin's popular songs published that same year. For comparison, "Oh, Lady Be Good" (Harms 7271-3) sold 22,184 copies the same quarter when *Rhapsody in Blue* first became available as sheet music, more than ten times the number of *Rhapsody* copies sold that entire year.[14] Nonetheless, the composer earned a 15 percent royalty on each copy of the *Rhapsody* sheet music sold. This income immediately outpaced that from recordings of the work. In the first year alone, Gershwin earned more from sheet music ($864, approximately $11,530 today) than he did from three years of recording sales ($798, approximately $10,730 today).

Due to a renewed interest generated by the flurry of *Rhapsody* recordings produced in 1927, two additional published arrangements of the

Table 2.5. SALES OF *RHAPSODY IN BLUE* SHEET MUSIC, ORIGINAL TWO-PIANO VERSION, 1925–1928 (HARMS 7266-41).

Year	Copies Sold	Total Sales	Total Sales 2013 Equivalent	Total to Gershwin	Gershwin Total 2013 Equivalent
1925	1,920	$ 5,760.00	$ 76,870.00	$ 864.00	$ 11,530.50
1926	2,914	$ 8,742.00	$ 115,347.97	$ 1,311.30	$ 17,302.20
1927	4,515	$ 13,545.00	$ 181,803.48	$ 2,031.75	$ 27,270.52
1928	479	$ 1,437.00	$ 19,626.06	$ 215.55	$ 2,943.91

piece appeared on the market that year. Harms hired Jesse Crawford, the well-known Wurlitzer organist at the Paramount Theatre, to prepare the first of these arrangements.[15] His version exploits the full capabilities of a standard two-manual theatre organ—clarinet ranks, chorus effects, and even bells. It sold just over 600 copies during the first three years of availability, a respectable number given that it emerged the same year as the "talkie" and the resulting demise of theatre organ performances.[16] Crawford recorded an abridged version of his arrangement for Victor Records on February 25, 1930 (Victor 22343) 🔊. Crawford's performance on the grand Wurlitzer theatre organ employs idiomatic techniques and preserves one interpretation made possible by his published organ arrangement of *Rhapsody in Blue*. He introduces multi-note slurs, alters registration settings, and improvises melodies, including a quasi-prelude employing the love theme.

New York pianist Isadore Gorn prepared the second arrangement of *Rhapsody in Blue* published in 1927, a solo-piano reduction of the original two-piano/four-hand version (Harms S-109-29). It retailed for between $1.25 and $2.00 (approximately $16.75 to $26.85 today), making it cheaper than the $3.00 original sheet music. Because of its ease of performance and low cost, it quickly became the best-selling edition of the *Rhapsody* (see table 2.6). Gorn's arrangement introduced its own set of unique cuts, reducing the piece as a whole by some 60 measures. As discussed in chapter 3, this 1927 solo-piano version had a significant impact on the reception of the *Rhapsody* over the course of the twentieth century in the concert hall and in recordings, since it is the arrangement Leonard Bernstein acquired as a teenager. Gorn's arrangement also introduced some performance indications that continue to appear in print today.[17] For example, on the final eighth beat of measure 156 [R. 20-5], Gorn inserts a fermata where none previously appeared in any of the source documents for the piece. This addition corresponds to the exact point where a cut occurs on both the 1924 and 1927 Whiteman recordings.

Table 2.6. SALES OF *RHAPSODY IN BLUE* SHEET MUSIC, SOLO-PIANO
VERSION, 1927–1931 (HARMS S-109-29).

Year	Quarter	Copies Sold	Total Sales	Total to Gershwin	Gershwin Total 2013 Equivalent
1927	3	2,891	$ 3,613.75	$ 542.06	$ 7,260.77
1927	4	3,799	$ 7,375.25	$ 1,106.29	$ 14,818.50
1928	1	5,157	$ 6,446.25	$ 966.94	$ 13,179.17
1928	2	2,969	$ 3,711.25	$ 556.69	$ 7,587.55
1928	3	2,509	$ 3,136.25	$ 470.44	$ 6,411.99
1928	4	2,494	$ 3,117.50	$ 467.63	$ 6,373.69
1929	1	2,464	$ 3,080.00	$ 462.00	$ 6,296.95
1929	2	1,579	$ 1,973.75	$ 296.06	$ 4,035.23
1929	3	1,644	$ 2,055.00	$ 308.25	$ 4,201.38
1929	4	1,959	$ 2,448.75	$ 367.31	$ 5,006.35
1930	1–2	3,143	$ 3,928.75	$ 589.31	$ 8,224.54
1930	3	2,029	$ 2,535.25	$ 380.29	$ 5,307.41
1930	4	2,391	$ 2,988.75	$ 448.31	$ 6,256.72
1931	1	2,336	$ 2,974.95	$ 446.24	$ 6,842.42
1931	2	2,431	$ 3,107.74	$ 466.16	$ 7,147.86
1931	3	1,947	$ 2,434.00	$ 365.10	$ 5,598.26
1931	4	1,910	$ 2,387.50	$ 358.13	$ 5,491.38
	Total	43,652	$ 57,314.69	$ 8,597.20	$ 120,040.17

All of these versions and figures reframe understandings of the *Rhapsody in Blue* and reveal the potential of a history viewed through the lens of arrangements. First and foremost, arrangements allowed the *Rhapsody* to circulate widely. The Paul Whiteman Orchestra alone had sold more than 150,000 recordings by 1930; the extent to which these records received radio airplay remains unknown. By that same time, almost 1,500 full sets of stock arrangement parts and more than 50,000 copies of the solo- and two-piano arrangements were in the hands of professional and amateur musicians. Such prevalence allowed the *Rhapsody* to gain popularity across the country. It also lent a perception of financial success. During the ten years following the premiere of *Rhapsody in Blue*, Gershwin earned $17,000 from sheet music sales of the piece. When combined with mechanical royalties, his total earnings from the *Rhapsody* over the duration of this period amount to approximately $23,000. No small compensation to be sure, but significantly less than the quarter-million dollars that David Ewen claims the piece earned for Gershwin during its first decade, even accounting for inflation. Gershwin's earnings would have equated to less than $50,000 at the time of Ewen's initial claim in the 1950s. But success also opened up the piece to criticism, particularly with respect to its participation in the appropriation of black musical culture by popular and classical traditions.

THE EARLIEST USES OF *RHAPSODY IN BLUE* IN FILM

Tension surrounded the "civilizing of jazz"—sometimes referred to as the "whitewashing" of a tradition developed by black artists—that *Rhapsody in Blue* embodied.[18] Indeed, such commentary resides in a 1929 film called *St. Louis Blues*, which features the earliest cinematic use of the *Rhapsody* 🎵.[19] This two-reel fifteen-minute depiction of African-American life and music interpolates the piece in an unexpected and acerbic way. With the exception of the *Rhapsody*, all other music heard in the movie, which was arranged by W. C. Handy and J. Rosamond Johnson, draws on Handy's popular song "St. Louis Blues" as performed by blues legend Bessie Smith.

St. Louis Blues was the only film appearance by Smith, who plays the part of an unrequited lover, Bessie, to a duplicitous gambler named Jimmy. She confronts Jimmy after finding him alone with another woman, and quickly finds herself battered and alone on the floor of a run-down apartment. While lying on the floor, she intones a single, unaccompanied line from "St. Louis Blues": "My man's got a heart like a rock cast in the sea." Each subsequent repetition of this phrase outlines a phrase of the twelve-bar blues form. Between the second and third iterations, as the harmony moves to the inherent tension of the dominant, a cross-fade relocates Bessie on a lonely barstool. Only as she concludes the fourth occurrence of the text does the camera reveal the all-black club setting and its powerful musical potential: tables filled with patrons who happen to be members of the Hall Johnson Choir, as well as a small jazz band populated by musicians from Fletcher Henderson's Orchestra and stride pianist James P. Johnson. The chorus hums a unison note that emerges as the new dominant for the commanding rendition of "St. Louis Blues" that follows. The performance offers a striking combination of Smith's well-known vocal proclivities with the multifaceted choral arranging of the Hall Johnson Choir. Eventually, Jimmy appears in the club, and Bessie immediately takes him back. The two embrace on the dance floor as the band strikes up an instrumental arrangement of "St. Louis Blues." Unbeknown to the love-struck Bessie, Jimmy carefully picks her pocket and with the final cadence of the piece, unmercifully shoves her back onto her barstool.

Past considerations of the film by scholars like Angela Y. Davis, Krin Gabbard, and Peter Stanfield focus on its shortcomings, particularly with respect to its stereotypical portrayal of African-American culture and the lack of agency on the part of Smith's character.[20] In the late 1920s and early 1930s, however, all-black musical films were nearly as scarce as their Broadway counterparts. The few such films that appeared during this time came from a group of independent white "Negrophile" filmmakers like Dudley Murphy, who directed both *St. Louis Blues* and the Ellington feature of the same year, *Black and Tan*. (The Hall Johnson Choir appeared in both of these short films.) To deny the inherent stereotyping that appears in such films would be a mistake, despite Thomas Cripps's observation in *Slow Fade to Black* that in the hands of directors like Murphy, "old stereotypes took on new dimension."[21] Angela Davis notes in *Blues Legacies and Black Feminism*, that the film "deserves criticism not only for its exploitation of racist stereotypes but for its violation of the spirit of the blues. Its direct translation of blues images into a visual and linear narrative violates blues discourse, which is always complicated, contextualized, and informed by that which is unspoken as well as by that which is named."[22]

Regardless of its representation of race or infidelity to blues aesthetics, Davis and others have overlooked one centrally important "unspoken" element in the film: *Rhapsody in Blue*. After Jimmy flashes his newly acquired bankroll and tips his hat to the distraught Bessie, the opening clarinet glissando of *Rhapsody in Blue* begins. During this brief twenty-second cue, Jimmy boastfully backs out of the club, bowing and again tipping his hat like a performer acknowledging an ovation. A half-diminished chord punctuates Jimmy's exit at the end of the cue, ushering in a particularly mournful reprise of "St. Louis Blues" performed by the full ensemble.

In one sense, the interpolation of the *Rhapsody* at this point offers a contrasting musical characterization of Jimmy, one that distinguishes his sound from that of the spurned Bessie. At the same time, this explicit introduction of Gershwin's famous piece complicates, contextualizes, and informs larger contemporary considerations of black music. Connecting the *Rhapsody* to the errant actions of Jimmy effectively links the piece to concurrent discourses regarding the appropriation (i.e., theft) of jazz from the black community. Jimmy not only strips Bessie (an actual black musician) of her agency, but he also literally deprives her of her financial standing. Given the parties involved, it seems unlikely that such a coupling was a matter of coincidence. Whether the decision to reference *Rhapsody in Blue* was Handy's, Johnson's, or Murphy's, the end result is the same. The first instance of *Rhapsody in Blue* on film offers a subtle but astute commentary on the racial economics and politics of popular music, one rather different from the image of the piece as it appeared in *King of Jazz* one year later. In light of the fact that Gershwin received a well-publicized $50,000 for the use of the *Rhapsody* in *King of Jazz*, its inclusion in *St. Louis Blues* becomes all the more poignant.[23]

The racialized tensions inherent in *St. Louis Blues* have long accompanied both the reception of the *Rhapsody* and the genre of concert jazz in general, due in large part to bandleader Paul Whiteman. In his 1930 film *King of Jazz*—heretofore celebrated as the first appearance of *Rhapsody in Blue* in film—Whiteman hoped to disseminate his vision of jazz as widely as possible. The movie has received criticism since its premiere for its one-sided telling of jazz history. Krin Gabbard observed that "a more elaborate, more thorough denial of the African American role in jazz is difficult to imagine."[24] Given that the film originated out of Paul Whiteman's autobiography, such an approach should come as no surprise. The film offers a revue-style retrospective of Whiteman's career, from his earliest days to the then present, featuring lavish production numbers oriented around performances by his famous orchestra. Director John Murray Anderson worked with designer Herman Rosse and cinematographers Ray Rennahan, Hal Mohr, and Jerome Ash to create cutting-edge sequences incorporating the latest color and cinematic effects of the day. Each musical vignette emerges from the *Paul Whiteman Scrap Book*, a two-story prop whose "pages are crowded by melodies and anecdotes" and brought to life "by the magic of the camera."[25] Taking advantage of the latest technologies, *King of Jazz* begins with a first-of-its-kind, full-color animated segment—directed by Walter Lantz of Woody Woodpecker fame, but much in the style of Disney's *Steamboat Willie* (1928). The cartoon suggests that Whiteman earned his "King of Jazz" moniker while hunting in the jungles of Africa. As historian Donna Cassidy notes, "the cartoon portrays the 'King of Jazz' as both explorer and colonizer of Africa: the white man who takes control and possession of jazz and its 'primitive' source and civilizes it."[26]

A similar sense of musical control emerges later in the film, when Whiteman describes the origins of *Rhapsody in Blue*: "The most primitive and the most modern musical elements are combined in this rhapsody, for jazz was born in the African jungle to the beating of the voodoo drum" ⬤.[27] The subsequent scene visualizes these words by placing a solo male dancer, masked completely in a dark skin-tight body suit and adorned with a large feather headdress, atop a gigantic African drum. Front-lit to create a striking shadow effect, he stomps out a regular rhythmic pattern with a steadily increasing tempo.[28] Filmed from a single, uninterrupted point of view over the course of a minute and a half, the gaze of the camera makes this visual and sonic objectification explicit.

The "voodoo drum" segment provides a marked contrast to the introduction of *Rhapsody in Blue* that follows. As the scene transitions from the supposed sounds of Africa to the opening of the *Rhapsody*, the viewer passes through the ruffled feathers of a cadre of showgirls, emerging to see a tuxedo-and-cape-adorned clarinetist. As the camera pulls away from its close-up on the musician, the ornate grand piano visible behind him reveals its enormous proportions. With its lid down, the blue instrument measures approximately twelve feet high and twenty-four feet long. Five pianists—sounding together as one—occupy the twenty-foot-long keyboard, playing the opening ritornello passages in synchronization with one another. Up to this point, the orchestra is heard but not seen. As the ritornello theme is first played by the full orchestra [R. 3], the massive lid of the piano opens, and nineteen musicians under the baton of Paul Whiteman emerge as the soundboard lifts them into position. The entire sequence conveys messages of refinement, grandeur, and excess: the enormous blue piano, the multiple, synchronized pianists, the elaborate entrance of the celebrated Whiteman ensemble.

According to *King of Jazz* director John Murray Anderson, Gershwin had no "preconceived ideas as to how [the *Rhapsody* sequence] should be photographed," but offered his blessing.[29] The upwardly mobile staging of the *Rhapsody*—simultaneously overshadowing and reinforcing its use in *St. Louis Blues*—visually represents the piece in a way that connects closely to the presumed biography of Gershwin, a young musician whose career remained on the rise in 1930 when *King of Jazz* appeared. The producers of the 1984 Olympic opening ceremonies—discussed at the beginning of this book—may very well have had this film in mind when they staged *Rhapsody in Blue* in the Los Angeles Memorial Coliseum. In both, the musicians appear as if from nowhere, and both feature multiple, synchronized male pianists dressed identically in tuxedos with tails. Such images set to the strains of the *Rhapsody* complement impressions of Gershwin's life and career. He too has been presented as a figure that emerged miraculously and suddenly from nothing and brought jazz along on his meteoric rise to the heights of sophistication. These biographical arrangements of Gershwin and his *Rhapsody* took root during his lifetime in large part due to Isaac Goldberg's 1931 biography—a book that continues to influence conceptions of Gershwin and his music.

THE PROBLEM OF BIOGRAPHY AND THE STUDY OF GERSHWIN'S MUSIC

Gershwin's relatives, friends, and associates quickly began to tell his story, often with their own interests at heart, following his untimely death at the age of thirty-eight. The broad-based popularity of his music and a general fascination with his all-too-short life prompted a multitude of biographies. Wayne Schneider is likely correct in his assumption that Gershwin "must be the most biographied composer of the twentieth century."[30] Writing in 1999, Schneider identified sixteen books on Gershwin in English and eleven more in other languages.[31] In the fifteen years since his tally, an additional six English-language biographies have emerged with more currently under preparation.[32] Rather than focus on aspects of musical analysis, these biographical assessments—which continue to dominate writings on Gershwin—reiterate the same sets of stories, many of which appeared only after Gershwin's death. Because of the deeply personal connection that many felt with Gershwin, these anecdotes offer compelling visions of his career but fall short when it comes to specific discussion of his music.

Most narrative accounts of Gershwin's career introduce individual works as waypoints along the well-traveled path of his life, rather than allowing the music to guide the journey. As a result, their discussions of compositions and compositional process provide little inspiration for further investigation. Although similar issues arise in virtually all composer biographies, in the case of Gershwin, the results have significantly affected scholarly interest in his music. Not until 2007, for example, did James Wierzbicki unravel the "genesis myth" for Gershwin's other rhapsody. He observed that "[t]he idea that the *Second Rhapsody* is a derivative work likely owes to a misleading statement that appeared in Isaac Goldberg's 1931 *George Gershwin: A Study in American Music* and subsequently was echoed in press reports surrounding the *Second Rhapsody*'s premiere."[33] Accordingly, interest in the piece waned, and seventy-five years passed before anyone bothered to provide an analysis of this substantive composition that went beyond Goldberg's passing summation.

The foundational assessment of Gershwin offered by Goldberg continues to shape both scholarship and reception of *Rhapsody in Blue*. "Perhaps more than any other single source," note the editors of *The George Gershwin Reader*, "[Goldberg's] biography provides a timeless glimpse of Gershwin during his lifetime, a uniquely valuable document given its dependence on the composer's own thoughts about his life and music that are contained in the letters exchanged between the author and composer."[34] All subsequent biographers have drawn on Goldberg's contemporary account, from its narratives of Gershwin's childhood to the roughly twenty pages of quotations attributed to Gershwin himself. The biography incorporates specific discussion of the music more extensively—*Second Rhapsody* included—than subsequent writings on Gershwin, largely because it appeared in the presumed middle stage of his career. The narrative arc of his life remained unseen, perhaps contributing to the sense of timelessness observed by the editors of *The George Gershwin Reader*. At the same time, given the degree to which Goldberg's biography infused all impressions of Gershwin, this timeless quality may emerge only in retrospect. That is, a sense of the book's importance results from how central it has become in writings on Gershwin, musical and biographical, scholarly and otherwise.

Isaac Goldberg's book set in motion much of the mythologizing of Gershwin that emerged in the years following his premature death, but little is known about Goldberg himself. What perspectives and prejudices did he bring to the study of Gershwin? Goldberg's background is key to understanding the Gershwin legend and its ultimate effect on the reception of the *Rhapsody*. The paucity of knowledge about Goldberg is surprising given the continued reliance on his work. In writing on Gershwin, if elements of Goldberg's own biography emerge at all, one finds allusions to his standing as a Harvard University professor or his authorship of an earlier book on Tin Pan Alley, but little else. Goldberg's correspondence and non-Gershwin-related publications reveal that his own childhood, training, and vision for American music affected his narrative construction of Gershwin. Probing Goldberg's biography and musical ideology provides insight into his promotion of Gershwin at the same time as it forces a critical reconsideration of his book's location in present-day conceptions of the composer.

Goldberg's artistic vision took shape in the industrial haze of the Gilded Age. His Boston upbringing during the late nineteenth and early twentieth centuries directly influenced his attitudes toward American music. The Goldberg family lived on Lowell Street in the city's West End, a now-defunct working-class neighborhood then populated by Jewish and Italian immigrant families.[35] His preference for municipal band concerts and Gilbert and Sullivan highlights the noticeable absence during his adolescence of the Boston Symphony Orchestra and other so-called highbrow entertainments. Goldberg recalled that "the first music I wrote was inspired immediately by the orchestras at the burlesque houses. I had composed a great deal as an adolescent, mostly for the piano, which in a very crude manner I had taught myself."[36]

Like Gershwin, his future biographical subject, the core of Goldberg's musical training took place outside of formal educational systems. During his second year of high school in 1904, Goldberg played hooky for an entire month, having "conceived a violent distaste for [his] studies." He continues:

> What was I doing during that month? It was a busman's holiday. I was chiefly
> at the Public Library, studying harmony and counterpoint in the silences of the

music room. Had I been caught at the time, I should have been doubly denounced as a wayward and undisciplined child. In sober fact I was intensely purposive and excessively disciplined, as any one will recognize if he is at all acquainted with the unnecessary rigors of counterpoint.[37]

Goldberg hoped to attend the New England Conservatory of Music upon graduation from high school; however, his Russian immigrant father forbade his eldest son from becoming a musician. Instead, with the assistance of academic scholarships, Goldberg enrolled at Harvard during the fall of 1907. There he became a comparative literature major, completing a thesis on the theatre of Spanish and Portuguese America. He graduated summa cum laude in 1910 and remained at Harvard where, only two years later, he earned a Ph.D. in Romance Languages and Literatures.

After completing his formal education, Goldberg began his career as a critic of contemporary culture. His impressive academic pedigree did little to alleviate his discomfort and discontent with public speaking. Goldberg would eventually lecture for two semesters at Harvard in the 1930s, whence his professor status originates, but he preferred to disseminate his knowledge in written form. He published biweekly essays in the *Boston Evening Transcript* throughout World War I, covering a wide range of cultural topics from abroad including art, architecture, literature, poetry, theatre, and music. Since he never left the United States and rarely ventured beyond New England, his coverage of foreign cultural events and figures during this time relied heavily on work appearing in European- and South American-language journals. His staggering facility with foreign languages—he knew at least eight by this point in his life—allowed him to establish an "armchair" working method that he followed for the rest of his career. Even though he largely relied on source material provided by others, Goldberg's insightful interpretations made unfamiliar and otherwise inaccessible subjects available and relevant to his readership. This approach continued as his criticism attained national circulation in the mid-1920s, particularly with respect to his writings on musical modernism.

In the debate that surrounded the role of jazz in American classical composition, Goldberg emerged in opposition to critics like Paul Rosenfeld, who famously quipped, "American music is not jazz. Jazz is not music."[38] From Goldberg's point of view, the incorporation of jazz in contemporary composition "actually educated the public. Educated, that is, in a physical as well as a musical sense. It has accustomed the popular ear to rhythmic intricacy, to a certain amount of contrapuntal and polyphonic involution, to shifts of key, even to harmonic modernism."[39] Goldberg saw popular music as a valuable tool of mediation in helping the American public adjust to modernist innovations. Much in the same way that he interpreted foreign-language culture and texts to World-War-I-era readers of the *Boston Evening Transcript*, Goldberg used his interwar writings on music to decipher unfamiliar aspects of contemporary composition. At the same time as he educated his readers, Goldberg revealed his own hopes for American music.

In an *American Mercury* article from September 1927, Goldberg identified a "young man who seems to hold out the greatest hopes for a *jazz that shall be music as well.*"[40] This fledgling musician was not George Gershwin, but rather a man popularly conceived as his compositional complement: Aaron Copland. At this stage in his career, Copland remained relatively unknown and certainly less famous than Gershwin. To provide his readers with as complete a portrait of Copland as possible, Goldberg asked the composer not only for copies of his scores, but also for suggestions on published writings on his music, which remained scarce. Copland obliged both requests in a letter from April of that year, directing Goldberg to the writings of Paul Rosenfeld in *The Dial*. In particular, he drew attention to a January 1926 review of *Music for the Theatre* in which Rosenfeld declares Copland's use of popular music to be "ironic" and "barbaric."[41] Rosenfeld ultimately reinforces the close connection Copland maintained with the contemporary European-music scene even as he developed a personal idiom representative of a new American tradition.

Despite Copland's hints, Goldberg's article paints a wholly contrasting portrait of the young Copland. He highlights the ways jazz dominates the composer's music, stating that Copland incorporates it "not as an adopted tongue, but in the only language that he knows. . . . [He] weaves it into his writing as naturally as one employs the rhythms and accents of one's childhood."[42] This nicely aligned with Goldberg's vision of an American music arising from its vernacular roots. However, upon reading the published article, Copland sent the following rather prickly response to Goldberg:

> If I advanced any criticism it would be that in spite of everything you say I am afraid the general impression is given that you are treating a jazz composer, which we both know is not true. The point is, that from my standpoint, as the first article to be devoted to my work as a whole, it rather overstresses the jazz element. It is very possible that (to all outward appearances) I am now finished with jazz, but I can't consider this a tragedy since I feel I was a composer before jazz and remain a composer without its aid. I'm sure you sense this too. But I'm not so sure about the readers of the Mercury. Not that they matter, of course— but we must be clear on this point.[43]

Copland leaves little doubt over his preference for Rosenfeld's portrayal, which framed the composer as incorporating popular music sparingly and from the top-down point of view of a traditionally (i.e., classically and formally) trained composer. Following this communication, Goldberg decisively backed away from both Copland and his music.

Goldberg needed to find a composer more willing to accompany his vision of American music. Two years later, in June 1929, he met George Gershwin for the first time. Their backstage encounter at Symphony Hall followed the Boston premiere of *An American in Paris*, and Goldberg described it as one of those typical "green-room introductions; the celebrity shakes your hands, murmurs that he is pleased to meet you, and then proceeds at once to forget you. Why shouldn't he? As for Gershwin, I knew him thoroughly before I met him; knew, that is, his music, from the first days to the present moment."[44] Gershwin and Goldberg's meeting was a fortunate occurrence. With a rhapsody, a concerto, a tone poem, and more than a dozen musicals under his belt, Gershwin's reputation and celebrity continued to climb. Goldberg desired a musician to champion, and Gershwin was happy to fill that role. A few months after their 1929 introduction, the *Ladies' Home Journal* commissioned a series of extensive profile articles by Goldberg on Gershwin. Appearing in the spring of 1931, these represented the first in-depth consideration of Gershwin and subsequently formed the basis for the biography published later that same year. Although the extent to which the composer was familiar with Goldberg's writings before this time or actively looking for an authorial advocate remains unknown, his association with Goldberg was particularly judicious. Both in his biography and beyond, Goldberg became an ardent promoter of Gershwin's music, not only communicating the spirit of his compositions, but also demonstrating their musical value through analysis.

Gershwin's music certainly appealed to Goldberg, but extra-musical reasons for his promotion of Gershwin also existed. The two had much in common. Like Goldberg, Gershwin was born into a Jewish immigrant family and spent his youth playing in the rough-and-tumble streets of an urban working-class neighborhood; both discovered music on their own while playing hooky from school; both received their musical educations outside a traditional pedagogical setting. At this point, however, their paths diverged. Goldberg's father prevented his son from following his musical ambitions, whereas Gershwin's did not. Gershwin stood as a manifestation of Goldberg's unfulfilled aspirations. This tension motivated many aspects of the biography that ultimately emerged, including the integration of particular quotations by Gershwin himself.

Biographers of Gershwin value Goldberg's book for its dependence on extended conversations and correspondence between the two of them (i.e., for its primary source material). However, evidence of significant direct collaboration between the two men remains scant. Only twelve letters from Gershwin to Goldberg survive in Harvard University's Houghton Library, and little of the information provided therein finds its way into the book's twenty pages of quotations.[45] Goldberg prepared his manuscript for the biography in much the same way as his early *Transcript* articles, collecting information about his subject from the comfort of his home in Boston. Although the two met in person at least twice while the book was in process, a New York-based research assistant named John McCauley conducted much of the interviewing. Little is known about McCauley's role, other than Edward Jablonski and Lawrence Stewart's claim that he spoke more with George's brother Ira than with the composer himself.[46] What is more, technological limitations precluded the recording of these conversations, forcing McCauley and Goldberg to reproduce Gershwin's statements from either their own notes or memory.

The degree to which the quotations appearing in Goldberg's book reflect what Gershwin actually said may never be fully clarified. Evidence suggests, however, that Goldberg provided certain modifications, injecting a bit of dramatic license in service of a more compelling narrative. The effect of such alterations becomes apparent when comparing the 1931 *Ladies' Home Journal* articles with Goldberg's published biography. Quotations attributed to Gershwin in the magazine appear to be altered, either slightly or extensively, in the subsequent book. Some changes affected biographical data. For example, Gershwin's telling of his discovery of music with little Maxie Rosenzweig (later violinist Max Rosen) expands from a paragraph to a page in the book, introducing new tales of treacherous truancy and torrential downpours. Other alterations had to do with musical-historical issues. This includes two brief amendments within a frequently quoted passage on the genesis of *Rhapsody in Blue* that have long framed understandings of Gershwin's compositional process.

In the first, Gershwin recounts the now-famous train ride from New York to Boston following the premiere of *Sweet Little Devil* when the "steely rhythms" and "rattle-ty-bang" supposedly inspired the musical construction of the *Rhapsody*.[47] As the story appeared in *Ladies' Home Journal*, Gershwin recalled that he "suddenly heard—and even saw on paper—the *opening* of the rhapsody."[48] The book reports Gershwin as saying, "Suddenly I heard—and even saw on paper—the *complete construction* of the rhapsody, *from beginning to end*."[49] A significant gulf exists between an opening and a complete work. Such a transformation provides a sense that the composition of the *Rhapsody* resulted instantaneously and effortlessly, a happenstance of Gershwin being on that train at that very moment. Although manuscript evidence presented in chapter 1 disproves such formations of the piece, this particular origin story for the *Rhapsody* has long dominated considerations of both its timeline of creation and the debate concerning its piecemeal versus organic construction.

A second distortion by Goldberg occurs when Gershwin discusses the origins of the *Rhapsody*'s love theme. In the context of the *Ladies' Home Journal* article, Gershwin's words imply that the theme came to him in Boston while he was tinkering at the piano "at the home of a friend."[50] As it appears in the book, however, the appended quotation places this event "at the home of a friend, *just after I got back to Gotham*."[51] At no other point in Gershwin's writings or correspondence does he refer to New York City as "Gotham." However, it would not be unlike Goldberg to interject the word, as he used it frequently in publication.[52] Even more significant is that the alteration of this statement emphasizes the centrality of New York City in the creation of this piece. It reinforces Goldberg's ongoing depiction of Gershwin as a "young man of Manhattan," closely attuned to the rhythms and accents of his childhood.[53] As will be explored in chapter 6, this connection to New York City remains a considerable aspect of perceptions of the *Rhapsody*, particularly as depicted in popular visual culture in America.

Goldberg arranged Gershwin and the *Rhapsody* to fit his particular vision of American music and, like any construction, the process involved a bit of mythmaking. In the process, Gershwin emerges as a figure with natural musical intuition and self-taught abilities. The cumulative effects of these and other biographical tidbits were longstanding conceptions of the composer—particularly images of Gershwin as naïve and unlearned—that have influenced both reception and scholarship. Howard Pollack's substantial biography of Gershwin demonstrates the abatement of such assessments within academic circles.[54] However, these impressions remain well entrenched in the public imagination due in large part to a film about Gershwin's life that appeared just eight years after his death.

RHAPSODY RETURNS TO THE SCREEN

The memorialization of George Gershwin through his music, particularly through performances of *Rhapsody in Blue*, began immediately after his passing on July 11, 1937. Radio responded first, with tributes broadcast from coast to coast. The evening after Gershwin's death, David Broekman's orchestra along with Bing Crosby and Victor Young appeared on the Mutual Broadcasting System, originating from Los Angeles. Simultaneously, the NBC Blue Network in New York City featured a concert by Paul Whiteman and his Orchestra. The next day, the Chicago Philharmonic Orchestra, under the direction of Richard Czerwonky, included *Rhapsody in Blue* in their CBS broadcast from Grant Park, reaching over one hundred stations. They followed their performance of the piece with Siegfried's funeral march from Wagner's *Götterdämmerung*. The audience held its applause, "sealing with silence its appreciation of a composer of popular music whose influence knew no barriers either of musical caste or of national boundary."[55]

The 1945 Warner Brothers film biography *Rhapsody in Blue: The Story of George Gershwin* translated such sentiments to the silver screen, but concerned itself more with entertainment than an accurate representation of the past. David Schiff calls the film a "questionable biopic," and Howard Pollack provides several critiques that reveal the "film as trite and implausible," yet it has long shaped popular conceptions of both Gershwin and the *Rhapsody*.[56] The film cast actor Robert Alda as Gershwin. To combat "any slight difference between the appearance and actions of the actor and the real-life person he portrays," the production team cast celebrities like Paul Whiteman, Al Jolson, Oscar Levant, and Hazel Scott as themselves.[57] This choice did not necessarily assuage age-discrepancy issues. A fifty-five-year-old Whiteman, for example, played himself at the premiere of the *Rhapsody* some twenty years earlier, and Al Jolson, then approaching his seventh decade, appears even more anachronistic in the scene depicting the 1919 debut of Gershwin's first popular-song success, "Swanee."

Such details fall by the wayside, however, when considering the artistic license taken in portraying other elements of Gershwin's biography. Despite the presence of real-life characters, the authors of *Rhapsody in Blue* invented several fictional characters to heighten the film's dramatic narrative. These include the two female love interests, Julie Adams and Christine Gilbert, as well as the elderly German Professor Franck, whom film music scholar Charlotte Greenspan identifies as the "designated representative of all of Gershwin's teachers."[58] With these characters come several plot lines foreign to those familiar with Gershwin's actual biography. But as Greenspan instructs, "the most useful critical question to ask about a biographical film is not how truthful it is but how truth and fiction are blended."[59]

The music of Gershwin features heavily, but as both the title of the picture and Gershwin's best-known work, *Rhapsody in Blue* emerges most frequently. Nine different scenes offer visualizations of the *Rhapsody*, including two staged performances: the 1924 premiere and the 1937 memorial concert at Lewisohn Stadium. In all instances, the viewer encounters *Rhapsody* in arrangement. For the non-concert scenes, this includes a brooding, minor-key setting of the love theme foreshadowing the death of Professor Franck, as well as an *agitato* rendition of the otherwise-tranquil love theme tag [R. 31] as Gershwin becomes infuriated at friend and publisher Max Dreyfus for suggesting that he reunite with his ex-girlfriend, the fictional Julie Adams. With the exception of the opening credits and the premiere performance, the *Rhapsody* accompanies scenes related to love or death. In the case of the final scene, the restaging of the Gershwin memorial concert at Lewisohn Stadium—discussed at the beginning of chapter 6—it accompanies both.

The film's creative team struggled to depict both the composition and premiere of *Rhapsody in Blue*—arguably the central scenes of the movie. Drafts of the screenplay reveal a stronger initial focus on the genesis of the *Rhapsody* than ultimately appears in the film. Two documents survive in the Gershwin Collection at the Library of Congress that represent separate points in an extended development process. The first is a draft completed by playwright Clifford Odets and dated August 28, 1942, that runs more than 300 pages, due in large part to the intricate shot and action details provided for each scene. It contains the fictionalized characters—here named Julie Evans, Alma Gilbert, and Mr. Frank—and a reduced number of real-life figures. The second draft, authored by Howard Koch and based on a subsequent revision of Odets's draft to which Sonya Levien contributed, bears a date of June 16, 1943. It is marked "final," but significant differences remain between it and the film as ultimately released, particularly with respect to its representation of *Rhapsody in Blue*.

Both screenplays highlight the anecdote that Gershwin forgot about his commission for Whiteman and depict the rapid compositional process that followed—central components of the *Rhapsody* legend more broadly. In the Odets draft, Whiteman halts Gershwin outside of a "Dinty Moore's Type" restaurant. As Gershwin complains about the downpour in which they find themselves, Whiteman declares, "I'll drown you in horseradish if you don't get that piece in time." Met with a blank stare, Whiteman continues, "Don't tell me you forgot my concert at Aeolian Hall! I'm emancipating jazz. You'll louse me all up if you don't come through."[60] Gershwin promises to work on the piece as soon as he returns from Boston. The subsequent composition scene—clearly indebted to the questionable passage from Goldberg's biography discussed above—unambiguously connects the *Rhapsody* to its supposed train-inspired origins. The scene features Gershwin in a Pullman car, presumably on his way home from Boston: "George is at a loss. But for the title the page before him is blank. He is absently whistling the clicking rhythm of the train wheels. . . . On sound track is heard the opening clarinet glissando of the Rhapsody, repeating itself, marking time, as if it were a turning wheel."[61] The montage that follows features close shots of various train-related images—a locomotive whistle, flying car wheels, crossing signals, pistons, and gleaming steel rails—each intercut with "George writing feverishly and filling many sheets of manuscript paper."[62]

The "final" screenplay by Koch relocates the encounter between Whiteman and Gershwin to a telephone conversation, with the camera cutting between the separate locations. The first part of the conversation features a close-up shot of Whiteman: "How's that blues piece coming George. . . for the concert at Aeolian Hall? What? (a pause—then looks worried) You haven't started! Are you kidding, George? The concert's February twelfth. We'll need a week's rehearsal. That only gives you three weeks."[63] The next shot finds Gershwin in his apartment as he exclaims, "Holy mackerel—three weeks!" Wary of this advanced deadline, he looks at brother Ira and love-interest Julie, who are in the room with him. They both nod, "vigorously confirming their confidence," and George confirms to Whiteman that the piece will be delivered in time. The composition scene that follows shows Gershwin at work on the first page of the Rhapsody. "He hums, searching for a phrase, then reaches over to try it on the piano. As he tries several different phrases, he gazes off as though looking into the distance."[64] With the exception of his final contemplative stare, the effect is substantially less dramatic than the train montage encountered in the previous draft of the screenplay.

Ultimately, the final cut of the film did away with such business between Whiteman and Gershwin, as well as the compositional process. It put the focus on the premiere of the work rather than its creation. Backstage following the dismal debut of Blue Monday Blues, Whiteman announces his intention to hold a concert in Aeolian Hall to "make a lady out of jazz." He invites Gershwin to compose a "serious concert piece based on the blues." Staring into the distance, Gershwin contemplates the proposal aloud: "A serious piece that's blue too? Blue themes and jazz rhythms? Of course!" With eyes still unfocused, he almost whispers, "A Rhapsody in Blue." The inspirational gaze seems to be all Gershwin needs. Without depicting any part of the compositional process, the film segues to the piece's debut in Aeolian Hall.

The premiere performance of the Rhapsody is the most intricate sequence in the entire film ◐. Both screenplays provide a detailed shot-by-shot outline for filming this staged performance—Odets provides twenty-five shots and Koch lists eighteen—but neither matches the ultimate complexity of the sequence as it appears in the movie. Lasting just under ten minutes, it includes nearly one hundred individual cuts, comprised of shots filmed from a variety of angles and depths of field. In addition to steady shots, the scene incorporates long tracking shots in which the camera pans over the audience, pausing on individual characters, or reverses from a long shot of the orchestra through the open lid of the piano to an over-the-shoulder view of Gershwin performing a cadenza. The sequence as a whole is carefully cut to highlight specific transitions in the music, conferring a great deal of visual excitement and energy upon this restaging of the premiere performance. Accounts of the actual response of Whiteman's audience to the *Rhapsody* vary, but in the film, the performance earns thundering applause and an immediate standing ovation.

With an emphasis on the performance and success of the premiere of *Rhapsody in Blue* rather than its genesis, the film arranges the piece as the launching pad for Gershwin's success. The performance itself offers a representation of the then twenty-five-year-old as a refined, tuxedoed composer and pianist, receiving the highest accolades and with only the brightest of futures ahead of him. For this reason, the filmmakers ultimately jettisoned scenes from both screenplays that cast Gershwin as full of doubt following the premiere concert. For example, the Odets draft depicts Gershwin stammering to Ira as they depart the hall for a local watering hole: "I'm depressed and I'm thirsty. I'da written something good if I knew it was such an important occasion."[65] His brother praises the ingenuity of the music, calling it simultaneously "significant and popular," but George hotly replies, "Excuse me, Ira, don't you think you're making mountains outa mole hills?"[66] A similar sequence exists in the final screenplay by Koch, but this portrayal of Gershwin appears to have been left on the cutting room floor—if such self-doubt was ever filmed at all. The end result is the portrayal of a confident musician at the start of his ascent to fame and fortune. It is an image of Gershwin with which subsequent composers and performers have had to contend.

CONFRONTING AN ICON

The lore surrounding *Rhapsody in Blue*, introduced by figures like Goldberg, significantly contributed to the piece's popular appeal. Nonetheless, the essential point here remains that both before and after Gershwin's death, his life and music were subject to a great deal of mythologizing. Shifting the focus from Gershwin's biography to arrangements of *Rhapsody in Blue* forces a reconsideration of conventional wisdom, and reframes preconceived impressions of Gershwin's musical achievements. Pushing beneath the surface of myths such as the million-copy status of Whiteman's record-ings reveals that the *Rhapsody* as premiered by Whiteman certainly did not corner the market in the way that existing historical accounts suggest. Confronting representations of the piece in film and print provides an understanding of how certain tropes about Gershwin, the *Rhapsody*, and its composition came to be enshrined for future generations. Multiple ver-sions of *Rhapsody in Blue* existed from the start, and the circumstances of their creation and distribution contributed to the initial reception of the piece. As a whole they reveal how individual musicians—beyond George Gershwin—shaped and continue to shape conceptions of the *Rhapsody* over the course of time, bringing to light a different story than the one told before. And one of the principal characters in that story is Leonard Bernstein.

CHAPTER 3

From Camp to Carnegie Hall

Leonard Bernstein and Rhapsody in Blue

Each man kills the thing he loves.

—Leonard Bernstein (1955)

During the summer of 1937, instead of spending time at the family's lake house in Sharon, Massachusetts, an eighteen-year-old Leonard Bernstein took a job at Camp Onota, a recently established Jewish all-boys camp in the Berkshires.[1] Bernstein served as a swimming counselor and was in charge of a cabin of campers from New York. Not surprisingly, he also organized all musical activities. He staged productions of Gershwin's *Of Thee I Sing* and Gilbert and Sullivan's *Pirates of Penzance*, the latter of which featured Adolph Green with whom Bernstein formed a close friendship that eventually led to the collaborative creation, with Betty Comden, of both *On the Town* (1944) and *Wonderful Town* (1953).[2] Bernstein also formed small musical ensembles and wrote camp songs. The text of one surviving example reads:

Onota Camp, the end is near
And soon we'll have to say goodbye to you, we fear.
Our hearts are sad, our eyes are damp,
Because we have to part with you Onota Camp.
Adon, adieu, and au revoir,
Better time we never saw;
We got the things we came here for—

So adon, adieu, auf wiedersehen
And au revoir![3]

Creating new words to an existing tune was common practice at camps such as Onota, much as it remains today. Here the melody of *Auld Lang Syne*, the song marking significant endings and beginnings such as the New Year, seems a likely and appropriate—if not slightly awkward—accompaniment for this particular set of lyrics. On the surface, they commemorate the end of a summer, a tearful farewell to fellow campers and friends. But these words may have resonated more deeply for Bernstein given the recent and sudden passing of George Gershwin.

Gershwin's death had a profound and permanent effect on the young Bernstein. He later divulged, "The great tragedy for me, the musical tragedy of my life, was I never met him."[4] The Sunday of Gershwin's passing coincided with parents' visiting day at Camp Onota. During lunch that day, Bernstein played Gershwin's *Second Prelude* as a musical tribute.[5] He requested that there be no applause at the conclusion of the performance. Instead, he rose from the piano bench and left the room in silence. "I discovered a lot of things that day," recounted Bernstein in an interview from the early 1970s. "I discovered the essence of tragedy; I didn't know anything about that. And I discovered the power of music."[6] Although Bernstein's grandiose personality occasionally led to melodramatic statements, Gershwin's death remained an emotional subject throughout his life. He often lamented the music that remained unwritten because of Gershwin's premature death.[7]

However, Gershwin's passing meant more to Bernstein than just music left unheard. In the same midlife interview, after recalling his performance of the *Second Prelude* at Camp Onota, Bernstein went on to discuss Gershwin's musicals, as well as *An American in Paris* and the *Concerto in F*. His responses become increasingly emotional and uncharacteristically inarticulate. Overcome by grief, Bernstein abruptly declared the interview over and exclaimed, "I have never in my life done an interview in tears. I don't know what the hell has happened to me. I thought I was more professional than that. . . . He [Gershwin] just touched something." Pressing on, the interviewer asked, "Are you OK?" Bernstein's response: "No. I loved him so much."[8] In addition to a loss of music, Bernstein also mourned the loss of a person with whom he connected intensely.

Bernstein's multifaceted arrangement of *Rhapsody in Blue* becomes a vehicle for considering his most profound anxieties—professional and personal—and how such tensions came to bear on the musical priorities of one of the piece's most famed interpreters. Two recently discovered musical arrangements from Bernstein's adolescence reveal the previously unknown narrative behind not only his polemical presentations of the *Rhapsody* in both print and performance, but also his emotional bond to Gershwin. The first primary source is Bernstein's personal copy of the published solo-piano sheet music that he acquired in 1932 at the age of thirteen. The second document is an arrangement of the *Rhapsody* prepared by Bernstein for an ensemble of teenagers at Camp Onota in 1937, the summer of Gershwin's passing. These youthful sources reveal that Bernstein had a particular vision of how the *Rhapsody* operated long before his infamous 1955 essay "A Nice Gershwin Tune" and his celebrated 1959 recording of the piece for Columbia Records. These latter arrangements— Bernstein's most public statements on the *Rhapsody*—emerge anew, not as a perceived critique of Gershwin and his music, but rather as a manifestation of Bernstein's struggles to integrate into the status-quo environment of the New York Philharmonic.

"A NICE GERSHWIN TUNE"

Rhapsody in Blue owes much of its global popularity and academic insecurity to Leonard Bernstein. He engaged with the work continually over the course of his multifaceted career, leaving his interpretive mark through copious concerts, broadcasts, recordings, and writings. The reach of his performative and analytical approaches to the *Rhapsody* can be observed most clearly during his 1958–59 inaugural season as music director at the New York Philharmonic. Even within the context of his yearlong "root and branch exploration of American music"—an undertaking that celebrated his appointment as the first American-born musician to the premier position with the nation's premier orchestra—the *Rhapsody* figures prominently.[9] In December 1958, Bernstein conducted the *Rhapsody* from the piano, as he always would, in a set of subscription concerts. The *Rhapsody* received attention on three separate televised *Young People's Concerts* that year, which considered the piece in the context of American music, orchestration, and symphonic forms, respectively.[10] In January 1959, Bernstein featured the *Rhapsody* on a CBS program titled "Jazz in Serious Music," which addressed an older audience and broadcast Bernstein's commentary and performance into the homes of millions of Americans.[11] And during the summer of 1959, after the close of the Philharmonic's season, Bernstein brought the *Rhapsody* to the international stage, featuring the work throughout the orchestra's tour of Eastern Europe and the Soviet Union. His performances abroad left quite an impression. Philharmonic President David M. Keiser reported in a letter to the board that in Istanbul, "the theatre was packed and after some respectful listening at first, the audience broke into greater and greater enthusiasm. . . *Rhapsody in Blue* [brought] stamping feet and cries of 'Bis, bis' [encore]."[12]

Bernstein's June 1959 recording of the *Rhapsody*, made for Columbia Records just before the Philharmonic embarked on its summer tour, provides a sense of what these eager audiences encountered.[13] Gershwin biographer Howard Pollack declared this recording "perhaps the best-known performance of the piece in the later twentieth century."[14] Its popularity and staying power result in part from Bernstein's unparalleled and ongoing celebrity status. Musically, much of what makes this version well liked involves the very same features that critics find problematic: Bernstein's exaggerated piano performance, his sudden and dramatic transitions between passages, and his elongation of particular melodic motifs, including the shuffle [R. 25] and the love themes [R. 28]. Even with two cuts that remove some sixty bars of the piece, the recording runs more than sixteen minutes—still one of the longest recordings of the piece to use Grofé's symphonic arrangement. Although some find Bernstein's performance "galvanizing" or "overwrought," the recording continues to have authority and remains the "quintessential" *Rhapsody* for a generation of Americans.[15] With this arrangement, Bernstein demonstrates control and authority over the piece—precisely the commanding image expected of the maestro of the foremost symphony orchestra in the world. But anxieties abound beneath the recording's polished surface.

By the time Bernstein recorded *Rhapsody in Blue* in 1959, he was a full-blown celebrity, the likes of which American music had not witnessed since George Gershwin. Indeed, the two had much in common. Both came from Jewish immigrant families, were remarkable pianists from an early age, and got their professional start in the sheet-music publishing houses of New York City. They both ultimately composed for Broadway and the concert hall, merging popular music with classical traditions. Bernstein was born after Gershwin, enjoyed a longer lifespan, and therefore had to deal with these comparisons on his own as he rose to fame in the years following Gershwin's death. One attempt by Bernstein to assert independence from his musical predecessor—a man to whom he nonetheless felt a deep personal connection—appears in a 1955 essay published in *The Atlantic* titled "A Nice Gershwin Tune."[16]

When reprinted in Bernstein's compendium of writings titled *The Joy of Music* in 1959—the year of his *Rhapsody* recording with the New York Philharmonic—the essay appears under a more derisive title: "Why Don't You Run Upstairs and Write a Nice Gershwin Tune?"[17] It presents an imaginary conversation between Bernstein and his Professional Manager. Before the two men speak, a prologue sets the scene: "Through the windows of the English Grill in Radio City we can see the ice skaters milling about on the rink, inexplicably avoiding collision with one another."[18] Such uneasy imagery is acutely appropriate given the frequency with which the lives and careers of these two men have been located on the same plane. Against this backdrop, Bernstein calls Gershwin's compositional abilities into question. Although he could write "inspired" and "God-given" melodies, he was not a true composer.[19] Professional Manager (P.M.) argues that Gershwin was "every inch a serious composer," offering *Rhapsody in Blue* as proof.[20] Interrupting, Bernstein responds with a passage that has since become infamous:

> Now, P.M., you know as well as I do that the *Rhapsody* is not a composition at all. It's a string of separate paragraphs stuck together—with a thin paste of flour and water. Composing is a very different thing from writing tunes, after all.[21]

Gershwin aficionados are quick to point out Bernstein's subsequent influence on the reception of the *Rhapsody*. Biographer Howard Pollack suggests that "A Nice Gershwin Tune" sullied the reputation of the work, particularly since it directly "informed" performance decisions made in Bernstein's 1959 recording.[22] In spite of its tremendous popularity, David Schiff called the recording a "crisis in the performance history of the piece."[23] As musicologist Larry Starr observes, such considerations typically "function as a kind of 'received wisdom' or even 'party line' on Gershwin in academic and critical circles."[24] Upholding this doctrine, however, assigns a degree of indifference to Bernstein when one does not exist. It also ignores the more complex relationship that ultimately existed between Bernstein, Gershwin, and Gershwin's music. Bernstein's essay did not simply beget Bernstein's recording, nor did either represent a hasty interpretation of the *Rhapsody*. They both resulted from his multi-decade relationship with the piece.

A BOSTON BOY MEETS *RHAPSODY IN BLUE*

Bernstein had an early and fervent attraction to the music of Gershwin, which circulated widely during the late 1920s and early 1930s through recordings, sheet music, and live performances. As a young teenager, Bernstein purchased Gershwin's scores, staged his musicals with friends, and attended presentations of his concert works given by the Boston Pops at Symphony Hall. After seeing the 1935 pre-Broadway tryout production of *Porgy and Bess* in Boston when he was seventeen years old, Bernstein permanently checked the score out from the Newton Public Library. "I admit freely, *pec-cavi*, I stole it," he later confessed. "But it was mine, it had torn pages where I'd turned too fast, and it was my copy. I'd written things in the margins and I marked it up."[25] The only Gershwin composition of which Bernstein felt more possessive than *Porgy and Bess* was *Rhapsody in Blue*.

The precise date when Bernstein first heard the piece is unknown, but the *Rhapsody* was certainly "in the air" during the years following its February 1924 premiere. As considered in the previous chapter, recordings by Paul Whiteman and a host of lesser-known ensembles disseminated the work widely. Bernstein's first acquaintance with the piece occurred either through these recordings (via phonograph or radio) or through performances by the Boston Pops. By the early 1930s, Bernstein was a teenager, and the Pops regularly programmed songs from Gershwin's Broadway shows, as well as his growing collection of orchestral works. Over the course of this decade, it presented *Rhapsody in Blue* a total of fifty-three times.[26] Bernstein regularly attended concerts and reveled in experiencing the *Rhapsody* live at Symphony Hall.

Given the extent to which the piece would occupy his musical adolescence, it could not have been too long after his first encounter with the *Rhapsody* that he obtained a copy of the sheet music, which he did by mid-1932. Bernstein's father agreed to pay for the two-dollar score. Lifelong friend and colleague Sid Ramin was with the thirteen-year-old Lenny the day that he made the purchase. Ramin recalled:

> We went back to Lenny's place and he opened it, and at sight he started to play it. Because he was, as you know, a prodigious sight-reader. He could read anything immediately. Then he got to a certain part and he said, "You know? I wonder why Gershwin wrote in this key." And he started to play it in another key![27]

Bernstein had an exceptionally attentive musical ear by this early age, as well as remarkable fluency at the keyboard. Ramin also noted that when playing through large scores, "What [Lenny] couldn't play he would sing, and what he couldn't play and sing he would stamp."[28]

Remarkably, Bernstein's own copy of this sheet music survives in the Leonard Bernstein Score Collection in the New York Philharmonic Archives (see figure 3.1). The version he purchased that day in 1932 was the solo-piano arrangement of *Rhapsody in Blue* first published by Harms of New York in 1927 (Harms S-109-29). The score shows signs of frequent and animated use by its scotch-tape binding repairs and smudged corners. Scrawled across the top of the front cover are taunting remarks about Bernstein's sister: "Shirley B. has a crush on Clark Gable." Further down, an

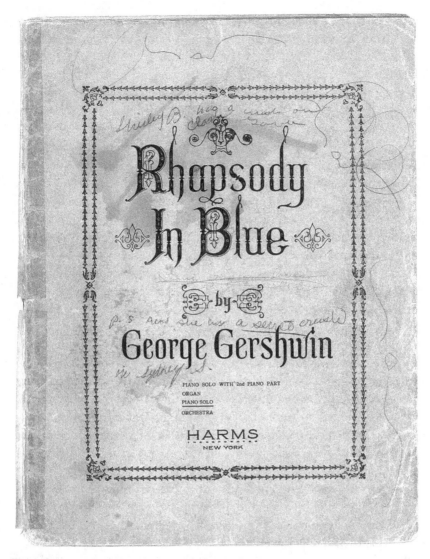

Figure 3.1
Front cover of Leonard Bernstein's childhood copy of the 1927 solo-piano arrangement of *Rhapsody in Blue*. Image courtesy of the New York Philharmonic Archives.

addendum announces: "P.S. Also she also has a <u>secret</u> crush on Sydney S."[29] Although the Sydney referenced here is not Sid Ramin, such comments remind us that this document is a product of adolescence. Annotations within the sheet music itself, however, reveal that Bernstein's approach to the *Rhapsody* was anything but juvenile.

The sheet music captures Bernstein's earliest arrangement of the *Rhapsody*, which he recalled fondly some years later: "We went home and played it with tears till dawn. The excitement! We made our own sort of arrangement so we could do it four hands and try to sound like an orchestra."[30] Pencil annotations throughout this score record this process. Most prominent are brackets that set off specific passages. These brackets document one way the two boys might have performed the *Rhapsody* together. The first of these sections begins with the opening clarinet glissando and concludes at the close of measure 18 [R. 2+2]. It is followed shortly thereafter by another set of brackets that contain the pickups for measures 21 through 23 [R. 3 to R. 4]. These two demarcated passages articulate orchestral passages without the soloist, following the well-known Whiteman recordings. The unbracketed measures that follow each of these sections correspond to solo piano portions. The twelve sets of brackets found throughout the score begin to give shape to the four-hand arrangement that Bernstein remembers playing with Ramin.

Not content simply alternating passages with Ramin, Bernstein also indicated obbligato sections in his copy of the *Rhapsody* score. Abbreviated as "obbl.," each of the five such occurrences found here specifies a section where the piano and orchestra (meaning both pianists in four-hand performance) play together. One particularly interesting example accompanies Bernstein's treatment of the love theme. Following the key change to E major at measure 244 [R. 28], a bracket indicates performance by the orchestra throughout the first presentation of this twenty-two-measure theme. The closing bracket does not appear until the end of measure 267 [R. 30+1], two measures into the second presentation of Gershwin's love motif. An "obbl." designation follows this bracket indicating the addition of the piano, which plays the countermelody while the orchestra sustains the whole notes of the main melody. This pattern repeats throughout the rest of this passage, with the piano joining the orchestra only when the countermelody is present. In combination, the brackets and obbligato markings suggest a procedure by which Bernstein and Ramin might actually play together and "sound like an orchestra."

Bernstein may have been unaware that he had acquired an abridged version of the *Rhapsody*; he was certainly unaware of the future implications of this circumstance. Given his desire to perform four-hand versions of the piece, Bernstein should have purchased the available two-piano edition. However, with a three-dollar price tag, this latter score may have cost more than Bernstein's father was willing to contribute. The solo-piano edition that he ended up with, the one published by Harms in 1927, contains a pair of unique cuts that do not appear in previous or subsequent publications of the score. At 451 measures long, it is nearly sixty measures shorter than the two-piano arrangement issued by Harms in 1925 (Harms 7206-41). When Bernstein first learned how to play the *Rhapsody*, he did so with these cuts in place.

The first revision responds to a similar cut encountered at the midpoint of the Paul Whiteman Orchestra's 1924 and 1927 recordings. Due to the space limitations of the 78-rpm format, four minutes and thirty seconds into the performance, it is necessary to flip the disc over. Side one of the record ends with the crash of a cymbal at measure 137 [R. 14-1] in the published orchestra score. The second side begins with start of the piano cadenza at measure 170 [R. 17+4], thirty-two bars later. The first iteration of the shuffle theme disappears as a result. The 1927 solo-piano version of the sheet music includes this cut and extends it slightly by excising seven bars of rapid-fire, hand-crossing arpeggios [R. 17+4 to R. 18+5]. It represents an editorial choice made by someone at Harms to appeal not only to those familiar with Whiteman's rendition, but also to less-than-virtuosic sheet-music consumers. As a result, thirty-nine measures of music ceased to exist between measures 137 and 138 of the solo-piano score purchased by the young Bernstein.

The second cut found in the 1927 *Rhapsody* score suggests that Bernstein had also familiarized himself with versions of the piece other than Whiteman's recordings. At the end of measure 187 [R. 22-2], a twenty-measure passage is omitted—an embellished presentation of the ritornello theme played by the piano alone. Bernstein has written the word "cadenza" above the measure where this cut occurs. Neither of the Whiteman recordings includes the portion of the score from which these measures are removed [R. 22-2 to R. 24+3].[31] Therefore, another source is necessary to clarify both the missing measures and Bernstein's annotation. In July 1935, under the direction of Arthur Fiedler, the Boston Pops made the first complete recording of *Rhapsody in Blue*.[32] That recording not only included this twenty-measure passage, but also at its conclusion, Jesús María Sanromá (official pianist of the Pops from 1924 to 1943) introduced his own elaborate cadenza. It is unclear when Bernstein added the cadenza indication to his copy of the 1927 score, but the connection of this annotation to performances of the work by the Pops suggests a familiarity with Sanromá's virtuosity, as well as openness to alternative interpretations of the *Rhapsody* during his time in Boston.

Attending performances of the Boston Pops with the teenaged Bernstein was an exciting, if potentially harrowing, experience. Sid Ramin recalled a performance of the *Rhapsody* featuring Sanromá at some point after he and Bernstein had acquired the sheet music:

> In the *Rhapsody in Blue* there's a chord that's [an E flat] pregnant ninth—whatever you want to call it. Lenny and I were in the balcony. . . . We got closer and closer to that chord—we were both waiting for it. Sanromá played it and Lenny grabbed my thighs and squeezed them during that chord! I couldn't walk afterwards![33]

The 1935 recording of Sanromá's performance captures the enthusiasm and excitement Bernstein found in *Rhapsody in Blue* during his adolescent years. At times, it sacrifices accuracy for intensity, and as a result, Sanromá's playing unlocks the raw power bound up in the *Rhapsody* itself. Annotations such as "cadenza" in his copy of the published solo-piano score suggest that the young Bernstein also found ways to realize the energy he clearly saw in this piece. As Bernstein transitioned from adolescence to young adulthood, his early experiences of the *Rhapsody*—through recordings, sheet music, and concerts—informed his first public interpretations of the piece. But as would emerge in the wake of Gershwin's death, such practical understandings of the piece formed only one consideration in his performance of the *Rhapsody*.

THE *RHAPSODY* GOES (TO) CAMP

Bernstein's impromptu memorialization of Gershwin with the lunchtime performance of the *Second Prelude* at Camp Onota might have been a powerful moment in his musical development, but it seems unlikely to have taken place as reported. According to Bernstein, he "just went to pieces" when he heard the news of Gershwin's death on the radio when he woke up at 7:00 a.m. that Sunday in July 1937.[34] However, Gershwin had died at 10:35 a.m. on the West Coast. Given the three-hour time difference, news of Gershwin's death would not have been broadcast until 1:35 p.m. at the very earliest on the East Coast. It is unlikely that Bernstein would have known about Gershwin's passing before lunch on visitors' day.

A more tangible tribute survives in an arrangement of *Rhapsody in Blue* completed by Bernstein on August 10, 1937, almost one month to the day after Gershwin's death. The final page of the manuscript appears as figure 3.2. The orchestration seems to be largely delineated by the availability of particular instruments and performers at the camp. Beyond the traditional piano and clarinet, this score requires recorder, accordion, three male voices (which also must whistle), two ukuleles, and a percussion ensemble. The arrangement is whimsical to say the least, yet it captures Bernstein's musical conception of the *Rhapsody* at this particular point in time. Furthermore, through the inherent musical humor of this camp arrangement, the stage is set for understanding Bernstein's deep emotional connection to Gershwin, as well as his equivocal engagement with the *Rhapsody* as he rose to prominence in the American concert world.

The manuscript itself is more of a draft for performance than a finished score, perhaps something developed piecemeal while his campers were

Figure 3.2
Final manuscript page of Bernstein's Camp Onota arrangement of *Rhapsody in Blue*. By permission of The Leonard Bernstein Office, Inc.

otherwise occupied. Written entirely in pencil, it fills the first seventeen pages of his Schirmer's Harmony Tablet—a staff-paper music notebook intended for student use—now located in the Leonard Bernstein Collection at the Library of Congress.[35] At times, Bernstein's notation is careful and measured, but at other times, his work appears hurried. The sketchy quality of the document suggests that Bernstein was not working directly from the 1927 sheet music but rather from his memory of it. Cross-outs and erasures appear throughout the manuscript, which make it nearly impossible for professional musicians, let alone teenaged campers, to perform from this score. Furthermore, Bernstein leaves large portions of the piano solo part unnotated—at times simply writing "Piano Cadenza"—likely owing to his memorization of the piano part and his intention to play the solo himself. Bernstein added rehearsal letters to the *Rhapsody* arrangement after the score was completed.[36] Their inclusion suggests the need to communicate specific locations in the score to performers. If the work ever received a performance at camp, Bernstein must have copied out parts for the campers.

Although no official record documents such a performance, Bernstein clearly prepared it while at Camp Onota. His "Onota Camp, the end is near" song lyrics are scrawled on the back cover of the Harmony Tablet in which the *Rhapsody* arrangement appears. Within this notebook are other original compositions by Bernstein that call for some of the same camp

Figure 3.3
Leonard Bernstein conducting the Camp Onota "Rhythm Band," summer 1937. © *The Berkshire Eagle*, used with permission.

instruments featured in his *Rhapsody* interpretation, including two movements of a recorder sonata. But it is a photograph taken at camp that summer—the earliest known image of Bernstein conducting—that provides the strongest evidence that Bernstein intended this arrangement for his campers (see figure 3.3).[37] In his Camp Onota tank top, Bernstein directs a group of seven young musicians who are playing a battery of percussion instruments, including two triangles, claves, chimes, cymbals, a tambourine, and even a kalimba. The caption for this photograph reads "Onota Rhythm Band and Leonard Bernstein—1937," the same ensemble name given to the percussion line on the first page of Bernstein's camp arrangement of the *Rhapsody*. Based on the instruments required by the score, it is entirely possible that the boys seen here with the tambourine, cymbal, and claves took part in a performance of this arrangement.[38]

Despite the number of performers required—a total of eleven campers plus Bernstein conducting from the piano—the texture of the arrangement remains relatively light throughout. In fact, the only point where all twelve musicians play at the same time is the final chord. The piano largely carries the arrangement, not only as the expected solo instrument, but also by filling in the harmonies, which the accordion also occasionally plays. The clarinet, recorder, and accordion cover the solo instrumental passages, much in the same way the clarinet, trumpet, and trombones function in Grofé's original Whiteman arrangement. Had more standard orchestral voices (such as strings or brass) or more advanced musicians been available, Bernstein's final product might have sounded quite different. However, his conception of the *Rhapsody* at this point would likely have remained the same in terms of its formal construction and thematic organization.

Pages nine through twelve of the arrangement reveal particularly salient aspects of Bernstein's musical and performative approaches to the *Rhapsody* in 1937, decisions that would come to influence his later interpretations of the work. Figure 3.4 shows the beginning of this passage.[39] This excerpt begins at rehearsal I [R. 17+4], which corresponds to the point in Whiteman's recording where side two commences. Here Bernstein has written "Piano Cadenza" followed by an arrow pointing to the four notes (F-sharp4, A4, F-sharp4, and D4) found in measure 183 [R. 21+7], indicating the conclusion of this solo passage. At this point, the arrangement jumps to measure 197 [R. 25-4], the first introduction of the shuffle theme—appearing at letter J as a *largo* clarinet solo.[40] Instead of proceeding with the clarinet or returning to the traditionally expected piano solo, Bernstein completely recasts the theme by assigning it to "3 male voices backstage" accompanied by two ukuleles. The orchestration changes again sixteen measures later, when Gershwin repeats the shuffle theme, now

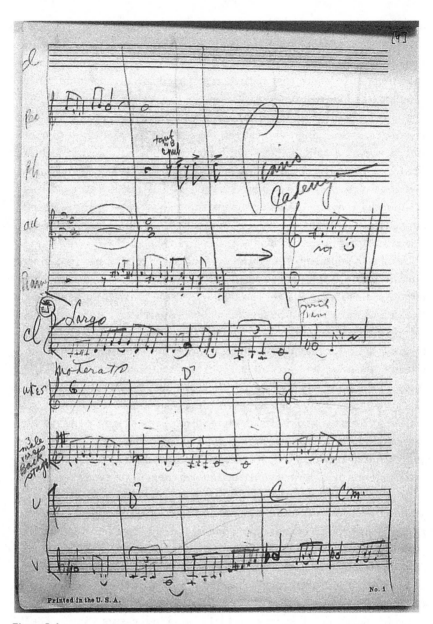

Figure 3.4
Page nine of Bernstein's Camp Onota arrangement of *Rhapsody in Blue*. By permission of The Leonard Bernstein Office, Inc.

dramatically modulating up a minor third every two measures. Here, at rehearsal K [R. 26], Bernstein has the clarinet play the melody with the support of accordion and percussion.[41] The piano and recorder join in at letter M [R. 26+12] with the continuation of the upward minor third sequence.

The ensemble makes a gradual crescendo to measure 238 [R. 27], where Bernstein indicates the start of another extended piano solo by again writing "Piano Cadenza." This point marks the end of page twelve of the manuscript, just before the entrance of the love theme at rehearsal N [R. 28].

The arrangement demonstrates Bernstein's continued conceptual compartmentalization of Gershwin's themes, much the same way as the annotated brackets did in Bernstein's 1927 solo-piano score. The orchestration alone suggests four distinct passages: piano solo, clarinet solo, voices with ukuleles, and full ensemble. The physical layout of this passage in the manuscript itself, where each section receives its own clearly defined system of staves, makes such thematic segregation explicit. Bernstein distinctly demarcates passages throughout the arrangement using fermatas, grand pauses, and dramatic shifts in dynamics or instrumentation. In one particularly striking instance, Bernstein separates the themes with the introduction of a transposition. This modification occurs at rehearsal N [R. 28], with the entrance of the love theme. In Gershwin's original, this theme is preceded by a piano cadenza that culminates with a B dominant seventh chord that sets up a V7 to I modulation to the key of E major. When Bernstein's arrangement reaches this same transition, instead of moving to E major, he begins the passage a third higher, in the key of G major (see figure 3.5). This transposition continues throughout the twenty-two-measure

Figure 3.5
Transition into the love theme from *Rhapsody in Blue* as it appears in the 1927 solo-piano sheet music (top system) and as transposed by Leonard Bernstein in his Camp Onota arrangement (bottom system). By permission of The Leonard Bernstein Office, Inc.

theme and returns to the original key only at the repeat of the theme at rehearsal O [R. 30].

Why might Bernstein have made this transposition? Such a move typifies a Broadway show-tune style of modulation, the kind that further heightens the dramatic effect of the melody. It also continues the motivic transposition by thirds, which precede this passage and allow a similar modulation to take place when the arrangement returns to the original key (rehearsal O [R. 30]).[42] In addition, such transposition allows the melody to begin on the same pitch with which the preceding cadence concluded. Looking ahead, Bernstein employs this mode of modulation throughout the score of *West Side Story*.[43] Looking to the past, however, Sid Ramin's observations regarding Bernstein's first read-through of the solo-piano sheet music gain additional significance. At a specific point, Bernstein paused, questioned Gershwin's choice of key, and then proceeded to transpose the passage in question. The transposition in the camp arrangement likewise built on that initial impulse. In addition, Bernstein scored it for male voices, which echoes another of Ramin's observations about Bernstein's sight-reading practices. The widely spaced intervals within the chords at this point in the score may have proven difficult for the thirteen-year-old pianist. Since Bernstein had a tendency to "sing. . . what he couldn't play," it is possible that he used his voice to render this passage.[44] Such a scenario becomes all the more likely since the chordal texture thickens, becoming more challenging, on the repetition of this particular theme.

On the one hand, over the course of his adolescent years, the *Rhapsody* became a musical space for Bernstein to explore aspects of compositional process, and the Camp Onota arrangement reveals Bernstein's facility with *Rhapsody in Blue*. Even with an instrumentally limited ensemble, he clearly articulated Gershwin's various themes, presented an unexpected and entertaining interpretation of the work, and made room to showcase his pianistic abilities while assuming the role of conductor. These qualities set the stage for performances of the work throughout his career and reveal an increasing sense of control and ownership over the *Rhapsody* that would fully emerge in his later performances with orchestras around the world.

On the other hand, the campiness of Bernstein's Camp Onota arrangement serves as a creative outlet for anxieties emerging during a particularly important year in his personal and professional development. The arrangement as a whole is humorous and irreverent, as witnessed in the over-the-top instrumentation of the passage seen in figure 3.4. Since it replaces what would otherwise be an extended solo-piano passage, choices made here are free from the influences of preexisting renditions of the *Rhapsody*—in other words, they are all Bernstein. The drama of the *largo* clarinet solo sets up a playful reinterpretation of the standard campfire sing-along, presented by disembodied, wordless voices and ukuleles. This arrangement received its world concert premiere on October 12, 2006, as part of Harvard University's symposia, *Leonard Bernstein: Boston to Broadway*, and the entrance of the singers received the largest laugh (of many) from the audience.[45] Such amusement also likely emerged from those who witnessed its performance at Camp Onota, where Bernstein found himself employed for the first time as a working musician.

Camp, a deliberately exaggerated and theatrical performance style often employed for humorous effect, has long been considered an outlet for gay male artists seeking integration into society. As an aesthetic, camp comes in a wide range of forms. In terms of Bernstein's arrangement of *Rhapsody in Blue*, Christopher Isherwood's 1954 conception of "High Camp" may be most applicable: "You're not making fun of it; you're making fun out of it. You are expressing what's basically serious to you in terms of fun and artifice and elegance."[46] Bernstein's musical humor belies a certain degree of respect toward the *Rhapsody*. At the same time, critic Jack Babuscio observes that the humorous side of camp serves as "a means of dealing with a hostile environment and, in the process, of defining a positive identity."[47]

The development of an identity—musical and sexual—was at the forefront of Bernstein's experience the year he and the *Rhapsody* went to camp. In 1937, Bernstein first became acquainted with two homosexual musicians who had a profound impact on his career as a conductor and composer, respectively. In January, Bernstein met the then-forty-year-old conductor Dimitri Mitropoulos, an encounter described in his college essay "The Occult."[48] In November, Bernstein was introduced to Aaron Copland at a concert in New York City, where they struck up a conversation. Copland subsequently invited him to his thirty-seventh birthday party that evening at his apartment where Bernstein impressed those in attendance by playing Copland's *Piano Variations* from memory. Mitropoulos and Copland became important mentors and close friends. The intimate nature of Bernstein's relationship with both men remains largely speculative, but biographers Humphrey Burton and Merle Secrest suggest a sexual relationship between Copland and Bernstein during their early acquaintance.[49] The Camp Onota arrangement of *Rhapsody in Blue* emerges in the midst of Bernstein's exploration of his sexuality and musicality through encounters with older male musicians. The playful camp aesthetics may serve to mask the deeper—perhaps unexplainable or unspeakable at the time—musical and personal connections Bernstein ultimately felt toward Gershwin in the wake of his passing.

If reviews of Bernstein's first performance of the *Rhapsody* with full orchestra are any indication, the musical and emotional toll of his Camp Onota arrangement seems to have carried over into the concert hall as well. Bernstein performed *Rhapsody in Blue* on January 2, 1938, at Harvard's Sanders Theatre the winter following his stint at Camp Onota. It featured the State Symphony Orchestra under the sponsorship of the Works Progress Administration's Federal Music Project. Alexander Thiede directed the ensemble (also known as the Commonwealth Symphony of Boston), which was one of several dozen federally funded community and professional symphonic ensembles. The program highlighted music by American composers and included *Rhapsody in Blue* as a memorial to the late George Gershwin. Several reviews from the local press provide a sense of the performance itself. The *Boston Herald* reported that "although the performance was not as finished as could be hoped for, it did have a good amount of spirit. Mr. Bernstein's playing was adequate for the performance, and he was recalled several times to acknowledge the enthusiasm of the audience."[50] However, a review from the *Boston Post* critiqued Bernstein's performance as "hardly up to those we are in the habit of hearing at the Pop Concerts, and the music suffered accordingly."[51]

Despite such a mixed response, Bernstein continued to perform the *Rhapsody* with the State Symphony Orchestra during his years in Boston. One such appearance took place during the summer of 1938, for which he reportedly received $150 (almost $2,500 today).[52] A press release from Bernstein's scrapbooks announces a similar engagement one year later: "Youth will be the keynote of this concert, for the soloist of the evening is young Leonard Bernstein, brilliant pianist, just barely into his twenties and a senior at Harvard. He will play his own colorful interpretation of the beloved George Gershwin's 'Rhapsody in Blue.'"[53] For many reasons, not the least of which is instrumentation, it is unlikely that audiences heard his Camp Onota arrangement that evening. Since the precise nature of his "colorful interpretation" remains lost to the past, looking to his future performances provides clarification.

Bernstein's 1959 recording of the *Rhapsody* demonstrates the ways that his experiences with the piece as a teenager continued to exert their influence. Charles Hamm unfavorably referred to this recording as "lush, rhythmically insipid and erratic, [and] neoromantic."[54] He is not the only one to call into question the conductor/pianist's interpretation. Most frequently, critics take issue with Bernstein's tempo decisions. Highlighting Bernstein's solo piano "slow and drunken blues" presentation of the shuffle theme [R. 25], David Schiff observes that "everything is dragged out ponderously to the point of (intended?) parody."[55] He compares this moment to Bernstein's blues "Big Stuff" from the opening of his 1944 ballet *Fancy Free*. Although a similarity undoubtedly exists between this recording and the song written fifteen years earlier, Schiff's observation about intended parody makes more sense in the context of the camp aesthetics of Bernstein's formative experiences with the *Rhapsody*.

Bernstein's copy of the 1927 solo-piano score provides evidence that Bernstein preferred to perform this passage slowly from an early point in his life. At measure 197 [R. 25-4], four bars before the shuffle-theme piano solo begins, Bernstein penciled in a "4/4" time signature. Additionally, the measure itself is subdivided by the annotation "1 + | 2 + | 3 + | 4 + |," in which the vertical lines divide the eighth-note melody into distinct beats (see figure 3.6). Bernstein made the decision to draw out the theme here even though these measures should be *a tempo* as originally published and performed. This ritardando reemerges in his Camp Onota arrangement (rehearsal J), where the clarinet melody receives a *largo* designation. Four bars later, the shuffle theme (sung by three males accompanied by ukuleles) saunters in with a *moderato* indication. Camp, parody, or otherwise, Bernstein's 1959 recording follows these early tempo assignments to the letter.

An additional critique often leveled at Bernstein's interpretation of the *Rhapsody* has to do with his cuts—namely, the excision of a statement of the shuffle and ritornello themes.[56] Here too, such choices have deeper roots, as a 1986 interview reveals:

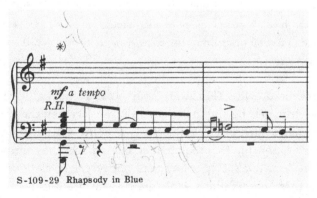

Figure 3.6
Measures 197–198 of Bernstein's childhood copy of the 1927 solo-piano sheet music of *Rhapsody in Blue*. Image courtesy of the New York Philharmonic Archives.

I have to confess to you and, even if this is a public confession, that is the way I have always played it, so that when I do play it with orchestras, and I have played it with many orchestras, I have to re-do the score to fit the way I learned it because that is the way I love it. That is the way I know it and I think it works better.[57]

Bernstein is true to his word. With the exception of two *grandioso* measures that introduce the final presentation of the stride theme [R. 39], his 1959 recording adheres note for note to the 1927 solo-piano sheet music of the *Rhapsody* that he learned as a teenager with its unique pair of cuts. Such cuts may have prompted the mixed response of his post-camp performances with the State Symphony during the late 1930s. In any event, with respect to both tempo and form, Bernstein's lifelong interpretations of the *Rhapsody* resulted from an adolescent infatuation with the piece and with Gershwin himself.

MORE THAN JUST "A NICE GERSHWIN TUNE"

Gershwin advocates maintain that the interpretation offered by Bernstein's recordings "arguably undermined the work's structural integrity."[58] However, using his essay "A Nice Gershwin Tune" as an example, Bernstein clearly saw the structural flexibility of the work as one of its greatest strengths. Bernstein states of *Rhapsody in Blue*:

> You can cut out parts of it without affecting the whole in any way except to make it shorter. You can remove any of these stuck-together sections and the piece still goes on as bravely as before. You can even interchange these sections with one another and no harm is done. You can make cuts within a section, or add new cadenzas, or play it with any combination of instruments or on the piano alone; it can be a five-minute piece or a six-minute piece, or a twelve-minute piece. And in fact all these things are being done to it every day. It's still the *Rhapsody in Blue*.[59]

Both voices in "A Nice Gershwin Tune"—Bernstein and Professional Manager—ultimately belong to Bernstein. Taken together, they reveal the affectionate ambivalence that lies at the core of his relationship with the *Rhapsody*, a relationship that took root at an early age. The considerations advanced in Bernstein's 1955 essay were not recent revelations. Rather, he formed these observations while growing up. He documented them in both his copy of the 1927 solo-piano sheet music and the 1937 Camp Onota arrangement. The latter makes various cuts, connects separate delineated sections, and alters the orchestration. Furthermore, it goes so far as to change the key of one of the work's most famous themes—something Bernstein discovered was a possibility at the age of thirteen. Even when the work was performed by a quirky ensemble of teenaged campers, Bernstein's later remarks hold true: Regardless of the alterations made to the piece, it remains the *Rhapsody in Blue*.

At the same time, Bernstein's performances of the work did not embrace such a supple approach to the *Rhapsody*. Given his deep-rooted belief in the flexibility of the piece, it is ironic that he always followed the same tempo and editorial choices. This is true of the 1959 recording, a 1976 televised broadcast at the Royal Albert Hall in London, and his 1983 Deutsche Grammophon recording with the Los Angeles Philharmonic. A review of his presentation of the piece at Carnegie Hall during the bicentennial year called his performance "perfumed," noting that "there were all kinds of Romantic shadings and rubatos; there were more long ritards than a subway trip between Times Square and Coney Island."[60] In many respects, Bernstein's Camp Onota arrangement set in stone a version of *Rhapsody in Blue* at the time of Gershwin's passing—not only with respect to cuts and tempo choices but also in terms of its dramatic presentation—to which Bernstein would hold steadfastly throughout his career. Based on his deep emotional connection to Gershwin, it would seem that Bernstein faced an interpretive lock with the *Rhapsody* that he was unable to open.

Bernstein acknowledges this impassioned bond in "A Nice Gershwin Tune." Although he articulates what he believes are the inherent flaws of the piece, Bernstein admits that he adores the *Rhapsody*. Professional Manager challenges this assertion by asking, "How can you adore something you riddle with holes?" Bernstein retorts, "Each man kills the thing he loves."[61] The gay subtext of Bernstein's relationship with *Rhapsody in Blue* emerges from his campy Onota arrangement, but it comes to the foreground with this allusive reference.[62] His reply quotes directly from Oscar Wilde's *The Ballad of Reading Gaol*. Wilde authored this extended poem in July 1896, following a two-year prison term for homosexual offenses in London. Appearances of the phrase "Each man kills the thing he loves" fittingly bookend a section of Wilde's poem apropos to Bernstein's irresolute treatment of *Rhapsody in Blue* and, by extension, George Gershwin:

Yet each man kills the thing he loves
By each let this be heard.
Some do it with a bitter look,
Some with a flattering word.
The coward does it with a kiss,

The brave man with a sword!
Some kill their love when they are young,
And some when they are old;
Some strangle with the hands of Lust,
Some with the hands of Gold:
The kindest use a knife, because
The dead so soon grow cold.
Some love too little, some too long,
Some sell, and others buy;
Some do the deed with many tears,
And some without a sigh:
For each man kills the thing he loves,
Yet each man does not die.[63]

The uneasy relationship with *Rhapsody in Blue* acknowledged by Bernstein in "A Nice Gershwin Tune" reveals the piece as a musical stand-in for personal relationships he had to keep behind closed doors. As Nadine Hubbs observes in an article on Bernstein and historiographical homophobia, "the acute and overt homophobia of midcentury American culture dictated that gay truths and desires could not be expressed."[64] In order to attain his position with the New York Philharmonic, Bernstein needed the "heterosexual identity credentials" that came with marriage and children.[65] "A Nice Gershwin Tune" may not really be about Gershwin or *Rhapsody in Blue* at all, but like the Camp Onota arrangement, an essential outlet for his personal and professional impulses as he navigated the American classical music scene during the 1950s.

As an American-born conductor taking the reins of an orchestral institution steeped in the European classical tradition, Bernstein had to tread lightly in his presentation of American music, much of which remained outside the canon of classical masterworks.[66] When *Rhapsody in Blue* appeared on a regular subscription concert program in December 1958 focusing on music of the 1920s, it followed Darius Milhaud's *La création du monde* and Gershwin's *An American in Paris*. In a preview concert talk comparing Milhaud and Gershwin, Bernstein observed that "in their different ways, they are both doing the same thing: fusing jazz with serious music. Only they came from different sides of the tracks: Gershwin from Tin Pan Alley, and Milhaud from the more sophisticated alleys behind the Eiffel Tower."[67] In doing so, Bernstein locates the European Milhaud above the American Gershwin. Almost as an afterthought, Bernstein concludes his remarks: "As for the *Rhapsody in Blue*, there is nothing I have to tell you about that. It's almost become the American National Anthem."[68] Perhaps owing to the ubiquity of the piece or his previously published comments on the work in "A Nice Gershwin Tune," he positions the *Rhapsody* as of central importance but not worthy of formal consideration. He also might have chosen not to talk about the *Rhapsody* for the sake of keeping his composure onstage at Carnegie Hall.

In the end, there remains an enigmatic depth to Bernstein's relationship with Gershwin. Following his declaration that "each man kills the thing he loves," Bernstein concedes to Professional Manager: "Yes, I guess you can love a bad composition. For noncompositional reasons. Sentiment. Association. Inner meaning. Spirit."[69] The specter of Gershwin loomed large for Bernstein. It cast a shadow over the music of his youth, his rise to musical prominence, and the construction of his own legacy as an American musician. It also affected Bernstein's public performance of the piece. His 1959 recording of the *Rhapsody* with the New York Philharmonic marks a pivotal point in the work's transition from a piece for classical piano with a jazz ensemble to one for jazz piano with a classical ensemble. The next chapter begins with a consideration of an arrangement recorded by Duke Ellington and his ensemble in 1963. This recording seems to respond to Bernstein's classicization of the piece. Rather than return to the origins of the *Rhapsody* with Ferde Grofé's Whiteman arrangement, Ellington offered an original interpretation that "swings" the pendulum as much toward the jazz end of the symphonic-jazz continuum as Bernstein's inclined toward the symphonic.

CHAPTER 4

Rearranging Concert Jazz

Duke Ellington and Rhapsody in Blue

The true story has not been told, because most of the histories have been written from too great a distance.

　　　　　　　　　　—Duke Ellington (1960)

Duke Ellington begins his foreword for the 1960 edition of *The Encyclopedia of Jazz* with the following admission: "It is strange that I should be contributing the foreword to Leonard Feather's book, because at one time I was involved in a similar project myself; I almost did a history of jazz."[1] In 1941, Orson Welles approached Ellington for a film project on jazz history, tentatively titled *It's All True*. Welles commissioned Ellington to write both the score and the book, as well as conduct his orchestra for the soundtrack. However, the project fell through after only twelve weeks of work. The only music composed—a twenty-eight measure trumpet solo performed by a musician playing the part of Buddy Bolden in a scene depicting the arrival of the King of the Zulus in an annual coronation celebration in New Orleans—did not survive. However, Ellington eventually found a home for the scenario in *A Drum Is a Woman* (1956), his allegorical history of jazz.[2]

This brief vignette encapsulates Ellington's concern with historical narratives and their realization through musical arrangements. In addition to *A Drum Is a Woman*, other suite-based works like *Symphony in Black: A Rhapsody of Negro Life* (1935), *Black, Brown, and Beige* (1943), *Deep South Suite* (1946), and *My People* (1963) depict the social, cultural, and political history of African Americans.[3] In these concert-jazz works,

Ellington incorporates compositional elements, or what he referred to as "tone parallels," that convey a sense of African-American musical history. Gestures to work songs, spirituals, stride piano, and big-band arranging techniques signify both the passing of time and the development of jazz. Ellington increasingly turned to the practice of representing music of earlier traditions through the musical lens of the present as his career went on, often with significant assistance from his collaborator Billy Strayhorn. Such musical reconfiguration occurs not only with arrangements of classical compositions, such as the *Peer Gynt Suites* and Tchaikovsky's *Nutcracker* (1960), but also with jazz standards of the past.

During the spring of 1963, Duke Ellington released an album titled *Will Big Bands Ever Come Back?*[4] Issued amid the post-bop musical backdrop of the jazz avant-garde, which itself took a back seat to the dominance of rock 'n' roll, this tribute to the popular hits of ensembles led by the likes of Glenn Miller, Benny Goodman, and Les Brown offers a wistful recollection of music from a bygone era. Most of the selections hark back to the late-1930s and mid-1940s, tunes known well by the generation of middle-aged Americans to whom this recording was directed. In fact, a full appreciation of the performances offered on this album requires a familiarity with the original big-band renditions. The version of "One O'Clock Jump," for example, replicates the well-known recording by Count Basie from 1937.[5] Ellington channels his inner Basie throughout the introduction with sparse piano riffs. Later, tenor saxophonist Paul Gonsalves pays homage to Lester Young, not only quoting his original 1937 solo but also, as audibly evident on the recording, adopting the same technique of false fingerings for the repeated notes. Other songs on the album, such as Woody Herman's "Woodchoppers Ball," emerge anew through the unique transformational choices of the arrangers. The crisp trumpet soli introduction becomes a boogie-woogie line, staggered and syncopated by the trombone section. The playful melody emerges from the strings of Ray Nance's violin through (appropriately enough) a combination of chopping *pizzicati* and sawing *arco* double-stops. With the original big-band arrangements echoing in the sonic memory of the listener, each selection on *Will Big Bands Ever Come Back?* affords the opportunity for reflection on music of the past.

Rhapsody in Blue represents not only the oldest selection on the album, but also the one most significantly altered from its original presentation ◗. Starting with the opening measures of the arrangement offered by the Ellington orchestra, very little remains of the *Rhapsody* as first performed and recorded by the Paul Whiteman Orchestra. Baritone saxophonist Harry Carney stylishly remaps the famous opening clarinet swoop. As he reaches the top of his meandering ascent, the band sets into a mid-tempo groove, which it maintains for the duration of the five-minute-long arrangement. Gone too are the elements that mark the *Rhapsody* as an exemplar of "symphonic jazz" as conceived by midcentury: no episodic development of various themes, no dramatic shifts of dynamic and tempo, no orchestral instrumentation, and no virtuosic piano cadenzas. Rather, the power of this performance comes from the creative redistribution of Gershwin's themes among the timbres and talents of the Ellington ensemble. David Schiff rightfully dubbed this recording of *Rhapsody in Blue* a "brilliant act of deconstruction—and renewal."[6]

Why might Ellington and Strayhorn have wished to retrofit the *Rhapsody* so thoroughly? By the time they recorded it in the early 1960s, and certainly in the context of the album on which it was released, performing a version more akin to Ferde Grofé's original 1924 arrangement of the piece would have been an act of recovery and renewal in its own right. After all, Leonard Bernstein's 1959 recording with the New York Philharmonic performing Grofé's symphonic arrangement of the work was in wide circulation at the time. Rather, the Ellington ensemble's 1963 recording of *Rhapsody in Blue* detaches the "symphonic" from the "jazz" through the rearrangement and re-orchestration of Gershwin's musical themes. Furthermore, it suggests to the listener how Ellington might have performed the piece early in his career, had he played it.

Much like *A Drum Is a Woman, Symphony in Black*, and *Black, Brown, and Beige*, this 1963 arrangement of *Rhapsody in Blue* represents a musicalized retelling of the past. Here that past is specifically concerned with narratives about concert jazz in the 1920s and 1930s. The *Rhapsody* remains the quintessential example of symphonic jazz in now-loaded definitions of the term. The "racial tensions between white and black 'jazz' aesthetics in the 1920s symphonic jazz vogue," writes musicologist John Howland, "fed into an emerging critical discourse that defined black jazz aesthetics as art and [Paul] Whiteman-style symphonic jazz as commercial kitsch."[7] Such discourses emerged in the 1930s and continue into the present day. This sentiment infuses conceptions of Ellington's music in this arena as distinct from that of his white contemporaries. Ellington's output—referred to as "extended jazz compositions" rather than "symphonic jazz"—offers a counter-narrative deeply embedded in Ellington's 1931 proclamation on the eve of his composition of *Creole Rhapsody* that he intended to create "an authentic record of my race *written by a member of it*."[8] Accordingly, a racialized barrier between the black "authentic" extended jazz compositions of Ellington and the white "inauthentic" symphonic jazz of Gershwin emerged in critical discourse around these traditions.[9] However, when considering Ellington and *Rhapsody in Blue* in tandem, these barriers become more complex and permeable.

As it turns out, this 1963 recording was not Ellington's first engagement with the *Rhapsody*, but rather his third and final arrangement of the
piece. The parts for two additional arrangements of the *Rhapsody* survive
in the Duke Ellington Collection at the Smithsonian National Museum of
American History. These interpretations, which date to 1925 and 1932
respectively, align more closely with the Whiteman-style symphonic-jazz
traditions that the 1963 recording assiduously elides. The presence of
Rhapsody in Blue at the outset of Ellington's compositional output of
extended jazz compositions raises some important questions: How distinct were the differences between the concertized jazz of Gershwin and
Ellington? What role did the *Rhapsody* play in Ellington's development of
extended forms? These 1925 and 1932 arrangements also force a closer
examination of Ellington's 1963 recording of *Rhapsody in Blue*. What motivated Ellington to return to the piece more than forty years into his career?
Why did the *Rhapsody* receive such a thorough reworking? Insights into
each of these questions emerge when considering these arrangements as
both historical and historiographical documents, informing understandings of the past at the same time that Ellington and his musicians were
constructing it through performance.

TWO EARLY ARRANGEMENTS OF *RHAPSODY IN BLUE*

"The recording bias of the jazz canon," notes Jeffrey Magee, "leads historians to construct artifices of musical evolution."[10] This observation presents
a double bind in the case of Ellington and *Rhapsody in Blue*. First, accepting Ellington's 1963 recording as his valedictory musical statement on the
Rhapsody—a recording that highlights the perceived historical priorities
of big-band-era jazz and Ellington's approach to concert jazz—results in
an oversimplification of the actual development of both. Second, until
the regular recording of radio broadcasts began in the late 1930s, most
of the music heard in clubs, including Ellington's early performances of
Rhapsody in Blue, did not survive on disc. While current catalogues document every piece recorded by Ellington beginning with his first studio session in July 1923, similarly consistent data do not exist for works heard at
Ellington's club and concert appearances until about a decade and a half
later.[11] From the time Ellington arrived in New York through his years at
the Cotton Club, it is unclear exactly what was heard when the band performed live. The two early arrangements of *Rhapsody in Blue* that reside in
the Ellington Collection at the Smithsonian originate during this thinly
documented period.[12] They not only illuminate this largely unconsidered

era of live performance, but also provide a sense of the role of the *Rhapsody* in Ellington's early development as a bandleader and arranger.[13]

The origins of the earliest arrangement of the *Rhapsody* performed by Ellington remain hazy. Ellington and his band held a regular gig at the Kentucky Club in New York City from September 1923 to the spring of 1927, as documented by early jazz scholar Mark Tucker.[14] As their reputation grew, their audiences increasingly consisted of celebrities from the world of popular entertainment. According to reports in the black press, Paul Whiteman attended Ellington's performances as early as February 1924 (the month of *Rhapsody in Blue*'s premiere).[15] Ellington and his musicians relied heavily on tips, which often constituted a greater share of their earnings than what they actually received from the club.[16] On one occasion, Whiteman asked Ellington's band to play a popular tune called "I Love You" in "their own inimitable way."[17] There was a lot at stake in such a request because it supposedly came with a hundred-dollar bill attached to it and because this very song had recently received its own unique treatment by Whiteman's ensemble when it appeared on the same Experiment in Modern Music program at which *Rhapsody in Blue* debuted.[18] Since this Tin Pan Alley song by Harry Archer (1886–1960) is not particularly complex, Ellington likely came up with something. It would not be so easy, however, to meet a similar request for the *Rhapsody*, which consists of a variety of contrasting melodies and harmonic progressions.

As considered in chapter 2, *Rhapsody in Blue* grew in popularity during the mid-to-late 1920s, and requests to hear the work—or at least its main themes—became increasingly common at clubs throughout New York City. Since published stock arrangements of the *Rhapsody* were not available until nearly a year and a half after the work's premiere, bandleaders and arrangers created their own renditions in the interim. Although there are no contemporary reports that Whiteman requested the *Rhapsody* specifically, Ellington and his band were under both financial and musical pressure to please their audiences and needed to be prepared to perform virtually any piece at a moment's notice. With respect to the *Rhapsody*, added pressure may have come not only from the presence of Whiteman, but also from Whiteman's musicians, whom Ellington drummer Sonny Greer recalled "would want to sit in and play with the band."[19]

Bob Sylvester, a regular orchestrator for the white New York bandleader Hal Kemp, prepared the oldest *Rhapsody* arrangement that resides in the Ellington archives.[20] Based on the extant manuscript and Ellington's personnel at the time, it likely originated in late 1925. Parts survive for a banjo, a trombone, and three reed players. In addition to the rest of the rhythm section, at least one trumpet likely performed this arrangement as well, bringing the total number of required musicians to nine (see table 4.1). In early 1925, Ellington's ensemble, then known as The Washingtonians, had only six musicians: Sonny Greer (drums), Charlie Irvis (trombone), Bubber Miley (trumpet), Fred Guy (banjo), Otto Hardwick (clarinet/saxophones), and Ellington (piano). Hardwick could have easily managed the requirements of the first saxophone part, which calls for a combination of soprano, alto, and baritone saxophones in addition to clarinet. To play this *Rhapsody* arrangement fully, however, two additional reed players had to be added to the standing ensemble. By the summer of 1925, Prince Robinson became a regular member of the group and Sidney Bechet regularly sat in with the band after hours at the Kentucky Club and when it performed in larger spaces.[21] It was also during the late summer or early fall of 1925 that Ellington hired tuba player Henry "Bass" Edwards. Regardless of whether or not the *Rhapsody* was a regular request, the ensemble likely had this arrangement at the ready by at least that date.

In this arrangement, Sylvester reorganized Gershwin's themes and removed large passages of the *Rhapsody* altogether; however, it still closely resembles the version of the piece premiered by Paul Whiteman in 1924 (see table 4.2). The arrangement's woodwind doublings and its reliance on Gershwin's written transitions connect it to the arrangement that Grofé prepared for the Whiteman Orchestra. Unlike future arrangements of the *Rhapsody* played by Ellington, there are no unexpected reharmonizations of the musical themes—after all, Ellington is not the arranger here. At 306 measures—some 200 bars shorter than the version premiered by

Table 4.1. PROPOSED PART ASSIGNMENTS FOR BOB SYLVESTER'S 1925 ARRANGEMENT OF *RHAPSODY IN BLUE*; MISSING PARTS BRACKETED.

Instrumentation	Musician
Saxophone 1: Alto/Soprano/Baritone Saxophones, & Clarinet (with optional Bass Clarinet & Oboe)	Otto Hardwick
Saxophone 2: Alto/Baritone Saxophones, & Clarinet	Sidney Bechet
Saxophone 3: Tenor Saxophone & Clarinet	Prince Robinson
Trombone	Charlie Irvis
[Trumpet]	Bubber Miley
Banjo	Fred Guy
[Piano]	Duke Ellington
[Bass/Tuba]	Henry Edwards
[Drums]	Sonny Greer

Table 4.2. THEMATIC ORGANIZATION FOR BOB SLYVESTER'S 1925
ARRANGEMENT OF *RHAPSODY IN BLUE*.

Rehearsal Letter	Measure Number	Theme	Key	Notes
--	1–10	Love	Bb major	New introduction
B-D	11–48	Ritornello	Bb major	Original introduction
--	49–84	Love (AAB...)	Eb major	Brass
E	85–92	Love (...C)		Brass/reeds
--	93–110	Love (AAB...)		Reeds
--	111–114	Transition		Solo horn
F	115–140	Ritornello (AAB...)	Ab major	
G	141–152	Transition + Ritornello (...A)	Bb major	
H-I	153–178	Stride	Bb major	Open solo section (?)
J	179–198	Shuffle (AAB...)	G major	
--	199–206	Transition: Gershwin's		
--	207–222	Shuffle (AA...)	Db major	
--	223–224	Transition: unnotated		Piano solo (?)
--	225–268	Love (AABC)	Eb major	Reeds
--	269–280	Transition: Gershwin's		
--	281–298	Love (AA...)		
--	299–306	Coda	Bb major	

Whiteman in 1924—this reworking of the *Rhapsody* remains the longest by
far of the arrangements performed by Ellington, probably lasting between
eight and ten minutes. A new ten-bar introduction appears at the outset, a
surprising choice given the *Rhapsody*'s now-famous opening clarinet ascent
(see figure 4.1). It is a modified presentation of the love theme that serves
to highlight the central location of this particular theme in the arrangement as a whole. In fact, this theme occupies half of the total measures
in the arrangement, as opposed to only a fifth in the premiere version of
Rhapsody in Blue.

Although on paper this 1925 arrangement appears similar to the one
performed by Whiteman, it probably took on its own "inimitable" tone
in performance. As figure 4.1 reveals, a trombone played the introductory presentation of the love theme through an open Harmon mute that
was further augmented with a hat on the long notes. The combination
of these elements allowed Charlie Irvis or "Tricky Sam" Nanton (after
June 1926) to produce a timbre often associated with the "jungle style"
of Ellington's ensemble. Nanton's well-known solo in this mode on the

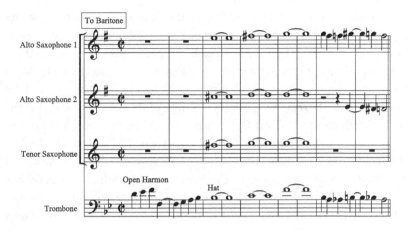

Figure 4.1
The ten-bar introduction for Bob Sylvester's 1925 arrangement of *Rhapsody in Blue*, from the Duke Ellington Collection, Archives Center, National Museum of American History, Smithsonian Institution. Used by permission of the Estate of Edward K. "Duke" Ellington.

1927 recording of "Black and Tan Fantasy" provides a sense of the unique treatment that this famous theme of the *Rhapsody* might have received.[22] Bubber Miley's growling trumpet fills on "The Mooche" (1928)—which closely resemble the *Rhapsody*'s tag motif in both melody and rhythm— provide an even stronger sense of how the individual contributions of Ellington's musicians likely resulted in a distinctive sonic transformation of the piece.[23]

The very fact that Ellington had an arrangement of *Rhapsody in Blue* on hand gives pause. The piece has long been characterized as "white" jazz because of its close association with the Paul Whiteman Orchestra. Historical representations of Ellington in the mid-to-late 1920s and 1930s, supported by statements made by Ellington himself, highlight his serious and systematic attempts to give voice to the African-American experience through music, similar to the efforts of other artists of the Harlem Renaissance. Despite the *Rhapsody*'s ubiquitous presence in dancehalls and clubs during this time, Fletcher Henderson remains the only other contemporary black bandleader thought to have engaged this piece.[24] The arrangement likely used by Ellington's musicians suggests that a black band—one that would become one of the most celebrated ensembles of the century— performed *Rhapsody in Blue* from the moment of its public emergence. Due to a lack of recorded evidence, the extent to which Ellington played the *Rhapsody* during the 1920s may never be known. Nonetheless, the piece continued to be part of his development as a bandleader and composer of concert jazz.

The other early arrangement of *Rhapsody in Blue* emerged during the late spring or early summer of 1932. Based on certain Ellingtonian devices used throughout, it appears that the bandleader prepared this particular arrangement himself. After completing several successful years as the house band at Harlem's famous Cotton Club (from 1927 to 1931), Ellington and his ensemble began touring the country. In spite of (or perhaps owing to) the economic effects of the Great Depression, the band prospered. A December 1931 report in the *Pittsburgh Courier* noted that "Ellington has broken attendance and box office records for the season, and in most instances has added new life and vigor to the institutions [in which the band has appeared]."[25] They provided music for dancers, supported various revues, and served as featured performers in their own right for eager audiences from coast to coast. The audience requests continued, and Ellington began to dedicate entire programs to suggestions from members of his audience.[26]

Perhaps in response to this increased popularity and prosperity, Ellington enlarged his ensemble to a total of fourteen musicians—the precise number required by this second arrangement of *Rhapsody in Blue* (see table 4.3). While performing in Los Angeles in March of 1932, Ellington successfully convinced trombonist Lawrence Brown to join his ensemble. Various reports in the black press note the significance of Ellington's addition of Brown, whom many bandleaders had attempted to lure away from the West Coast.[27] This feat increased the trombone section from two to

Table 4.3. PART ASSIGNMENTS FOR DUKE ELLINGTON'S 1932 ARRANGEMENT OF *RHAPSODY IN BLUE*; MISSING PARTS BRACKETED.

Instrumentation	Musician
"Jonny" [sic]: Alto/Soprano Saxophones	Johnny Hodges
"Carney": Baritone/Alto Saxophones	Harry Carney
"Bigard": Clarinet, Tenor Saxophone	Barney Bigard
"Otto": Bass/Alto Saxophones	Otto Hardwick
[Cornet 1]	Arty Whetsol
Cornet 2	Cootie Williams
Cornet 3	Fred Jenkins
Trombone 1	Lawrence Brown
[Trombone 2]	Joe "Tricky Sam" Nanton
Trombone 3	Juan Tizol
Banjo	Fred Guy
[Piano]	Duke Ellington
Bass	Wellman Braud
[Drums]	Sonny Greer

three, a move soon emulated by many other bands. Otto Hardwick had left four years previously, but he rejoined the band toward the end of May 1932, increasing the saxophone section from three to four. The name of each saxophonist appears on their respective parts from the 1932 arrangement of the *Rhapsody*: Barney [Bigard], Jo[h]nny [Hodges], [Harry] Carney, and Otto [Hardwick]. The expansion of these two sections of the band allowed Ellington to achieve more complex harmonies, as well as a greater range of timbral and harmonic color, all of which he explores in this arrangement of the *Rhapsody*.

Dance may represent one impetus for Ellington's 1932 arrangement of *Rhapsody in Blue*. Recall that social dancing played a large part in early recordings of the *Rhapsody* by groups such as the Victor Irwin Orchestra. Beginning in late May of that year, Ellington and his orchestra played a series of one-night dances along the northeastern seaboard before heading to the Midwest for engagements between June and August.[28] They spent the month of July at the Lincoln Tavern in Chicago, where they accompanied a floor show featuring "Harlem's sweet dance queen" Louise Cooke, the "sensational dance team of note" Fredi Washington and Al Moiret, and an "eccentric dancer" from California named Kid Charleston.[29] Ellington had recently reported: "When I'm making my arrangements or composing something new, I try to think of something that will make my hearers feel like dancing."[30] This *Rhapsody* arrangement contains no specific tempo markings, as is the case with most of Ellington's arrangements. But with the possible exception of an improvised piano solo, the arrangement can be played with a steady, danceable tempo making it an appropriate accompaniment for any of these performers or a ballroom full of social dancers.

However, Ellington's 1932 arrangement of the *Rhapsody* stands as more than just an example of a dance arrangement for a newly expanded ensemble . It demonstrates several hallmarks of Ellington's emergent compositional style. In the span of just over 200 cut-time measures (one-third shorter than Sylvester's 1925 arrangement), Ellington reinterprets the *Rhapsody* while maintaining the familiar structure and thematic unfolding of the recorded and published versions of the piece (see table 4.4). He begins with the famous clarinet glissando and introduction of the expected ritornello theme, played by Bigard over a foundation of trombones and bass saxophone in the key of Bb major. These first twenty-one measures follow the original Whiteman arrangement by Grofé. At rehearsal B, Ellington recasts the first piano solo as a fourteen-bar saxophone and trombone interlude that excises sixty-two measures of piano-heavy thematic development. For the next fifty-six measures (rehearsals C to H), Ellington again largely follows Grofé's arrangement, apart from transferring the melody

Table 4.4. THEMATIC ORGANIZATION OF DUKE ELLINGTON'S 1932
ARRANGEMENT OF *RHAPSODY IN BLUE.*

Rehearsal Letter	Measure Number	Theme	Key	Notes
A	1–21	Ritornello	Bb Major	Original introduction
B	22–35	Transition		Orchestration of written piano solo
C & D	36–54	Ritornello (AABA)	A Major	
E	55–68	Train (AABA)	C Major	
F	69–78	Transition: Gershwin's		
G	79–93	Stride (AABA)	C Major	(A) - reeds (A) - reharmonized brass (B) - brass/reeds (A) - reeds
	94–101	Transition: Gershwin's		Improvised piano solo?
H	102–123	Love (AABC)	Eb Major	
	124–145	Love (AABC)		Reharmonized saxophone breaks
I	146–155	Transition		Orchestration of written piano solo
J	156–181	Love (AABC)	F Major	Episodic parade of themes
K	182–185	Transition: Gershwin's		
L	186–203	Stride (AABA)	Eb Major	
	204–210	Coda	Bb Major	

between different sections of the ensemble and adding a few extended harmonies, particularly at points of transition. For example, Ellington moves
the final two bars of the train theme (just prior to rehearsal F) from the
reeds to the brass, recasting what would otherwise be an octave presentation of the melody over a tonic/dominant harmony with a series of altered
ninth and thirteenth chords (see figure 4.2). A similar change occurs during a section of the stride theme. Here the melody is reharmonized as a
series of minor and diminished tritone substitutions (see figure 4.3). Both
of these examples result in parallel-motion, extended-harmony passages,
which would become a trademark of the Ellington sound.[31]

The 1932 arrangement reveals a reliance on traditional models at the
same time as Ellington begins to move beyond them. John Howland has
explored the various archetypes that Ellington used in his development
of concert jazz compositions during the 1930s.[32] Howland concludes
that Ellington's early efforts reveal "the adaptation, expansion, and ultimate transcendence of a formal model that was popular among his white

Figure 4.2
The train theme from *Rhapsody in Blue* as originally written by Gershwin (top staff) and as reharmonized by Ellington (bottom system) in his 1932 arrangement, from the Duke Ellington Collection, Archives Center, National Museum of American History, Smithsonian Institution. Used by permission of the Estate of Edward K. "Duke" Ellington.

arranger peers."[33] This formal model was episodic in nature and emerged from the popular song-arranging aesthetics of ensembles such as Paul Whiteman's as witnessed in the work of Ferde Grofé. The episode-driven organization and development of Ellington's 1932 arrangement stands as one example of his adaptation of such a model. Nonetheless, certain decisions—compositional choices that would come to be labeled as characteristically "Ellingtonian"—form an expansion of concert jazz techniques encountered in other arrangements of the *Rhapsody*.

One such example emerges in Ellington's treatment of the episodic love theme, where he fully realizes the sonic possibilities of his expanded saxophone and trombone sections for the first time in the arrangement. The theme first enters at rehearsal H in Eb major, modulating up a half-step from the preceding cadence on D major. In its first appearance, Ellington

Figure 4.3
The stride theme from *Rhapsody in Blue* as originally written by Gershwin (top staff) and as reharmonized by Ellington (bottom system) in his 1932 arrangement, from the Duke Ellington Collection, Archives Center, National Museum of American History, Smithsonian Institution. Used by permission of the Estate of Edward K. "Duke" Ellington.

presents the theme according to Gershwin's original harmonic scheme, with the second alto saxophone and third trumpet providing the counter-melody. A notable shift in orchestration and harmonization occurs when the theme is played for a second time twenty-two bars later. Rather than continue to carry the melody, the four saxophone players enclose the solo line—played by Juan Tizol on the valve trombone—within a series of altered ninth chords, similar to those found in his earlier treatment of the train theme (see figure 4.4).

In addition to the incorporation of creative reharmonizations and instrumental color combinations, Ellington also utilizes unexpected transpositions and reiterations of previously heard themes. When the love theme recapitulates at rehearsal J, it enters in F major. Both here and at rehearsal H, Ellington avoids the expected modulation to E major, choosing instead to set this famous melody on either side of it—Eb and F major, respectively—perhaps to avoid a significant number of sharps in the saxophone key signatures. Following this transition to F major at rehearsal J, instead of assigning the expected countermelody to the saxophones, Ellington substitutes brief two-bar reiterations of the train and stride themes followed by the tag motif (see figure 4.5).

This repetition of melodies heard at an earlier point in the arrangement functions as allusion, and as with any allusion, it falls upon the receiver to interpret the intention of this parade of themes. On the one hand, it exists as pure novelty, a performative device that subverts the expectations of his audience. On the other hand, this clever maneuver may serve to highlight his abilities as an arranger, pointing in the direction of future works like

Figure 4.4
The love theme from *Rhapsody in Blue* as originally written by Gershwin (top staff) and as reharmonized by Ellington (bottom system) in his 1932 arrangement, from the Duke Ellington Collection, Archives Center, National Museum of American History, Smithsonian Institution. Used by permission of the Estate of Edward K. "Duke" Ellington.

Figure 4.5
An episodic parade of themes (train, stride, and tag) at rehearsal J of Ellington's 1932 arrangement of *Rhapsody in Blue*, from the Duke Ellington Collection, Archives Center, National Museum of American History, Smithsonian Institution. Used by permission of the Estate of Edward K. "Duke" Ellington.

Reminiscing in Tempo (1935) that rely on the juxtaposition of themes as countermelodies. Regardless, this passage indicates one way that extended forms allowed for a greater degree of compositional flexibility for Ellington than the shorter pieces that comprised a majority of his recorded output up to that point.

In 1931, the year before this *Rhapsody in Blue* arrangement, Ellington released his recordings of *Creole Rhapsody*, which reference Gershwin in both title and musical content.[34] Critics such as A. J. Bishop, Gunther Schuller, and David Schiff have noted Ellington's "borrowings" from Gershwin in the *Creole Rhapsody*.[35] Yet the composition has long been identified as Ellington's move away from the symphonic jazz of Gershwin and Whiteman toward an extended form that was uniquely his own. However, as Ellington's 1932 arrangement of *Rhapsody in Blue* reveals through its use of episodic development, he may not have ventured away from Whiteman-style symphonic jazz as quickly as previously assumed. To this end, the *Rhapsody in Blue* functioned as a sort of sandbox wherein Ellington mixed traditional structural models with harmonic and instrumental techniques that would eventually come to be considered markers of his style—elements that certain critics would come to associate with "authentic" jazz.

REWRITING THE *RHAPSODY* FOR THE 1960s

In certain circles, by the time Ellington recorded *Rhapsody in Blue* in 1963, the piece had become decidedly not jazz. The traditional narrative of jazz history divides its development into discrete styles as they evolved one into another, decade by decade, from the 1920s through the 1960s: New Orleans jazz, swing, bebop, cool jazz and hard bop, free jazz and fusion. In an essay on the historiography of jazz, Scott DeVeaux explains that a "seamless narrative" such as this emerges as those styles that came before get remapped to construct an evolutionary bridge to the present.[36] During the 1960s, notions of authenticity in jazz became progressively more linked to ethnicity and race as figures like Amiri Baraka (formerly LeRoi Jones) assertively positioned black music against the dominant white mainstream.[37] Accordingly, critics, historians, and musicians began to actively reinforce the separation of black, authentic jazz from its inauthentic white counterpart, reforming perspectives on music of the past accordingly.[38] This revision had a devastating effect on the reception of symphonic jazz and *Rhapsody in Blue*, which had firmly secured its place in the white mainstream—due in no small part to Leonard Bernstein—by this point in time.

"As we can now appreciate," proclaimed jazz critic Eric Larrabee in *Harper's Magazine* during the summer of 1962, "nothing about the *Rhapsody in Blue* is right. It is pseudo-Lisztian pastiche, with a Tchaikovsky-like major theme, which borrows from jazz only those few blue notes and dance rhythms necessary to make it seem fresh and keep it moving. As proper jazz, it is nonexistent."[39] That same year, historian Neil Leonard wrote: "*Rhapsody [in Blue]* seems to be traditional music dressed in jazz costume and coloring—Liszt, as it were, in blackface, a rented tuxedo, and battered top hat."[40]

In this context, the arrangement of the *Rhapsody* recorded by Ellington for his 1963 album *Will Big Bands Ever Come Back?* accomplishes two related endeavors of jazz discourse in the 1960s. First, it rewrites the piece to form a seamless continuum from Ellington of the past to Ellington of the then present. Large-scale reissues of out-of-print recordings by Ellington and his ensemble were not yet in circulation at this time. With these earlier sonic documents effectively lost to history, Ellington and Strayhorn were free to arrange the *Rhapsody* so that it more closely aligned with current impressions of the historical Ellingtonian style. Second, the arrangement authenticates the *Rhapsody* by deemphasizing particular aspects of the piece aligned with prevailing conceptions of symphonic jazz in favor of instrumental and improvisational choices that ultimately reinforce Ellington's approach to concert jazz as distinct from that of white composers.

The liner notes for *Will Big Bands Ever Come Back?* highlight the singular genius of Ellington among his contemporaries. The opening sentence proclaims his longstanding preeminence: "Ellington is one of the wonders of our day, and of yesterday, and of a couple of days before yesterday." The notes continue, affirming that "hardly a man is now alive. . . who can remember a time when the Duke was not surprising and delighting us with music which above all else has refused to be set, pat or predictable."[41] The "pat or predictable" observation could be directed at any number of Ellington's contemporaries, but it seems particularly pertinent when separating him from musicians like Gershwin. Given the historical import that the liner notes assign to Ellington, it may not be surprising that arranger Billy Strayhorn's name appears nowhere on the album. Although awareness of Strayhorn's manifold contributions to Ellington's success and legacy continues to grow, at the time of this album's release, he received no credit.[42] Rather the liner notes proudly declare, "What the Duke has done is essentially to create eleven new Ellington originals."[43]

Mark Tucker initially identified Strayhorn as the one responsible for the "playful foiling of listener's expectations" arising from this arrangement of the *Rhapsody*.[44] He based his conclusion on sketches found by musicologist

Walter van de Leur in the Strayhorn archive, as well as a "Strayhorn touch" in the "falling chromatic sequence of chords in the coda that closely resembles a figure heard at the end of *Blood Count*."[45] Manuscript parts used by the ensemble during the recording session, bearing the title "Rhap-in Blue," reside in the Ellington archives at the Smithsonian National Museum of American History.[46] Whereas the reed parts are identified only by instrument, the trumpet parts identify the name of the individual musician (see table 4.5). The only rhythm section part that survives is the bass; it is unlikely that piano or drum parts were ever prepared. Rehearsal letters appear throughout, generally signaling the start of a new musical theme. Strayhorn condenses the *Rhapsody* into a presentation that lasts just under five minutes, the shortest of the three Ellington band renditions. Accordingly, he incorporates only three of Gershwin's five themes—ritornello, stride, and love—recasting their duration, order, and instrumental distribution (see table 4.6).

Despite a host of alterations to the organization and presentation of the *Rhapsody* as a whole, the first minute of the arrangement resembles Grofé's original scoring of the piece—although cast in a different key and infused with a swing sensibility. The opening clarinet line, as mentioned earlier, becomes a baritone saxophone solo played by Harry Carney. It begins as might be expected with a trill on the dominant, appearing in the

---

Table 4.5. PART ASSIGNMENTS FOR BILLY STRAYHORN'S 1963 ARRANGEMENT OF *RHAPSODY IN BLUE*; MISSING PARTS BRACKETED.

Instrumentation	Musician
Alto Saxophone – I	Johnny Hodges
Alto Saxophone – III	Russell Procope
Tenor Saxophone – II (also Clarinet)	Jimmy Hamilton
Tenor Saxophone – IV	Paul Gonsalves
Baritone Saxophone	Harry Carney
Trumpet – "Cat"	Cat Anderson
Trumpet – "Cootie"	Cootie Williams
Trumpet – "Roy"	Roy Burrows
Trumpet – "Ray"	Ray Nance
Trombone – I	Lawrence Brown
Trombone – II	Buster Cooper
Trombone – III (bass)	Chuck Connors
[Piano]	Duke Ellington
Bass	Ernie Shepard
[Drums]	Sam Woodyard

Table 4.6. THEMATIC ORGANIZATION OF BILLY STRAYHORN'S 1963
ARRANGEMENT OF *RHAPSODY IN BLUE*.

Rehearsal Letter	Measure Number	Record Timing	Theme	Key	Notes
--	1	0:00			Baritone cadenza
A	2–13	0:14	Ritornello (A)	Ab Major	Introduction
B	14–15	0:51	Transition		Sectional swells
C	16–18	0:57	Ritornello (A)	Eb Major	Saxophones
--	19–34	1:06	Stride (AABA)		Trumpet solo
D	35–38	1:51	Transition		Piano solo
E	39–44	2:04	Love (AABC)	F Major	(A) piano
--	45–56	2:23			(ABC) saxophones
F	57–65	3:00	Love (AABC)		(AA) trumpets
G	66–69	3:28			(B) alto solo
--	70–73	3:40			(C) clarinet ad lib
H	74–77	3:52	Ritornello (A)	Bb Major	Clarinet/tenor
--	78–84	4:08	Tag		Ensemble coda
[I]	85–87	4:26			Piano coda/final chord

manuscript part as a whole note followed by a glissando to the concert Ab
that begins the ritornello theme. However, instead of a smooth ascent,
Carney improvises, pausing for additional trills on the tonic and dominant
(see figure 4.6). The initial presentation of the ritornello theme follows that
of Grofé's Whiteman arrangement, with the melodic line gaining support
from other members of the ensemble, including the rhythm section and
an alternation between two instrumental combinations: three trombones
and tenor saxophone, or clarinet, tenor saxophone, and trumpet with
plunger. At rehearsal B, a series of transitional alternating swells from the
saxophone and trumpet sections replace what would otherwise be the first
entrance of the piano playing the tag motif [R. 2+3]. This moves the piece
into Eb major for the subsequent tutti presentation of the ritornello theme
at rehearsal C [R. 3], cast in five-part saxophone harmony. Four bars later,
the entrance of the piano—the start of its first cadenza [R. 4]—is again
elided. It is replaced by the stride theme, presented as a polite yet snarky
trumpet solo by Ray Nance.

The removal of the piano, the traditionally featured instrument, is
bound up in the process of authenticating Ellington's approach to concert
jazz and the *Rhapsody*. In fact, throughout the arrangement, the piano is
conspicuously absent, with its first entrance not occurring until the conclusion of Nance's trumpet solo. By the time the stride theme played by Nance

Figure 4.6
The opening baritone saxophone line as played by Harry Carney on Ellington's 1963 recording of *Rhapsody in Blue*. Transcription by David Berger.

appears in the version of the *Rhapsody* premiered by Whiteman, the piano has performed two virtuosic cadenzas and a multitude of passagework. In Ellington's recording, the piano is present for only twelve measures out of eighty-seven in total, comprising less than 15 percent of the piece. In comparison, the piano appears in 70 percent of the *Rhapsody* in both the initial Whiteman and symphonic arrangements.

Removing all of Gershwin's notated piano solos allows the instrument to maintain its expected jazz role as a comping and improvisational instrument while allowing Ellington to be true to his own pianistic style. After the two brief tremolos that punctuate Nance's trumpet solo, the piano disappears again until it provides a four-bar segue between the stride theme in Eb major and the love theme in F major that follows. This moment corresponds to rehearsal D in each of the manuscript parts, which consist simply of a single, double-bar-lined measure with "piano?" written above it. This notation—likely from Strayhorn—suggests confidence that Ellington could accomplish this rather uncomplicated harmonic transition, but also uncertainty about how many measures it might take. Apparently this was determined during the recording session because about half of the surviving parts indicate in one form or another that this was to be a four-measure piano solo. The only passage where the piano plays a melodic rather than transitional phrase is the love theme at rehearsal E. Here Ellington reduces it to only two notes at a time, adorning the melodic line with harmonies at intervals of the third and fifth. Finally, a two-bar improvised piano coda prepares the final chord—a Bb7-#9-13 (add M7)—presented by the full ensemble.[47]

The presence of improvisation in this arrangement of *Rhapsody in Blue* serves as another important mode of authenticating it. Improvisation emerges in Carney's opening baritone saxophone line and Nance's realization of the stride theme, but comes to the foreground during the love theme. Rather than place the focus on the melody of the love theme alone, the arrangement treats it as a foundation for two contrasting improvised solos. Though barely noticeable at first, a solo by tenor saxophonist Paul Gonsalves emerges as the remaining saxophones take over the love theme after Ellington's brief piano solo. Gonsalves weaves intricate and increasingly chromatic figures around the central theme as the band enters the second presentation of the love theme at rehearsal F. Here the ensemble builds toward a dramatic brass-dominated climax, topped off with the lead trumpet popping a double-high B—just the sort of virtuosic sound expected from the Ellington ensemble. Rising from the sonic ashes four bars later is an ad-libbed clarinet solo performed by Jimmy Hamilton—the first and only appearance of this instrument in the arrangement. Hamilton gracefully runs up and down scales in accordance with the changes, possibly paying homage to Sidney Bechet, who had passed away just a few years earlier. The reinforcement of the instrument's connection to jazz of the past also emerges from the marked difference in rhythmic and melodic contours between the tenor and clarinet solos—transcriptions of each over the same descending chord progression appear in figures 4.7 and 4.8.

This 1963 arrangement is not the only to use improvisation to make *Rhapsody in Blue* conform to modern expectations of jazz. In 1995, jazz pianist Marcus Roberts recorded a thirty-minute version of the *Rhapsody* prepared by frequent Jazz at Lincoln Center arranger Robert Sadin. This re-envisioning of the *Rhapsody* features extended improvised solos not only by Roberts, but also by other members of an ensemble that consisted of symphony orchestra and jazz trio. As Roberts conceived it, the goal was to offer a rendering of the *Rhapsody* that Gershwin might have composed had he experienced many of the later trends that form present-day conceptions of jazz. In a similar manner to the version recorded by Ellington in 1963—though on a much broader scale with respect to both instrumentation and duration—it serves as a primer on the history of jazz as envisioned by historicist-minded bandleaders of the 1990s.

The most overtly historical reference in Strayhorn's arrangement of the *Rhapsody* emerges thirty seconds from the end of the recording. The final scalar ascent of the aforementioned clarinet solo dovetails into the familiar ritornello theme heard in the traditional symphonic jazz arrangement of the *Rhapsody*. The familiar opening clarinet gesture is finally encountered, and its effect is like that of the parade of themes found in the 1932 arrangement: It forces an allusion to the past. Along with the other previously discussed instrumental and improvisatory choices made within this 1963 arrangement, it serves to remind the listener that a transformation has taken place—not just within the context of the recording itself, but also with respect to the perceived development of jazz in the intervening years.

Figure 4.7

An excerpt of the tenor saxophone solo as played by Paul Gonsalves on Ellington's 1963 recording of *Rhapsody in Blue* over stepwise descending changes. Transcription by David Berger.

Figure 4.8

An excerpt of the clarinet solo as played by Jimmy Hamilton on Ellington's 1963 recording of *Rhapsody in Blue* over stepwise descending changes. Transcription by David Berger.

"Once upon a time there was a Big Band Era. Ellington pre-dated it, shaped it, and now has outlasted it," affirm the liner notes of *Will Big Bands Ever Come Back?*[48] Ellington and Strayhorn's 1963 reworking of the *Rhapsody* might be read as a moment of great import in the jazz canonization movement—the cumulative efforts of musicians, scholars, and critics of the late 1950s and early 1960s to define jazz with respect to emerging social and academic currents. At the time, the Ellington ensemble was one of the last remaining big bands with roots in the 1920s or 1930s. This arrangement— the entire album on which it appears, in fact—might represent their best effort to preserve the music of the past, albeit through their unique musical lens. Regardless, the musical choices made in the 1963 arrangement mark Ellington's *Rhapsody in Blue* as distinct and distanced from the version premiered by Paul Whiteman in 1924 and the later symphonic arrangement as performed by Leonard Bernstein. In sum, it reaffirms Ellington's approach to concert jazz as separate from George Gershwin's.

The historiography of Ellington suggests that he maintained a marked distance from the concert works of Gershwin. One of the most prominent examples comes from Ellington's 1935 interview with Edward Morrow titled "Duke Ellington on Gershwin's 'Porgy and Bess.' "[49] Published shortly after the premiere of Gershwin's folk opera, Morrow intended to counterbalance recent reviews by the "cult of critical Negrophiles," white reviewers whose "huzzas filled the columns, were quoted by second-hand *intelligentsia*, and echoed in the banalities of the subscribers."[50] Morrow sought out Ellington's opinions on *Porgy and Bess* as a means of articulating an African-American position on the opera, which from Morrow's point of view could only be negative. Although historians such as Allen Woll, and more recently, George Cunningham and Ray Allen have revealed the varied and dynamic response of the black community, Morrow's leading line of questioning with Ellington provoked a series of polemical statements by the bandleader.[51] Morrow concluded his article by declaring that the opera offered little more than "lamp-black Negroisms," stereotypes in serious need of debunking. Despite the fact that these words were Morrow's and not Ellington's, critics and scholars continue to attribute this statement to Ellington when discussing his supposedly adverse response to Gershwin's concert music.[52]

Ellington's only direct commentary on *Rhapsody in Blue* comes from this same interview. Morrow asked Ellington why he thought that the music of *Porgy and Bess* remained "grand," despite his concerns about its particular representations, and reported the following response:

"Why shouldn't it be," he smiled amiably, "It was taken from some of the best and a few of the worst. Gershwin surely didn't discriminate: he borrowed from everyone from Liszt to Dickie Wells' kazoo band." Ellington turned to the piano, and playing said: "Hear this? These are passages from *Rhapsody in Blue*. Well, here is where they came from—the Negro song *Where Has My Easy Rider Gone?*"[53]

This and other examples of appropriation that appeared in Morrow's published interview have fueled a larger, decades-long backlash against Gershwin's music as inauthentic and irrelevant to considerations of Ellington's music, particularly with respect to his development of extended jazz forms.

Rather than relying solely on mercurial remarks from Ellington or those of a host of contemporary observers, greater insight into the past can be gained from the musical commentary residing in Ellington's own interpretations of Gershwin's works. In this way, musical practice as captured by the preparation and performance of the three arrangements of *Rhapsody in Blue* under consideration here shapes and reshapes narratives related to the development of jazz in the United States more broadly. The presence of the 1925 arrangement removes a long-held assumption that the *Rhapsody* was the provenance of only white bands. The 1932 arrangement provides insight into the role that the *Rhapsody* played in Ellington's own development of concertized jazz. This narrative might otherwise remain obscured by the arrangement recorded by Ellington in 1963, which re-envisioned the band's history through musical choices such as instrumentation and improvisation. Perhaps most important, each of these arrangements of *Rhapsody in Blue* alters conventional wisdom regarding Ellington's stated, implied, or otherwise imposed positions on the music of Gershwin.

Considering the connection between Ellington and Gershwin in this way offers an important intervention given Ellington's demonstrated interest in and concern with representing the past through musical performance rather than written or spoken narratives. The following chapter turns its attention to harmonica virtuoso Larry Adler, a figure whose career relied heavily on such narrative constructs. Although Adler may seem like a liminal figure in comparison to Leonard Bernstein and Duke Ellington, examining the harmonicist's lifelong engagement with *Rhapsody in Blue* reveals a dynamic musical career as carefully arranged as those of his more famous musical peers.

CHAPTER 5

"It Ain't Necessarily So"

Larry Adler and Rhapsody in Blue

If you would hear Larry Adler at his absolute best, the music to call for is Gershwin's *Rhapsody in Blue*. . . . The virtuoso of the harmonica is a man of wit and impudence and what he wants is a chance to give them play.

—Concert review (1942)

In August 1994, an album titled *The Glory of Gershwin*, featuring a symphonic arrangement of *Rhapsody in Blue* for harmonica soloist, debuted in the top ten of British popular music albums, eventually rising to the penultimate slot. This same album received a write-up in the January 1995 issue of *Rolling Stone*, the cover of which featured the smirking faces of Green Day, the pop-punk group selected as its best new band of the year. "Of all the tribute albums around," noted the review, "*The Glory of Gershwin* holds the distinction of being the only one to feature an 80-year-old harmonica player *and* Meat Loaf."[1] A peculiar observation, but perhaps less curious than the fact that an album of Gershwin's music resonated within the international sphere of popular music at the close of the twentieth century. Part of the album's success resulted from the cast of characters assembled on the recording, a veritable "who's who" of entertainment industry musicians: Jon Bon Jovi, Kate Bush, Cher, Elvis Costello, Peter Gabriel, Elton John, Sinead O'Connor, and Sting, among others. The individual Gershwin songs performed by these singers—ranging from "Somebody Loves Me" (1924) to "Embraceable You" (1930) to "My Man's Gone Now" (1935)—certainly contributed to the appeal as well. But what lent this particular tribute album an aura of intrigue and authority was the man at the center of it all: Larry Adler, the octogenarian harmonica player prominently present on every track.

Adler was once known as "the best harmonica player in the world."[2] Nearly every article published about Adler from the late 1930s forward acknowledges his unmatched virtuosity and singular standing among harmonica players. Adler's popularity resulted from the novelty of his playing both popular and classical repertoires on such an unexpected instrument, which he preferred to call a "mouth-organ." His performance style concurrently embraced aesthetic elements from both sides of the highbrow/lowbrow divide. This versatile boundary-crossing ultimately propelled him from vaudeville to Carnegie Hall. At the height of his popularity in the 1940s, Adler frequently appeared on a bare stage, dressed in a tuxedo with tails standing beneath a single spotlight that reflected off the metallic sheen of the chromatic harmonica cradled in his hands. This setting drew complete focus to his manipulation of the instrument, elegant and refined one moment and raucous and unrestrained in the next, producing a seemingly boundless range of timbres and tones. It was not uncommon for a Bach partita to precede "Smoke Gets in Your Eyes" and for both to garner equal applause. Adler gave solo recitals, presented collaborative duo concerts with the dancer Paul Draper, and appeared with symphony orchestras, netting upward of $250,000 per year.[3] Adler's celebrity quickly cooled, however, when allegations of his communist affiliations resulted in him being unemployable in the United States by 1950. Blacklisted, he moved to London, which became his home for the remaining fifty years of his life.

The Glory of Gershwin emerged late in Adler's career not as a stand-alone tribute, but rather as the capstone in a multi-decade devotion to George Gershwin. Adler spoke often of various encounters with Gershwin in interviews and in concerts during the last twenty years of his life. One of his favorite anecdotes involved an impromptu performance of *Rhapsody in Blue* at a Manhattan society party at the home of Cartier executive Jules Glaenzer in 1934. Adler recalled the event in his typically charming narrative style:

> Then Jules shushed everybody—he was known as The Great Shusher—and announced: "Larry and George are going to play the *Rhapsody in Blue*." I certainly hoped that I'd do a number with George but *Rhapsody*? I had never played it through but I knew the Paul Whiteman recording (Paul was also there that night) and had it in my head. George looked dubious; he didn't know whether I could handle it or not, nor did I. He sat at the piano, I began the run usually taken by the clarinet and George came in at the top of the run. It was one of

those times when two musicians had complete rapport. I knew when to lay out and let the piano take over, George would signal me back in at the right moment. When we finished, with the piano taking the five chord climax while I held a high F, everybody cheered. . . Gershwin looked at me oddly. "Goddam thing sounds as if I wrote it for you," he said. The goddam thing still does. . . . . I'm sorry it went so well. Whenever, after that, I would raise the idea of George writing for the mouth-organ he'd tell me he already had.[4]

This story is one of several Gershwin-related accounts found in Adler's 1984 autobiography *It Ain't Necessarily So*—a book that takes its title from Sportin' Life's cautionary song and dance number in Gershwin's 1935 opera *Porgy and Bess*. If we follow Adler's lead, his career-long association with the *Rhapsody* resulted from his close personal and professional relationship with Gershwin.

Arrangements of *Rhapsody in Blue* figured prominently in the manufacturing and maintenance of Adler's career. He used the piece in two important ways: to build a career performing on a nontraditional concert instrument and to rebuild that same career in the aftermath of his blacklisting. The various interpretations of *Rhapsody in Blue* offered by Adler between 1934 and 1949 capture his development as a musician and entertainer in pursuit of a professional career as a harmonica player. Two different arrangements of the *Rhapsody* performed by Adler during this period—one accompanied by theatre orchestra and the other a special symphonic version prepared by the famed Broadway orchestrator (and frequent Gershwin collaborator) Robert Russell Bennett—reveal the challenges presented by the adaptation process. In the case of the first arrangement, the challenges were of a technical nature, yielding idiomatic solutions that promoted his virtuosity. The Bennett arrangement navigates similar challenges while at the same time confronting the increasingly rigid aesthetics of symphonic-soloist performance in the late 1940s.

While Adler's career benefited from his performance of the *Rhapsody* in the years before his blacklisting, he came to rely on the piece's reputation during the final decades of his life. When Adler mounted his comeback in the United States in the early 1980s, rather than arranging the piece itself, Adler rearranged his personal history with frequently repeated anecdotes about his encounters with George Gershwin. Unlike musicians such as Oscar Levant, Adler did not immediately hitch his wagon to Gershwin's celebrity in the wake of Gershwin's death in 1937. Rather, each of these stories emerged more than forty years later, when Adler very much needed to associate himself with a figure and a work viewed as quintessentially American in the collective cultural afterglow of the United States bicentennial. However, Adler's actual connection to Gershwin and *Rhapsody in Blue* may have been just as the title of his memoir indicates: not necessarily so.

LARRY ADLER BEFORE *RHAPSODY IN BLUE*

"Adler was as talented a storyteller as he was a musician," commented National Public Radio host Linda Wertheimer, a fact born out by his 1984 autobiography *It Ain't Necessarily So*.[5] Adler's book recounts his meetings with a plethora of likely and unlikely historical figures, ranging from Al Capone to Zero Mostel. In the preface, Adler acknowledges his propensity to exaggerate or misremember the events of his life. Accordingly, Adler's published memoirs make it difficult to get a straightforward sense of his biography. Rather than rely on his entertainingly subjective autobiography, details of Adler's early career emerge from correspondence—hundreds of letters sent home while touring the country and the world—housed in the Larry Adler Collection at the American Heritage Center at the University of Wyoming. These personal and candid reports document Adler's determination and efforts to succeed free from much of the embellishment and aggrandizement that would eventually become the hallmarks of his public persona.

Aspects of Adler's adolescence beyond his autobiographical recollections are scarce. Like George Gershwin and Leonard Bernstein, Lawrence Cecil Adler was born the son of Russian Jewish immigrants to Louis Adler (a plumber) and his wife Sadie Hack (a homemaker) on February 10, 1914, in Baltimore, Maryland. Adler's family members often referred to him as "Bushie" rather than Larry in their correspondence, a nickname related to the thick, tousled hair of his youth. Precisely when he began to play the harmonica remains unknown. However, his early involvement appears consistent with the general popularity of the instrument in the mid-1920s. During this time, Borrah Minevitch and his Harmonica Boys (later the Harmonica Rascals) came to prominence. Concurrently, harmonica ensembles became a means for keeping adolescent males out of trouble, providing them with an outlet for aggression. "Once they learn to play a simple tune, our worry as to their behavior decreases greatly," noted a 1926 article in the *Los Angeles Times*. "It might be termed a case of harmonica music soothing the boyish breast."[6] Local harmonica bands and competitions popped up and flourished; Adler participated in one such ensemble based in Baltimore. In 1928, he became the harmonica champion of Maryland after participating in a contest sponsored by the *Baltimore Evening Sun*.[7] He later attributed his win solely to his decision to play Beethoven's Minuet in G, which stood out amid the popular song selections performed by his fellow contestants.

With stars in his eyes, Adler moved to New York the following September hoping to launch his career; he was fourteen years old. As the motion picture replaced vaudeville, film companies employed a "unit," or standing roster of performers to entertain audiences prior to film screenings in theatres across the United States. Adler landed his first such contract with Paramount Pictures in June 1929. His act initially consisted of well-known popular songs like W. C. Handy's "St. Louis Blues" and came to include "When Day Is Done" and "I Wanna Be Loved by You." In what would become the first tall tale of Adler's career as an entertainer, he performed under the pretence that he was a newly discovered "local boy." He was a local boy regardless of where they were performing. This bit remained popular until too many repeat engagements revealed the gimmick. A *Washington Post* review of the unit supporting MGM's 1931 film *Flying High* casually remarked, "Larry Adler and his harmonica are 'discovered' for the third or fourth time."[8] As Adler's popularity increased, so did the duration of his act and the range of his repertoire, including a move toward light classical works like Ravel's *Bolero*.

During the late fall of 1933, not yet twenty years old, he traveled to Hollywood to perform before films at Grauman's Chinese Theatre. There, he first appeared in "Sidewalks of New York," a prologue to screenings of Eddie Cantor's musical film *Roman Scandals*. One opening night review notes that "it was difficult to tell which of the numerous [prologue] acts achieved the most favor with the audience, but certainly the harmonica player, Larry Adler, may be credited with receiving a sensational ovation."[9] Adler's introduction of *Bolero* into his act at this time contributed greatly to such favorable reception. In the popular-entertainment milieu of Grauman's Chinese Theatre, the work stood out in much the same way as his contest-winning performance of Beethoven's Minuet in G: such classically oriented works defied audience expectations and prompted an enthusiastic response. Following one particularly well-received performance, Adler wrote to his parents: "Last night I asked the audience what they wanted to hear and don't you think that six or seven people didn't yell *Bolero*!"[10] The newness of the composition, which had premiered only five years earlier in Paris, surely contributed to this popularity. But, as Adler reported, what kept audiences clamoring for more was his creative adaptation and energetic performance.

The central challenge faced by Adler in adapting *Bolero* was to reflect Ravel's original orchestration through idiomatic harmonica techniques. Much of *Bolero*'s fame resides in Ravel's virtuosic buildup of orchestral timbres as a means of dissipating the inherent repetition of the piece. For percussionists, it presents a significant performing challenge, since the snare drum plays a continuous crescendo for the entire piece, repeating a two-bar ostinato more than 150 times. Over the course of the work, Ravel subtly and skillfully transitions from a single *pianissimo* flute to the rich sonority of the full orchestra at full volume. The *Los Angeles Times* reported that Adler "achieved the crescendo effect [in *Bolero*] by lung control, by using his free hand for tremolos, and by just, as he says, 'faking it.'"[11]

The chromatic harmonica allows for a wide range of tonal possibilities. Adler played a twelve-hole instrument manufactured by the M. Hohner Company in Germany. As opposed to diatonic harmonicas, which are restricted to playing the scale and fundamental chords of a particular instrument's given key, a chromatic harmonica can perform in and through any major of minor tonality. A performer creates tones on either type of harmonica by blowing or drawing air through an individual hole over metal or plastic reeds contained within the body of the instrument. The chromatic variety possesses a lever called a "key" that directs the passing air toward one of two different reeds tuned a half-step apart. This construction allows the possibility of up to four different pitches for any given hole, depending on the direction of the passing air and the position of the key (see table 5.1). The full chromatic scale repeats every four holes, which means that Adler's instrument of choice possessed a range of three octaves.

Table 5.1 CHART OF POSSIBLE PITCHES ON FIRST FOUR HOLES OF A CHROMATIC HARMONICA.

Pitch	Hole	Breath	Lever (key)
C	1	Blow	out
C#/Db	1	Blow	in
D	1	Draw	out
D#/Eb	1	Draw	in
E	2	Blow	out
F	2	Blow	in
F	2	Draw	out
F#/Gb	2	Draw	in
G	3	Blow	out
G#/Ab	3	Blow	in
A	3	Draw	out
A#/Bb	3	Draw	in
B	4	Draw	out
C	4	Draw	in
C	4	Blow	out
C#/Db	4	Blow	in

Adler's animated 1935 recording of *Bolero*—recorded a little over a year after he incorporated it into his act—provides a sense of the textural range of the chromatic harmonica ◐.[12] With the accompanying ensemble providing the familiar two-measure harmonic and rhythmic ostinato, Adler begins the piece much like Ravel: a single melody line, played crisp and clean, in the reedy middle portion of the harmonica's register. In the second statement of the main theme, Adler gives the line a rounder, almost flute-like tone by presenting the melody up an octave. As the second theme emerges, the tempo increases and the woodwinds provide additional accompaniment support by playing in parallel with the harmonica. Here Adler moves air through the instrument at an increased rate, creating a double-reed sound. The space between phrases becomes increasingly filled in with harmonica improvisations. Faster still, the first theme returns with the support of the strings and Adler's addition of harmonies to the melody line. As the piece reaches its final climax, Adler provides a series of glissando flourishes that lead to a dramatic trill on the final cadence.

Insight into Adler's creation of additional instrumental timbres appears in a 1942 profile in *The New Yorker*:

> For a trumpet effect, for instance, he stands three feet back of the microphone, opens his hands over the harmonica, and blows a sharp, brassy tone; for a wah-wah muted-trumpet sound he opens and closes his hands slowly, closer to the mike; a violin tone is achieved by fluttering the hands fast and playing into the mike from a distance of ten or twelve inches, a 'cello tone by blowing softly over the first three holes of the harmonica, about six inches from the mike, and an oboe effect by vibrating the tongue rapidly.[13]

Performances of *Bolero* left Adler literally breathless. It is little wonder that as his rendition grew in popularity, he lamented to his family: "I'm thoroughly knocked out—haven't enough energy to get out on the stage—let alone play a number that takes as much out of me as the Bolero. I simply can't do that tune five times a day."[14] Perhaps to stave off exhaustion, other classical favorites soon became part of Adler's performances. In the mid-1930s, *Bolero* was joined by Ernesto Lecuona's *Malagueña*, George Enesco's *Roumanian Rhapsody*, and George Gershwin's *Rhapsody in Blue*.

THE *RHAPSODY* AND ADLER'S RISE TO FAME

An April 1934 notice in the *Chicago Daily Tribune* reported that "Adler, who plays the harmonica at one of the better night-life spots, has an ambition to be a soloist with the Symphony some day."[15] Moving from the vaude-ville stage to the concert hall was a big leap for a popular entertainer, especially for one who performed on a nontraditional concert instrument. But this transition became Adler's focus from the mid-1930s forward, and *Rhapsody in Blue* figured prominently. From early April to late July 1934, Adler appeared nightly in the Empire Room at Chicago's Palmer House Hotel, the better night-life spot alluded to by the *Tribune* reviewer (see figure 5.1). On Independence Day 1934, Adler reported to his family that "The Rhapsody is definitely established as a hit. I played it last night to a noisy crowd and it stopped everything."[16] He often used the *Rhapsody* as a closer—a "sock finish" in Adler's words—along with other tried-and-true pieces such as "Day Is Done," "St. Louis Blues," and *Bolero*. His program also included "Sophisticated Lady," "Smoke Gets in Your Eyes," and "The House Is Haunted," which rotated through as openers, with "Mood Indigo," "Carioca," "Ain't Misbehavin" and "The Last Roundup" filling out the set. The inclusion of *Rhapsody in Blue* among these selections represents his conscious transition from being a popular-song, vaudeville-style performer to becoming a classical solo artist capable of appearing with an orchestra.

A sense of Adler's adaptation of *Rhapsody in Blue* for performance on the chromatic harmonica emerges from his May 1935 recording of the piece.[17] Capitalizing on Adler's originality and rising status as a soloist, British

Figure 5.1
Postcard image of the Empire Room at the Palmer House in Chicago, circa 1940. Personal collection of the author.

impresario Charles B. Cochran—the so-called Ziegfeld of England—brought Adler to London in November 1934 where he appeared in a revue called *Streamline* and made his first recordings ⊕.[18] The show was not popular, but Adler's performances were. Adler reported to his family: "General opinion around London is that Streamline stinks. It does."[19] Nevertheless, Columbia approached Adler to record material for two 78-rpm discs the week after his *Streamline* debut. He would receive twenty-five pounds and 5 percent of the royalties to record *Bolero* and *Rhapsody in Blue* for the first disc and "Smoke Gets in Your Eyes" and "The Continental" for the second. Columbia arranged for Charles "Jock" Prentice, conductor of *Streamline*, to lead the ten-piece band (presumably *Streamline*'s pit orchestra) accompanying Adler. They were able to get through only half of the intended material when they entered the recording studio on December 12, 1934: "We were a bit too optimistic—Smoke and Bolero went off OK because we knew them, but Continental was phoo and Rhapsody was impossible."[20] He found greater success with *Rhapsody in Blue* upon his return to Columbia's studio on May 28, 1935.

The subsequent recording documents Adler's ability to recast Gershwin's famous melodies and selected piano solos on the chromatic harmonica—but accomplishing this task was not as simple as he made it sound ◕. The recording captures a host of technical and musical obstacles faced when adapting the *Rhapsody* for harmonica soloist. Although the various themes of the *Rhapsody* are basic enough to be performed individually on the harmonica, the biggest challenge Adler confronted was the adaptation of Gershwin's piano solos and lengthy cadenzas. Adler met this challenge with simple yet striking idiomatic methods. These techniques ultimately lent Adler the veneer of virtuosity within the limits of his performance abilities at this early stage in his career.

The seemingly simple opening trill of the *Rhapsody* reveals the copious challenges faced by Adler in adapting the piece for harmonica performance. At the very outset of his 1935 recording of the *Rhapsody*, his trill peculiarly consists of a half-step interval, rather than the expected whole step. As typically performed by the clarinet, the first measure of the piece begins on a concert F and alternates with increasingly frequency between that pitch and the G above it before the seventeen-note glissando ascent. A clarinet produces this trill through the simple flutter of the right-hand ring finger, but no such easy solution exists on the chromatic harmonica. There are two different methods to produce an F: blowing into hole two while pressing the lever, or drawing on hole two without the lever. Neither allows for a graceful or rapid trill with G, which requires blowing into hole three without the lever. Although both are technically possible, the first option is inhibited by motion in opposite directions, and the second quickly leads to hyperventilation. Adler solves this dilemma by playing the opening trill on F and F sharp, which he achieves by simply pressing and unpressing the lever while drawing air through the second hole.

More challenging for Adler than the opening trill of *Rhapsody in Blue*, however, were the abundant and extended piano cadenzas. Playing melody and harmony simultaneously on the harmonica poses difficulty even for simple diatonic passages. Rendering such aspects of Gershwin's intricate, chromatic, and highly idiomatic piano cadenzas is all but impossible. Rather than rescore the solo piano passages for the ensemble to accompany the harmonica soloist, Adler's 1935 recording omits large sections of the *Rhapsody* (see table 5.2). Several of the cuts, including two extended solo piano passages [R. 18 to R. 22 and R. 32 to R. 34], result in awkward transitions that likely contributed to the challenges faced in the unsuccessful initial studio session. Regardless, the editorial emendations resulted in a recording of the *Rhapsody* that was a full two and a half minutes shorter than those released by Whiteman in 1924 and 1927.

Despite his elimination of these larger solos and cadenzas, Adler reproduced many of the shorter piano fills in a highly dramatic fashion. One such example occurs at rehearsal 11, where a pair of two-bar arpeggiated passages introduces and links excerpts of the stride theme. In the first of these, when played on the piano, the left hand plays the notes of a B major

Table 5.2. CUTS IN ADLER'S 1935 RECORDING OF *RHAPSODY IN BLUE* (COLUMBIA 35513).

Timing	Cut	Total Bars Removed	Comments
1:25	R. 4+6 to R. 6	42	Omits piano cadenza; incorporates "Optional Cut A to B" + 7 bars
3:07	R. 14-1 to R. 28-4	161	Occurs at break between sides 1 and 2 of record; incorporates "Optional Cut C to D" and "E to F" + 63 additional bars
4:38	R. 31 to R. 33-8	32	First half of omitted piano cadenza
4:55	R. 33 to R. 36	65	Second half of omitted piano cadenza; incorporates "Optional Cut G to H" + 28 additional bars. Two measures are added just before the cut to allow for transition from E major to C major
5:35	R. 39 to R. 39+2	2	Removal of 2-bar "Grandioso" passage
5:47	R. 39+9 to R. 40	8	Omits repeat of "stride" theme before final coda

triad on each beat of the measure while the right hand arpeggiates differ-ent inversions of a C major triad (see figure 5.2). Replicating this idiomatic passage on a sixteen-hole chromatic harmonica is possible, with the excep-tion of the final E. However, given the fast tempo at which it is performed, as well as the fact that Adler's harmonica had only twelve holes, this solu-tion remained less than ideal.

Instead, Adler opts for a more practical and flashy solution. Blowing through any three adjacent holes on a chromatic harmonica, with excep-tions at the points where octaves repeat, produces the intervallic pitches of a C major triad. Starting with hole one, Adler plays chords, moving his embouchure one hole higher on each beat (skipping the fourth hole in each octave). He rapidly trills each chord by pressing and releasing the lever as quickly as possible. The result is a shimmer of sound as the chord alternates between C and C sharp major. Adler made this all the more impressive in live performance by operating the key while wiggling his outstretched fingers, an effect not unlike "jazz hands" (see figure 5.3). Though not the same combination of chords as given by the B and C major combination of Gershwin's original, this half-step-removed alternative accomplishes a similar effect.

Adler received quite favorable reviews for his 1935 recording of *Rhapsody in Blue*. One critic noted that "Adler has achieved the unbelievable. Already, this amazing young virtuoso has given us such diverse and seemingly impossible items as Ravel's *Bolero*, de Falla's *Fire Dance* and Kreisler's *Caprice Viennois*, but here, surely, is his magnum opus! It is a triumph of mouth organ playing that will be long remembered."[21] Indeed, the appeal of this recording is similar to that of Adler's live performances at the time: the newness of hearing these famous melodies on the harmonica coupled with Adler's ability to represent characteristically Gershwinian piano passages

Figure 5.2
Solo-piano arpeggio fill at rehearsal 11 of *Rhapsody in Blue* with corresponding chromatic harmonica tabular notation. Numbers correspond to the particular hole through which air is passed either as a blow (+) or a draw (-); numbers with a strikethrough indicate that the lever (key) is to be pushed in.

Figure 5.3
Larry Adler in action. Larry Adler Papers, American Heritage Center, University of Wyoming.

on his chosen instrument. In the process of adaptation, Adler convincingly made the piece his own.

SYMPHONIC ASPIRATIONS AND THE ROBERT RUSSELL BENNETT ARRANGEMENT

Adler's desire to be taken seriously as an artist and to play as a soloist with a symphony orchestra persisted. Following his first attempt to record the *Rhapsody* with Jock Prentice in 1934, Adler wrote to his parents:

> [Prentice] told me that he's the big boss at Columbia, and that he records the big twelve-inch records with a hundred and fifty piece symphony! His latest idea is for me to record the big classic[s] such as Beethoven's 5th Symphony and Caesar Franck's Symphony! If I agree, which means if I think I can master those tremendous works, it'll put me on the map as a real artist, in the concert class![22]

Prentice's vision of recording harmonica renditions of these works never came to fruition. However, over the course of the mid-to-late 1930s, Adler successfully parlayed his status from fourth billing to headliner. He continued to live and perform abroad, returning to Hollywood only briefly in February 1937 to appear in the film *The Singing Marine*. The majority of his repertoire continued to be popular songs of the day, largely because of audience expectations in the venues in which he appeared. However, alongside the *Rhapsody*, Adler gradually integrated additional classical and light classical works. He performed Vivaldi's Violin Concerto in A Minor in concert appearances and recorded portions of Strauss' *Blue Danube* and Liszt's second *Hungarian Rhapsody*. By the start of 1939, Adler was earning more money than ever before as evidenced by his refusal of a generous offer from the Coconut Grove in Los Angeles that would have paid him $500 a week (approximately $8,150 in 2013). Adler informed his family why he turned down such a sum: "It's silly to start as a small act in America when I'm a star in the United Kingdom."[23] But it may have been artistic aspiration rather than finances that ultimately motivated his decision.

Adler's symphonic dreams became a reality on the night of January 26, 1939, just a few weeks after turning down the Coconut Grove engagement: "Last night I achieved an ambition that has beset me since first I took up the mouth-organ. To play serious music with a full symphony orchestra."[24] The Sydney Symphony invited Adler to play Vivaldi's Violin Concerto in A Minor—the only solo symphonic work that he knew—at a benefit concert. An excerpt from his extended letter home about the performance captures the excitement of the experience, as well as his comedic wit:

I hold the harmonica as if its a charged lightning rod. . . c'mon dope, start the orchestra. . . somebody once said the hardest thing in the world is to start an orchestra and the 2nd hardest is to stop them. I'll stop them. Right in their tracks. Where's the fellow who was going to play the Vivaldi? There he is under a spittoon. He's not looking well, is he? Something he ate.

Oh, so he's finally started. Well, its about time. What was he waiting for, a weather report? They sound pretty snappy, those fiddles. No wonder. They're sitting down. No need to worry about their knees giving way. Where are my knees? Oh, better wait a minute, mister, I've lost my knees. Oh, there they are. Cripes, its my cue now. Up she goes, whoops!

Look, I'm playing the Concerto. Right in front of everybody. With a hey nonny nonny and a first time bar. Don't look now but I think I've spit in the harmonica.

The first movements over. What are you clapping for, dopes. You're not supposed to clap until the whole thing is finished. I'll learn you.

Now the second movement. The slow one. Put an itsy bit of Rubinoff. Why shouldn't Vivaldi have his bit of shmaltz.

Now the last movement. Here's where I throw a fit. He's taking it too fast. When we get to that fast part, I'll go off the rails, I just know I will. Bzzz, bzzz, whang, bang—migawd, its over!

Now you can clap. Lets hear it. There's several thousand of you out there and you ought to be able to whip up some mean noise. Yeah man! Boy, I feel weak![25]

As this animated passage suggests, Adler put himself fully into his first appearance with a complete symphony orchestra. The event left him energized and paved the way for repeat experiences in the years that followed. However, he still had much to learn about the nuances and expectations of classically oriented performance.

Reviews of Adler's annual concerts at Lewisohn Stadium during the early 1940s, following his return to the United States, document responses to his technique over the course of this period. These appearances with the New York Philharmonic under the direction of Alexander Smallens drew enthusiastic audiences of 5,000 to 6,000 people. At his August 1941 concert, Adler performed Vivaldi's Violin Concerto in A Minor, the second movement ("Siciliana") of Bach's Flute Sonata in Eb Major, and Rachmaninoff's *Vocalise*. As encores, Adler played selections from Strauss's *Blue Danube* and the popular song "When Day Is Done." One review of this concert highlighted the "monotony" of Adler's timbres and tones and questioned whether a harmonica could attain "the status of a legitimate solo instrument capable of holding its own on a symphonic program."[26] The same critic located such potential in "the refinement of the sound [Adler] was able to draw from the harmonica when used to outline melodies in single notes and by the rapid passage-work he proved could be negotiated on the humble instrument."[27] A review of Adler's 1946 appearance at Lewisohn Stadium showcases interpretive improvements made over the course of five years:

The high point. . . was Larry Adler's performance on the harmonica of his third and last encore, the Bach *Gavotte in E major* from the *Partita No. 3* for unaccompanied violin, which he played in the key of C, where it lies better for the double-stop playing. In this performance was high art. After the virtuosity of a concerto for harmonica and orchestra and the Enesco *First Rumanian Rhapsody*, the beautiful little eighteenth-century piece was played with a simplicity, a rhythmic charm, a subtle and lovely tone color and a grace that set it apart from the rest of the program.

Mr. Adler's mastery long ago passed beyond the "freak" stage of a technique that achieves standard instrumental effects, into the realm of sound and remarkable musical interpretation.[28]

In negotiating the boundary between popular song and classical works that led to success in the concert hall, Adler suppressed many of the bread-and-butter effects that had contributed to his initial appeal as a performer. He could unleash a full battery of pyrotechnics on the music of Jerome Kern, but not on J. S. Bach. In light of this tension, *Rhapsody in Blue* emerges as Adler's solution to the problem of balancing symphonic performance with crowd-pleasing techniques in the concert hall.

The theatre orchestra arrangement of *Rhapsody in Blue* that Adler had been performing since the mid-1930s was not appropriate for the concert hall. He needed a more refined arrangement, one suitable for the instrumentation afforded by a full symphony orchestra. Concurrently, he needed an arrangement that did not rely exclusively on flashy idiomatic harmonica passagework but allowed space for a greater degree of musical subtlety. By the end of 1946, Adler had commissioned Robert Russell Bennett to craft such a version of the piece. The earliest known performance of the Bennett arrangement by Adler took place on January 6, 1947, with the Pittsburgh Symphony Orchestra.[29]

Bennett's career spanned most of the twentieth century, but as is the case with all arrangers of this period, his significant contributions to the history of American music remain ripe for consideration.[30] He was active as a composer in his own right and had studied with Nadia Boulanger in Paris between 1926 and 1929, though he was better known as a Broadway arranger and orchestrator. Bennett began as a stock arranger for T. B. Harms in 1919—where he prepared the arrangement of Gershwin's "Do It Again" discussed in chapter 1—which soon led to work in theatre. He orchestrated several of Gershwin's shows, including *Oh, Kay* (1926), *Girl Crazy* (1930), and *Of Thee I Sing* (1931) and went on to become the primary orchestrator and arranger for the musicals of Rodgers and Hammerstein. The "Dream Ballet" sequence from *Oklahoma!* (1942) stands as just one example of the degree to which Bennett's arrangements became integral to the dramatic action of the American musical.

Unfortunately, the whereabouts of the *Rhapsody in Blue* score that Bennett prepared for Adler during the mid-1940s remain unknown. In a letter to Ira Gershwin in June 1974, Adler confessed that his orchestral score for the *Rhapsody* had been misplaced: "I've lost—lost!—the scores and parts of 2 works; 1, the orchestration Robert Russell Bennett did of the *Rhapsody in Blue* for me, the other the Enesco *Roumanian Rhapsody*. This comes of changing wives and residences. I phoned Bennett when I was in NY in April but he doesn't have even a sketch of his score."[31] After the call from Adler, Bennett managed to produce a replacement manuscript that is now in the Robert Russell Bennett Collection in the Northwestern

University Music Library.[32] Although Bennett penned this version more than a quarter-century after his original arrangement, it closely resembles the one captured on Adler's earliest known recording of this symphonic *Rhapsody* arrangement from 1957.[33] It includes the same cuts and the slight variations in instrumentation that exist between the two, including an increased use of strings and a closer adherence to Grofé's orchestration, merely lend Bennett's reconstructed arrangement a more symphonic sound than had originally been the case. These differences, however, do not interfere with the most musically interesting and important portions of this arrangement, namely the passages that showcase Adler.

The arrangement prepared by Bennett in the late 1940s simultaneously takes advantage of advances in Adler's technique, while relying on idiomatic "tricks" like those found in the version of *Rhapsody in Blue* recorded by Adler in 1935. The clearest example of the former is the opening trill, which is both written and performed using the original whole-step interval. As suggested, Adler faced two equally challenging methods for rendering this difficult F to G trill. A video from a late-career performance of the *Rhapsody* at a concert in Japan reveals that he opted for the first solution, which requires moving the mouth to the right while simultaneously pushing the lever or key to the left.[34] At the same time, the passage that begins at measure 63 [R. 11] reveals one way that Adler continued to rely on idiomatic shortcuts. As was the case with his 1935 recording, Adler plays these arpeggiated piano fills as a series of trilled chord tones (see figure 5.4).

Bennett faced the challenge of rendering the solo piano passages omitted from Adler's 1935 recording for performance by the harmonica and orchestra. From these previously un-orchestrated sections emerge a sense of Bennett's overall approach to arranging the *Rhapsody* as well as his creative solutions for recasting the otherwise unaccompanied piano solos. The first passage follows the harmonica's presentation of the final four bars of a cadenza [R. 19-4], where the piano would typically repeat the AABA stride theme twice. Gershwin provided a "slower and marked" indication at this point in his original pencil score, a tempo change that continues to accompany published versions of the piece along with "*Meno mosso e poco*

Figure 5.4
Harmonica solo from Robert Russell Bennett's arrangement of *Rhapsody in Blue*, from the Robert Russell Bennett Papers, Music Library, Northwestern University. Used by permission of the Estate of Robert Russell Bennett.

scherzando." Bennett simplifies matters with his indication: "rather deliberate." The harmonica plays the melody previously located in the right hand of the piano, while the strings, clarinet, oboe, and bassoon fill in the accompanimental stride-patterned rhythm of the left-hand part. Bennett punctuates each of Adler's phrases—presented in a full, round tone with ample vibrato on the 1957 recording—with a short brass and woodwind fill based on the solo-piano line.

Bennett maintains momentum in this extended and otherwise repetitive section by expanding on the single horn line from measure 120 to 127 of Ferde Grofé's symphonic arrangement [R. 20 to R. 20+7]. He infuses this passage with the additional accompaniment of strings, woodwinds, and brass, which maintain their presence past the point at which the solo horn line concludes in the Grofé orchestration (m. 128 [R. 20+8]). This extension of the horn part adds a degree of continuity to the passage, maintaining the syncopated line that would otherwise emerge from the lowest notes of the piano solo. Cellos, clarinets, and bass clarinet join the horns, while the trumpets and upper strings play on the beat to highlight Gershwin's rhythmic interplay. Adler articulated the melody clearly above the increasing texture of the orchestral accompaniment by producing a brighter tone and decreasing his use of vibrato in the restatement of the theme.

Such alterations to the well-known symphonic *Rhapsody* received mixed reception. When Adler performed the *Rhapsody* with the Cleveland Summer Orchestra in June 1947 (in front of a capacity audience of 8,057), one review noted that although Bennett's arrangement "gave the Adler mouth-organ magic full play, it strayed often from the Gershwin path."[35] Highlighting the infidelity of Adler's performance reveals the extent to which Grofé's symphonic arrangement of the *Rhapsody* had become "the" composition in audiences' minds by the late 1940s. Although this particular critic did not give specific nomadic moments, two likely candidates emerge from the Bennett arrangement. In the first, Bennett provides an overtly romantic treatment of the love theme. Bennett writes in indications of "*molto animato*" at instances of the countermelody throughout this section. During the first iteration of the love theme, he assigns the countermelody to the flutes and horns. The second time, however, Adler plays the countermelody himself. Additionally, while the brass and woodwind instruments play the theme, Bennett adds a dramatically cascading, scalar, quarter-note descent in the strings (mm. 211–212 [R. 30 to R. 30 +1]; see figure 5.5). This moment of over-scoring lends the already lush theme an additional level of late nineteenth-century romanticism.

Another portion with which the critic may have taken issue occurs at the point in the score where Bennett's voice as an arranger emerges most fully.

Figure 5.5
Reduction of the love theme featuring descending string section countermelody from
Robert Russell Bennett's arrangement of *Rhapsody in Blue*, from the Robert Russell Bennett
Papers, Music Library, Northwestern University. Used by permission of the Estate of Robert
Russell Bennett.

This modification falls in measure 134 [R. 21-1], where a sequential repetition of the final two bars of the solo-piano stride theme begins to transition the piece from A to G major. Here Bennett's orchestral accompaniment
becomes sparse, yet elegant, reflecting the thinned piano line and, at the
same time, enhancing it greatly. Viola, cello, bass clarinet, and clarinet play
half notes (as originally arpeggiated by the left hand on the piano), while the
horns and bassoons play the offbeat (see figure 5.6). In the second iteration
of this descending melodic line (m. 136 [R. 21 + 1]), at the moment when
the harmonica line leaps up an octave, the accompaniment drops down a

Figure 5.6
The solo-piano presentation of the stride theme from *Rhapsody in Blue* as originally written
by Gershwin (top staff) and as orchestrated by Robert Russell Bennett (bottom system)
in his arrangement, from the Robert Russell Bennett Papers, Music Library, Northwestern
University. Used by permission of the Estate of Robert Russell Bennett.

fifth into the lowest register of these instruments. These notes must be played on the C-string of the cello and viola, the string that produces the heaviest tone on these instruments. Simultaneously, the bass clarinet and the clarinet move to the bottom of the *chalumeau* register, producing the darkest and richest color. These choices result in a thick and warm timbral foundation over which the harmonica solo floats several octaves above.

This register leap may represent a typically Robert Russell Bennett "moment." Bennett's 1942 arrangement and recomposition of music from Gershwin's opera, titled *Porgy and Bess: A Symphonic Picture*, contains similar instances. For example, at rehearsal 27, the melody of the B section of the AABA tune "I Got Plenty o' Nuttin'" moves into the strings and low clarinets. This alteration provides a strong timbral and registrational contrast to the banjo-led melody of the A sections. Bennett's *Symphonic Picture* has received criticism for lending Gershwin's original score a "glossier sound that altered somewhat the music's basic character."[36] However, in neither the *Symphonic Picture* nor *Rhapsody in Blue* does Bennett alter Gershwin's original rhythms or harmonies. Rather, his choices as an arranger draw out such elements in new and unanticipated ways.

Bennett's arrangement also showcased improvements in Adler's technical abilities, particularly in the passages that would otherwise feature solo piano. The most striking instance occurs between rehearsals 36 and 37 in the published orchestral score, where the orchestra builds to a climax over the course of ten measures. In the 1935 recording, Adler flubs his way through these chords alongside the orchestra. By the time of Bennett's arrangement, Adler's precision has increased to the point that the orchestra drops out after four bars (m. 246 [R. 36+4]), allowing him to render the block chords of this passage completely on his own (see figure 5.7). This grand cadenza, which Adler would certainly have imbued with a great deal of dramatic stage movement in performance, made for a thrilling climax in Bennett's symphonic arrangement of the *Rhapsody*, certainly warranting the ovations it frequently received.

Figure 5.7
Adler's "grand cadenza" from Robert Russell Bennett's arrangement of *Rhapsody in Blue*, from the Robert Russell Bennett Papers, Music Library, Northwestern University. Used by permission of the Estate of Robert Russell Bennett.

Although Adler's performance of Bennett's symphonic arrangement of *Rhapsody in Blue* presented the harmonica player with a new level of virtuosity, critics remained skeptical. A review of his performance with the Milwaukee Symphony Orchestra in 1948 observed that "conductor [Victor Alessandro], orchestra and soloist all were first rate, and the occasionally clownish effects of the solo instrument were in the mood of the piece. But it still needs a piano more than a harmonica."[37] It remains possible that, given more time, Adler might have won over such detractors, and his association with the piece during the 1940s might have become better known. However, Larry Adler soon found himself completely unemployable in the United States.

THE BLACKLISTING OF LARRY ADLER

The roots of Larry Adler's downfall took shape long before he ever performed or recorded *Rhapsody in Blue*. Shortly before his relocation to California where he would transfix audiences with *Bolero*, Adler shared the stage at Radio City Music Hall with the dancer Paul Draper. At the time, neither could have predicted the notoriety generated by their future collaboration. Like Adler's harmonica performance, Draper's dancing combined classical and popular elements. He began as a ballroom instructor at the Arthur Murray Dance Studio in the 1930s and later studied at George Balanchine's School of American Ballet. His resultant style combined tap dance with "the elegance of manner, precision of execution, arm movements, and turns and jumps of ballet."[38] The program in which Adler and Draper appeared at Radio City Music Hall found them dueling for the affections of a young woman as they showed off their respective talents.

Adler and Draper came to rely on a similar back-and-forth format for their duo recitals when they reunited seven years later in Chicago. In concert, each man would perform a solo portion (accompanied by a pianist) in addition to doing several pieces together. In the joint portions of their program, Adler and Draper often performed Gershwin's song "I Got Rhythm" and also improvised on suggestions made by the audience. The remaining repertoire of these concerts largely consisted of classical compositions. The program from their 1945 concerts at the Opera House in Chicago, for example, featured Schubert's Sonatina No. 1 in D Major, a bagatelle from Beethoven's Opus 119, and Brahms's Intermezzo in Eb Minor. Other frequently heard classical compositions included Mozart's Oboe Quartet, Bach's first *Brandenburg Concerto*, and Debussy's prelude *La fille aux cheveux de lin* (*Girl with the Flaxen Hair*).

These recitals were so popular that their engagements were frequently held over. A planned seven-day run often extended to several weeks of sold-out performances. Such was the case at their celebrated City Center performances in New York during January and February 1946. *Billboard* magazine reported that Adler and Draper booked seventy additional concerts around the country following this engagement.[39] Their intended audience aligned with Adler's classically oriented trajectory. "We elected to concentrate on the smallest, the most elite, public," observed Adler in March 1947. "It was tough, but we've worked ourselves up to becoming one of the 10 leading concert attractions in the country."[40]

With greater success, however, came greater scrutiny, which proved disastrous for Adler and Draper as segments of the American population grew evermore anxious over communism. In December 1948, a community concert series in Greenwich, Connecticut, scheduled Larry Adler and Paul Draper to perform a recital the following spring. Following the announcement of this program, local resident Hester McCullough wrote a letter to the board of the concert series. She lobbied for the cancellation of their concert, exclaiming, "These two men, while fine artists, have been openly denounced in the press as being pro-Communist. . . . I deeply resent having any money from a community project in this town going into the hands of those unsympathetic to our democracy."[41]

Indeed, Adler and Draper had been denounced as being pro-communist. On his own, Adler had become increasingly involved in fighting the mounting injustices facing artists of the day. In late 1947, he joined the Committee for the First Amendment, which met initially and incidentally at Ira Gershwin's house in Los Angeles. The group, which was "in the business of supporting *rights*, not causes," formed to express support for the "Hollywood Ten." The committee maintained that "no member of our group is a Communist or sympathetic to the totalitarian form of government practiced or advocated by Communist parties in different parts of the world."[42]

Hester McCullough's accusations resulted from conservative press coverage of Adler and Draper's participation in a September 1948 rally for Henry Wallace following a concert in Birmingham, Alabama. They spoke in support of his candidacy for president under the auspices of the Progressive Party, which maintained no connection to its initial incarnation as the nominating party for Theodore Roosevelt in 1912. The primary aim of the Progressive Party in 1948 was to secure Wallace's run for the presidency. It became closely associated with the American Labor Party and also received the support of the U.S. Communist Party, which did not forward a candidate. Although Adler and Draper's concert performance was unrelated to their appearance at the rally, the press implied what McCullough made explicit: that Adler and Draper used proceeds from their performances to support pro-communist causes. Hoping to ease the situation, the two men issued a joint statement: "We have done our best as artists and do not intend to let anything stop us from doing our best as citizens."[43]

But in the wake of the Hollywood Ten hearings in 1947 before the House Un-American Activities Committee, the anti-communism movement continued to gain momentum and ultimately derailed Adler and Draper. The national papers quickly relayed Hester McCullough's outrage, and several supported her position. William Randolph Hearst's publications gave particular prominence to the allegations due to prominent gossip columnist Igor Cassini at the *New York Journal-American*, who communicated directly with McCullough. The cumulative effect of these allegations resulted in the cancellation of all scheduled appearances by Adler and Draper at venues throughout the United States scheduled for 1950. Adler and Draper each filed a $100,000 civil suit against McCullough for libel, but this move only drew increased ire from the anti-communist movement. Although the case ended in a hung jury in May 1950, the damage had already been done. Adler soon found himself in *Red Channels*, the so-called blacklister's bible. Because of his name's unfortunate alphabetical position, Adler appeared at the top of the list.

Broke and unable to find work in the United States, Adler relocated his family and career to London, where his reception remained as favorable as it had been some twenty years earlier. Composers from the United Kingdom took advantage of Adler's presence there and created pieces specifically for him. Between 1952 and 1954, he premiered new works by Ralph Vaughan Williams, Arthur Benjamin, and Malcolm Arnold at the annual BBC Promenade Concerts. Adler also composed music for film during this time, including the score for *Genevieve* (1953), which was nominated for an Academy Award. However, as was typical for blacklisted artists of the time, his name was absent from prints of the movie shown in the United States and the award nomination itself. Sustained success abroad throughout the 1960s did little to alter Adler's standing in his home country.

REMAKING A CAREER WITH *RHAPSODY IN BLUE*

Nearly two decades after his blacklisting, Adler voiced concern about becoming a "footnote in musical history."[44] With his status still largely unchanged by the mid-1970s, Adler attempted to reemerge as a performing artist in the United States. He appeared in a highly anticipated reunion concert with Paul Draper in Carnegie Hall in June 1975. Adler presented a condensed rendition of *Rhapsody in Blue*, just as he had done with great regularity during his concerts with Draper in the 1940s. The *New York Times* review noted that this particular piece "suffered somewhat from a running debate between John Coleman, the pianist[,] and the page-turner over what was being cut, a distraction that even Mr. Adler's hypnotic skill could not overcome."[45]

Such quibbles aside, Adler could no longer rely on the novelty of his instrument or the pure technical ability of his performance. The classical music world in the United States had changed radically in the quarter-century since his blacklisting. Changes in post-war socioeconomics coupled with a new generation of musically conservative conductors and audiences stratified the symphonic concert life. Although often featuring the same instrumentalists, serious "program" concerts featured a separate and distinct repertoire from the symphonic "pops" performances.

As Adler quickly discovered, few concertgoers or critics would take him or his harmonica seriously in either realm. A review of an October 1977 performance with the Chicago Symphony questioned Adler's choice to perform "a piece of unmitigated kitsch like Francis Chagrin's 'Roumanian Fantasy'" when a repertory of harmonica pieces—many composed specifically for Adler—existed.[46] Performances of such selections by Adler were also poorly received, including the U.S. premiere of Milhaud's *Suite for Harmonica and Orchestra* (Opus 234). "The Milhaud proved rough going," noted one critic, due in part to perceived weaknesses in the composition itself, but also because "Adler's contribution, microphoned bravura notwithstanding, was hardly impeccable either."[47] Even his performances of *Rhapsody* were dogged by criticism: "Adler's technique and expressivity in Gershwin's *Rhapsody in Blue* were admirable, but still he couldn't make his arrangement much more than a curio what with adapting everything in sight—familiar piano, clarinet, trumpet and string parts—and linking it all rather episodically."[48]

Adler found greater success and acceptance with a different, less formal approach, one that brought him full circle to his early career: cabaret-style performances infused with engaging narrative. In concert, he introduced each piece of music with an amusing anecdote from his career and told it in his typically effusive style. Adler's storytelling had grown out of his early experience as a vaudeville-style entertainer but had gained additional polish through his biweekly radio broadcasts for the Australian Broadcasting Commission, which began in November 1938. In an effort to fill up time in the twenty-five-minute Saturday night broadcasts (the Wednesday programs were only ten minutes), Adler decided to "do a short dramatisation

[sic] of some episode of my life. This is for about 7 minutes and includes a solo. For example, this Saturday I'm doing the Baltimore harmonica contest. That works into Minuet in G. . . . I'm doing the scripts for these."[49] Following the first broadcast, Adler reported, "The talking seems to go over very well. Someone said that I make it sound as if I was right in the room with the listener."[50] As his career became more formalized in the United States throughout the 1940s, room for story-infused performance abated. But when Adler mounted his comeback in the late 1970s and early 1980s, his retrospective narrative style reemerged. His increasingly popular cabaret concerts became as much about the narratives that accompanied his performances as they were about the music itself. These stories established a connection with more prominent American musicians and entertainers, including Duke Ellington, Billie Holiday, and George Gershwin. In fact, the music of Gershwin and anecdotal accounts of Adler's association with the composer received increasing emphasis in his cabaret performances.

Adler frequently introduced performances of the *Rhapsody* with a story about his first encounter with Gershwin. According to Adler, in an attempt to advance his fledgling career in May 1930, he managed to get backstage at New York's Roxy Theatre to audition for Paul Whiteman, who was performing there with his orchestra in support of the film *King of Jazz*. He recounted this amusing encounter in June 1987 on National Public Radio's then-new program *Fresh Air*:

> I played "Poet and Peasant" and when I finished playing it, Whiteman said, "Let me hear you play the *Rhapsody in Blue*." I was fifteen; I couldn't handle the *Rhapsody in Blue*. But I was a very arrogant, snotty little kid (and success has not changed me). I couldn't let him know that I didn't know *Rhapsody in Blue* and that it was too tough for me. So I said, "I don't like *Rhapsody in Blue*." He [Whiteman] turns to a young man I hadn't noticed before and he says: "How do you like that, George?" That's how I met George Gershwin.[51]

During the last twenty years of his life, Adler spoke more of this first encounter with Gershwin than he did about any other event in his career ◗. Although the story remained unpublished for nearly thirty years, Adler shared it with renowned chronicler Studs Terkel as early as 1976.[52] It first publically appeared in a 1982 article by Leonard Feather and subsequently emerged not only in Adler's 1984 autobiography but also in nearly every newspaper, television, and radio interview given by Adler until his death in 2001.[53]

Adler's frequently told tale served multiple purposes. When taken at face value, it captured an amusing moment from early in Adler's career, combining humor and humility. Simultaneously, it offered an inauspicious starting point for what would become a career-long association with the piece. By Adler's own admission, the piece was "too tough." The anecdote situated the *Rhapsody* beyond Adler's capacities as a teenaged performer and reinforced the difficulty inherent in adapting the piece for harmonica. But most important, the story linked Adler to important figures in the history of American music who were unaffected by political blacklisting. It is no coincidence that the story first materialized at the very moment when Adler mounted his comeback in the United States. Furthermore, this anecdote was only one of several supposed interactions with Gershwin that Adler ultimately revealed during the 1980s.

In January 1986, Adler began to perform *Rhapsody in Blue* to the disembodied accompaniment of Gershwin's 1925 piano roll—an "eerie" effect, according to Adler himself.[54] The press publicized these concerts as a celebration of the fiftieth anniversary of "the time [Adler] performed *Rhapsody in Blue* with the composer at the piano," the impromptu recital at the home of Jules Glaenzer introduced at the outset of this chapter.[55] Despite a slight chronological misalignment—the impromptu performance reportedly took place in 1934—the accompanying anecdote underscores Adler's musical talent and aptitude in at least two ways. First, it suggests that in the span of just four years, between his 1930 encounter with Gershwin at the Roxy Theatre and the performance at Glaenzer's home, Adler went from an inability to play even a portion of the *Rhapsody* to the point where he could perform it spontaneously and in its entirety with Gershwin himself at the piano. Adler's assertion that although he knew Whiteman's recording of the *Rhapsody* in November 1934 but had "never played it through" directly contradicts the fact that he had been performing it as a regular and highly popular part of his act since July of that year. Regardless, this aspect of the story highlights Adler's claim to an inherent ability to instantly perform a piece without practice. This capacity to reproduce music effortlessly—a prized skill attributed to virtuosi such as Mozart and Liszt—became one of the more prominent aspects of Adler's musical legacy.

Perhaps most important, this anecdote about the impromptu performance with Gershwin lends a degree of authenticity to Adler's subsequent adaptations of the *Rhapsody* for performance on the harmonica. Recall Adler's report that after the two finished playing the *Rhapsody*, Gershwin ceremoniously announced: "Goddamn thing sounds as if I wrote it for you."[56] Since this supposed encounter took place a few months before his first recording of the *Rhapsody* in 1935, Adler's story implies that Gershwin approved of his harmonica interpretation from the outset. Such backdated endorsement became particularly important given the patchy reception received by his orchestral performances of the *Rhapsody* during the 1980s.

Another anecdote to emerge at this time relates specifically to such symphonic renditions of the *Rhapsody*. In his 1987 autobiography, Adler recalled the following about a Gershwin memorial concert from 1937:

> I was asked to play *Rhapsody in Blue*. Robert Russell Bennett, Gershwin's friend, who had orchestrated several Gershwin musicals and also arranged the *Porgy and Bess Suite*, had re-orchestrated the *Rhapsody in Blue* for mouth-organ and orchestra, this with Gershwin's permission.[57]

Adler proceeds to tell of a run-in with pianist Oscar Levant, who was "in such a rage that I thought he'd hit me," over the fact that Adler was scheduled to play the *Rhapsody* at the memorial.[58] Despite Levant's protests, the nationally broadcast concert went as planned with Adler performing the Bennett arrangement.

The inaccuracies within this reminiscence reveal another case of Adler bestowing authority upon his harmonica renditions of the *Rhapsody*. First and foremost, Adler likely never took part in the memorial concert. Transatlantic passenger ship manifests suggest that Adler was outside of the United States from March 1937 to July 1939.[59] Furthermore, none of the memorial broadcasts that took place during the late summer and early fall of 1937 or on the one-year anniversary of Gershwin's death name Adler as a participant.[60] Adler's assertion that Gershwin authorized Bennett's symphonic arrangement also seems unlikely since it did not materialize until the mid-1940s. Given the difficulties displayed by Adler on his 1935 recording—just two years prior to the date of this supposed memorial concert—it seems unlikely that he would have been proficient enough to perform Robert Russell Bennett's challenging arrangement even if it did originate nearly a decade before the evidence suggests.

Such claims, however, bestow a twofold legitimacy upon the symphonic arrangement of the *Rhapsody* performed by Adler: that it was prepared by a frequent Gershwin collaborator and that it received the composer's seal of approval. The addition of Levant provides the icing on the cake, implying that Adler's harmonica version took precedence over one offered by the man who would become the foremost interpreter of Gershwin's music following his death. By this time, Levant himself had been dead for fifteen years, allowing Adler to not only freely hitch his proverbial wagon to Gershwin but also place it firmly in front of Levant's.

There remains little evidence to support Adler's late-career anecdotes about his associations with Gershwin. None of these stories or encounters appears in contemporary correspondence with his family. Given the level at which Adler documented aspects of his life in these letters, including various encounters with other celebrities, an event as significant as performing *Rhapsody in Blue* with the composer at the piano should have been documented in detail. But no such record exists. It remains possible that these particular letters are missing or that Adler may have shared such news with his family by telephone. However, information garnered from elsewhere within Adler's correspondence raises additional questions about the veracity of his many Gershwin-related anecdotes.

Gershwin's name appears only twice in Adler's correspondence. These cursory appearances suggest a tenuous relationship, at best, between the two men. In the first, from January 30, 1935, Adler informs his parents about the possibility of a new composition by Gershwin prepared specifically for Adler and his harmonica:

> Did I tell you that two newspapers have rumored that Gershwin, having been impressed by hearing my playing, is writing me a harmonica concerto? It sounded important enough to cable Cochran about it which I did last night. Even if he isn't, perhaps it could be arranged—gad, what a stunt![61]

Adler does not clarify how or when Gershwin heard his playing, which leaves open the possibility that the two actually did perform the *Rhapsody* together at Glaenzer's home, as his anecdote claims. However, there remains no evidence that Gershwin was in fact at work on such a composition. During the winter of 1934–35, Gershwin gave his focus over completely to *Porgy and Bess*. He had completed its condensed score in January 1935 and immediately set about orchestrating the work while wintering in Palm Beach at the home of Emil Mosbacher. The Gershwin harmonica concerto rumor appears to have been just that.

The other mention of Gershwin in Adler's correspondence appears two years later, when Adler returned briefly to the United States to appear in a film.[62] As a special treat for his twenty-third birthday on February 10, 1937, Adler attended a concert featuring Gershwin at the Hollywood Bowl. He reported that the event was "not too good but sold out completely. [Alexander] Smallens, who conducted some of the numbers, was hammy, and Gershwin[']s pianistics sounded like WCBM on Yom Kippur."[63] Adler's reference to his hometown radio station on a Jewish high holy day suggests an at-times dissonant and chromatically inflected performance on the part of Gershwin that might have been an early indicator of the brain tumor that would take his life only five months later. Adler makes no mention of seeing Gershwin outside of this performance. This omission makes suspect the claim in Adler's autobiography that the two men were concurrently dating Hollywood starlet Simone Simon at the time—a dubious detail that remains unchallenged in accounts of Gershwin's love life.[64]

Adler strategically overstated his interactions with Gershwin—an American icon whose music and career never acquired the taint of communism—as a way of reintegrating himself into the American music scene. Yet his *Rhapsody*-related tales contain an element of accuracy. For example, he *did* perform the *Rhapsody* following Gershwin's death in August 1937, but these broadcasts took place in Ireland and were not specifically presented as memorial concerts.[65] Likewise, Adler *did* attend a party at the home of Jules Glaenzer, but this event was for Cole Porter, and it took place two years after Gershwin's death.[66] In the preface of his book *It Ain't Necessarily So*, Adler cautioned: "Something that must worry any autobiographer is the treachery of memory. I find in too many instances that it's completely unreliable. I think I'm writing the truth; I'd even swear to it, but how can I be sure?"[67] Adler's anecdotes should not be set aside, however, since they function as important arrangements—of history rather than music—in their own right.

ADDING UP ADLER'S ARRANGEMENTS AND ANECDOTES

Following the release of the 1994 tribute album *The Glory of Gershwin*, Adler stated that the recording was "For our moments together. For the fun and the laughter."[68] Regardless of the veracity of Adler's anecdotes, the fact remains that he did spend copious amounts of time with the music of Gershwin, *Rhapsody in Blue* in particular. As Ronald Radano affirms in his book *Lying up a Nation: Race and Black Music*, "the notion of lying. . . is meant to convey the sense that stories, whether literary or musical, are always to an extent made up, and in this way they stretch the truth. But the best of them capture something of the texture of living and in the end seem the truest of all."[69] In the aftermath of his blacklisting, Adler came to rely on the associative capacities of the *Rhapsody* to a greater degree than its performative aspects. Questions arise from Adler's tales and the way they connect him to an American icon. Whether or not Adler actually knew Gershwin is a moot point. The important observation to be made here is that Adler specifically chose to identify himself with *Rhapsody in Blue*, more so than with any other composition, and with Gershwin, more so than with any other figure, musical or otherwise. Adler's memorialization of Gershwin through narrative and performance reveals, on one hand, the significant debt that Adler felt toward him and the *Rhapsody* for their role in his development as a musician. On the other hand, these stories represent Adler's attempt to reclaim his former status through the retroactive remanufacturing of his image.

In a certain respect, the process paid off. At the age of eighty, Larry Adler had a hit record. However, it was not his rendition of *Rhapsody in Blue* that brought him to the attention of the popular music world, but rather the famous musicians he assembled to perform with him. These artists might have recorded an album with Adler regardless of his actual past with Gershwin. However, performing side by side with Adler placed these celebrities that much closer to Gershwin themselves, effectively granting them access to the success and prestige that came with such an association. To this end, Larry Adler and the artists featured on *The Glory of Gershwin* album demonstrate the recursive attraction of Gershwin and his music for those musicians who never knew him but were nevertheless influenced by him. As emerges in the final chapter, promoting such a connection to Gershwin became a major occupation of visual media representations of *Rhapsody in Blue* from the late twentieth century to the present.

CHAPTER 6

Selling Success

Visual Media and Rhapsody in Blue

Rhapsody in Blue stands for quality, elegance, and class—and that's what we want United to stand for.

—United Airlines spokesperson (1988)

Memorial performances of Gershwin's music sprung up all over the country in the weeks and months that followed his death, but the most highly anticipated concert took place in New York City at Lewisohn Stadium on August 9, 1937. This summer concert venue had a long history with Gershwin, from his first appearance as a piano soloist in 1927, to his conducting debut with the Philharmonic-Symphony Society in 1929, to the premiere of his *Cuban Overture* in 1932, a concert that set an attendance record for the stadium with 17,835 in attendance. The evening of the Gershwin Memorial Concert, a crowd of more than 20,000 resoundingly surpassed that record.[1] In an attempt to make the event accessible to as many as possible, Mayor La Guardia ordered his police force to keep "ticket speculators" away.[2] Regardless, demand far exceeded the capacity of the venue. Attendees "lined both extension walls of the shell and occupied every point of vantage," according to the *New York Times*. Thousands were turned away at the door, but "hundreds stood by the stadium fences on Convent Avenue." Together, they celebrated Gershwin's success and mourned the "abundant potentiality" of a life cut short.[3] In this time of grief, the public attended en masse to be in the presence of Gershwin's music and, by extension, the man himself. The final piece on the program was *Rhapsody in Blue* performed by pianist Harry Kaufman with Alexander Smallens conducting the Philharmonic-Symphony Orchestra.

The final scene of the 1945 biopic *Rhapsody in Blue* dramatically recreates this particular performance, albeit with a different cast of characters. Paul Whiteman leads a massive one-hundred-member orchestra with Oscar Levant providing an extravagantly theatrical piano performance. As the opening ritornello unfolds, dramatic lighting effects highlight individual sections of the ensemble. The camera slowly pulls back to an extreme long shot capturing not only the vastness of the audience but also the skyline of Manhattan as it stretches out behind the stadium itself—neon signs flash in the dark distance. The closing shot offers an equally dramatic representation of the space. To the strains of the love theme [R. 30], an overhead camera tracks back from a close-up on the hands of pianist Oscar Levant and rises to a bird's-eye view high above the stadium. As the arrangement cuts to the coda of the *Rhapsody* [R. 40+4], the screen fills with clouds as if to provide the perspective of Gershwin looking down from heaven.

Although those in attendance could not have experienced the *Rhapsody* from these two cinematically constructed vantage points, the *Rhapsody* has come to be largely connected to such visual imagery in the present day. These shots immediately call to mind the opening sequence of Woody Allen's *Manhattan* and the "friendly skies" of United Airlines' commercial advertising. Despite the abundant appearances of *Rhapsody in Blue* on film, television, and beyond, one skyline and one airline dominate visual representations of the piece in the present era. But even these seemingly simple images carry with them a more complex story with respect to their arrangements of *Rhapsody in Blue*. As introduced in chapter 2, movies such as *King of Jazz* (1930) and *Rhapsody in Blue* imbued the *Rhapsody* with notions of success—both potential and realized. Together with future filmic framings of the piece from *Manhattan* (1979) to *Fantasia 2000* (1999) to *The Great Gatsby* (2013), a consensus developed on the inherent meaning and visual potential of the *Rhapsody*. These films promote and reinforce the American Dream trope of the piece with a modern, urban, and specifically New York sensibility.

At the same time, United Airlines has spent hundreds of millions of dollars over the course of nearly thirty years to ensure that it comes to mind when *Rhapsody in Blue* is heard. When the company began its association with *Rhapsody in Blue* in 1987—fifty years after Gershwin's death—it drew on visions of the piece inherited from visual media, including films such as *Rhapsody in Blue* and the then-recent opening ceremonies of the Los Angeles Olympics. Such "upwardly mobile" and "elevated" conceptions are, after all, also germane to images of flight. However, the flexible identity of the *Rhapsody* as a concept and a collection of tunes has become of greatest significance to the success of its branding. United Airlines has incorporated aspects of *Rhapsody in Blue* into more than fifty different television advertisements, the soundscape of its terminal at O'Hare International Airport, and even the underscoring of pre-flight safety announcements. Looking at United's commercial and architectural use of *Rhapsody in Blue* reveals how it has transformed the piece from a national symbol of success into an internationally applicable anthem—one that quite literally circles the globe, non-stop daily.

UNITING VISIONS OF *RHAPSODY IN BLUE* ONSCREEN

After the *Rhapsody* appeared in multiple scenes for Warner Brothers' 1945 biopic on George Gershwin, the use of the piece as a narrative device in Hollywood film was long restricted by Ira Gershwin, trustee of his late brother's estate. Following George Gershwin's death in 1937, requests to use his music were frequent, and Ira was judicious about granting such permission, particularly when it came to *Rhapsody in Blue*. A 1939 letter from Ira to his lawyer, A. M. Wattenberg, regarding a request from bandleader Glenn Miller to create a dance arrangement of the *Rhapsody*, made his concerns clear: "I have the greatest respect for Mr. Miller's work but do not believe the time is propitious for such an undertaking. . . . I wouldn't like too much of the 'Rhapsody' done just now especially after the new Whiteman recording just put out, the [José] Iturbi recording etc. etc. No use doing the thing to death. . . . A dance arrangement, true, will give the 'Rhapsody' additional performances, but it really doesn't need them and might injure the work by overexploitation."[4] Ira eventually relented, allowing Miller to perform and record Bill Finegan's arrangement of the *Rhapsody*.[5] However, after the 1945 *Rhapsody in Blue* movie, he granted no further permissions for filmic use of the piece until the final years of his own life.

In 1979, four years before Ira Gershwin's death, Woody Allen submitted a request to use *Rhapsody in Blue* in his new film *Manhattan*. As he had in the past, Ira initially resisted the notion. But Al Kohn, licensing vice president for Warner Brothers at the time, eventually convinced his friend Ira to allow Allen to use the *Rhapsody*.[6] It proved to be a shrewd move. Due in part to the decades-long absence of *Rhapsody in Blue* from the screen, Allen's powerful visualization of the piece resonates into the present. Although both Gershwin and his *Rhapsody* have long been connected to New York City—due in no small part to biographer Isaac Goldberg as discussed in chapter 2—it was not until the opening sequence of Allen's film that both became explicitly correlated with the grandeur of its skyline.

In this comedic drama, Allen plays Isaac Davis, a TV comedy writer with an inability to maintain a relationship with anyone except Manhattan itself. Gershwin's music features throughout the film, often as a means of providing wordless commentary on the action taking place onscreen. Allen noted that he "filmed scenes that in themselves might not mean anything" until "I put music behind it."[7] For example, in a scene taking place at a black-tie cocktail-party fundraiser, a small jazz combo plays "Let's Call the Whole Thing Off" quietly in the background. Isaac happens upon Mary, the mistress of his best friend, played by a spirited Diane Keaton. When first introduced earlier in the film, the two clash immediately while debating art, music, and philosophy. Isaac and Mary remain somewhat dismissive toward each other when they meet again in this later cocktail-party scene. But the unsung lyric of the song foretells their future: "For we know we need each other, so we better call the calling off off. Let's call the whole thing off." The two soon find themselves in a romantic relationship that, reflecting the triple negative of the lyric, ultimately meets its demise.

As central as Gershwin's songs become in achieving dramatic moments throughout *Manhattan*, Ferde Grofé's symphonic arrangement of *Rhapsody in Blue* sets the stage for the film as a whole during its famous opening montage. The introductory four-minute sequence—filmed like the rest of the movie in black-and-white Panavision—consists of sixty separate shots, ranging from expansive skylines to busy city streets. Allen includes no opening credits; the only clue that this is the title sequence comes in the fourth shot: a neon "Manhattan" marquee illuminating the night. Soon thereafter, the voiceover begins the first of five possible opening vignettes for a novel written by Allen's yet-unidentified character:

> Chapter 1: He adored New York City. He idolized it all out of proportion. Uh, no. Make that: He romanticized it all out of proportion. Better. To him, no matter what the season was this was still a town that existed in black and white and pulsated to the great tunes of George Gershwin. Uh. . . no. Let me start this over.[8]

On the words "idolized" and "romanticized," Allen cuts to shots of the iconic 59th Street Bridge and the Empire Diner respectively. The word "season" coincides with an extreme long shot down a snow-covered Park Avenue toward the viaduct around Grand Central Terminal (see figure 6.1). Allen does not mention Gershwin by name again, but the continued presence of *Rhapsody in Blue*—performed here by Zubin Mehta and the New York Philharmonic with Manhattan native Gary Graffman at the

Figure 6.1
Screenshots that respectively accompany the words "idolized," "romanticized," and "season" from the opening montage of Woody Allen's 1979 film *Manhattan*.

piano—underscores each narrative attempt and extends beyond his final declaration: "New York was his town and it always would be." Although the phrase ostensibly applies to Allen's character, as the sequence unfolds over the course of the next two minutes, the connection between Gershwin's music and Manhattan becomes increasingly clear. By this point, the *Rhapsody* has reached the triumphant full ensemble version of the ritornello theme [R. 6]. Images of uptown abound, including the west side skyline at sunrise, Central Park covered in snow, and Lincoln Center. A flashing "Broadway" sign accompanies the flutter tongue trumpet just before the entrance of the train theme [R. 9-2]. At this point, the arrangement jumps to the accompanied piano cadenza at rehearsal 37, visually accompanied by the frenetic action of midtown. As the music speeds up, so does the frequency of images, as well as the activity that fills the frame. On the verge of overwhelming the viewer, the final fifty seconds of the montage is a single shot: fireworks over the downtown skyline. The *grandioso* reintroduction of the stride theme [R. 39] provides a nearly in-sync accompaniment to each brilliant pyrotechnic explosion, firmly imprinting *Rhapsody in Blue* on

New York City and vice versa. At the time, film critic Gene Siskel rightly called this overture a "masterfully edited. . . contribution to the 'I Love New York' campaign."[9] Little did he or anyone else know just how far into the future such publicity would extend.

Twenty years later, Martin Scorsese paid homage to Allen's opening sequence in his 1999 film *Bringing Out the Dead*. The movie is about a New York City EMT named Frank Pierce, played by Nicholas Cage, who attempts to keep his life and career together after a series of dramatic failures. In one scene, he works to rescue an acquaintance improbably impaled on a wrought-iron balcony railing, which dangles several stories above the street below. While Pierce holds the man as his colleagues work to free him with a metal-cutting torch, sparks erupt into the night sky behind them. The delirious victim declares the view beautiful, screaming into the darkness: "I love this city!" Pierce also gazes out at the vista as hints of *Rhapsody in Blue* emerge from the underscoring. Rather than using the *Rhapsody* itself—perhaps in order to avoid a hefty royalty payment—film composer Elmer Bernstein rearranges the notes of the tag motif to form a new melody: Bb-C-Eb-Db-C-Bb-Bb. Colorful fireworks suddenly appear amid the sparks and buildings, making the reference to *Manhattan* explicit.

That same year, similar associations between the New York skyline and *Rhapsody in Blue* featured prominently in Disney's *Fantasia 2000*, albeit in a much more lighthearted manner. Disney commissioned a new recording of Grofé's symphonic arrangement by the Philharmonica Orchestra under the baton of Bruce Broughton and featuring pianist Ralph Grierson. They trimmed the running time of the piece down to approximately twelve minutes by excising 125 bars of piano solo from three different sections [R. 19-4 to R. 22-5; R. 25-4 to R. 28-4; and R. 32+10 to R. 33]. *Fantasia 2000* attempted to capture the visual-musical magic of the 1940 original film ("designs and pictures and stories that music inspired in the minds and imaginations of a group of artists") updated for audiences of the new millennium.[10] Although striving for the modern, the *Rhapsody in Blue* sequence reinforces established narrative tropes of the past from the very outset. Quincy Jones introduces the segment observing that Gershwin "took jazz off the streets, dressed her up, and took her to the concert hall."[11]

The story that accompanies the *Rhapsody* follows a day in the lives of four inhabitants of New York City during the early 1930s, all longing for a change in their current situation. Director Eric Goldberg observed, "We devised a story where they all help each other achieve their goals—without ever realizing that they're helping one another."[12] Accompanying the opening clarinet glissando, the *Rhapsody in Blue* sequence begins with an Al Hirschfeld-inspired line drawing of the New York skyline, which unfolds as if created on an Etch-a-Sketch toy. As day breaks over the subsequent iteration of the ritornello theme, the buildings fill in with deep shades of purple, pink, and blue just before the sunrise washes them out. In quick succession, two of the four central characters that inhabit the cityscape are introduced: Duke, an African-American construction worker who dreams of being a jazz drummer, and Sad-Eyed Joe a well-dressed, but clearly down-on-his-luck white man. During the more energetic portions of the first piano cadenza, a late-for-work Duke arrives at his jobsite and operates a riveting hammer in time with the music; the more languid portions accompany Joe as he sips coffee in a lonely diner.

As the *Rhapsody* continues, the Hirschfeldian imagery maintains a close connection to its musical and thematic contours, ushering in two more central characters (and a special cameo) in the process. The train theme accompanies a crowded subway at rush hour; the beat of the stride theme aligns with the pile driver at Duke's construction site; an up-tempo shuffle theme (reorchestrated to feature more brass) accompanies the introduction of Rachel, a bright-eyed little girl being rushed from activity to activity by her nanny. Rachel's piano lesson is interrupted by George Gershwin seen playing the solo-piano climax of the ritornello theme [R. 22-4] through the window of his uptown apartment in the same building.[13] The ensuing "Orientalist" ritornello section [R. 22 as discussed in chapter 1] accompanies the antics of an inattentive organ grinder's monkey. The final character, John, briefly mimics the dancing simian before his overbearing and overspending wife chastises him. During the four-bar piano-solo transition to the love theme [R. 28-4], each of the four main characters gazes longingly into the distance.

Recalling the opening scene of Leonard Bernstein's essay "A Nice Gershwin Tune," the love theme [R. 28] accompanies a pair of figure skaters twirling around the ice rink at Rockefeller Center. In turn, each character envisions him or herself on the ice, fulfilling their respective dreams: Rachel skates hand in hand with her parents; Joe glides to a time clock and punches his card; Duke skips from drum to drum, playing the rolls of the snare in sync with the music; and John takes to the air, literally free as a bird. Returning to reality, during the subsequent piano cadenza [R. 33], a frustrated Duke throws his construction equipment from the top of the building site. This action sets in motion a series of events that allows each character to find resolution. As Joe catches Duke's discarded equipment, the foreman offers him a job on the night shift. Joe causes a crane hook to pick up and haul away John's wife. John sees a sign for "Harlem Jazz Talent Night" and heads off to the show. On his way to the same venue to play with his jazz quartet, Duke accidentally bumps Rachel's ball into the street. The girl runs into traffic, only to be rescued by and reunited with her parents. She is hoisted up onto the shoulders of her father as the full orchestra presents the final iteration of the ritornello theme [R. 40]. As the piano plays the final tag [R. 40+4], the camera zooms out to reveal Times Square around them, full of the hustle and bustle of traffic and neon signs. It simultaneously recalls images from the opening sequence in *Manhattan* and sets the stage for future visual representations of the piece.

During the fall of 2010, the long-running animated series *The Simpsons* drew on such associations in the premiere episode of its twenty-second season, titled "Elementary School Musical." Inspired by a week at arts camp and frustrated by the musical limitations of her hometown of Springfield, Lisa Simpson runs away from home to pursue her dream of becoming a professional jazz musician. As she bicycles her way out of town with her saxophone strapped to her back, she pauses at an intersection that features a multi-paneled street sign indicating the five boroughs of Springfield: Spanhattan, The Spronx, Spueens, Spaten Island, and Sprooklyn (see figure 6.2). A close-up shot of the sign ushers in the *Rhapsody* from the triplet pickups of the initial three-measure symphonic statement of the ritornello theme [R. 3]. Triumphantly, the camera pans left in the direction of Sprooklyn as Lisa makes her way across a gothic revival suspension bridge clearly modeled on the Brooklyn original.

A 2011 episode of *Glee*—an immensely popular series about the trials and tribulations of a high school show choir—also highlighted the close visual connection between *Rhapsody in Blue* and New York City. In the finale of its second season, the ensemble travels to New York for a competition. The episode begins with a close-up of an American flag in the middle

Figure 6.2
Screenshot of character Lisa Simpson heading toward Sprooklyn from *The Simpsons* episode 465, "Elementary School Musical."

of Times Square accompanied by the opening trill and glissando of the *Rhapsody*. As the clarinet reaches the top of its melodic ascent and is joined by the orchestra for the presentation of the ritornello theme, the camera offers a slow 360-degree pan of the mesmerizing environment. The shot ends with a close-up of Rachel Berry soaking it all in (see figure 6.3). A high school junior, Berry's sole ambition is to appear on the Broadway stage. With sheer delight visible in her wide smile and tightly clenched fists, she breathlessly declares, "I made it."

The recent television appearances of *Rhapsody in Blue* not only further connect the piece with narratives of success taking place in and around New York, but also form a direct link to biographical arrangements of George Gershwin. Both *The Simpsons* and *Glee* used *Rhapsody in Blue* as a narrative device that underscores the ambitions of young musicians as they seek artistic success. Lisa Simpson and Rachel Berry are performers of jazz and musical theatre respectively—the very genres in which George Gershwin operated. Such representations connect to tropes that accompany conceptions of Gershwin from Isaac Goldberg and onward: a young musician who struck out on his own to find success through jazz and popular song in the heart of New York City.

The connection of the *Rhapsody* to this image of self-madeness continued into 2013 with the release of Baz Luhrmann's lavish adaptation of *The Great Gatsby*. Just as in F. Scott Fitzgerald's original novel, the action takes place in the fictional town of West Egg on Long Island in 1922—two years prior to the actual premiere of *Rhapsody in Blue*. Approximately thirty minutes into the film, protagonist Nick Carraway finds himself in attendance at one of Jay Gatsby's extravagant parties. Eager to meet his neighbor and

Figure 6.3
Screenshot of character Rachel Berry in Times Square from *Glee*, season 2, episode 22, "New York."

host, Carraway makes his way through the throng of guests—dancing to an anachronistic yet fitting upbeat soundtrack produced by hip-hop mogul Jay-Z that is brought to life onscreen by a dozen string players—only to discover that none of the people gathered have ever met the mysterious Gatsby.

During a pause in the musical entertainment, the conductor calls out like a midway barker: "Ladies and Gentlemen: A jazz history of the world and accompanying fireworks!" The crowd rushes outside to witness the spectacle as *Rhapsody in Blue* begins in the middle of the final piano cadenza [R. 34-10].[14] Carraway makes his way to the balcony and strikes up a conversation with an unknown individual. Just as the piece reaches the flutter-tongue brass climax two bars before rehearsal 37, the camera reveals the face of Jay Gatsby, played by actor Leonardo DiCaprio. The *Rhapsody* immediately cuts to the final seven bars of the piece [R. 40] as fireworks simultaneously erupt into a dazzling display behind him (see figure 6.4). In slow motion, Gatsby raises his martini glass and beams, as Carraway's voiceover says, "[It was] one of those rare smiles that you may come across four or five times in life. It seemed to understand you and believe in you just as you would like to be understood and believed in." Gatsby's smile is made even more potent by the presence of *Rhapsody in Blue*, one of those rare pieces with the power to affect and inspire those who encounter it.

Visual arrangements of the *Rhapsody* by and large reinterpret and reaffirm longstanding tropes related to George Gershwin, using the music to sell an image of success. Such recurrent associations contrast markedly with the first cinematic appearance of the piece in *St. Louis Blues*, which, as discussed in chapter 2, tied *Rhapsody in Blue* to questions of appropriation and financial gain. Instead of complicating the narrative of the *Rhapsody* as

Figure 6.4
Screenshot of character Jay Gatsby as he first appears in the 2013 film *The Great Gatsby*.

such, film and television formations of the piece from the last quarter of the twentieth century to the present smooth over complexities that emerge from its arrangement by figures like Ferde Grofé, Leonard Bernstein, Duke Ellington, and Larry Adler. Rather, in popular visual culture, the *Rhapsody* has become a sonic stand-in for the urban experience, one closely connected to the hopes and dreams of specific individuals, as well as the realization of these ambitions through action—just the sort of imagery that might appeal to an airline in need of a marketing makeover.

BRANDING THE FRIENDLY SKIES

The establishment of *Rhapsody in Blue* as the corporate soundtrack for United Airlines in 1987 coincided with a major attempt on the part of the company to revamp its image. It had long been branded as the "friendly skies," but that impression had become strained in recent years. The Leo Burnett Company of Chicago first pitched the "Fly the Friendly Skies" slogan while competing for the United account in 1965 amid a rapidly expanding leisure and business travel industry. United had been the largest commercial carrier since 1961. Following the deregulation of the industry in 1978, for which United had lobbied heavily, the airline became the first to serve all fifty states in the nation in 1984. As new competition forced expansion and cost-cutting measures, United fell victim to a month-long strike by its pilots in May 1985. The company had spread itself thin and witnessed a decline in customer satisfaction as a result. The behemoth airline turned to *Rhapsody in Blue* to improve its brand image. Initially, United capitalized on the "quality, elegance, and class" that had come to accompany visual representations of the *Rhapsody* through its various arrangements over time.[15] While maintaining a connection to this original impulse, over the course of the past twenty-five years, the commercials of United Airlines have come to document a broad visual and sonic slice of American life, capturing its cultural priorities and fixations in the process, all to the strains of *Rhapsody in Blue*.

The licensing of preexisting music—as opposed to creating brand-specific jingles—increased dramatically over the course of the 1980s. As the expiration of copyrights attached to music of the Tin Pan Alley era drew ever closer, the estates of such composers and the companies that managed their distribution sought out opportunities to capitalize on these works while they remained part of the public consciousness yet out of the public domain. For example, in 1986, the Kurt Weill estate licensed "Mack the Knife" to McDonald's for its "Mac Tonight" campaign. At the same time, a rise in consumption by the American population as a whole—roughly twice the goods and services were purchased in the 1980s as they were in the 1950s—resulted in increased market segmentation.[16] Advertisers turned to music selected to resonate with the values, beliefs, and lifestyles of specific demographics. Pepsi reached out to the "new generation" through music-video-styled commercials featuring Michael Jackson and popular hits like "Bad." Nike turned to "Revolution" by The Beatles to sell edgy athletic apparel to baby boomers—a move that turned out to be as successful as it was controversial. Critics, fans, and even former members of the band itself spoke out against its commercial use, complaining that the advertisement cheapened the song.[17] The use of preexisting music became a double-edged sword.

As with film and television, rarely did the music of George Gershwin accompany commercial advertising before the death of Ira Gershwin in 1981. But in 1985, the Gershwin estate allowed Toyota to use an instrumental version of the 1930 song "I Got Rhythm" in the promotion of the company's redesigned four-door Camry. Even when Toyota ceased using the full song, its tagline endured as the company slogan for the remainder of the decade: "Who could ask for anything more?" Such long-term relationships were clearly on the mind of Warner Brothers chairman Chuck Kaye, who stated in 1985, "If you get one of your songs on a United Airlines commercial you're talking about $200,000 to $300,000 in income over three years."[18] At the time, Kaye suggested that his company was in negotiation with Volvo for the use of *Rhapsody in Blue*. Had that deal worked out, the *Rhapsody*'s association with United Airlines might never have gotten off the ground.

Both United Airlines and the Leo Burnett advertising agency were aware of the potential challenges and costs associated with acquiring commercial use rights for *Rhapsody in Blue*, which it did in 1987. For a reported $300,000 that first year alone, the airline secured the right to use the various themes of the *Rhapsody* as it pleased. The company made clear that it would treat the piece with respect from the start. Bill Alenson, an advertising executive at United at the time, said that their "intention was to use it in a way that Gershwin, were he still alive, would be pleased with."[19] Carla Michelotti, the Burnett executive and lawyer who negotiated the initial licensing deal with the Gershwin estate, reported that they "were very well informed of our intent. We wanted them to approve the commercial. We wanted them to feel comfortable with it."[20]

It some respects, it was in the best interests of the Gershwin estate to license *Rhapsody in Blue* to United. The advertising agency could have easily created new music that closely resembled the *Rhapsody* and paid no royalties, just as Elmer Bernstein would later do for Scorsese's *Bringing Out the Dead*. Marc Gershwin, George Gershwin's nephew and current trustee of his estate, agreed: "We'd rather have the real theme than a lousy theme that was close, and that is often what you're up against."[21] Less pessimistically, he also acknowledged that commercial use of the piece could educate the public, introducing them to a bit of American music history they might not otherwise experience. However, the educational component accompanying arrangements of *Rhapsody in Blue* in United Airlines commercials ultimately has more to do with corporate representations of American culture than its musical past.

The autumn after United Airlines acquired the rights to the *Rhapsody*, it launched its fifteen million dollar "Rededicated" campaign, featuring the piece in a commercial titled "Nation's Business" ◐. The goal was to reaffirm the quality of its customer service and commitment to business travelers, an essential market during the economic boom of the late 1980s that represented approximately 80 percent of its revenue stream at the time. Directed by Leslie Dektor, this first commercial of the campaign has a no-nonsense, documentary-film aesthetic—not unlike Nike's "Revolution" advertisement that had premiered just six months earlier. Here United presents members of white-collar America—stock traders, engineers, architects, lawyers, even suit-wearing cowboys—traveling to various parts of the country to carry out their work. As accompaniment to the business-like approach of the commercial, Burnett executives envisioned a modernized arrangement of the *Rhapsody*. They turned to composer Terry Fryer, a principal with the Chicago-based commercial music firm Colnot/Fryer Music and a pioneer in digital music technologies, who re-presented the love theme amid the synthesized sonic sensibilities of the 1980s. If not for the soaring love melody, the arrangement might easily be mistaken for the title theme from the 1981 movie *Chariots of Fire*, with its steadily pulsing reverb-enhanced electric bass and the heavy punctuation of the floor tom.[22]

Although perhaps not as sonically recognizable as *Rhapsody in Blue*, United called upon the talents of actor Gene Hackman to provide the commercial's voiceover. "We are a nation of business and to bring us together there is the airline of business," Hackman's narration begins. He assuredly concludes: "United Airlines: Rededicated to giving you the service you deserve." His participation reflected a growing trend in media advertising during the late 1980s to hire professional actors rather than pitchmen to give voice to the ad copy. Although celebrity spokespeople had been used to promote products for decades, nothing in these voiceover spots specifically disclosed Hackman's identity. "Probably only movie buffs will know it's Hackman," Burnett's creative director Greg Taubeneck said at the time.[23] Similar to connotations emerging from past representations of the *Rhapsody*, Hackman's voice had a certain familiarity and trustworthiness due in no small part to his critically acclaimed performance as Coach Norman Dale in the 1986 film *Hoosiers*. Hackman earned a reported annual sum of $200,000 for his uncredited voiceover work—almost as much as the company initially paid for the rights to use *Rhapsody in Blue*.

Terry Fryer's arrangement of the *Rhapsody* received the award for best adapted commercial music of 1987 by *Advertising Age* magazine, but prompted mixed reviews in the popular press. *Washington Post* television critic Tom Shales rhetorically asked, "Is it sacrilegious to use what is almost a patriotic anthem by now in a TV commercial?" Focusing on the arrangement itself, composer Randy Newman, who had recently sold four of his own songs as commercial theme music, voiced a critique similar to that of Shales. He complained that the synthesized *Rhapsody* "really bothered me. . . they changed the tempo, cut bars, cut beats. Bad! They screwed up the music."[24] Ira Gershwin's former attorney, Ronald Blanc, went on record on behalf of his late client following the appearance of the *Rhapsody* in the commercial campaign: "I doubt that [Ira] would have approved it. Obviously there were many requests to use it. He always resisted and was very firm about it." Even Leopold Godowsky III, another of Gershwin's nephews and part of the estate that granted permission to United to use the *Rhapsody*, admitted: "I'm not crazy for it, but it's alright. If it were bad, I would be upset about it. But I don't think this music could be devalued."[25] Undeterred by such appraisals, United continued to arrange the *Rhapsody* in unexpected visual and sonic ways.

In addition to promoting domestic business travel, United Airlines initially used *Rhapsody in Blue* to highlight the elegance of its hard-earned foreign destinations. Following the deregulation of the airline industry, United successfully acquired Pan American's Pacific division, providing them with routes to thirteen countries in Asia. The Leo Burnett agency put Ron Condon and Jim Dyer in charge of promoting United's newly expanded transpacific routes. In 1989, the team developed a commercial that adapted *Rhapsody in Blue* using musical instruments from a variety of Asian cultures with the tag line "All over the Pacific they're playing our song."[26] The slogan claimed *Rhapsody in Blue* for America, as well as United Airlines, and intimated the popularity of both around the world. The resulting commercial reflected a revived cultural fascination with Asia during the late 1980s, akin to what accompanied the origins of the *Rhapsody* in the 1920s.

Titled "Pacific Song" 🔊, the commercial's visuals interspersed markedly Asian scenes—a junk sailing through Hong Kong harbor, dancers in ornate headdresses in a Southeast Asian palace, the Great Wall of China—with shots of United aircraft. Gene Hackman's voice pronounces: "Flying to three hundred cities on five continents with a 747 transpacific fleet and the warmth of an Asian smile. We're in harmony with you all the way." The double meaning intended by the use of the word "harmony" emerged from the consonance of the arrangement provided by Com/Track composer Manny Mendelsohn and the images seen onscreen. The music establishes an Asian sensibility in the opening moment: A taiko drum roll accompanies a shakuhachi flute playing a single note. This brief statement functions as the harmonic dominant to the love theme that follows. With its synthesized bass line and soaring brass melody, the theme receives a setting similar to that in the "Nation's Business" commercial. Here Mendelsohn replaces the punctuating floor toms with further use of the taiko, as visualized by a twirling Japanese woman in a white kimono. The sounds of other Asian instruments adorn the *Rhapsody*'s theme whenever shots of musicians are shown. Aligned with the voiceover word "harmony," three Chinese women dressed in colorful robes strum pipas that supplement the timbre of the piano in the love theme's countermelody.

Advertisements from the "Playing our Song" campaign contributed to an upsurge in passenger traffic to and from United's Pacific destinations. The company increased service from 31,000 seats each week in 1988 to nearly 50,000 just two years later.[27] This 60 percent increase represented more than a third of its business overall. Understandably, United continued to place strong emphasis on this particular market over the next several years, not only in commercials for American audiences but also for those in Asia. Just as "Pacific Song" provided a glimpse into Asian cultures, albeit through the streamlined gaze of corporate advertising, commercials designed for broadcast in Asian markets offered correspondingly reductive depictions of America.

A 1994 commercial promoting United's "mileage plus" program to Japanese business travelers rearranged the *Rhapsody* to reflect the musical environment of a variety of destinations ◐. The spot features a Japanese puppet of the traditional Bunraku style seated on an airplane as the voiceover announces a series of locales that travelers could visit at ever-increasing award levels. The puppet appears in a succession of wardrobes representative of each destination. The accompanying *Rhapsody*, starting with the final B section of the love theme [R. 29-4], receives a modified instrumentation with each costume change, timed to occur every two measures. First, the puppet appears in a traditional Japanese kimono representing its point of origin. Here a shamisen, the traditional instrumental accompaniment for Bunraku, plays the theme. Next, the puppet's clothing changes to a silk Chinese robe and an erhu replaces the shamisen. Two measures later, a Hawaiian slide guitar picks up the melody as the outfit becomes a bright floral-patterned shirt adorned by a yellow lei. Representing mainland United States, the puppet next wears a brown jacket with a bolo tie and waves a black cowboy hat in time to the *Rhapsody*, which now takes the form of a fiddle-driven two-step. With the puppet finally appearing in a white Italian sports coat with a pair of dark sunglasses—a clear reference to Don Johnson and *Miami Vice*—the rest of the commercial features a steel-drum calypso version of the *Rhapsody*. The only English words heard come at the very end: "Friendly Sky: United Mileage Plus." The commercial not only effectively promotes United's frequent flyer program but also reinforces its corporate logos—both motto and music—to an international market. Through easily identifiable visual and sonic representations of destinations in the United States from Hawaii to Texas to Florida, it also promotes a positive—and stereotypical—view of American culture using one of its most recognizable musical works.

By the time of this particular mileage plus commercial, the company had been in a period of decline, due in part to the recession of the early 1990s, but also as a result of poor management. As reported in the *Washington Post*, "United had the worst on-time record of major airlines, and callers to its reservation lines typically endured several minutes of 'Rhapsody in Blue'" (the average connection time before an agent picked up was seven and a half minutes).[28] In July 1994, the employees of United Airlines gained majority control of the company after agreeing to the acquisition of stock in exchange for a reduction in salary. It became the largest employee-owned company in the world. Accordingly, United immediately amended its slogan to the more inviting and communal "Come fly our friendly skies." Soon thereafter, the company solicited bids from other advertising agencies, effectively ending its thirty-year association with Leo Burnett. In October 1996, United awarded its approximately $120 million account to two separate firms: Fallon McElligott in Minneapolis to manage domestic marketing and Young & Rubicam in New York to service foreign markets. The "friendly skies" moniker became the first casualty of the shift in agencies and initially the *Rhapsody* appeared to be not far behind.

The first television commercial produced by Fallon in May 1997, titled "Rising," ◉ addressed the perennially pertinent concern of customer service. Produced to look like a silent movie, with grainy black and white shots, the advertisement restages the Wright Brothers' first flight at Kitty Hawk but with an overlay of travel delay announcements and frustrated passengers. The voiceover states plainly, "If Orville and Wilbur had to go through what you do just to fly, they would have stayed in the bicycle business." It represented a stark departure not only from the "friendly skies" motto and its colorful presentation of the travel experience but also the company's use of *Rhapsody in Blue*. Rather than include a creative arrangement of the piece as an underscore, the *Rhapsody* enters only briefly at the end of the advertisement. A monophonic piano presentation of the tag motif accompanies a silhouetted bird flying by itself across a suddenly yellow background representing the dawn of a new day.

United received an underwhelming response to its "Rising" campaign, which it attempted to salvage in part by reintroducing *Rhapsody in Blue*. A series of advertisements released during 1999 incorporated the phrase "Rising is. . ." with one or more concluding concepts: astonishing, imagination, leading, etc. Intricately shot and assembled, each featured a jet moving slowly across the sky at cruising altitude as seen from the ground below and worked into a secondary shot. The commercial featuring the "Rising is imagination" tagline was titled "Day Dream" ◐. It features a young boy looking out the window of a diner accompanied by the sounds of a cool-jazz piano trio. He spots the jet and raises his hand to the glass, appearing to hold the aircraft in the palm of his hand. As he does so, the piano begins to play a transitional figure from the *Rhapsody* [R. 32]. Just before he casts off the aircraft like a paper airplane, the jazz combo transitions into the love theme. Each of the various commercials in this campaign utilized a different arrangement of *Rhapsody in Blue*, ranging from a symphonic version based on Ferde Grofé's orchestral setting to an adult contemporary popular music adaptation. However, in October 1999, United announced that it would retire the "Rising" campaign because it felt that it was "too intellectual and esoteric for general customers."[29]

United briefly ran a new campaign that focused its attention on the company name, instilling a feeling of togetherness—one that became all the more important following the events of September 11, 2001, in which two of its own aircraft were involved. United responded to the tragedy with commercials that tried to capture the spirit of unity in the nation after the terrorist attacks. A solo-piano arrangement of the love theme provides an appropriately subdued yet uplifting soundtrack. Under the banner "We Are United" ◐, the commercials feature members of the employee-owned company—pilots, flight attendants, gate agents, and ground crew—talking about their longstanding relationships with the airline. They speak of the airline as a family enterprise, both figuratively and literally. Captain Dennis E. Fitch, an icon within the company in his own right for his heroic efforts during the crash landing of flight 232 in Sioux City, Iowa, in 1989, proudly lists members of his immediate family who work for United.

As poignant as the commercials were, they had only a brief run. Two months later, American Airlines flight 587 crashed into the Atlantic Ocean shortly after its departure from JFK Airport in New York, killing everyone on board. Out of respect, United placed all television advertising on hold— a move that lasted longer than the company might have intended. In the severe economic downturn that followed the 2001 attacks, several airlines filed for Chapter 11 bankruptcy. United did the same in December 2002 to begin a more than three-year reorganization process. At the time, one critic questioned what was next for United's multi-decade effort to create "an orchestrated aura of supremacy, pride and grandeur" through the musical application of *Rhapsody in Blue*.[30]

The answer came fourteen months later with a campaign titled "It's Time to Fly." These four television spots, according to senior vice president of marketing Martin White, were intended to "harken back to a time when the customer had an emotional bond between them and an airline."[31] Providing a sonic association with United's past, *Rhapsody in Blue* featured prominently in each. Robert Redford became the voice of the airline; executive vice president of marketing John Tague selected him based on his narration of the film *A River Runs Through It* (1992). Tague observed that "[h]e has a way of delivery that makes you stop and take note of it," a central consideration given that only seven seconds of voiceover occur in the sixty-second spots.[32] The only words appear at the end of the commercial: "Where you go in life is up to you, and we're the airline to take you there. United. It's time to fly."

With little narration, the success of each spot rested on the message communicated by the interaction of the images onscreen and the arrangement of *Rhapsody in Blue* heard on the soundtrack. The first commercial, titled "Interview" ◐, appeared during the February 2004 Academy Awards broadcast. Various sections of the *Rhapsody*'s solo piano cadenzas accompany shots of a man nervously getting ready for [R. 25], traveling to [R. 26+12], and undergoing [R. 6-14] a job interview. He leaves the interview conveying a sense of failure, as confirmed by the solitary solo violin playing the coda of the love theme [R. 29]. Suddenly, he receives a call on his mobile phone, whose ringtone happens to be in the same key as the violin melody, informing him that he did indeed get the job. As the full orchestral setting of the love theme [R. 30] triumphantly reemerges, Redford begins the closing voiceover. The final shot is of the man returning comfortably home aboard a United Airlines flight.

"Interview" and the three other spots that debuted with it—"Light Bulb," "Rose," and "A Life"—ushered in an era of animation for the airline. Possibly taking a cue from Disney's use of the piece in *Fantasia 2000*, marketing vice president John Tague wanted to see animation become as closely connected to the airline as *Rhapsody in Blue*, which he considered to be "an audio icon" for the company.[33] United hoped to distinguish the look of its advertising from that of their competitors, and Fallon executives challenged members of their agency "to depict the life experience of [United's] frequent business travelers in a thoughtful and differentiated way."[34] The first thirty seconds of "A Life" ◐, which features original solo-piano music not related to the *Rhapsody*, portray the lifespan of a businessman from boyhood through retirement—riding his bike, graduating from college, traveling to meetings—all the while looking to the sky as if searching for something more. The tag motif enters during his retirement party and follows him as he ponders his next move while on a stroll in a park. An airplane soaring high above ushers in the fast-paced shuffle theme from its piano cadenza presentation [R. 26+12], which inspires the man to make the most of retirement by traveling the world with his wife. In the final seconds, Redford's voiceover repeats the same message that closed "Interview." The critically acclaimed commercial earned a spot in the permanent collection of the Museum of Modern Art in New York, and its incorporation of the *Rhapsody* garnered a Clio award for best music adaptation.

Perhaps inspired by such success, United continued to produce animated commercials for the next several years—each one more fanciful than the next. "Dragon" ◐ premiered during the 2006 Super Bowl as the company prepared to emerge from bankruptcy protection. It depicts a child's dream wherein his father's business trip transforms into an incredible adventure. Created with intricate paper cutouts and stop-motion filming, the father travels on the wings of a giant white bird to a table full of noble knights in a dark forest. With tidbits of the stride theme filtering into the fantasy-movie-inspired soundtrack, a battle commences between the men and a pack of fire-breathing fairytale dragons. Victorious, the father appears atop a majestic throne accompanied by the climax of the love theme [R. 31-4] before the bird returns him home to his awaiting son.

A journey of a different sort, but no less spectacular, takes place in the 2008 commercial "Sea Orchestra" ◐, which ran during the Olympic Games in Beijing. It was commissioned by Barrie D'Rozario Murphy—a startup agency founded by former Fallon executives—and featured music by Trivers Myers. The commercial composition duo of John Trivers and Elizabeth Myers previously had created arrangements of *Rhapsody in Blue* for "Interview," "A Life," and "Dragon."[35] At the outset of the advertisement, an orchestra is heard tuning up as a reef inhabited by a bevy of animated sea creatures emerges from below the surface of the ocean. A crustacean conductor gives the downbeat, and a piano glissando ushers in the reprise of the love theme [R. 34] performed initially by a herd of seahorses bowing themselves as if they were violins before transitioning four bars later to a group of trumpet fish. The octopus pianist plays a bed of mussels while a cheerful orca pats its belly like a timpani. Trivers Myers expanded Grofé's symphonic arrangement to highlight the visuals at hand. Violins and timpani were added to accompany the seahorses and orca, providing a musical texture as layered as the animation on the screen. Likewise, Trivers Myers added chimes to highlight another moment in the commercial where starfish bounce off of suspended stingrays. Following the climatic, flutter-tongued dominant thirteen chord [R. 37-2], the *Rhapsody* arrangement cuts to the *grandioso* finale [R. 39]. The camera draws back horizontally from the triumphant reef to capture the shadow of a jetliner passing overhead as Robert Redford announces: "Crossing the ocean will never be the same." The commercial ends before the final cadence of the piece, sonically suggesting that the journey carries on.

Trivers Myers took a more modest musical approach to "Heart," ◑ another advertisement from the 2008 campaign. Directed by Jamie Caliri, who created the "Dragon" commercial two years earlier, the stop-motion animated "Heart" spot begins as a man and woman say their goodbyes at the airport. The woman removes a cutout in the shape of a heart from her chest and slips it into the man's pocket. The heart-shaped hole remains visible as she travels away, makes a business presentation, and then does a bit of sightseeing. She encounters a small sparrow, which flies through the opening and ushers in the stride theme of the *Rhapsody* and her return home. The two-piano arrangement prepared by Trivers Myers represents the ability of the couple to function independently yet maintain a harmonious connection. Furthering this notion, United called on high-profile musicians Herbie Hancock and Lang Lang to record the arrangement. The African-American jazz pianist and the Chinese classical pianist had performed a six-minute version of the *Rhapsody* on the Grammy Awards earlier that year and would soon embark on a worldwide tour together. Their collaboration highlighted the fusion of jazz and classical inherent in the *Rhapsody*, while reestablishing the cultural melting-pot ideals long associated with the piece. While an oversimplification of the concept, such a fusion worked wonderfully as a marketing tactic as the airline actively sought out opportunities to consolidate its operations and expand its presence in the international marketplace.[36]

With the ultimate merger of United and Continental Airlines in 2010—a sort of modern-day corporate melting pot—the future of the *Rhapsody*'s association with the company once again seemed uncertain.[37] However, new commercials, beginning with the 2012 Summer Olympic Games and extending into recent spots promoting both the customization of its long-range aircraft and wireless Internet capabilities, have revived the connection between United and *Rhapsody in Blue*. In December 2013, United posted a video to its YouTube channel, which soon received heavy rotation on the seatback video monitors of its aircraft ◉. It begins with Jeff Smisek, chairman, president, and CEO of the company, affirming, "When our customers hear *Rhapsody in Blue*, they think of United. And you'll be hearing a lot more of it with this new recording made especially for us by the London Symphony Orchestra."[38] By highlighting the exclusivity of the recording as "especially" for United by one of the most illustrious ensembles in the world, the company has re-staked its claim on the *Rhapsody* not as an American anthem but as a global one.

RHAPSODY AMBIANCE

For all of the exposure generated by United Airlines' commercial advertising, the arrangement of *Rhapsody in Blue* heard by its greatest number of customers is played in a neon-lit tunnel at O'Hare International Airport. United has served approximately thirty million passengers annually at O'Hare since 2000.[39] Conservatively speaking, more than half a trillion travelers have passed through its concourses since it completed its five hundred million dollar "Terminal of Tomorrow" in 1987—the same year United began to use the *Rhapsody* in its commercials. A 744-foot long underground corridor connects the B and C concourses and is one of the most striking—and controversial—features of the building. With its near constant presence in the space for more than twenty-five years, it seems safe to say that this arrangement of the *Rhapsody* is the single most encountered version of the piece ever, regardless of whether or not all those who traverse the passageway are even aware of the music.

To distract passengers from the fact that they are effectively in a tunnel under the airport's busy taxiway, the airline commissioned a lumetric sculpture for the ceiling. Titled "Sky's the Limit" and created by artist Michael Hayden, the installation consists of more than 400 neon-light tubes in an array of colors that run the length of the tunnel—more than one mile of neon in total ◉. As travelers descend escalators to the underground passageway, the sculpture unfolds before them, first at eye level and then above them as they continue downward to the floor of the tunnel. More than 23,000 square feet of mirrors adorn the ceiling above the sculpture, providing an extra level of dimensionality. Passengers first enter the cool zone, consisting of curved neon in calm colors. Vertically oriented white waves transition to more horizontally positioned curves of purple and then turquoise. Never static, each colored set of neon flashes, brightens, or dims in sequence, beckoning people toward the moving walkways in front of them. Above the first 350-foot conveyor belt, the colors transition from dark green to light, then yellow and white as the neon tubes dissipate into seemingly random squiggles. Here, in the middle of the tunnel, the hot zone begins: neon shaped into diamonds with sharp angles and a warmer color palette consisting of oranges and reds that become purple at the very center. From the middle of the tunnel, expanding outward to either end, the sculpture offers a mirror image of itself. As travelers step onto the second moving walkway, they pass through a mirror image of the cool zone into which they initially descended.

Although an arrangement of *Rhapsody in Blue* has served as the sonic accompaniment to this visual odyssey for more than a quarter-century, this was not the music originally commissioned for the space. At the suggestion of artist Michael Hayden, composer and former Los Angeles Philharmonic percussionist William Kraft provided the original environmental music that accompanied the neon installation. Just like the sculpture, the music was presented in two distinct zones through forty-eight speakers mounted into the ceiling. As travelers passed from the cool to the hot sections of the space, the music became liveliest at the center. A United executive described the music as "an incredible winner," noting that passengers were "thoroughly enchanted" by the experience. However, a series of scathing articles by *Chicago Tribune* columnist Bob Greene presented evidence to the contrary. He quoted United employees describing the music as a "funeral march" or inducing a "bad drug trip." They observed passengers moving through the space "in a daze. . . like they entered the Twilight Zone."[40] Greene even went so far as to suggest that the music was responsible for elderly people falling off the walkway's end. When asked about the situation in a 1988 interview, Kraft attributed the demise of his music to improper volume levels and declared, "My statement to [United] is that art is not to be judged by the Nielsen ratings."[41] But in the corporate and competitive world of United—then in the midst of its "rededicated" advertising campaign—the last thing it needed was bad press. The airline scrapped the music and fired the executive who had approved it.

United decided to replace the music with *Rhapsody in Blue* and, as in its television commercials, desired an arrangement suitable to the neon visuals already a part of the tunnel. The company wanted a high-tech sound that contributed to a pleasing experience but did not draw attention to itself. The goal was for passengers to feel relaxation in the initial cool zone, a bit more motion in the hot zone at the center, and a renewed sense of relaxation as they entered the second cool zone and exited the space. To achieve this effect, they turned to Gary Fry, a principal composer for Com/ Track Incorporated. Fry had provided underscoring for several United Airlines radio spots during the pre-*Rhapsody in Blue* era and would later develop music for national campaigns such as "There's More For Your Life at Sears" and McDonald's "Food, Folks, and Fun."

The Leo Burnett advertising agency contacted Fry not for his jingle-creating abilities but for his reputation as a sound designer fluent in the latest digital sampling and synthesizer technologies. His approach to sound design is to "tear apart music into its basic elements and recombine them in unusual and sometimes random ways to create an overall texture and atmosphere."[42] In preparation for his arrangement, he went to experience the tunnel space at O'Hare Airport for himself. He noted the separate visual and sound zones as well as the amount of time it took to traverse the tunnel while standing on the moving walkways: four and a half minutes. Respecting that timeframe, Fry decided that each of the four central *Rhapsody* themes selected for inclusion should be experienced during that span of time. Since United had requested thirty minutes of non-repeating music but provided him with only a brief period of time in which to complete it, he employed the looping capabilities of his Synclavier—a digital music workstation that formed the centerpiece of his production studio. Each loop utilized a different synthesized instrument and lasted for a duration ranging from ninety seconds to nine minutes.

Taking advantage of the existing speaker setup, Fry created two separate movements—"Curves" and "Angles"—for the respective cool and hot zones in an arrangement titled *Rhapsody Ambiance*. Travelers entering the space from either end of the tunnel experience "Curves" first (see figure 6.5). Two brief *Rhapsody* fragments form the melodic content of this movement: the first eight notes of the love theme and the thirteen-note tag motif. These familiar phrases appear on the first loop of the arrangement on an acoustic piano. The other loops include harmonic and rhythmic support through the introduction of synthesized strings, bells, and piano in addition to the sounds of a struck wine glass and a suspended cymbal. The glass and cymbal were not preexisting sounds on the Synclavier, but recorded into the system through its advanced sampling capabilities. The electronic instrumentation, in Fry's words, contributed "an open, airy, light and bright atmosphere to the environment."[43] "Angles" uses two additional melodies from the *Rhapsody*: the first four bars each of the ritornello and stride themes (see figure 6.6). These melodic phrases also appear in the first loop on the acoustic piano, but unlike the motifs heard in "Curves," these themes receive a greater

Figure 6.5
Excerpt from "Curves" from *Rhapsody Ambiance* with tag motif in top staff line. Used by permission of Gary Fry.

degree of fragmentation and overlap. The other loops of "Angles" feature an electric koto, two harps, a synthetic piano, and a sampled bell tree. These digitally rendered plectrum instruments, whose acoustic counterparts are all struck to produce sound, lend the movement a sharper, more

Figure 6.6
Excerpt from "Angles" from *Rhapsody Ambiance* with stride theme in top staff line. Used by permission of Gary Fry.

pointillist sensibility—one that aligns with the busier visual stimuli of the hot zone that it accompanies.

Because of the sonic overlap between the hot and cool zones, travelers experience no distinct moment when the audio for one movement ends and another begins. For this reason, the two movements of *Rhapsody Ambiance* needed enough common elements to make the transition from "Curves" to "Angles" as seamless as possible. To provide harmonic continuity, Fry constructed both movements around the C overtone series, which contains not only the flattened seventh degree, but also additional jazz extensions such as the ninth and the flat thirteenth. This uniform foundation supports the various blues-inflected melodic fragments from the *Rhapsody*. Consistency between the movements also occurs in the tempo of each: "Angles" is exactly twice as fast as "Curves," one hundred twenty versus sixty beats per minute—roughly that of a march tempo and the human heart at rest, respectively. The changes in tempo—slow, fast, slow—support the experiential goal of motion through the space.

Fry's replacement music for the O'Hare tunnel received a positive initial response, but its reception has faded over time, just like the neon sculpture itself. In a column titled "United Airlines Faces the Music," Bob Greene declared an immodest victory following the initial adoption of *Rhapsody Ambiance*. He noted that even though the arrangement was created using synthesizers, it was "made to sound like real, pleasant music."[44] A spokesperson for United said that feedback from employees was "very upbeat." Passengers felt the same way. Whenever travelers wrote to United's corporate headquarters praising the music, the airline mailed them a compact disc of the arrangement. However, some ten years after the installation, a reporter described a scene reminiscent of Greene's initial critique: passengers moving through the tunnel with the same expression on their faces, "unemotional, drained of feeling, as if suspended in animation." Rather than offering passengers an escape from the airport experience, he called it "a perfectly devised exaggeration and apotheosis of that experience."[45] At the turn of the twenty-first century, theorist Matthew Butterfield further extended such an assessment, calling the music a "sonic adornment conditioning movement through the corporate world of United Airlines."[46] Devoid of the typical advertising that lines the walls of airport terminals, piping in the sonic signifier of United Airlines maintains the musical capital long ago established by the airline.

As someone with nearly four decades of commercial advertising experience, *Rhapsody Ambiance* arranger Gary Fry is surprised that United still uses the piece—both in the tunnel and in its commercials. It is "very smart, but it is very rare in contemporary American business that they do not just revolve into new advertising campaigns with a totally different feel every few months."[47] When the airline first began to use *Rhapsody in Blue*, this may well have been the plan, particularly following the mixed reception of its initial commercial. But in ways similar to those of musicians like Duke Ellington and Larry Adler, the variable arrangement of the *Rhapsody* has allowed the company to adapt to changing markets and audience expectations. Originally, United selected the piece for its associative values, meanings closely connected to representations of the piece through film: the upwardly mobile tropes long associated with biographical depictions of Gershwin. However, as copious arrangements of the *Rhapsody* encountered through the commercial advertising of United Airlines make clear—only a few of many possible examples have been considered here—such associations have not been absolute over time.

The now-global company has arranged the *Rhapsody* to accompany a wide range of narratives about life in America, from job interviews to business meetings, from childhood fantasies to retirement expeditions, and all manner of personal and professional relationships. Therein lies the brilliance of selecting *Rhapsody in Blue* as a musical icon for United Airlines in the first place. Although advertising executives at Burnett or United were probably unaware of it at the time, the musical and conceptual adaptability of the piece has allowed it to become the most successful corporate musical campaign of all time. In 1988, television critic Tom Shales lamented, "Children will henceforth think of [*Rhapsody in Blue*] not as Gershwin's masterwork but as the song of the friendly skies."[48] While in many respects, Shales's concern has become a reality, United Airlines has simultaneously opened up conceptions of the *Rhapsody* beyond the consensus view of the piece as encountered in narrative arrangements of it in film and television from the past through the present—representations that continue to provide overly simplified representations of the *Rhapsody*, George Gershwin, and American culture more broadly. But as arrangements of *Rhapsody in Blue* considered over the course of this book have illuminated, narratives surrounding the piece and its "composer" are far from straightforward.

Epilogue

Arranging on Multiple Levels

If I were an Asian or a European, suddenly set down by an aeroplane on this soil and listening with fresh ear to the American chorus of sounds I should say that American life is nervous, hurried, syncopated, ever *accelerando*, and slightly vulgar.

—George Gershwin (1926)

At some point in January 1924, George Gershwin handed the first pages of *Rhapsody in Blue* to Ferde Grofé, and the rest, as they say, is history. Or is it? David Schiff observed in the late 1990s that *Rhapsody in Blue* "evolved from a lively experiment to a national icon and then a dutifully worshiped relic."[1] Yet the *Rhapsody* should not be considered as a fixed entity emerging from a distant past. Its history materializes only through the study of arrangements. In this way, the piece continues to live an active and, at times, surprising life, allowing for investigations into the development of American identities, musical and nonmusical alike, over the course of the twentieth century and into the present. This epilogue uses one concluding example, prepared in 2005 by Bay Area percussionist, composer, ethnomusicologist, and bandleader Anthony Brown, to highlight several of the themes running throughout this book.

When Anthony Brown watched the *Rhapsody* segment of *Fantasia 2000* with his then-nine-year-old daughter, he thought: "These aren't quite the images I associate with this piece."[2] He had previously reinterpreted works by Thelonious Monk and Duke Ellington, including the latter's *Far East Suite*, for which he received a Grammy nomination. Likewise, Brown saw in *Rhapsody in Blue* "an opportunity to have twenty-first-century America reflected in something that we all identify as American."[3] He named his subsequent recomposition of the piece *American Rhapsodies*, which he prepared for his Asian American Orchestra. On the surface, the title references Gershwin's reported working title for the piece, *American Rhapsody*.[4] But on a deeper level, Brown's pluralized title encapsulates a central tenet of this book: No single interpretation of *Rhapsody in Blue* captures the full essence of the piece. Rather, the accumulation of arrangements over the course of the past ninety years has shaped the iconic status of both the *Rhapsody* and George Gershwin. Beyond its title, however, *American Rhapsodies* plays with the concept of arranging on multiple levels.

Anthony Brown's musical outlook lies very much in his own ethnic makeup. "It informs everything I do," he once stated.[5] The son of an African-American serviceman with South Carolina Choctaw ancestry and a woman from Tokyo, Brown—a self-described army brat—grew up multiracial in cities around the world.[6] He has been involved with the Asian-American jazz movement since its origins in San Francisco during the 1980s. Asian-American jazz emerged as an artistic outlet for the growing awareness of the population's longstanding presence and ongoing struggles. Brown's musical treatment of *Rhapsody in Blue* merges the spirit of this movement with his personal background and experience. In a radio interview with KQED's Nina Thorsen, he observed that, with the *Rhapsody*, Gershwin "was primarily presenting a very progressive view of race relations by combining the musical languages he knew best, the European and African American. I thought. . . why not bring in the entire demography of America and have it reflected in what I would consider America's vernacular anthem."[7]

Brown gives voice to this demography in his arrangement through the introduction of a range of musical instruments beyond those encountered in Grofé's various renditions of *Rhapsody in Blue*. First, Brown includes the electric guitar and the drum set, which he considers "the heart and soul of American popular music."[8] Similar to arrangements performed by Duke Ellington and Larry Adler, Brown eliminates the piano's presence entirely and replaces many of the cadenzas with electric guitar solos. As he stated in his KQED interview, "Gershwin himself as a kid would have been noodling around on the piano in the way that, you know, now a kid would be noodling on a guitar out in the garage."[9] Brown also uses pan-Asian instruments like the Chinese yangqin (hammered dulcimer) and the Japanese shakuhachi (end-blown flute). Additionally, he includes Caribbean percussion such as the Cuban cajón (box drum) and steel pans from Trinidad and Tobago.

These varied instruments contribute to the sonic modernization and diversification of the *Rhapsody* at the same time that they allow Brown to arrange his place within American concert jazz traditions. Brown considers his version of the *Rhapsody* a "wellspring for the fifth stream."[10] His concept of the "fifth stream" originates from "third-stream music," a term coined by composer Gunther Schuller in 1957 to describe a genre of music combining, but distinct from, jazz and classical mainstreams. To distinguish third-stream music from the so-called symphonic jazz of Gershwin, Schuller highlighted improvisation as an integral component. The fifth stream, according to Brown, proffers "a new musical language blending instruments, conventions and sensibilities of world and popular music into the third stream."[11]

Each of the six individual movements of Brown's *American Rhapsodies* operates within a fifth-stream consciousness. In "Exposition," Asian birdcalls are heard before the listener encounters the opening clarinet glissando. The dizi, a traditional Chinese flute, provides the lead chirps with two Japanese flutes, a fue and a shakuhachi, responding and filling out the sonic space. The movement unfolds as might be expected by those familiar with Grofé's arrangement for the Paul Whiteman Orchestra, but with slight modifications. Over the course of the initial presentation of the ritornello, the ride cymbal plays steady yet slightly swinging quarter notes. A pair of Chinese hammered dulcimers replace the piano's initial presentation of the tag motif [R. 2+3], and an electric guitar supplants the arpeggiated figures of the first piano cadenza [R. 4+6]. In a sequence that might be termed "East Meets West," the guitar and dulcimers begin to alternate phrases, coming together for the first full statement of the ritornello theme [R. 5-3] where they are joined by the bass and percussion reasserting a swing sensibility. As the theme unfolds, the dulcimers play the melody straight while the guitar improvises around them, eventually completely taking over the melodic theme.

Having transitioned from the general feel of the original Grofé jazz band arrangement and through an Afro-Cuban rendition of the train theme in a subsequent movement titled "Rumba," Brown's arrangement arrives at its farthest point of departure in a section titled "Gagaku" (see figure 7.1). This ancient form of Japanese imperial court music is a style that Brown used in a 1996 composition titled *E.O. 9066*, named after the executive order issued by President Franklin Roosevelt in 1942 that resulted in the internment of more than 120,000 people of Japanese ancestry during World War II. Brown incorporated *gagaku* into this earlier work because it is a "voice that's over a thousand years old. . . with pacing that is very measured and very stable."[12] Brown uses *gagaku* in his arrangement of the *Rhapsody*

Figure 7.1
Manuscript copy of "Gagaku" from *American Rhapsodies* based loosely on the shuffle theme. Used by permission of Anthony Brown.

to achieve a similar contemplative effect. The movement opens with the stroke of a gong and an overlay of Chinese dulcimers and a waterphone. Because no set meter exists in *gagaku*, the length of phrases is set by the lead instrument. Here the shakuhachi freely presents the stride theme over the continuous harmonic foundation of a pair of Chinese shengs (free-reed mouth-organ). Gradually, additional Western instruments, including the clarinet and a muted trumpet, offer their own presentations of the theme.

Although "Gagaku" is the shortest movement in Brown's arrangement, its freedom from the rhythmic emphasis of the rest of the piece gives the listener an opportunity to reflect on the musical representation at hand. It offers a rejoinder to Gershwin's impression of American life as it might be described by a person of Asian heritage "suddenly set down. . . on this soil."[13] It also provides a more nuanced Asian treatment of the *Rhapsody* than that of United Airlines.

The rest of the arrangement introduces the remaining *Rhapsody in Blue* themes, each filtered through Brown's multicultural musical lens. The sounds of imperial Japan fade into the distance, replaced by an adagio shuffle drumbeat that serves as the background for a blues guitar presentation of the stride theme in "Scherzando." In the next movement, "Andantino/ Adagio," an erhu (two-string fiddle) and two Chinese dulcimers present the love theme. The countermelody emerges from a set of Trinidadian steel pans. Japanese percussion and a train whistle usher in the last movement titled "Taiko Trane/Finale," which quotes a portion of *Rhapsody in Blue* as recorded by Duke Ellington in 1963—an arrangement of an arrangement of an arrangement.

In the twenty-first century, *Rhapsody in Blue* remains an infinitely recursive space for developing, exploring, and promoting identities. To this end, Anthony Brown's *American Rhapsodies* draws out three overlapping themes that have emerged from arrangements of the *Rhapsody* considered in this book. First, *Rhapsody in Blue* serves as an outlet for individuals to arrange their personal and professional identities within American music and American culture more broadly. Leonard Bernstein arranged the *Rhapsody* as means of confronting his status as an American-born, homosexual conductor and composer in midcentury classical performance. Although a business and not an individual, United Airlines has constructed its corporate identity around the piece for nearly three decades. In *American Rhapsodies*, Brown arranges aspects of his multiethnic heritage in each movement, providing a musical montage reflecting the broader demographics of his personal experience living in the Bay Area after the turn of the millennium. Simultaneously, as with arrangements performed by Bernstein and Larry Adler, Brown's identity as a performer—a multi-instrumental percussionist, dynamic bandleader, and activist musician—takes center stage in *American Rhapsodies*.

Second, *Rhapsody in Blue* provides an outlet for individuals to arrange themselves within the course of American music history. Situating *American Rhapsodies* within the "fifth stream," Brown locates himself within the broad continuum of concert jazz, not unlike Duke Ellington, Ferde Grofé, and George Gershwin before him. Brown's explicit reference to Ellington's 1963 recording of the *Rhapsody* makes such arrangement unmistakable. The self-awareness of musicians operating within a bigger history in which Gershwin looms large is also apparent in Bernstein's "A Nice Gershwin Tune" and Adler's anecdotal efforts to revive his career in the United States. In each of these examples, musical arrangements become biographical ones as well.

Arranging Gershwin—both his life and legacy—stands as the third overarching theme of this book to emerge from Brown's arrangement. Gershwin said of *Rhapsody in Blue* that he "heard it as a sort of musical kaleidoscope of America—of our vast melting pot."[14] Brown's observation that Gershwin presented "a very progressive view of race relations" through a merger of African-American and European musical traditions echoes the "melting pot" ideals promulgated in descriptions and interpretations of *Rhapsody in Blue* from the earliest moments. Through his arrangement, Brown imbues Gershwin's black and white kaleidoscopic aesthetics with an all-encompassing spectrum of cultural colors—black, white, brown, yellow, and red—all blending together to form a deep shade of blue. In this way, Brown's arrangement of *Rhapsody in Blue* connects to one of America's most popular and enduring myths. Gershwin's celebrated fusion of popular and classical traditions, black and white musical cultures, highbrow and lowbrow performance, all endear this piece to the myth of the melting pot. It is important to remember, however, that Gershwin's commentary ultimately emerges from the same passage of Isaac Goldberg's biography that features several interventions by Goldberg himself about the origins of the *Rhapsody*.[15] Is Brown's vision of the *Rhapsody* ultimately an extension of Gershwin's or Goldberg's? Or does his impulse stem from the inherent malleability of the *Rhapsody* and, by extension, George Gershwin, as witnessed by countless others over the past ninety years?

Like a rhapsody itself, the story of the *Rhapsody in Blue* continually unfolds. It moves from one musician, venue, or conception to the next without formal design or intent, all the while revealing new perspectives on what has come before and providing a platform for understanding future encounters with the piece. A different collection of arrangements than those considered here might result in different themes, raise different concerns, and provide alternate narratives about the past and the present. Nonetheless, the ultimate point of approaching the *Rhapsody* through arrangements would remain much the same. Shifting emphasis away from a centralized composer and text does not rescind the iconic status of either Gershwin or *Rhapsody in Blue*. Rather, it provides insight into why their elevated standing persists in American culture.

ENDNOTES

INTRODUCTION

1. *I Won't Play*, Crane Wilbur, dir., Warner Brothers Pictures, 1944.
2. Since few readers will have access to the arrangements described and analyzed within this book, references to specific passages, measure numbers, or rehearsal letters include a bracketed correspondence to their respective locations in the readily available orchestral or two-piano/four-hands scores (Alfred Music M00013 and 31859). Here, for example, R. 4+1 refers to one bar after rehearsal number 4. Likewise, R. 6-4 refers to four bars before rehearsal number 6.
3. An overview of existing approaches to Liszt's arrangements as well as new modes of integrating such music into formations of Liszt and the construction of social and music history music in the nineteenth century appears in Kregor, *Liszt as Transcriber*.
4. Magee, "Fletcher Henderson," 63.
5. Eco, *Role of the Reader*, 56.
6. Goldberg, *George Gershwin*, 162.
7. Ira Gershwin to Edward Jablonski, December 18, 1941, Box 65, Folder 26, GC.
8. Wierzbicki, "The Hollywood Career of Gershwin's *Second Rhapsody*," 134, note 3.
9. Pollack, *George Gershwin*, 314; Columbia ML-5413, recorded June 1959.
10. Goehr, *Imaginary Museum of Musical Works*, 8.
11. Fourteen individual forklift drivers, cued by radio headsets and guided only by taped lines on the floor beneath them, moved the risers into position.
12. *Opening Ceremonies of the Games of the 23rd Olympiad*, ABC national broadcast, July 28, 1984.
13. Schiff, *Rhapsody in Blue*, 6.
14. Ibid., frontispiece.
15. Ibid., 10–25.
16. David Schiff, pers. comm., December 3, 2013.
17. See, for example, Howland, *Ellington Uptown*; Rapport, "Bill Finegan's Gershwin Arrangements"; and Crawford and Hamberlin, *Introduction to America's Music*.
18. Deleuze and Guattari, *A Thousand Plateaus*, 158. Their conception of plateaus draws on Gregory Bateson's work on Balinese culture. See Bateson, *Steps to an Ecology of Mind*, 107–127.
19. See, for example, Ewen, *Journey to Greatness*, 114–115; Jablonski and Stewart, *The Gershwin Years*, 90–91; Schwartz, *Gershwin*, 92; Pollack, *George Gershwin*, 296.

CHAPTER 1

1. George Gershwin, letter to J. C. Rosenthal, August 18, 1928, ASCAP, New York City. Punctuation and spelling in original.
2. "Whiteman Judges Named: Committee Will Decide 'What Is American Music,'" *New York Tribune*, January 4, 1924: 11. Reprinted in Wyatt and Johnson, *George Gershwin Reader*, 44–45.
3. See Shirley, "George Gershwin: Yes, the Sounds as Well as the Tunes Are His," in ibid., 301–308.
4. Jablonski, *Gershwin*, 66. See also Rayno, *Paul Whiteman*, 77–78.
5. Goldberg, *George Gershwin*, 153.
6. Alicia Zizzo, ed., *The Annotated Rhapsody in Blue* (Secaucus, NJ: Warner Brothers, 1996), 2.
7. Pollack, *George Gershwin*, 301.
8. Schwartz, *Gershwin*, 80.
9. Rayno, *Paul Whiteman*, 78.
10. Fair-copy holograph for *Rhapsody in Blue*, Box 201, FGC. I am deeply indebted to Ray White, senior music specialist at the Library of Congress for bringing this manuscript and its peculiarities to my attention.
11. Goldberg, *George Gershwin*, 142.
12. Howland, "Jazz Rhapsodies," 486–493.
13. Bañagale, *"Rhapsodies in Blue,"* 49–118.
14. Microfilm, MUSIC 1350, GC.
15. Farrington, "Ferde Grofe," 66, note 2. Ferde Grofé Jr. suggests that the lawsuit was specifically directed at his father and that the manuscript was donated to the Library of Congress to fend off such litigation (pers. comm., August 3, 2012).
16. Jeff Sultanof, ed., *Rhapsody in Blue: Commemorative Facsimile Edition* (Secaucus, NJ: Warner Brothers, 1987).
17. Jablonski, *Gershwin*, 71; Neimoyer, 293.
18. Ray White, pers. comm., August 8, 2008.
19. One such example appears on page thirty of the manuscript where Gershwin originally indicated "Bells/Celeste." Grofé used the latter in his initial arrangement for Whiteman, but opted for the former in his theatre- and symphonic-orchestra versions.
20. Hyland, 58.
21. George Gershwin, "Making Music," *Sunday World Magazine*, May 4, 1930. Reproduced in Wyatt and Johnson, *George Gershwin Reader*, 135–136. For more on Gershwin's working methods, see Pollack, *George Gershwin*, 176; Jablonski, *Gershwin*, 285.
22. Tape 115, Ferde Grofé Audio Collection, Warren D. Allen Music Library, Florida State University, Tallahassee, FL. Quoted in Rayno, *Paul Whiteman*, 78.
23. Grofé's indication to "copy piano solo part 45 bars" at this point reveals another moment when Gershwin took a break from composing the *Rhapsody*.
24. Magee, *Uncrowned King of Swing*, 40.
25. Farrington, "Grofé, Ferde," *Grove Music Online, Oxford Music Online*, accessed July 26, 2010, http://www.oxfordmusiconline.com/subscriber/article/grove/music/42029.
26. Carl Engel, "Jazz: A Musical Discussion," *Atlantic Monthly* 130, no. 2 (August 1922), accessed July 26, 2010, http://www.theatlantic.com/past/docs/unbound/jazz/cengel.htm.

27. For more on Grofé's musical development prior to his work with Art Guerin, see Farrington, "Ferde Grofe," 5–17.
28. Ibid.,18.
29. Magee, "Revisiting Fletcher Henderson's 'Copenhagen,'" *Journal of the American Musicological Society* 48, no. 1 (1995): 42–66.
30. A detailed account of the period under consideration in this brief biographical paragraph appears in Rayno, *Paul Whiteman*, 32–54.
31. "Japanese Sandman" (recorded August 19, 1920) and "Whispering" (recorded August 23, 1920) were released on the same disc, Victor 18690. According to Rayno, this disc sold nearly two million copies within the first year, an almost unheard-of achievement given that million-copy sellers were rare. Rayno, *Paul Whiteman*, 448. This figure appears throughout the Whiteman literature, and like *Rhapsody in Blue*, as discussed in chapter 2, may have been inflated for the sake of self-promotion.
32. Pollack, *George Gershwin*, 89–91.
33. Ibid., 236–241.
34. Farrington, "Ferde Grofe," 28. Farrington references Tape 120, Ferde Grofé Audio Collection.
35. Magee models this approach in his work on the early arrangements of the Fletcher Henderson Orchestra, *Uncrowned King of Swing*, 7–8.
36. Osgood, *So This Is Jazz*, 169.
37. Ibid.
38. Ibid.
39. A copy of Bennett's "Do It Again" stock arrangement, published by Harms in 1922, resides in Box 47, FGC.
40. The "South Sea Isles" arrangement (Victor 18801, November 1921) integrates the refrain of "She's Just a Baby" into presentations of its own refrain. Likewise, "Drifting Along with the Tide" becomes an intermediary refrain in a song called "When Buddha Smiles" by Nacio Herb Brown (Victor 18839, February 1922). *The French Doll* was an adaptation of the French play *Jeunes filles de palaces* that ran for 120 performances. Only one other song was included: "When Eyes Meet Eyes (When Lips Meet Lips)" by Gus Edwards.
41. The published sheet music, stock arrangement, and recording are all in F major.
42. This fourth installment of White's annual *Scandals* opened on August 28, 1922, and ran for eighty-nine performances. Gershwin's *Blue Monday Blues*, sometimes considered to be his first opera, was unceremoniously dropped after the first performance. See Pollack, *George Gershwin*, 268–275.
43. The precise origins of this quotation remain unclear. Walter Rimler's *A Gershwin Companion* cites Kimball and Simon's *The Gershwins*, which provides no information beyond that it was "written on George's 25th birthday," which took place on September 26, 1923.
44. No holograph manuscript exists for "Stairway." A copyist's score can be found in Box 7, Folder 20, GC.
45. Though the 1922 score for "Stairway to Paradise" did not survive, Whiteman scholar Don Rayno has encountered several instances of this notation in the scores he examined from this period. Rayno, pers. comm., August 12, 2010.
46. Tape 114, Ferde Grofé Audio Collection. Quoted in Von Glahn, *Sounds of Place*, 324, note 132.
47. Goldberg, *George Gershwin*, 153.
48. Duke, "Gershwin, Schillinger, and Dukelsky: Some Reminiscences," *Musical Quarterly* 33 (1947), 107.

49. See, for example, Neimoyer, 128–179.
50. As noted previously, the instruments listed in the piano score at this point (clarinet, cello, and violin) were subsequent additions.
51. Quoted in Farrington, "Ferde Grofe," 64. Originally in William Roberts Tilford, "Carve Out Your Own Career: From a Conference with the Well-known Composer, Orchestral Arranger and Radio Conductor, Ferde Grofe," *Etude* 56, no. 7 (July 1938), 425.
52. Osgood, *So This Is Jazz*, 169.
53. Magee, *Uncrowned King of Swing*, 39–71.
54. For a consideration of Gershwin's Orientalist songs and their influence on his musical purview, see Bañagale, "An American in Chinatown."
55. Schiff, *Rhapsody in Blue*, 9, 11.
56. The precise date of this orchestral arrangement remains unknown. However, Grofé must have completed it before its performance by orchestras like the Boston Pops, which regularly featured the piece during the early 1930s.
57. For example, in measures 11–14 [R. 1 to R. 2-1], the bass clarinet and tenor saxophone both play the conclusion of the ritornello theme. Schiff, *Rhapsody in Blue*, 9.
58. Goldberg, *George Gershwin*, 153.
59. Gershwin, "Mr. Gershwin Replies to Mr. Kramer," 18; reproduced in Wyatt and Johnson, *George Gershwin Reader*, 98–100.

CHAPTER 2

1. Ewen, *Journey to Greatness*, 114. Emphasis added.
2. Ibid., 115. Emphasis added.
3. Ibid., 116.
4. Schiff, *Rhapsody in Blue*, 62; Pollack, *George Gershwin*, 304.
5. Record E 589226, CCC. The *Rhapsody in Blue* copyright deposit score is a ten-page solo-piano reduction of the piece, which consists of measures 1–105. Microfilm MUSIC 1350, GC.
6. Harms earned mechanical royalties in the amount of $0.02 per side for recordings. For the first ten years, the *Rhapsody* generally appeared abridged on two sides of a 12-inch, 78-rpm disc, earning Harms $0.04 per recording sold. Harms subtracted 10 percent from the total amount earned from the record companies; it remains unclear why this was the case. Gershwin then received 50 percent of that reduced figure.
7. Here and throughout the rest of the book, 2013 figures have been calculated using the Bureau of Labor Statistics Consumer Price Index inflation calculator. See http://www.bls.gov/data/inflation_calculator.htm.
8. Royalty statement, December 12, 1924, Box 114, GC.
9. Nauck, *American Record Labels*, xvii.
10. Account summary, February 25, 1933, Box 114, GC.
11. "Miscellaneous," *Gramophone*, October 1927, 26.
12. Goldberg titles his chapter on *Rhapsody in Blue* "Beyond the Dance" in *George Gershwin*, 136–167.
13. Record E 2982, CCC.
14. Royalty statement, March 31, 1925, Box 114, GC.
15. Harms did not provide an individual catalogue number for this edition, which received its copyright on November 9, 1927. Record E 675967, CCC.
16. The smaller electric-organ market would not emerge in the United States until the mid-1930s when the Hammond Organ Company released its Model A.

17. Gorn's arrangement also corrected a few of the errors found in the "original" publication, such as the E natural that should be an F natural in the bass on the final eighth beat of measure 66 [R. 6-6].

18. Ake, *Jazz Cultures*, 162.

19. *St. Louis Blues*, Dudley Murphy, dir., Paramount Pictures, 1929.

20. Davis, *Blues Legacies*, 60–61; Gabbard, *Jammin' at the Margins*, 161–162; Peter Stanfield, "An Excursion into the Lower Depths: Hollywood, Urban Primitivism, and *St. Louis Blues, 1929–1937*," *Cinema Journal* 41/2 (Winter 2002), 84–108.

21. Cripps, *Slow Fade to Black*, 204.

22. Davis, *Blues Legacies*, 9.

23. Pollack, 193.

24. Gabbard, *Jammin' at the Margins*, 10.

25. *King of Jazz*, John Murray Anderson, dir., Universal Pictures, 1930.

26. Donna Cassidy, "Jazz Representations and Early Twentieth-Century American Culture: Race, Ethnicity, and National Identity," in James Leggio, ed., *Music and Modern Art* (New York: Routledge, 2002), 204.

27. Paul Whiteman in *King of Jazz*.

28. Krin Gabbard associates this sequence with the "*faux* Africanist dancing of Josephine Baker" (Gabbard, *Jammin' at the Margins*, 13).

29. Rayno, *Paul Whiteman*, 242.

30. Schneider, *Gershwin Style*, xii.

31. The English-language biographies identified by Schneider are (in chronological order): Goldberg, *George Gershwin: A Study in American Music* (1931); Armitage, ed., *George Gershwin* (1938); Ewen, *The Story of George Gershwin* (1946) and *A Journey to Greatness: The Life and Music of George Gershwin* (1956); Armitage, *George Gershwin: Man and Legend* (1958); Jablonski and Stewart, *The Gershwin Years: George and Ira* (1958); Payne, *Gershwin* (1960); Rushmore, *The Life of George Gershwin* (1966); Kimball and Simon, *The Gershwins* (1973); Schwartz, *Gershwin: His Life and Music* (1973); DeSantis, *Portraits of Greatness: Gershwin* (1987); Jablonski, *Gershwin: A Biography* (1987); Kendall, *George Gershwin: A Biography* (1987); Rosenberg, *Fascinating Rhythm: The Collaboration of George and Ira Gershwin* (1991); Jablonski, *Gershwin Remembered* (1992); and Peyser, *The Memory of All That: The Life of George Gershwin* (1993).

32. Greenberg, *George Gershwin* (1998); Hyland, *George Gershwin: A New Biography* (2003); Leon, *Gershwin* (2004); Pollack, *George Gershwin: His Life and Works* (2007); Rimler, *George Gershwin: An Intimate Portrait* (2009); and Starr, *George Gershwin* (2011). A biography by Richard Crawford is forthcoming.

33. Wierzbicki, "Gershwin's *Second Rhapsody*," 134.

34. Wyatt and Johnson, eds., *Gershwin Reader*, 14.

35. Writing in 1929, Goldberg stated that "Lowell street was not the sunless thoroughfare that it is today. The elevated structure had not yet risen to blot out the light of the sky" ("A Boston Boyhood," 354). Goldberg here refers to the Lechmere Viaduct, which today remains as Boston's only surviving elevated subway. The street on which he lived is no longer in existence—in 1930, the famous Boston Garden was constructed on the site of his former neighborhood.

36. Goldberg, "A Boston Boyhood," 360.

37. Isaac Goldberg, "Three Moral Moments," *American Mercury* 19, no. 73 (January 1930): 102.

38. Rosenfeld, *An Hour With American Music*, 11.

39. Isaac Goldberg, "The Lower Learning," *American Mercury* 5, no. 18 (June 1925): 158.

40. Carol J. Oja raises this issue in "Gershwin and American Modernists of the 1920s," 658. Originally in Goldberg, "Aaron Copland and His Jazz," *American Mercury* 12, no. 45 (September 1927): 63. Emphasis added.
41. Paul Rosenfeld, "Musical Chronicle," *The Dial* 80, no. 2 (February 1926): 175.
42. Goldberg, "Aaron Copland and His Jazz," 64.
43. Letter from Aaron Copland to Isaac Goldberg, September 15, 1927, Isaac Goldberg Papers, MSS. & Archive Section, N.Y.P.L., New York. Underline original. Reprinted by permission of The Aaron Copland Fund for Music, Inc., copyright owner.
44. Isaac Goldberg, "In the World of Books," *American Freeman*, July 1929.
45. George Gershwin Letters to Isaac Goldberg (MS Thr 222), Harvard Theatre Collection, Houghton Library, Harvard University.
46. Jablonski and Stewart, *The Gershwin Years*, 311–312.
47. Goldberg, *George Gershwin*, 139.
48. Goldberg, "Music by Gershwin," April 1931, 25. Emphasis added.
49. Goldberg, *George Gershwin*, 139. Emphasis added.
50. Goldberg, "Music by Gershwin," April 1931, 25.
51. Goldberg, *George Gershwin*, 139. Emphasis added.
52. See, for example, Goldberg, *George Gershwin*, 4, 20, 27, 133, 182, 217; Goldberg, *Tin Pan Alley*, 32, 65, 103, 133, 147, 197.
53. Goldberg, *George Gershwin*, 3–42. Goldberg titled the first chapter of his Gershwin biography "A Young Man of Manhattan."
54. Pollack, *George Gershwin*, 701–702.
55. Cecil M. Smith, "Park Concert Pays Tribute to Gershwin," *Chicago Daily Tribune*, July 14, 1937.
56. Schiff, 62; Pollack, 526.
57. Publicity booklet for the film. Reproduced in Greenspan, "A Study in Hollywood Hagiography," in Schnieder, ed., *The New Gershwin Style*, 146.
58. Ibid., 150.
59. Ibid., 146.
60. Clifford Odets, *Rhapsody in Blue* Draft Screenplay, August 28, 1942, Box 68/Folder 5, GC, 129.
61. Ibid., 130–131.
62. Ibid., 131.
63. Howard Koch, *Rhapsody in Blue* Final Screenplay, June 16, 1943, Box 68/Folder 6, GC, 68.
64. Ibid., 68.
65. Odets, *Rhapsody in Blue* Draft Screenplay, 138.
66. Ibid., 139.

CHAPTER 3

1. During previous summers in Sharon, Bernstein produced and performed in productions of *Carmen* (1934), *The Mikado* (1935), and *H.M.S. Pinafore* (1936). See Burton, *Leonard Bernstein*, 22–24.
2. Burton, *Leonard Bernstein*, 38.
3. Schirmer's Harmony Tablet, Box 18/Folder 3, LBC, reverse cover.
4. Bernstein, "Unidentified Interview, Transcript 1/Lmal 3787," Box 15/Folder 89, LBC, 4. This unidentified transcript dates to approximately 1972, placing Bernstein in his mid-fifties.
5. See Burton, *Leonard Bernstein*, 38–39.

6. Bernstein, "Unidentified Interview," 6.

7. Such lamentations appear, for example, in "A Nice Gershwin Tune," as part of his remarks during a January 1959 CBS television broadcast titled "Jazz in Serious Music," during his commentary for a 1972 WBGH program on Gershwin, and in the preface to Charles Schwartz's 1973 Gershwin biography.

8. Bernstein, "Unidentified Interview," 13–14.

9. Burton, *Leonard Bernstein*, 291.

10. "What Is American Music?" on February 1, 1958; "What Is Orchestration?" on March 8, 1958; and "What Makes Music Symphonic?" on December 13, 1958.

11. Titled "Jazz in Serious Music," January 25, 1959; script reproduced in *The Infinite Variety of Music*, 49–64.

12. Letter from David M. Keiser to the New York Philharmonic Board of Directors, August 31, 1959, Box: Tours, Europe 1959/Folder: Papers of the President, NYP.

13. Leonard Bernstein and The Columbia Symphony [New York Philharmonic], *Rhapsody in Blue/An American in Paris*, Columbia ML-5413, 1959, LP.

14. Pollack, *George Gershwin*, 314.

15. For "galvanizing," see Smith, *Curious Listener's Guide*, 202; for "overwrought" see Jablonski and Stewart, *Gershwin Years*, 362; for "quintessential," see Barry Singer, "Sounds of Gershwin: A Record Guide," *New York Times*, August 30, 1998.

16. Leonard Bernstein, "A Nice Gershwin Tune," *Atlantic Monthly* (April 1955): 39–42.

17. Bernstein, "Why Don't You Run Upstairs and Write a Nice Gershwin Tune?" All subsequent citations reference this 1959 publication of the essay.

18. Ibid., 52.

19. Ibid., 57.

20. Ibid.

21. Ibid.

22. Pollack, *George Gershwin*, 314.

23. Schiff, *Rhapsody in Blue*, 67.

24. Starr, "Musings on 'Nice Gershwin Tunes,'" in Schneider, ed., *The Gershwin Style*, 96.

25. Bernstein, "Unidentified Interview," 8.

26. Adler, "'Classical Music for People Who Hate Classical Music,'" 303.

27. Ramin, "Interview," 24.

28. Ibid., 25.

29. *Rhapsody in Blue* [1927], Leonard Bernstein Score Collection, NYP. Underlining original.

30. Burton, *Leonard Bernstein*, 18.

31. Whiteman's 1924 and 1927 recordings cut a total of 103 measures from this portion of the *Rhapsody*, from R. 20-4 to R. 28-4.

32. Adler, "Classical Music for People Who Hate Classical Music," 301–302. The recording was part of Victor's Musical Masterpiece Series (Victor M-358; rereleased as RCA Camden CAL 304) and appeared on three ten-inch discs. According to Adler, the Pops made this recording on July 1, 1935, the same day they played the *Rhapsody* in concert. The next major recording of the *Rhapsody* did not appear until Oscar Levant's performance with Eugene Ormandy and the Philadelphia Orchestra in the late 1940s (Columbia MX251).

33. Ramin, "Interview," 37. This chord occurs at measure 404 in the solo-piano sheet music [R. 37-2]. Ramin could not place exactly when they attended this performance. Adler's data reveal that throughout the 1930s Sanromá performed the *Rhapsody* with the Boston Pops forty-seven times, thirty-four of which took place after the boys acquired the sheet music.

34. Bernstein, "Unidentified Interview," 6.

35. Schirmer's Harmony Tablet, Box 18/Folder 3, LBC, 1–17.

36. Bernstein uses letters "A" through "Q." These indications were added at the end of the process because they overlap other previously notated elements of the score, such as tempo markings.

37. The image is also available through the Library of Congress's online American Memory Project, accessed December 10, 2013, http://hdl.loc.gov/loc.music/lbphotos.42a026.

38. The manuscript calls for "W. B." or wood block, but the claves offer an appropriate substitute.

39. Because the arrangement is closely bound to Bernstein's knowledge of the solo-piano sheet music, all measure numbers in the following description refer to that score.

40. In both the two-piano and full-orchestra scores, the shuffle theme is heard much earlier, at measure 137 [R. 14].

41. Schiff, Rhapsody in Blue, 21, notes the "harmonic jugglery" of this passage. It is possible Bernstein recognized that such rapid chromatic alterations would prove difficult on the ukulele. The accordion, with its chromatic keyboard, is better suited for this passage.

42. Schiff, Rhapsody in Blue, 29, indicates that a move to G major for the love theme is suggested by the half cadence on D major at the end of the preceding cadenza. However, three of the four bars appearing immediately before the entrance of the love theme close on a B major chord (the other is a tritone substitute), effectively undermining the harmonic implications of the aforementioned half cadence.

43. Such an example occurs in "Cool," where Bernstein elides his use of the traditional ABAC Tin Pan Alley song form by applying this type of transition between the A and B, as well as the A and C sections. See also measures 98–102 and 153–157 of Tony's song "Something's Coming."

44. Ramin, "Interview," 25.

45. This performance took place under the musical direction of Judith Clurman and with the permission of the Bernstein and Gershwin estates, using a performing edition prepared by myself.

46. Christopher Isherwood, The World in the Evening (New York: Random House, 1954). Reproduced in Cleto, ed., Camp, 51.

47. Jack Babuscio, "The Cinema of Camp (AKA Camp and the Gay Sensibility)," Gay Sunshine Journal 35 (Winter 1978): 27. Reproduced in Cleto, ed., Camp, 126.

48. Seldes, Leonard Bernstein, 12.

49. See discussion of Mitropoulos and Copland in Hubbs, "Bernstein, Homophobia, Historiography," 30.

50. "Music: State Symphony Orchestra," Boston Herald, January 3, 1938. Bernstein Scrapbooks, Vol. IA, Box SB1, LBC.

51. Untitled clipping, Boston Post, January 3, 1938. Bernstein Scrapbooks, Vol. IA, Box SB1, LBC.

52. Burton, Leonard Bernstein, 48.

53. Hand-dated press release. Bernstein Scrapbooks, Vol. IA, Box SB1, LBC.

54. Charles Hamm, "Towards a New Reading of Gershwin," in Schneider, ed., The Gershwin Style, 12.

55. Schiff, Rhapsody in Blue, 67.

56. See ibid., 7–9, 67; see also Pollack, George Gershwin, 312.

57. Leonard Bernstein, "My Musical Childhood," unpublished interview with Humphrey Burton, September 15 1986, Box 99/Folder 1, LBC, 13–14. Burton indicates that this interview was carried out as the first stage of a joint BBC Unitel project in which Bernstein was to have explored the many influences on his musical makeup. The project was never completed.

58. Pollack, *George Gershwin*, 312. Regarding structure and form, see Neimoyer, "*Rhapsody in Blue*," and Starr, "Musings on 'Nice Gershwin Tunes.'"

59. Bernstein, "Why Don't You Run Upstairs," 60.

60. Harold Schonberg, "Philharmonic Back at Carnegie Hall," *New York Times*, May 21, 1976.

61. Bernstein, "Why Don't You Run Upstairs," 59–60.

62. The intertextuality goes deeper still as Wilde's line twists the words of Bassanio in William Shakespeare's *The Merchant of Venice*: "Do all men kill the things they do not love?" (Act 4, Scene 1).

63. Wilde, *The Ballad of Reading Gaol*.

64. Hubbs, "Bernstein, Homophobia, Historiography," 40.

65. Ibid., 25.

66. Although he featured music by American composers on twenty-two of twenty-five programs under his baton during his first year as music director of the Philharmonic, a full-page *New York Times* advertisement for this 1958–59 season emphasizes the programming of "works from the standard repertoire" (September 7, 1958). Highlighted are "outstanding events" including Handel's *Ode for St. Cecilia's Day*, Beethoven's Ninth Symphony, and Debussy's *Pélléas et Mélisande*. Additionally, during his weeks off from conducting, Bernstein brought in four guest conductors presenting concerts of music from different European countries. Thomas Schippers, Herbert Von Karajan, Sir John Barbirolli, and Dimitri Mitropoulos performed the music of Italy, Germany, England, and France, respectively. Bernstein carefully planned his concerts so that the work of an American composer was placed alongside a more familiar work from the standard orchestral repertoire. Such was the case with the first program of the season, which paired Charles Ives's Second Symphony with Beethoven's Seventh.

67. Leonard Bernstein, Thursday Evening Preview Script, December 11, 1958, Box 76/Folder 7, LBC.

68. Ibid. Underline original to the document.

69. Bernstein, "Why Don't You Run Upstairs," 60.

CHAPTER 4

1. Duke Ellington, "Forward," in Leonard Feather, *The New Edition of the Encyclopedia of Jazz* (New York: Horizon Press, 1960), 13.

2. Cohen, *Duke Ellington's America*, 333–334.

3. See, for example, Kevin Gains, "Duke Ellington, *Black, Brown, and Beige*, and the Cultural Politics of Race," in Ronald Radano and Philip Bohlman, eds., *Music and the Racial Imagination* (Chicago: University of Chicago Press, 2000), 585–602. Gains sees *Black, Brown, and Beige* as a "self-conscious construction of historically situated narratives of African-American group consciousness as part of a progressive, antiracist agenda during World War II" (587).

4. Duke Ellington, *Will Big Bands Ever Come Back?* Reprise 6168, 1963, LP.

5. Count Basie and His Orchestra, "One O'Clock Jump," Decca 1363, 1937, 78 rpm.

6. Schiff, *Rhapsody in Blue*, 69.

7. Howland, *Ellington Uptown*, 101.

8. See, for example, Howland's chapter "Ellingtonian Extended Composition and the Symphonic Jazz Model," in ibid., 143–199. Duke Ellington, "The Duke Steps Out," *Rhythm*, March 1931, 61. Reproduced in Tucker, ed., *The Duke Ellington Reader*, 50. Emphasis original.

9. Alain Locke introduced such concerns in his book *The New Negro and His Music*, which formed the basis for subsequent critiques of white/black concert jazz. Overviews of such discourse appear in Anderson, *Deep River*, and Gennari, *Blowin' Hot and Cool*. See also Howland, *Ellington Uptown*, 144–150.

10. Magee, *Uncrowned King of Swing*, 8. See also Krin Gabbard, "Introduction: The Jazz Canon and Its Consequences," and Jed Rasula, "The Media of Memory: The Seductive Menace of Records in Jazz History," in Gabbard, ed., *Jazz Among the Discourses*, 1–28, 134–162.

11. For example, the only public performance before May 1936 listed in Timner's *Ellingtonia* is a fall 1932 broadcast featuring the songs "When It's Sleepy Time Down South" and "Double Check Stomp." The most complete account of Ellington's appearances in New York clubs, on tour, and in the studio appears in Vail's two-volume *Duke's Diary*. However, the book provides infrequent details about specific pieces heard during live performances.

12. Box 306, DEC.

13. The only substantial investigation of this period appears in Tucker, *Ellington: The Early Years*. Tucker's thorough account of Ellington's career before his tenure at the Cotton Club provides some sense of what his live performances entailed; however, much of his musical discussion relies on recordings from the era.

14. Originally called the Hollywood Club, it changed its name in March 1925. For more on this period in the ensemble's history, see Tucker, *Ellington: The Early Years*, 96–118.

15. "The Washingtonians 'Set New England Dance Crazy,'" *Chicago Defender*, August 27, 1927. Reproduced in Tucker, ed., *Duke Ellington Reader*, 26.

16. Tucker, *Ellington: The Early Years*, 116.

17. "The Washingtonians 'Set New England Dance Crazy.'"

18. For more on this premiere performance, see Schiff, *Rhapsody in Blue*, 51–62.

19. Hasse, *Beyond Category*, 81.

20. An "Arranged by Bob Sylvester" stamp appears at the top of several parts for this arrangement. Count Basie recalled a series of performances in a theatre on the north side of Chicago in early 1941 where his band performed a special arrangement of *Rhapsody in Blue* by Bob Sylvester. See Basie, *Good Morning Blues*, 136. It remains possible that the arrangement played by Ellington formed the basis of Sylvester's later arrangement for Basie.

21. Tucker, *Ellington: The Early Years*, 111–113.

22. The Washingtonians, "Black and Tan Fantasy," Brunswick 3526, 1927, 78 rpm.

23. Duke Ellington and His Orchestra, "The Mooche," Okeh 8623, 1928, 78 rpm.

24. Critic Roger Pryor Dodge recalled an improvised-laden dance arrangement of the work performed by the Henderson Orchestra during the winter of 1924–25. Nothing from this particular arrangement survives. See Magee, *Uncrowned King of Swing*, 6.

25. Floyd G. Snelson, "Story of Duke Ellington's Rise to Kingship of Jazz Reads Like Fiction," *Pittsburgh Courier*, December 19, 1931. Reproduced in Tucker, ed., *Duke Ellington Reader*, 55. For discussion of this tour, as well as Ellington's role in reviving failing vaudeville houses during this time, see Cohen, *Duke Ellington's America*, 94–100.

26. One such occurrence took place in July 1931 in Cleveland. See Archie Bell, "Duke Ellington's Orchestra Draws Big Crowds," *Cleveland News*, July 8, 1931. Reproduced in Tucker, ed., *Duke Ellington Reader*, 52.

27. See, for example, Howard Brown, "Duke Ellington Adds Two New Men to Band," *Chicago Defender*, May 21, 1932. See also Hasse, *Beyond Category*, 158.

28. Stratemann, *Day by Day*, 51.

29. "The King of Jazz," *Pittsburgh Courier*, July 9, 1932. See also Vail, *Duke's Diary*, vol. 1, 61–63. Fredi Washington, who made her debut as a chorus girl in the all-black musical *Shuffle Along* (1921), married Ellington's newly added trombonist Lawrence Brown the following August. She had previously appeared with Ellington in the short film *Black and Tan* (1929). See Cheryl Black, "Looking White, Acting Black: Cast(e)ing Fredi Washington," *Theatre Survey* 45, no. 1 (May 2004): 19–40.

30. Bell, "Duke Ellington's Orchestra Draws Big Crowds," 53.

31. "Sophisticated Lady" stands as a contemporary example, which the ensemble recorded for the first time at an RCA-Victor session in New York on September 21, 1932, just a few months after this *Rhapsody* arrangement emerged. This particular recording (Matrix BS73559) remains unissued.

32. Howland, *Ellington Uptown*, 143–199.

33. Ibid., 147.

34. Duke Ellington and His Famous Orchestra, *Creole Rhapsody Parts 1 & 2*, Brunswick 6093, January 1931, 78 rpm; Duke Ellington and His Orchestra, *Creole Rhapsody Parts 1 & 2*, Victor 36049, June 1931, 78 rpm.

35. See A. J. Bishop, "Duke's *Creole Rhapsody*," *Jazz Monthly* (November 1963). Reproduced in Tucker, ed., *Duke Ellington Reader*, 349; Schuller, *Early Jazz*, 354; Schiff, *Rhapsody in Blue*, 77–79.

36. Scott DeVeaux, "Constructing the Jazz Tradition: Jazz Historiography," *Black American Literature Forum* 25, no. 3 (1991): 525.

37. See Baraka, *Blues People*.

38. For a nuanced and well-crafted discussion of music criticism in the 1960s, including a thoughtful analysis of Baraka among his contemporaries, see Gennari, *Blowin' Hot and Cool*, 251–298.

39. Eric Larrabee, "Jazz Notes," *Harper's Magazine* 225 (July 1962), 96.

40. Leonard, *Jazz and the White Americans*, 84.

41. Charles Champlin, liner notes for *Will Big Bands Ever Come Back?*

42. See, for example, Hajdu, *Lush Life*; Van de Leur, *Something to Live For*.

43. Champlin, liner notes.

44. Mark Tucker, liner notes for *Duke Ellington: The Reprise Studio Recordings* (Mosaic MD5-1931999), 8–9.

45. Ibid.

46. Box 306, DEC. David Berger prepared a transcription of the 1963 recording for Essentially Ellington 2004: The Ninth Annual Jazz at Lincoln Center High School Jazz Band Competition and Festival (Alfred 00-JLCM03004C).

47. The prepared arrangement ends four bars before what is heard on the recording. As indicated by the pencil addition of a final pitch on each part, this last chord, like the duration of the piano solos, was not selected until the recording session.

48. Champlin, liner notes.

49. Edward Morrow, "Duke Ellington on Gershwin's 'Porgy,'" *New Theatre* (1935). Reproduced in Tucker, ed., *Duke Ellington Reader*, 114–115.

50. Ibid. Emphasis original.

51. Woll, *Black Musical Theatre*, 171–175; Ray Allen and George P. Cunningham, "Cultural Uplift and Double-Conciousness: African American Responses to the 1935 Opera *Porgy and Bess*," *Musical Quarterly* 88, no. 3 (2005): 342–369.

52. See, for example, Franceschina, *Duke Ellington's Music for the Theatre*, 170; Furia, *Ira Gershwin*, 112; Peress, *Dvorak to Duke Ellington*, 76; Peretti, *Lift Every Voice*, 108; Swain, *The Broadway Musical*, 62.

53. Morrow, "Duke Ellington on Gershwin's 'Porgy,'" 115–116. Written and published by Shelton Brooks in 1913 as "I Wonder Where My Easy Rider's Gone?" the song to which Ellington refers was initially performed by Sophie Tucker. In 1924, Ma Rainey recorded a blues titled "See See Rider" with some of the same lyrics and a similar melody. As a twelve-bar blues with a similar melodic contour, "Easy Rider" loosely resembles the *Rhapsody*'s shuffle theme, although the two are separated by distinctly different intervallic content in their melodies.

CHAPTER 5

1. Elysa Gardner, "The Glory of Gershwin," *Rolling Stone* 700, January 26, 1995. Emphasis in original.

2. Margaret Case Harriman, "Profiles: Big-Time Urchin," *New Yorker*, July 18, 1942.

3. Leonard Feather, "Larry Adler: Still the Survivor," *Los Angeles Times*, October 17, 1982.

4. Adler, *It Ain't Necessarily So*, 49. Spelling and punctuation in original.

5. Linda Wertheimer, "Larry Adler," *All Things Considered*, National Public Radio, August 7, 2001.

6. "Boys Skip Harm Via Harmonicas," *Los Angeles Times*, June 15, 1926.

7. "Baltimore's Harmonica Star Seeks Foreign Fame," *Baltimore Evening Sun*, September 1934, Box 2, Folder 3, LAP.

8. "The New Cinema Offerings," *Washington Post*, November 21, 1931.

9. Edwin Schallert, "'Roman Scandals' in Brilliant Premiere," *Los Angeles Times*, November 29, 1933.

10. Letter from Adler, "Monday" [December 25, 1933], Box 1, Folder 4, LAP.

11. Philip K. Scheuer, "A Town Called Hollywood," *Los Angeles Times*, December 17, 1933.

12. Larry Adler, *Bolero*, Columbia 35515, 1935, 78 rpm.

13. Margaret Case Harriman, "Big-Time Urchin," *New Yorker*, July 18, 1942.

14. Letter from Adler, "Sunday" [January 1934], Box 1, Folder 4, LAP.

15. June Provines, "Front Views and Profiles" *Chicago Daily Tribune*, April 13, 1934.

16. Letter from Adler, "Wednesday" [July 4, 1934], Box 1, Folder 4, LAP.

17. Larry Adler, *Rhapsody in Blue*, Columbia 35513, 1935, 78 rpm.

18. Adler uses this phrase in his 1984 autobiography *It Ain't Necessarily So*, 67, which is borrowed from Stearns, *Jazz Dance*, 162. In addition to recording for Columbia, Adler cut several sides for a short-lived British label called Rex.

19. Letter from Adler, December 6, 1934, Box 1, Folder 1, LAP.

20. Letter from Adler, December 13, 1934, Box 1, Folder 1, LAP.

21. "Rhapsody in Blue, and Other Records," *Northern Dispatch*, July 6, 1935, Box 2, Folder 3, LAP.

22. Letter from Adler, December 8, 1934, Box 1, Folder 1, LAP.

23. Letter from Adler, January 17, 1939, Box 1, Folder 4, LAP.

24. Letter from Adler, January 27, 1939, Box 1, Folder 4, LAP.

25. Ibid. All punctuation and spelling in original.

26. Noel Straus, "Harmonica Solos Heard at Stadium," *New York Times*, August 10, 1941.
27. Ibid.
28. R. L., "Larry Adler Plays At Stadium Concert," *New York Times*, June 30, 1946.
29. Donald Steinfirst, "Larry Adler Soloist on Symphony Program," *Pittsburgh Post-Gazette*, January 7, 1947.
30. Scholar George Ferencz has contributed greatly to our understanding of Bennett through the compilation of a bio-bibliography on the arranger, as well as an edition of Bennett's autobiography and selected writings. See Ferencz, *Robert Russell Bennett*; Bennett and Ferencz, *The Broadway Sound*.
31. Letter from Adler to Ira Gershwin, June 24, 1974, Ira and Leonore Gershwin Trust Archive, Library of Congress, Washington, DC.
32. Robert Russell Bennett Papers, Music Library, Northwestern University, Box 74, Folder 2.
33. Larry Adler, *Rhapsody in Blue*, EMI Classics CDM 7 64134 2, 1991, CD. The track released on this album was recorded live at Watford Town Hall with the Pro Arte Orchestra.
34. "Larry Adler—Rhapsody in Blue," YouTube, accessed December 23, 2013, http://youtu.be/4ZI8uB7KfSU.
35. Elmore Bacon, "Adler and Peterson Thrill 8,000 at Pop Concert," unknown Cleveland newspaper, June 19, 1947, Box 2, Folder 4, LAP.
36. Pollack, *George Gershwin*, 642.
37. Edward P. Halline, "8,500 Attend Park Concert," *Milwaukee Sentinel*, July 14, 1948.
38. Hill, *Tap Dancing America*, 190.
39. *Billboard*, January 5, 1946.
40. Philip K. Scheuer, "Larry Adler's Harmonica Art Leaves Union Cold," *Los Angeles Times*, March 23, 1947.
41. Excerpt reproduced in "Concert in Greenwich," *Time*, December 5, 1949.
42. Ceplair, *Inquisition in Hollywood*, 276–277.
43. Richard Severo, "Larry Adler, Political Exile Who Brought the Harmonica to the Concert Stage, Dies at 87," *New York Times*, August 8, 2001.
44. "Instrumentalists: Seeking a Mark," *Time*, June 30, 1967.
45. Donal Henahan, "Music: Adler and Draper," *New York Times*, June 17, 1975.
46. John Von Rhein, "Adler, Symphony Team Is Offbeat but Selections Don't Do Justice," *Chicago Tribune*, October 14, 1977.
47. Walter Arlen, "Music Reviews: Adler at UCLA," *Los Angeles Times*, December 4, 1979.
48. Chris Pasles, "Music Review," *Los Angeles Times*, August 4, 1986.
49. Letter from Adler, November 2, 1938, Box 1, Folder 4, LAP.
50. Letter from Adler, November 8, 1938, Box 1, Folder 4, LAP.
51. "Harmonica Legend Larry Adler," *Fresh Air*, National Public Radio, June 19, 1987; rebroadcast May 10, 2007.
52. Terkel, *And They All Sang*, 253.
53. Leonard Feather, "Larry Adler: Still the Survivor," *Los Angeles Times*, October 17, 1982; Adler, *It Ain't Necessarily So*, 67; see also a recording reissued on *Larry Adler Harmonica Rarities, Volume 1* (Prestige Elite, 2006) and an interview in an issue of *Tutti Magazine* (July 1995) dedicated exclusively to the music of Gershwin.
54. "Harmonica Legend Larry Adler," *Fresh Air*.
55. Stephen Holden, "It's Very Clear, the Gershwins Are Here to Stay," *New York Times*, January 10, 1986. Adler reprised this act in October of the same year.
56. Adler, *It Ain't Necessarily So*, 50.

57. Ibid., 115.
58. Ibid.
59. Digitized manifests for transatlantic travel from Ancestry.com, accessed June 29, 2009, http:///www.ancestry.com.
60. *Rhapsody in Blue* was performed at Gershwin memorial concerts by Harry Kaufman with Alexander Smallens at Lewisohn Stadium on August 9, 1937; by José Iturbi (soloist and conductor) at the Hollywood Bowl on September 8, 1937; and by Roy Bargy with Paul Whiteman on CBS on July 11, 1938. Oscar Levant appeared only at the Hollywood Bowl concert, where he performed Concerto in F.
61. Letter from Adler, January 30, 1935, Box 1, Folder 1, LAP.
62. The film was either Paramount's *The Big Broadcast of 1937* (with Jack Benny) or Warner Brothers' *The Singing Marine* (with Dick Powell).
63. Letter from Adler, February 13, 1937, Box 1, Folder 1, LAP.
64. Adler, *It Ain't Necessarily So*, 84–86; Pollack, *George Gershwin*, 115.
65. Letter from Adler, August 9, 1937, Box 1, Folder 4, LAP.
66. Letter from Adler, December 18, 1939, Box 1, Folder 1, LAP.
67. Adler, *It Ain't Necessarily So*, 7.
68. Adler, *Me and My Big Mouth*, 17.
69. Radano, *Lying up a Nation*, xiv.

CHAPTER 6
1. "Gershwin Concert Has Record Crowd," *New York Times*, August 10, 1937.
2. "Bars Ticket Speculators: Mayor Places Special Police in Area of Gershwin Concert," *New York Times*, August 10, 1937.
3. "Gershwin Concert has Record Crowd."
4. Letter from Ira Gershwin to Watty [Mr. A. M. Wattenberg], August 30, 1939, Box 126, Folder 32, GGC. Underline in original.
5. See Rapport, "Bill Finegan's Gershwin Arrangements."
6. Phil Rosenthal, "'Rhapsody' Remains Familiar Refrain at United," *Chicago Tribune*, January 8, 2012.
7. Björkman, ed., *Woody Allen on Woody Allen*, 35.
8. *Manhattan*, Woody Allen, dir., United Artists, 1979.
9. Gene Siskel, "Bergman, move over for Allen," *Chicago Tribune*, April 30, 1979.
10. *Fantasia*, Walt Disney, prod., Walt Disney Productions, 1940.
11. *Fantasia 2000*, Roy Disney and Donald Ernst, prods., Walt Disney Pictures, 1999.
12. Charles Solomon, "*Rhapsody in Blue: Fantasia 2000*'s Jewel in the Crown," *Animation World Magazine* 4, no. 9 (December 1999).
13. Director Eric Goldberg described the challenges in animating this eight-second shot of Gershwin: "Not only did the fingers have to hit the right keys at the right time, they had to look like Hirschfeld fingers—I had to curl one up or crack a knuckle in a way that resembles a Hirschfeld drawing." Solomon, "*Rhapsody in Blue*."
14. Howard Pollack believes F. Scott Fitzgerald intended such a reference to *Rhapsody in Blue* in this particular scene as it appeared in his 1925 novel, as evidenced in a draft from a year earlier titled *Trimalchio*. See Pollack, *George Gershwin*, 305.
15. Bob Greene, "United Airlines Faces the Music," *Chicago Tribune*, February 16, 1988.
16. Taylor, *Sounds of Capitalism*, 180–183.
17. Ibid., 199–202.
18. William K. Knoedleseder Jr., "Music Copyrights Can Be Gold Mines to Current Owners," *Los Angeles Times*, December 29, 1985.

19. Tom Shales, "Gershwin's Rhapsody: Perfect Pitch? Commercializing a Classic to Sell United's Friendly Skies," *Washington Post*, November 25, 1987.

20. Ibid.

21. Ibid.

22. The sonic similarity was probably not an accident given that the Academy-award winning instrumental piece by Vangelis became a symbol of aspiration and success because of its filmic associations with the Olympics. As the official airline of the U.S. Olympic team, such connections were likely purposeful as United geared up for the winter and summer games of 1988.

23. Ronald Alsop, "Listen Closely: These TV Ads Might Have a Familiar Ring," *Wall Street Journal*, October 22, 1987.

24. Reproduced in Patrick Goldstein, "Pop Eye," *Los Angeles Times*, December 13, 1987.

25. Alsop, "Listen Closely."

26. Susan Shahoda, "Ron Condon & Jim Dyer," *Back Stage*, June 16, 1989.

27. Eric Berg, "United Thrives Amid Turmoil," *New York Times*, October 2, 1990.

28. Michael J. McCarthy, "Risky Flight Plan," *Wall Street Journal*, March 6, 1995.

29. Aaron Baar, "Fallon going Tagless for United," *AdWeek*, January 10, 2000.

30. Michael McCarthy, "United's Next Pitch: Rhapsody in Red Ink?" *Wall Street Journal*, December 6, 2002.

31. Greg Griffin, "United Launches New Design Jet Colors, Ads Aim for Revived Image," *Denver Post*, February 19, 2004. Musicologist Joanna Love argues that these commercials depict a homogenized middle class with capitalistic aspirations and that such representation "deviates from the piece's original implications and illustrates its own ideals about American identities," namely "elitism and sophistication." Love-Tulloch, *Marketing American Identity*, 2.

32. Micheline Maynard, "Advertising: Campaign for United Airlines Uses Animation and Casts Robert Redford as the Voice of Reason," *New York Times*, March 4, 2004.

33. Ibid.

34. Aaron Baar, "Fallon Gives United Fanciful Destination," *AdWeek*, January 30, 2006.

35. Two of the advertising company's principals, Bob Barrie and Stuart D'Rozario, created the original "It's time to fly" campaign while working at Fallon.

36. Dave Carpenter, "United Still Looking for a Merger, CFO says," *USA Today*, June 14, 2007.

37. Rosenthal, "'Rhapsody' Remains Familiar Refrain at United."

38. "United—Behind the scenes with Rhapsody," YouTube video, accessed December 20, 2013, http://youtu.be/ZtUAidKQ88E.

39. Passenger statistics from Airports Council International, accessed December 12, 2013, http://www.aci.aero/Data-Centre/Annual-Traffic-Data/Passengers; performance data from Chicago Department of Aviation, accessed December 12, 2013, http://www.flychicago.com/OHare/EN/AboutUs/Facts/Performance-Data.aspx.

40. Greene, "United Airlines Faces the Music."

41. William Kraft, interview with Bruce Duffie from May 25, 1988, accessed July 1, 2013, http://www.bruceduffie.com/wm-kraft.html.

42. Interview by the author with Gary Fry.

43. Gary Fry, composer's notes for *Rhapsody Ambiance*.

44. Greene, "United Airlines Faces the Music."

45. Richard Rayner, "Nowhere, U.S.A.," *New York Times*, March 8, 1998.

46. Butterfield, "The Musical Object Revisited," *Music Analysis* 21, no. 3 (October 2002), 373.
47. Fry, composer's notes.
48. Tom Shales, "Critics Corner," reproduced in *Los Angeles Times*, July 9, 1989.

EPILOGUE
1. David Schiff, "Ado Over Plenty o' Nuttin,'" *New York Times*, June 29, 1997.
2. Anthony Brown, interview with Nina Thorsen on *Pacific Time*, KQED, November 17, 2005.
3. Ibid.
4. Pollack, *George Gershwin*, 298.
5. Anthony Brown, pers. comm., June 26, 2009.
6. "Anthony Brown: Biography," accessed June 15, 2013, http://www.anthony-brown.org/biography.html.
7. Brown, *Pacific Time* interview.
8. Anthony Brown, "The Director's Notes," accessed June 15, 2013, http://www.anthonybrown.org/cd_rhapsodies_dnotes.html.
9. Brown, *Pacific Time* interview.
10. Anthony Brown, "American Rhapsodies: Wellspring of the Fifth Stream," accessed June 15, 2013, http://www.anthonybrown.org/cd_rhapsodies_wellspring.html.
11. Ibid.
12. Anthony Brown, interview with *Inside Oakland* (1998), accessed June 12, 2013, http://jounalism.berkeley.edu/projects/oakland/culture/link1.html.
13. George Gershwin, "Jazz is the Voice of the American Soul," *Theatre Magazine* (June 1926). Reproduced in Wyatt and Johnson, eds., *George Gershwin Reader*, 93.
14. Goldberg, 139.
15. See chapter 2 for a discussion of this passage.

BIBLIOGRAPHY

ARCHIVAL SOURCES
Copyright Card Catalog, Copyright Public Records Reading Room, Library of Congress, Washington, DC (CCC)
Duke Ellington Collection, Smithsonian National Museum of American History, Washington, DC (DEC)
Ferde Grofé Collection, Library of Congress, Washington, DC (FGC)
George and Ira Gershwin Collection, Library of Congress, Washington, DC (GC)
Isaac Goldberg Papers, Manuscripts and Archive Section, New York Public Library, New York (IGP)
Larry Adler Papers, American Heritage Center, University of Wyoming, Laramie (LAP)
Leonard Bernstein Collection, Library of Congress, Washington, DC (LBC)
New York Philharmonic Archives, New York (NYP)

BOOKS AND ARTICLES
Adler, Ayden. "'Classical Music for People Who Hate Classical Music': Arthur Fiedler and the Boston Pops, 1930–1950." Ph.D. dissertation, University of Rochester, 2007.
Adler, Larry. *It Ain't Necessarily So*. London: Collins, 1984.
Adler, Larry. *Me and My Big Mouth*. London: Blake, 1994.
Ake, David. *Jazz Cultures*. Berkeley, CA: University of California Press, 2002.
Anderson, Paul Allen. *Deep River: Music and Memory in Harlem Renaissance Thought*. Durham, NC: Duke University Press, 2001.
Armitage, Merle, ed. *George Gershwin*. New York: Longmans, Green and Co., 1938. Reprint, New York: Da Capo Press, 1995.
Armitage, Merle. *George Gershwin: Man and Legend*. New York: Duell, Sloan and Pearce, 1958.
Bañagale, Ryan. "*Rhapsodies in Blue*: New Narratives for an Iconic American 'Composition.'" Ph.D. dissertation, Harvard University, 2011.
Bañagale, Ryan. "An American in Chinatown: Asian Representation in the Music of George Gershwin." M.A. thesis, University of Washington, 2004.
Baraka, Amiri [LeRoi Jones]. *Blues People: Negro Music in White America*. New York: William Morrow, 1963.
Basie, Count. *Good Morning Blues: The Autobiography of Count Basie*. New York: Random House, 1985.
Bateson, Gregory. *Steps to an Ecology of Mind*. New York: Ballantine Books, 1973.
Bennett, Robert Russell, and George Joseph Ferencz. *The Broadway Sound: The Autobiography and Selected Essays of Robert Russell Bennett*. Eastman Studies in Music. Rochester, NY: University of Rochester Press, 1999.

Bernstein, Leonard. "Why Don't You Run Upstairs and Write a Nice Gershwin Tune?" *The Joy of Music*. New York: Simon and Schuster, 1959.

Bernstein, Leonard. *The Infinite Variety of Music*. New York: Simon and Schuster, 1966.

Björkman, Stig, ed. *Woody Allen on Woody Allen*. New York: Grove Press, 1994.

Burton, Humphrey. *Leonard Bernstein*. New York: Doubleday, 1994.

Butterfield, Matthew. "The Musical Object Revisited." *Music Analysis* 21, no. 3 (October 2002): 327-380.

Ceplair, Larry. *The Inquisition in Hollywood: Politics in the Film Community, 1930–1960*. Berkeley, CA: University of California Press, 1983.

Cleto, Fabio, ed. *Camp: Queer Aesthetics and the Performing Subject: A Reader*. Ann Arbor, MI: University of Michigan Press, 1999.

Cohen, Harvey G. *Duke Ellington's America*. Chicago: University of Chicago Press, 2010.

Crawford, Richard, and Larry Hamberlin. *An Introduction to America's Music*, second ed. New York: W. W. Norton & Co., 2013.

Cripps, Thomas. *Slow Fade to Black: The Negro in American Film, 1900–1942*. New York: Oxford University Press, 1997.

Davis, Angela Y. *Blues Legacies and Black Feminism: Gertrude "Ma" Rainey, Bessie Smith, and Billie Holiday*. New York: Pantheon, 1998.

Deleuze, Gilles, and Félix Guattari. *A Thousand Plateaus: Capitalism and Schizophrenia*. Translated by Brian Massumi. Minneapolis, MN: University of Minnesota Press, 1987.

DeSantis, Florence Stevenson. *Portraits of Greatness: Gershwin*. New York: Treves, 1987.

Eco, Umberto. *The Role of the Reader: Explorations in the Semiotics of Texts*. Bloomington, IN: Indiana University Press, 1984.

Ewen, David. *A Journey to Greatness: The Life and Music of George Gershwin*. New York: Holt, 1956.

Ewen, David. *The Story of George Gershwin*. New York: Holt, 1946.

Farrington, James. "Ferde Grofe: An Investigation into his Musical Activitities and Works." M.A. thesis, Florida State University, 1985.

Ferencz, George Joseph. *Robert Russell Bennett: A Bio-Bibliography*. New York: Greenwood Press, 1990.

Franceschina, John. *Duke Ellington's Music for the Theatre*. Jefferson, NC: McFarland, 2001.

Furia, Philip. *Ira Gershwin: The Art of the Lyricist*. New York: Oxford University Press, 1996.

Gabbard, Krin, ed. *Jazz Among the Discourses*. Durham, NC: Duke University Press, 1995.

Gabbard, Krin. *Jammin' at the Margins: Jazz and the American Cinema*. Chicago: University of Chicago Press, 1996.

Gennari, John. *Blowin' Hot and Cool: Jazz and Its Critics*. Chicago: University of Chicago Press, 2006.

Goehr, Lydia. *The Imaginary Museum of Musical Works: An Essay in the Philosophy of Music*, rev. ed. New York: Oxford University Press, 2007.

Goldberg, Isaac. "A Boston Boyhood." *American Mercury* 17, no. 67 (July 1929): 354–361.

Goldberg, Isaac. *George Gershwin: A Study in American Music*. New York: Simon and Schuster, 1931.

Goldberg, Isaac. "Music by Gershwin" (series). *Ladies' Home Journal* 48/2 (February 1931): 12–13, 149, 151; 48/3 (March 1931): 20, 208–210, 212–213; 48/4 (April 1931): 25, 196, 198–199.

Goldberg, Isaac. *Tin Pan Alley: A Chronicle of the American Popular Music Racket*. New York: John Day, 1930.

Greenberg, Rodney. *George Gershwin*. London: Phaidon Press, 1998.

Hajdu, David. *Lush Life: A Biography of Billy Strayhorn*. New York: Farrar, Straus, Giroux, 1996.

Hasse, John Edward. *Beyond Category: The Life and Genius of Duke Ellington*. New York: Simon and Schuster, 1993.

Hill, Constance Valis. *Tap Dancing America: A Cultural History*. New York: Oxford University Press, 2010.

Howland, John. *Ellington Uptown: Duke Ellington, James P. Johnson, and the Birth of Concert Jazz*. Ann Arbor, MI: University of Michigan Press, 2009.

Howland, John. "Jazz Rhapsodies in Black and White: James P. Johnson's *Yamekraw*." *American Music* 24, no. 4 (2006): 438–493.

Hubbs, Nadine. "Bernstein, Homophonia, Historiography." *Women and Music: A Journal of Gender and Culture* 13 (2009): 24–42.

Hyland, William. *George Gershwin: A New Biography*. Westport, CT: Praeger, 2003.

Jablonski, Edward. *Gershwin Remembered*. Portland, OR: Amadeus Press, 1992.

Jablonski, Edward. *Gershwin: A Biography*. New York: Doubleday, 1987.

Jablonski, Edward, and Lawrence D. Stewart. *The Gershwin Years: George and Ira*. Garden City, NY: Doubleday, 1958.

Kendall, Alan. *George Gershwin: A Biography*. New York: Universe, 1987.

Kimball, Robert, and Alfred Simon. *The Gershwins*. New York: Atheneum, 1973.

Kregor, Jonathan. *Liszt as Transcriber*. New York: Cambridge University Press, 2010.

Lange, Arthur. *Arranging for the Modern Dance Orchestra*. New York: Robbins Music Corp., 1926.

Leon, Ruth. *Gershwin*. London: Haus, 2004.

Leonard, Neil. *Jazz and the White Americans: The Acceptance of a New Art Form*. Chicago: University of Chicago Press, 1962.

Locke, Alain. *The New Negro and His Music*. New York: Kennikat Press, 1936.

Love-Tulloch, Joanna. "Marketing American Identity: The Role of American Classical Music in Television Advertising." M.A. thesis, University of Nevada, Reno, 2006.

Magee, Jeffery. "Fletcher Henderson, Composer: A Counter-Entry to the *International Dictionary of Black Composers*." *Black Music Research Journal* 19, no. 1 (1999): 61–70.

Magee, Jeffrey. *The Uncrowned King of Swing: Fletcher Henderson and Big Band Jazz*. New York: Oxford Univeristy Press, 2005.

Neimoyer, Susan. "*Rhapsody in Blue*: A Culmination of George Gershwin's Early Musical Education." Ph.D. dissertation, University of Washington, 2003.

Nauck, Kurt. *American Record Labels and Companies: An Encyclopedia (1891–1943)*. Denver, CO: Mainspring Press, 2000.

Oja, Carol. "Gershwin and American Modernists of the 1920s." *Musical Quarterly* 78, no. 4 (Winter 1994): 646–668.

Oja, Carol. *Making Music Modern*. New York: Oxford University Press, 2000.

Osgood, Henry Osborne. *So This Is Jazz*. Boston: Little, Brown, and Co., 1926.

Payne, Robert. *Gershwin*. London: Hale, 1960.

Peress, Maurice. *Dvorak to Duke Ellington: A Conductor Explores American Music and its African American Roots*. New York: Oxford University Press, 2004.

Peretti, Burton. *Lift Every Voice: The History of African American Music*. Lanham, MD: Rowman & Littlefield, 2009.

Peyser, Joan. *The Memory of All That: The Life of George Gershwin*. New York: Simon and Schuster, 1993.

Pollack, Howard. *George Gershwin: His Life and Work*. Berkeley, CA: University of California Press, 2007.

Radano, Ronald. *Lying up a Nation: Race and Black Music*. Chicago: University of Chicago Press, 2003.

Rapport, Evan. "Bill Finegan's Gershwin Arrangements and the American Concept of Hybridity." *Journal of the Society for American Music* 2, no. 4 (2008): 507–530.

Rayno, Don. *Paul Whiteman: Pioneer in American Music, Volume I, 1890–1930*. Lanham, MD: Scarecrow Press, 2003.

Rimler, Walter. *George Gershwin: An Intimate Portrait*. Urbana, IL: University of Illinois Press, 2009.

Rimler, Walter. *A Gershwin Companion: A Critical Inventory and Discography, 1916–1984*. Ann Arbor, MI: Popular Culture, 1991.

Rosenberg, Deena. *Fascinating Rhythm: The Collaboration of George and Ira Gershwin*. New York: Dutton, 1991.

Rosenfeld, Paul. *An Hour With American Music*. Philadelphia: J. B. Lippincott, 1929.

Rushmore, Robert. *The Life of George Gershwin*. New York: Crowell-Collier Press, 1966.

Schiff, David. *Gershwin: Rhapsody in Blue*. Cambridge, UK: Cambridge University Press, 1997.

Schneider, Wayne, ed. *The Gershwin Style: New Looks at the Music of George Gershwin*. New York: Oxford University Press, 1999.

Schuller, Gunther. *Early Jazz: Its Roots and Musical Development*. New York: Oxford University Press, 1968.

Schwartz, Charles. *Gershwin: His Life and Music*. Indianapolis: Bobbs-Merrill, 1973.

Seldes, Barry. *Leonard Bernstein: The Political Life of an American Musician*. Berkeley, CA: University of California Press, 2009.

Smith, Tim. *The NPR Curious Listener's Guide to Classical Music*. New York: Perigee Trade, 2002.

Starr, Larry. *George Gershwin*. New Haven, CT: Yale University Press, 2011.

Stearns, Marshall Winslow. *Jazz Dance: The Story of American Vernacular Dance*. New York: Macmillan, 1968.

Stratemann, Klaus. *Duke Ellington: Day by Day and Film by Film*. Copenhagen: JazzMedia ApS, 1992.

Swain, Joseph P. *The Broadway Musical: A Critical and Musical Survey*, second ed. Lanham, MD: Scarecrow Press, 2002.

Taylor, Timothy D. *The Sounds of Capitalism: Advertising, Music, and the Conquest of Culture*. Chicago: University of Chicago Press, 2012.

Terkel, Studs. *And They All Sang: Adventures of an Eclectic Disc Jockey*. New York: New Press, 2005.

Timner, W. E. *Ellingtonia*. Lanham, MD: Scarecrow Press, 2007.

Tucker, Mark, ed. *The Duke Ellington Reader*. New York: Oxford University Press, 1993.

Tucker, Mark. *Ellington: The Early Years*. Urbana, IL: University of Illinois Press, 1991.

Vail, Ken. *Duke's Diary: The Life of Duke Ellington*, two vols. Lanham, MD: Scarecrow Press, 2002.

Van de Leur, Walter. *Something to Live For: The Music of Billy Strayhorn*. New York: Oxford University Press, 2002.

Von Glahn, Denise. *The Sounds of Place: Music and the American Cultural Landscape*. Boston: Northeastern University Press, 2003.

Wierzbicki, James. "The Hollywood Career of Gershwin's *Second Rhapsody*." *Journal of the American Musicological Society* 60, no. 1 (2007): 133–186.

Wilde, Oscar [C. 3. 3.]. *The Ballad of Reading Gaol*. London: Leonard Smithers, 1898. Reprinted as Project Gutenberg EBook, accessed December 11, 2013. http://www.gutenberg.org/files/301/301-h/301-h.htm.

Woll, Allen L. *Black Musical Theatre: From Coontown to Dreamgirls*. Baton Rouge, LA: Louisiana State University Press, 1989.

Wyatt, Robert, and John Andrew Johnson, eds. *The George Gershwin Reader*. New York: Oxford University Press, 2004.

INTERVIEWS BY THE AUTHOR

Anthony Brown, June 26, 2013

Gary Fry, June 28, 2013

Ferde Grofé Jr., August 3, 2012

Sid Ramin, February 21, 2006

David Schiff, December 3, 2013

INDEX

Adler, Ayden, 186n32
Adler, Larry
  blacklisting of, 138–140
  Draper and, 120, 138–140
  Ellington and, 142
  G. Gershwin and, 121–22,
    142–46
  I. Gershwin and, 133, 139
  The Glory of Gershwin and, 119–120,
    146–47
  as harmonica player, 120–21, 122–133,
    126, 137–38, 140–44
  photograph of, *130*
  Rhapsody in Blue and, 126–130, **128**,
    129, 133–38, *134*, 140–44, 178
Adler, Louis, 122
advertising
  Rhapsody in Blue in, 149–150, 158,
    159–168, 178
  use of music in, 158–59
Advertising Age (magazine), 161
"Ain't Misbehavin" (song), 126
Alda, Robert, 68
Alenson, Bill, 159
Allen, Ray, 117
Allen, Woody, 149, 150–53
American Airlines, 165
An American in Paris (Gershwin), 50, 94
American Labor Party, 139
American Mercury (magazine), 64
American Rhapsodies (Brown), 175–79, *177*
American Society of Authors,
    Composers, and Publishers
    (ASCAP), 14, 45
Anderson, John Murray, 59, 60
The Annotated Rhapsody in Blue
    (Zizzo), 16

Archer, Harry, 100
Armer, Albert, 33
Arnold, Malcolm, 140
arrangers, 4
ASCAP (American Society of Authors,
    Composers, and Publishers),
    14, 45
Ash, Jerome, 59
Asian-American jazz, 175. *See also*
    Brown, Anthony
Australian Broadcasting Commission,
    141

Babuscio, Jack, 89
Bach, Johann Sebastian, 132, 138
"Bad" (song), 159
The Ballad of Reading Gaol (Wilde), 93–94
Ballets Russes, 5
Baltimore Evening Sun (newspaper), 122
Baraka, Amiri (LeRoi Jones), 110
Barbirolli, John, 188n66
Bargy, Roy, 193n60
Barrie D'Rozario Murphy (advertising
    agency), 166
Basie, Count, 97, 189n20
BBC Promenade Concerts, 140
The Beatles, 159
Bechet, Sidney, 101, 115
Beethoven, Ludwig van, 122–23, 138,
    188n66
Benjamin, Arthur, 140
Bennett, Robert Russell
  Rhapsody in Blue and, 121, 133–38,
    134, *136–37*
  Sweet Little Devil and, 26
  Whiteman and, 36–37
Berger, David, 190n46

Bernstein, Elmer, 153, 160
Bernstein, Leonard
    at Camp Onota, 73–74, 82–89, *84*
    Gershwin and, 74–75, 77–78
    Rhapsody in Blue and: arrangements
        by, 73–74, 82–89, *86–87*;
        Grofé's arrangement and, 5,
        76; identity and, 178; "A Nice
        Gershwin Tune", 75, 76–77,
        92–94, 154, 179; performances
        of, 75–76, 90–92, 94–95;
        recordings of, 75, 76, 90, 92–93,
        95, 98; sheet music of, 55, 75,
        78–80, *79, 91*
"Big Stuff" (song), 91
Billboard (magazine), 138–39
Bishop, A. J., 110
Bizet, Georges, 185n1
Black, Brown, and Beige (Ellington), 96
Black and Tan (film), 58, 190n29
Blanc, Ronald, 161
Bloodworth, James, 2–3
Blue Danube (Strauss), 131, 132
Blue Monday Blues (Gershwin), 182n42
Blues Legacies and Black Feminism (Davis),
        58
Bolero (Ravel), 123–24, 125,
        126–28, 127
Bon Jovi, Jon, 119
Boosey & Hawkes (music
        publisher), 49
Boston Evening Transcript (newspaper),
        63–64
Boston Herald (newspaper), 90
Boston Pops, 77, 78, 81, 183n56
Boulanger, Nadia, 133
Brahms, Johannes, 138
Brandenburg Concerto (Bach), 138
Bringing Out the Dead
        (film), 153, 160
Broekman, David, 67–68
Brooks, Shelton, 191n53
Broughton, Bruce, 153
Brown, Anthony, 174–79, *177*
Brown, Lawrence, 104–5, 190n29
Brown, Les, 97
Brown, Nacio Herb, 182n40
Brunswick, 52
Burton, Humphrey, 89
Bush, Kate, 119

Butterfield, Matthew, 172
Byers, Hale, 33, 39

Cage, Nicholas, 153
Caliri, Jamie, 167
camp (performance style), 89
Cantor, Eddie, 123
"Carioca" (song), 126
Carmen (Bizet), 185n1
Carney, Harry, 97–98, 112–13
Cassidy, Donna, 59
Cassini, Igor, 140
CBS, 68, 75
Chariots of Fire (film), 160
Charleston, Kid, 105
Cher, 119
Chicago Daily Tribune (newspaper),
        125–26
Chicago Philharmonic Orchestra, 68
Chicago Symphony, 141
Chicago Tribune (newspaper), 169
chromatic harmonicas, 124–25, **124**
Clark, Donald, 33, 39
Cleveland Summer Orchestra, 135
Clurman, Judith, 187n45
Cochran, Charles B., 126–27
Colnot/Fryer Music, 160
Columbia Records, 52–53, 75, 127
Combattente, Fred, 31
Comden, Betty, 73
Committee for the First Amendment,
        139
Commonwealth Symphony of
        Boston, 90
Compo, 52
composers, 4
Concord Sonata (Ives), 8
Condon, Ron, 161
"The Continental" (song), 127
Continental Airlines, 167
Cooke, Louise, 105
"Cool" (song), 187n43
"Copenhagen" (song), 35
Copland, Aaron, 6, 64–65, 89
Costello, Elvis, 119
Crawford, Jesse, 55
La création du monde (Milhaud), 94
Creole Rhapsody (Ellington), 98, 110
Cripps, Thomas, 58
Crosby, Bing, 67–68

Cuban Overture (Gershwin), 148
Cunningham, George, 117
Czerwonky, Richard, 68

Davis, Angela, 57–58
"Day Is Done" (song), 126
Debussy, Claude, 138, 188n66
Deep South Suite (Ellington), 96
Dektor, Leslie, 160
Deleuze, Gilles, 9–10
DeVeaux, Scott, 110
The Dial (magazine), 64
diatonic harmonicas, 124
DiCaprio, Leonardo, 157, *157*
Disney. See *Fantasia 2000* (film)
"Do It Again" (song), 35–36, *37*, 40,
        133
Dodge, Roger Pryor, 189n24
Donahue, Jack, 5
Draper, Paul, 120, 138–141
"Drifting Along with the Tide" (song),
        182n40
A Drum Is a Woman
        (Ellington), 96
Duke, Vernon, 39
Dyer, Jim, 161

"Easy Rider" (song), 191n53
Eco, Umberto, 4–5
Edison, 52
Edwards, Gus, 182n40
Edwards, Henry "Bass", 101
Ellington, Duke
    Adler and, 142
    Black and Tan and, 58
    A. Brown and, 174, 178–79
    history of jazz and, 96–98
    on *Porgy and Bess*, 117–118
    Rhapsody in Blue and: arrangement
        of (1925), 99–103, **101–2**, *103*;
        arrangement of (1932), 99–100,
        104–10, **104**, **106**, *107–9*;
        commentary on, 117–18; in *Will
        Big Bands Ever Come Back?*, 97–99,
        110–17, **112–13**, *114*, *116*
"Embraceable You" (song), 119
Enesco, George, 125
Engel, Carl, 34
E.O. 9066 (Brown), 176
Ernst, Hugh C., 17

European American Music Distributors, 5
Ewen, David, 48, 56

Fallon McElligott (advertising agency),
        163–64, 166
Fancy Free (ballet), 90–91
Fantasia 2000 (film), 149, 153–55,
        165–66, 174
Far East Suite (Ellington), 174
Farrington, James, 20, 34, 36
Feather, Leonard, 96, 142
Ferencz, George Joseph, 192n30
Fiedler, Arthur, 81
La fille aux cheveux de lin (Debussy), 138
Finegan, Bill, 150
Fitch, Dennis, 164
Fitzgerald, F. Scott, 156, 193n14
Flute Sonata in Eb Major (Bach), 132
Flying High (film), 123
The French Doll (musical), 182n40
Fresh Air (radio program), 142
Fry, Gary, 170–73
Fryer, Terry, 160–61

Gabbard, Krin, 57–58, 59
Gabriel, Peter, 119
gagaku (Japanese imperial court music),
        176–78, *177*
Gains, Kevin, 188n3
Gautier, Eva, 30–31
Genevieve (film), 140
George Gershwin (Goldberg), 8, 47,
        61–62, 66–67, 150–51, 179
The George Gershwin Reader (Wyatt and
        Johnson), 61–62
George White's Scandals of 1922, 37–38,
        182n42
George White's Scandals of 1924, 49
Gershwin, George
    Adler and, 121–22, 142–46
    Bernstein and, 74–78
    biographies of, 8, 60–61
    death of, 67–68, 74
    Goldberg and, 65–67
    Grofé and, 35–36
    on Grofé's role, 14, 45–46
    Levant and, 121
    Whiteman and, 50
    See also *George Gershwin* (Goldberg);
        Rhapsody in Blue (Gershwin)

Gershwin, Ira
  Adler and, 133, 139
  Committee for the First Amendment
    and, 139
  Goldberg and, 66
  on *Rhapsody in Blue*, 5
  Rhapsody in Blue's creation and, 15
  as trustee of G. Gershwin's
    estate, 150
Gershwin, Marc, 160
Gershwin Memorial Concert (1937),
  148–49
Girl Crazy (musical), 133
Glaenzer, Jules, 120–21, 146
Glee (television series), 155–56, *156*
The Glory of Gershwin (album), 119–120,
  146–47
Godowsky, Leopold III, 161
Goldberg, Eric, 153, 193n13
Goldberg, Isaac
  biography and musical ideology of,
    62–65
  biography of Gershwin by, 8, 47,
    61–62, 66–67, 150–51, 179
  on Boston, 184n35
  on creation of *Rhapsody in Blue*, 16
  G. Gershwin and, 65–67
  I. Gershwin and, 66
  on Grofé, 39, 45
  on *Rhapsody in Blue*, 5, 53
Gonsalves, Paul, 97, 114–15
Goodman, Benny, 97
Gorman, Ross, 33, 39, 40–41, 43
Gorn, Isadore, 55
Götterdämmerung (Wagner), 68
Graffman, Gary, 151–52
The Great Gatsby (film), 149, 156–57, *157*
The Great Gatsby (Fitzgerald), 156,
  193n14
Green, Adolph, 73
Green Day (pop-punk group), 119
Greene, Bob, 169, 172
Greenspan, Charlotte, 68
Greer, Sonny, 100, 101
Grieg, Edvard, 97
Grierson, Ralph, 153
Grofé, Ferde
  arrangements of *Rhapsody in Blue*, 4,
    5–7, 15–17, 19–20, 38–46, **44**,
    151

  as arranger, 34–38, *37*
  Gershwin and, 35–36
  photograph of, *24*
Grofé, Ferde Jr., 181n15
Guattari, Félix, 9–10
Guerin, Art, 34–35
Guthrie, Woody, 6
Guy, Fred, 101

Hack, Sadie, 122
Hackman, Gene, 160–61, *162*
Hamilton, Jimmy, 115
Hamm, Charles, 90
Hammerstein, Oscar II, 133
Hancock, Herbie, 167
Handel, George Frideric, 188n66
Handy, W. C., 57, 123
Hardwick, Otto, 101, 105
harmony chorus, 36, 38, 40
Harms, Inc.
  Bennett and, 133
  Gershwin and, 36
  Rhapsody in Blue and, 43, 49, 53–55,
    78
Hayden, Michael, 168–69
head arrangements (huddle system),
  34–35, 36
Hearst, William Randolph, 140
Henderson, Fletcher, 34, 35, 103
Herman, Woody, 97
"Hey! Hey! Let 'Er Go!" (song), 26
H.M.S. Pinafore (comic opera), 185n1
Holiday, Billie, 142
Hoosiers (film), 161
"The House Is Haunted" (song), 126
Howland, John, 98, 106–7
Hubbs, Nadine, 94
huddle system (head arrangements),
  34–35, 36
Hungarian Rhapsody (Liszt), 131
Hyland, William, 25

"I Got Rhythm" (song), 138, 159
"I Love You" (song), 100
"I Wanna Be Loved by You" (song), 123
"I Wonder Where My Easy Rider's
    Gone?" (song), 191n53
I Won't Play (film), 1–3
"(I'll Build a) Stairway to Paradise"
    (song), 37–38

Intermezzo in Eb Minor (Brahms), 138
Irvis, Charlie, 101, 102
Irwin, Victor, 52–53, 105
Isherwood, Christopher, 89
It Ain't Necessarily So (Adler), 121, 122, 146
Iturbi, José, 193n60
Ives, Charles, 8, 188n66

Jablonski, Edward, 5, 22, 66
Jackson, Michael, 159
James, Etta, 6
"Japanese Sandman" (song), 35, 41, 182n31
"Jazz in Serious Music" (CBS program), 75
Jeunes filles de palaces (play), 182n40
John, Elton, 119
Johnson, Don, 163
Johnson, J. Rosamond, 57
Jolson, Al, 36, 68
Jones, Quincy, 153
The Joy of Music (L. Bernstein), 76

Karajan, Herbert von, 188n66
Kaufman, Harry, 148–49, 193n60
Kaye, Chuck, 159
Keaton, Diane, 151
Keiser, David M., 75–76
Kemp, Hal, 100
Kimball, Robert, 182n43
King of Jazz (film), 47, 58–60, 142, 149
Koch, Howard, 69, 70
Kohn, Al, 150
Kraft, William, 169

La Guardia, Fiorello, 148
Ladies' Home Journal (magazine), 65, 66–67
Lang Lang, 167
Lantz, Walter, 59
Larrabee, Eric, 111
"The Last Roundup" (song), 126
Lecuona, Ernesto, 125
Leo Burnett (advertising agency), 158, 159–163, 170
"Let's Call the Whole Thing Off" (song), 151
Leur, Walter van de, 112

Levant, Oscar
    Adler and, 144
    Gershwin and, 121
    Gershwin memorial concert and, 193n60
    Rhapsody in Blue and, 186n32
    in *Rhapsody in Blue* (biopic), 68, 149
Levien, Sonya, 69
Lewisohn Stadium (New York), 148–49
Liszt, Franz, 4, 131
Locke, Alain, 189n9
Los Angeles Olympics (1984), 6–7, 7, 60, 149
Los Angeles Times (newspaper), 122, 124
Love, Joanna, 194n31
Luhrmann, Baz, 156

"Mack the Knife" (song), 158
Magee, Jeffrey, 4, 34, 35, 99
Malagueña (Lecuona), 125
Manhattan (film), 149, 150–53, *152*
McCauley, John, 66
McCullough, Hester, 139–140
McDonald's, 158
Mehta, Zubin, 151–52
Mendelsohn, Manny, 162
Miami Vice (television series), 163
Michelotti, Carla, 159
Mikado, The (comic opera), 185n1
Miley, Bubber, 101, 103
Milhaud, Darius, 94, 141
Miller, Glenn, 97, 150
Milwaukee Symphony Orchestra, 138
Minevitch, Borrah, 5, 122
Minuet in G (Beethoven), 122–23
Mitropoulos, Dimitri, 89, 188n66
Mohr, Hal, 59
Moiret, Al, 105
Monk, Thelonious, 174
"The Mooche" (song), 103
"Mood Indigo" (song), 126
Morrow, Edward, 117–18
Mosbacher, Emil, 145
Mozart, Wolfgang Amadeus, 138
Murphy, Dudley, 58
Museum of Modern Art (New York), 166
Music for the Theatre (Copland), 64
Mutual Broadcasting System, 67–68
"My Man's Gone Now" (aria), 119

My People (Ellington), 96
Myers, Elizabeth, 166–67

Nance, Ray, 97, 113–14
Nanton, "Tricky Sam", 102–3
National Public Radio, 142
NBC Blue Network, 68
Neimoyer, Susan, 22
New York Journal-American (newspaper), 140
New York Philharmonic, 75–76, 94, 98, 132, 151–52
New York Times (newspaper), 141, 148
New York Tribune (newspaper), 15
The New Yorker (magazine), 125
Newman, Randy, 161
"A Nice Gershwin Tune" (Bernstein), 75, 76–77, 92–94, 154, 179
Nike, 159, 160
Ninth Symphony (Beethoven), 188n66
Novachord Orchestra, 43
Nutcracker (Tchaikovsky), 97

Oboe Quartet (Mozart), 138
O'Connor, Sinead, 119
Ode for St. Cecilia's Day (Handel), 188n66
Odets, Clifford, 69, 70
Of Thee I Sing (comic opera), 73, 133
Oh, Kay (musical), 133
"Oh, Lady Be Good" (song), 54
O'Hare International Airport (Chicago), 150, 168–173
Okeh Records, 52
Oklahoma! (musical), 133
Olympic Fanfare (Williams), 6
On the Town (musical), 73
"One O'Clock Jump" (song), 97
"Onota Camp, the end is near" (song), 73–74, 84
Opus 119 (Beethoven), 138
Ormandy, Eugene, 186n32
Osgood, Henry Osborne, 36

Paramount Pictures, 123
Pardon My English (musical), 50
Pathé, 52
Peer Gynt Suite (Grieg), 97
Pélléas et Mélisande (Debussy), 188n66
Pepsi, 159

Philadelphia Orchestra, 186n32
Philharmonic-Symphony Society, 148
Pirates of Penzance (comic opera), 73
Pittsburgh Courier (newspaper), 104
Pittsburgh Symphony Orchestra, 133
Pollack, Howard
  on Bernstein, 5, 76, 77
  on *The Great Gatsby*, 193n14
  on Grofé's role, 16
  on *Rhapsody in Blue* (biopic), 68
  on sales figures, 48
Porgy and Bess (opera), 77–78, 117–18, 121, 145
Porgy and Bess: A Symphonic Picture (Bennett), 137
Porter, Cole, 146
Prentice, Charles "Jock", 127, 130
Progressive Party, 139

"Quite a Party" (song), 26

Rachmaninoff, Sergei, 132
Radano, Ronald, 146
Rainey, Ma, 191n53
Ramin, Sid, 78–80, 81, 88
Ravel, Maurice, 123–24, 125, 126, 127
Rayno, Don, 16, 182n31, 182n45
Red Channels (report), 140
Redford, Robert, 165, 166, 167
Redman, Don, 34, 35
Reminiscing in Tempo (Ellington), 108–10
Rennahan, Ray, 59
"Revolution" (song), 159, 160
Rhapsody in Blue (biopic), 68–71, 149
Rhapsody in Blue (Gershwin)
  arrangements of, 3–5, 9–10; Adler and, 121, 133–38, *134*, *136–37*; by Bennett, 121, 133–38, *134*, *136–37*; by Bernstein, 73–74, *83*, 84–89, *86–87*; by Crawford, 55; Ellington (1925) and, 99–103, **101–2**, *103*; Ellington (1932) and, 99–100, 104–10, **104**, **106**, *107–9*; by Fryer, 160–61; by Gorn, 55; by Grofé, 4, 5–7, 15–16, 19–20, 38–46, **44**, 151; by Mendelsohn, 162; by Strayhorn, 111–16, by Sylvester, 100–103, **101–2**, *103*

commission for, 15, 30, 69–70
creation of, 14–16
debut of, 4, 15, 17
in films: in *Bringing Out the Dead*,
    153, 160; in *Fantasia 2000*, 149,
    153–55, 165–66, 74; in *The
    Great Gatsby*, 149, 156–57; in *I
    Won't Play*, 1–3; in *King of Jazz*,
    47, 58–60, 149; in *Manhattan*,
    150–53, *152*; in *Rhapsody in Blue*
    (biopic), 69–71, 149; in *St. Louis
    Blues*, 57–59, 60, 157
at Gershwin Memorial Concert,
    148–49
instrumentation timeline for, 33,
    40–41, *41*
Los Angeles Olympics and, 6–7, *7*
love theme: in *American Rhapsodies*
    (Brown), 178; Bennett and,
    136; Bernstein and, 87–88;
    Ellington and, 107–8, *108*,
    114–15; in *Fantasia 2000*,
    154–55; Goldberg on, 67;
    manuscript sources and, 32,
    33; name of, 9, *9*; in *Rhapsody
    in Blue* (biopic), 149; United
    Airlines and, 160, 162–63, 164,
    165, 166–67, 170
manuscript sources, 16–17, **16**, 18;
    Grofé/Whiteman manuscript,
    16, 18, 19–23, *41*; ink manu-
    script, 16, 18, 23–30, *24*, **25**,
    27, *29–30*, 40; pencil manu-
    script, 15–16, 18–19, *20–21*,
    26–27, *27*, 29–30, *29–30*, *31*,
    32, 39–40
"A Nice Gershwin Tune" and, 75,
    76–77, 92–94, 154, 179
performances of: by Adler, 126–130,
    128, *129*, 133–38, *134*, 141–44,
    178; by Bernstein, 75–76,
    90–92, 94–95
recordings of: Adler and, 127–130, **128**;
    by Bernstein, 75, 76, 90, 92–93,
    95, 98; Boston Pops and, 81;
    Ellington and, 97–99, 110–16,
    112–13, *114*, *116*; by Roberts,
    115; sales figures and, 48–53,
    50–52, 56–57; Whiteman and,
    49–50, **50–51**, 56

ritornello theme: in *American
    Rhapsodies* (Brown), 176;
    Bernstein and, 91; Ellington
    and, 112–13; in *Fantasia 2000*,
    154; in *Glee*, 156; in Grofé's
    arrangement, 39, 40, 41–42;
    in *I Won't Play*, 2; manuscript
    sources and, 32–33, *33*; name
    of, 8, *9*; in *Rhapsody in Blue*
    (biopic), 149; in *The Simpsons*,
    155; United Airlines and, 170
sales figures of, 48–57, **50–51**
sheet music of: Bernstein and, 55, 75,
    78–81, *79*, *91*; sales figures and,
    48–49, 53–56, **55–56**
shuffle theme: Bernstein and, 85–86,
    90–91; in *Fantasia 2000*, 154;
    manuscript sources and, *30*;
    name of, 9, *9*; United Airlines
    and, 166
stock arrangements of, 53, **54**, 56, 100
stride theme: Adler and, 128–29; in
    American Rhapsodies (Brown),
    177; Bennett and, *136*;
    Bernstein and, 92; Ellington
    and, 106, *108*, *109*, 113–14;
    in *Fantasia 2000*, 154; in
    Grofé's arrangement, 41–42; in
    Manhattan, 152–53; manuscript
    sources and, 24–25, 28–29, *29*,
    32, 33; name of, 8, *9*; United
    Airlines and, 167, 170, *171*
tag motif: in *American Rhapsodies*
    (Brown), 176; E. Bernstein,
    153; Ellington and, 108, *109*;
    in Grofé's arrangement, 39–40;
    in Irwin recording, 53; manu-
    script sources and, 26, 33; "The
    Mooche" and, 103; name of,
    8, *9*; United Airlines and, 164,
    166, 170, *171*
in television series: in *Glee*, 155–56, *156*;
    in *The Simpsons*, 155, *155*, 156
themes of, 8–9, *9*
title of, 17
train theme: in *American Rhapsodies*
    (Brown), 176; Ellington and,
    106, *107*, *109*; in *Fantasia 2000*,
    154; in *Manhattan*, 152; name
    of, 8–9, *9*

Rhapsody in Blue (Gershwin) (*Cont.*)
  tributes to Gershwin and, 67–68
  United Airlines and: in commercial
    advertising, 149–150, 158,
    159–168, 178; in soundscape at
    O'Hare International Airport,
    150, 168–173, *171*
Rhapsody in Blue (Schiff), 8–9
Rimler, Walter, 182n43
A River Runs Through It (film), 165
Roberts, Marcus, 115
Robinson, Prince, 101
Rodeo (Copland), 6
Rodgers, Richard, 133
Rolling Stone (magazine), 119
Roman Scandals (musical film), 123
Romeo and Juliet (Tchaikovsky), 9
Roosevelt, Franklin D., 176
Roosevelt, Theodore, 139
Rosenfeld, Paul, 63, 64
Rosenthal, J. C., 14
Rosenzweig, Maxie (Max Rosen), 66
Rosse, Herman, 59
Roumanian Rhapsody (Enesco), 125

Sadin, Robert, 115
Sanromá, Jesús María, 81
Schiff, David
  on Bernstein, 77, 90–91
  on Ellington, 98, 110
  on Grofé, 42, 44
  on *Rhapsody in Blue* (biopic), 68
  on *Rhapsody in Blue* (Gershwin), 8–9,
    9, 174
  on sales figures, 48
Schippers, Thomas, 188n66
Schneider, Wayne, 61
Schubert, Adrian, 52
Schubert, Franz, 138
Schuller, Gunther, 110, 176
Schwab, Laurence, 2–3
Schwartz, Jerome, 16
Scorsese, Martin, 153, 160
Scott, Hazel, 68
Second Prelude (Gershwin), 74, 82
Second Symphony (Ives), 188n66
Secrest, Merle, 89
"See See Rider" (song), 191n53
Seldes, Gilbert, 17
Seventh Symphony (Beethoven), 188n66

Shales, Tom, 161, 173
"She's Just a Baby" (song), 182n40
Shilkret, Nathaniel, 50
Shuffle Along (musical), 190n29
Simon, Alfred, 182n43
The Simpsons (animated series), 155, *155*,
  156
Singing Magazine (magazine), 45
The Singing Marine (film), 131
Siskel, Gene, 153
Smallens, Alexander, 132, 148–49,
  193n60
Smisek, Jeff, 168
Smith, Bessie, 57
"Smoke Gets in Your Eyes" (song), 126,
  127
So This Is Jazz (Osgood), 36
social dancing, 53, 105
"Somebody Loves Me" (song), 49, 119
Sonatina No. 1 in D Major (Schubert),
  138
"Sophisticated Lady" (song), 126
Sousa, John Philip, 6
"South Sea Isles" (song), 182n40
St. Louis Blues (film), 57–59, 60, 157
"St. Louis Blues" (song), 57, 123, 126
"Stairway to Paradise" (song), 182n45
Stanfield, Peter, 57–58
Starr, Larry, 77
State Symphony Orchestra, 90
Steamboat Willie (film), 59
Stewart, Lawrence, 66
Sting, 119
stock arrangements, 35–36, 53, **54**, 56, 100
Strauss, Richard, 131, 132
Strayhorn, Billy, 97, 98, 111–12,
  112–13, 114
Streamline (revue), 127
Suite for Harmonica and Orchestra
  (Milhaud), 141
"Swanee" (song), 36, 68
Sweet Little Devil (musical), 15, 26, 30, 66
Sylvester, Bob, 100–103, **101–2**, *103*,
  189n20
Symphony in Black (Ellington), 96
Synclavier, 170

Tague, John, 165–66
Taubeneck, Greg, 160–61
Tchaikovsky, Pyotr Ilyich, 9, 97

Terkel, Studs, 142
Thiede, Alexander, 90
"This Land Is Your Land" (song), 6
Thorsen, Nina, 175
Timner, W. E., 189n11
Toyota, 159
Trivers, John, 166–67
Trivers Myers, 166–67
Tucker, Mark, 100, 111, 189n13
Tucker, Sophie, 191n53
"Turkey in the Straw" (song), 6

Ueberroth, Peter, 6
United Airlines
  commercial advertising and, 149–150,
    158, 159–168, 178
  soundscape at O'Hare International
    Airport and, 150, 168–173,
    171
U.S. Communist Party, 139

Vail, Ken, 189n11
Victor Records, 35, 37, 49–50, 55
Violin Concerto in A Minor (Vivaldi),
  130, 131–32
Vivaldi, Antonio, 131–32
Vocalise (Rachmaninoff), 132
Volvo, 159

Wagner, Richard, 68
Wallace, Henry, 139
Washington, Fredi, 105
Washington Post (newspaper), 123, 161,
  163
"Washington Post March" (Sousa), 6
Wattenberg, A. M., 150
Weill, Kurt, 158
Welles, Orson, 96
Wertheimer, Linda, 122
West Side Story (musical), 88
"When Buddha Smiles" (song),
  182n40

"When Day Is Done" (song), 123, 132
"When Eyes Meet Eyes (When Lips Meet
  Lips)" (song), 182n40
"When the Saints Go Marching In"
  (song), 6
"Whispering" (song), 35–36, 182n31
White, Martin, 165
Whiteman, Paul
  Adler and, 142
  Ellington and, 100
  Gershwin and, 50
  Grofé and, 35–37
  King of Jazz and, 59–60
  Rhapsody in Blue and: commission
    for, 15, 30, 69–70; debut of,
    4, 17; manuscript and, 19–20;
    recordings of, 49–50, 50–51,
    56; tributes to Gershwin and,
    68, 193n60
  in Rhapsody in Blue (biopic), 68,
    69–70, 149
Wierzbicki, James, 61
Wilde, Oscar, 93–94
Will Big Bands Ever Come Back? (album),
  97–98, 111–16, 112–13, 114,
  116
Williams, John, 6
Williams, Ralph Vaughan, 140
Woll, Allen, 117
Wolper, David, 6
Wonderful Town (musical), 73
"Woodchoppers Ball" (song), 97
Wright Brothers, 163–64

Young, Lester, 97
Young, Victor, 67–68
Young & Rubicam (advertising agency),
  163
Young People's Concerts (New York
  Philharmonic), 75

Zizzo, Alicia, 16

10/10/2014

Ira didn't read music or play any instrument.

Kay Swift - composer: very close w/ Kay George
dated for a while while married to
Chapem

Ira, once he gave in & accepted his Pulitzer,
hung it up in his bathroom.

Stage version of 'An American in Paris'
in NYC & Paris in April 2015.

'Oscar Levant is one of the most neurotic
people I've met'

LORD
Send a Revival

CLARENCE SEXTON

CROWN
PUBLICATIONS
Royal Reading